*The Uncle's Story*

Witi Ihimaera is descended from Te Aitanga A Mahaki, Rongowhakaata and Ngati Porou tribes, with close affiliations with other Maori tribes.

His novels include the award-winning *The Matriarch*, winner of the Wattie/Montana Book of the Year Award in 1986, and its sequel, *The Dream Swimmer*, published by Penguin in 1997. He has won the Wattie/Montana on two other occasions for *Tangi* in 1974 and *Bulibasha, King of the Gypsies* in 1995, also published by Penguin. His other fiction includes *Pounamu, Pounamu, Whanau, The New Net Goes Fishing, The Whale Rider, Dear Miss Mansfield, Kingfisher Come Home* and *Nights In the Gardens of Spain*. Ihimaera has also edited a major five-volume collection of new Maori fiction and non-fiction, called the *Te Ao Marama* series. His first play, *Woman Far Walking*, was premiered in 2000 at the International Festival of Arts, Wellington.

Ihimaera is a former diplomat who has served with the New Zealand Ministry of Foreign Affairs in Canberra, New York and Washington. He now lives in Auckland and is a Professor of English at the University of Auckland, specialising in creative writing and the literatures of New Zealand and the South Pacific.

*For all the Sams and Cliffs*
*of the world*

# The Uncle's Story

Witi Ihimaera

PENGUIN BOOKS

PENGUIN BOOKS

Published by the Penguin Group
Penguin Books (NZ) Ltd, cnr Airborne and Rosedale Roads, Albany,
Auckland 1310, New Zealand
Penguin Books Ltd, 80 Strand, London, WC2R 0RL, England
Penguin Group (USA) Inc., 375 Hudson Street, New York, NY 10014,
United States
Penguin Books Australia Ltd, 250 Camberwell Road, Camberwell,
Victoria 3124, Australia
Penguin Books Canada Ltd, 10 Alcorn Avenue, Toronto,
Ontario, Canada M4V 3B2
Penguin Books (South Africa) (Pty) Ltd, 24 Sturdee Avenue, Rosebank,
Johannesburg 2196, South Africa
Penguin Books India (P) Ltd, 11, Community Centre, Panchsheel Park,
New Delhi 110 017, India
Penguin Books Ltd, Registered Offices: 80 Strand, London,
WC2R 0RL, England

First published by Penguin Books (NZ) Ltd, 2000
This edition published 2003
3 5 7 9 10 8 6 4 2

Copyright © Witi Ihimaera, 2000

The right of Witi Ihimaera to be identified as the author of this work in terms of
section 96 of the Copyright Act 1994 is hereby asserted.

Designed by Mary Egan
Typeset by Egan-Reid Ltd
Printed in Australia by McPherson's Printing Group

ISBN 0 14 301898 1
A catalogue record for this book is available
from the National Library of New Zealand.

www.penguin.co.nz

Alone I watch in the night
Over you who laugh in your dreams
Listen to my warning for someone comes . . .
Sleepers, wake up! Take care!
Soon the night will pass —

Brangäne's Warning
Richard Wagner's *Tristan and Isolde*

# PART ONE

# I,
# Michael

## CHAPTER ONE

———— 1 ————

The irony is that Jason began it all.

'It's about time your folks knew,' he said. 'If you don't tell them now, you'll never do it. You owe it to them, to yourself. You owe it to me.'

'Yes, I'll tell them,' I promised.

I stepped into the car, waved goodbye and headed out on Highway One. Four hours later I reached Hastings. It was dark and I could have pushed onward to Gisborne, but I decided to check into a motel for the night. I should have known that the night would bring with it the dream that always made me wake up screaming.

———— 2 ————

You know what it's like in nightmares, especially the ones you've had since you were a child. It's dark and you're always alone. You feel so foolish that you've made yourself vulnerable again. You've gone to sleep and you've put yourself in a perilous position. Nightmares never go away. They simply watch and wait. They have all the time in the world. They watch you as you laugh in the sunlight. They watch you with family and friends. Then one night, when you least expect it, they curl out of the darkness, and your sleep is filled with that very special dread.

I was walking along a black highway at midnight. I heard a thrumming sound. Something was coming from out of the darkness behind me. I

9

couldn't see it, but I knew it was the huge nightmare stallion that had pursued me all my life through countless years, countless beds and countless dreams.

I began to run but my limbs were leaden. I could move only in slow motion. I tried to concentrate. I knew I was grinding my teeth. I willed myself to run faster, escape from the blackness. Before I knew it, I was drenched with sweat.

I looked back. All I could see were the eyes of the stallion, and the sparks as his hooves struck the highway. He was all the more frightening because he was only half glimpsed. His shrill whinnying proclaimed that this time he would get me.

My heart began to race. I heard myself moaning, felt myself threshing, trying to run. I willed my arms and legs to pump me forward. It was too late. The stallion had struck out to the left and was taunting me, circling in the blackness, choosing its moment. The thrum, thrum, thrum was all around me, the hooves on fire, and then —

There he was. Coming towards me. There was nothing I could do.

Wake up, wake *up*.

But the stallion was rearing up on his hind legs. He was screaming his rage, his hooves slashing steel blades, shredding the blackness with arcs of fire. His eyes were bulging. The veins on his neck were like ropes.

The hooves descending. Slashing.

'*No.*'

I twisted clear of the falling hooves. Screaming, I threw myself out of the darkness and found myself falling into the light. The thrumming, palpable, taking shape, bounced around the walls of the motel and I listened as the shapes began to recede out of the room.

I leapt from the bed and followed the sounds towards the window. Opened it. The cold stung my face. In the early mist of that grey winter's morning, jockeys were at training on an adjacent racetrack. The sound of hooves ricocheted in the room. The riders rode high in the stirrups. Steam jetted from the horses' nostrils. I put my hands to my ears.

My heart was racing. I was still disoriented. I dialled Reception.

'My watch has stopped. Can you tell me the time?'

'Six-thirty, Sir.'

'Where the hell am I?'

'Hastings, Sir.'

'And who am I?'

The receptionist thought I was joking. I heard her whisper, 'The guy in 41 doesn't know who he is.'

'Neither would I if I had drunk as much at the bar last night,' someone said. 'Better humour him.'

A rustle of papers. A pause. 'You're Mr Michael Mahana, Sir. You booked in last night. From what I gather, you're on your way to your sister's wedding?'

'Oh. Yes. What time's checkout?'

'Ten.'

——— 3 ———

Just after midday I reached Gisborne. Half an hour later I saw the valley and the village ahead. Nothing seemed to have changed: the grape and kiwifruit vines on either side of the road; the same red-roofed houses in between — though, hello, somebody had a satellite in their back paddock. And was that a black Mercedes parked in beside the old meeting house? This was what Maori economic development was all about: extra, and expensive, toys for the boys.

A few kilometres past the village was the gateway to the farm. Somebody had given a new lick of paint to the gate and the sign: MAHANA WINES. No doubt Amiria had badgered Dad to do it. Make an impression on the prospective in-laws. Even the road to the homestead had been gradered and gravelled. I turned in at the gate and across the cattlestop, put my foot down and roared the car over the rise. There was the homestead and the complex of buildings and vats where Dad produced his Cabernet Sauvignon for export.

Amiria was coming down the steps. People say you can always tell a Mahana by the way we walk. As if nothing can stop us doing whatever we want to do. As if we own the world.

'I thought you only drove Japanese,' Amiria said, as I stopped the car. 'You must be making a lot of money. Or — is it my present?'

I got out, grabbed Amiria in a hug and kissed her. Wide handsome face; a thick, glossy mane of hair; eyes sparkling with good humour;

generous mouth and a gap in the middle of white teeth. When Amiria and I were younger we always used to argue over whose gap was bigger. Amiria liked to win — that is, until she read in a glossy magazine that the gap was a sign of a lascivious nature.

Mum came bustling down. 'You were supposed to be here last night.' She looked across my shoulders as if expecting to see somebody. 'Did you come by yourself? Why didn't you bring a girlfriend!'

Dad was at the top of the stairs. He shook my hand in greeting. 'The place is a bloody circus,' he whispered. 'Your mother has gone mad tying ribbons on everything. If I was you I wouldn't stand in one place too long.'

Wouldn't you just know it, Mum had been waiting for me to get home before letting slip to Amiria that the arrangements for the reception after the wedding had — well, changed. Mum hoped I would take her and Dad's side against Amiria's formidable anger.

'Are you telling me the reception's now at the marae?'

'Dear, the Starlight wasn't big enough,' Mum said.

'Wasn't big enough? It's a cabaret. It can take two thousand!'

Mum looked to Dad for support. 'You are from a family of mana,' Dad said. 'Everybody will expect to come to your wedding. They will come out of respect for your grandfather Arapeta's memory and they will come because of our standing as a family. We will not be able to deny them. What would Arapeta have said! He would turn in his grave if he knew we weren't doing the best to uphold the family's status.'

'I will not stand here, Daddy,' Amiria said, 'and let you drive over me as if you were a tank.'

'It's more appropriate for the wedding to be down at the marae. All of your kuia can come, and their mokopuna. And all your Mum's people from up the Coast with their kids.'

Dad was getting that stubborn look, his chin jutting further and further out.

'I told you I only wanted to have a small wedding,' Amiria said. 'I also told you I didn't want to have any kids at the wedding. How do you think Tyrone's parents will take all this! They'll think we're like Indians having a pow wow.'

'If they haven't been on a marae it's about time they did,' Dad answered.

'Dear,' Mum tried to explain, 'the real problem was that the Starlight had no place where your father could put his hangi.'

Amiria went into overdrive. She'd lived so long with passive Pakeha friends in Auckland she'd become accustomed to getting her own way.

'Look. Read my lips. When we first discussed this wedding, Mother, we agreed that it would be silver service, with knives and forks —'

'There'll be knives and forks,' Dad interrupted. 'We haven't used our fingers for years. Do you think we're cannibals or something!'

'I wanted it to be like — like — a Pakeha wedding! With waiters and a band! You promised me! When I rang from Auckland you said that —'

'We do have waiters, dear,' Mum said. 'Your cousins are getting dressed up in their flashest clothes and Uncle Bimbo is bringing his karaoke.'

Amiria's mouth dropped open. 'That's it!' she screamed. 'The wedding is off. Off, off, off.'

It was Dad who had the last word. 'Amiria,' he said. 'What kind of Maori are you!'


I decided to extricate myself with a quiet escape to the front room. I flipped the cellphone open. Dialled Wellington.

'Hello?'

'Hi.' It was Saturday afternoon but Jason's voice sounded smoky and half asleep. I thought of him in bed, the sheets slipping from his chest as he reached for the telephone.

'Oh, it's you,' Jason said. 'Hang on a minute. I was out clubbing. Didn't get in until late.' There was the sound of creaks and sighs: muffled mysteries. 'So you've arrived safely then? How goes it?'

'I'd forgotten what families are like. A Mum and a Dad and a sister. The usual screaming matches.'

'So you've told them.'

'Not yet. There hasn't been a chance. Soon.'

There was a pause. A hesitation. 'Maybe you shouldn't go through with it,' Jason said. 'If you don't want to, don't do it.'

'That's a change! After all these months of pestering me!'

'Yes. Well —'

'I miss you. I wish you were here.'

'I know. Listen, when you get back, let's talk. In the meantime, enjoy the wedding.'

13

Just before dinner tempers were still flaring. I was in the middle of the firing line.

'I don't know what's wrong with your sister,' Mum said. 'Talk some sense into her. She's always listened to you.'

Not today.

'Thanks for your help,' Amiria said with some sarcasm. 'You're supposed to be on my side and help me against them.'

There were eight for dinner: Mum and Dad, Amiria and Tyrone, Tyrone's parents, myself and Dad's elder sister Auntie Pat.

'Kia ora, Nephew,' Auntie Pat said. 'You better hurry up, your sister is leaving you behind. Or maybe you're waiting to grow up to marry me, eh? And don't you dare answer that question!'

'It's not that I wouldn't marry you,' I said. 'It's just that I'm not the marrying kind.'

'Michael, dear, you say the sweetest things. I'd quit while I was ahead if I was you.'

I gave Auntie Pat a quick hug. She never seemed to like close physical contact. How she'd managed to cope among such a tribal people as ours I'll never know. Perhaps that's why she had moved from Waituhi to a flat in nearby Gisborne city soon after Grandfather Arapeta had died.

'Don't forget,' Auntie Pat whispered, 'we have to behave for the prospective in-laws. So we better sit beside each other and make sure we are good.'

The in-laws in question, Mr and Mrs Henderson, were standing in the lounge where Dad was showing them the Military Cross awarded to his father, Arapeta. The family were still reeling from the shock that Amiria, who had met Tyrone while he was on a surfing trip to New Zealand, was marrying into a family of Texans who owned a casino in El Paso. No wonder Dad, for whom such things mattered, was trying to impress the Hendersons with facts that implied that our family history might not go back to Davy Crockett and the Alamo but was at least as distinguished.

'Arapeta was one of the first of 146 Maori trainees to go to Army School at Trentham. That was in 1939 and few had any previous military training. Dad relied on the warrior blood of his ancestors — their intelligence, their cunning and their ability to lead — to get him through. He was only 20. When he landed in Egypt to fight against Rommel, he had risen to sergeant. He was wounded at El Alamein where he was commanding his platoon. He arrived in Italy and fought at Monte Cassino as a major under Pita Awatere. By the time the war was over he had risen through the ranks to lieutenant colonel. He was only 23 when he was awarded his Military Cross.'

'Wow,' Mr Henderson said. 'I've heard that the Maoris were formidable foes.'

Dad nodded. He loved talking about Arapeta. 'When my father came back he married my mother, Florence. My sister was the firstborn and I was second. Dad named me after the battle at Monte Cassino — people call me Monty. I think my Dad was hoping that there would be a war for me to fight in, but I was just a little young for Vietnam. Had I been older I would have volunteered. Nevertheless I joined up in peace time and was three years in the Army as a gunner. Dad came to see me graduate and it was one of the proudest moments in my life. He told me that I had' — Dad took a quick glance at Auntie Pat — 'restored the family honour.'

Mr Henderson turned to me and smiled.

'And you, son? Have you kept up your family's military tradition?'

'Michael's the only one of the family to go to university,' Dad answered. 'He's taken after his mother's side. Anyway, there are no wars for him to fight.'

'So what is your degree qualification?' Mrs Henderson asked.

Dad intervened again. 'I wanted Michael to go into viticulture and to take over from me, but you know what boys are like! They'll always do what they want to do.'

'Like my boy, Tyrone.'

'Michael's always liked the arts. He's set up a consultancy. If people want advice on Maori or bicultural art he helps them. You work closely with government, don't you, son?'

I nodded. It was easy to become mute around Dad.

'Oh?' Mr Henderson said. 'Sounds pretty impressive, but what does it mean?'

'Whatever it means,' Dad answered, 'it sure as hell sounds easier than working with grapes!'

While everyone was laughing, Amiria arrived with Tyrone.

'Tyrone,' Amiria said, 'you've not met my brother Michael.'

He was all white teeth in a bronzed, open, face. He laughed, 'So you're the twin and it *is* true. I've seen photographs but never realised. You and Amiria do look alike.'

'Except I'm prettier,' Amiria said, 'and the gap between my front teeth is not as wide as Michael's.'

Mum had excelled herself with the dinner. Three courses, good wine and not a pork bone or pot of puha in sight. Every now and then I could see Amiria looking across at Mum and beaming a silent thank you. By the end of the second course, the dinner party could be counted a success. Dad and Mr Henderson had taken off their ties and were now on first-name terms. Mum and Mrs Henderson were walking down Memory Lane, swapping baby stories about Amiria and Tyrone. To top it all off, Mr Henderson had given the famous Alamo war cry.

Auntie Pat looked at me askance. 'Any minute now,' she said, 'and your father is going to follow suit with his equally famous rendering of the haka.'

For some reason, a shadow eased itself stealthily over the bonhomie and warmth. Perhaps it had something to do with my conversation with Jason.

'Maybe you shouldn't go through with it,' he'd said. 'If you don't want to, don't do it.'

Nothing is worse for a single man or woman than to go home for a family celebration at which all the conversation, all the codes, are involved with family. You have failed, have not conformed. You are isolated.

Auntie Pat must have sensed my mood. She looked at me with concern.

'By the way,' Dad said to Tyrone, 'has Amiria told you what to expect? The Mahana breed has a habit of having twins. There's seven sets distributed throughout your generation.'

'Uh oh,' Tyrone said. He hit himself on the forehead in a mock gesture.

'When Amiria gets pregnant,' Mum continued, 'make sure you get one of those big double prams!'

'Gee, thanks,' Tyrone said. 'You really make a fella feel good about getting married.'

'Stop telling Tyrone your horror stories,' Amiria said. 'You should count yourselves lucky the wedding is still on!'

At that moment, there was the sound of a couple of cars screeching to a stop outside the house. The front door banged open.

'Hello, everyone!' Denise, Amiria's matron of honour, came in. After her trailed Amiria and Tyrone's groomsmen and bridesmaids. They'd been having a couple of drinks at the pub.

'Gotta go,' Amiria said. She gave a look at Tyrone, who stood up and prepared to follow her.

'Where to, dear?' Mum asked.

'Me and the girls are celebrating my last night of freedom, and Tyrone and the boys are going back to the motel for their stag do.'

'It won't be much of a do,' Denise scoffed.

'How do you know we haven't got a female stripper coming along?' one of the groomsmen challenged.

'You wouldn't know what to do with her if she was!'

Dad and Mr Henderson smiled at each other knowingly. Mum and Mrs Henderson pretended not to understand what anyone was talking about. Weddings are such a pretence.

Then Amiria turned to Tyrone. 'Tyrone, why don't you take Michael with you. He won't want to spend all night with the older generation.'

The older generation clucked in protest.

'Sure,' Tyrone said.

'I'll take a rain check,' I answered. 'You guys go ahead.'

'After all,' Mum agreed, 'why should Michael want to watch a stripper? He's already got a girlfriend.'

The others smiled. Mum looked as pleased as punch.

'So you won't come with us?' Amiria asked. 'Okay.'

I watched Amiria as she moved around the table. Saw her red kiss being accepted by proffered cheeks like a reward for having done the right thing. And then I knew that this was it, the opening I had been waiting for. After all these years of Mum and Dad talking for me, and making up a history for me, it was time I talked for myself. It was now or never.

'I don't have a girlfriend.'

Amiria's lips wavered above my face and she stepped back.

'Of course you do!' she said.

Dad was staring at me with incomprehension.

'I don't have a girlfriend, I never had a girlfriend, I will never have a girlfriend. Ever. End of story.'

Mum looked at me and, at that moment, I realised she already knew. Perhaps she had always known. Always suspected. Isn't that what they say about mothers?

'Perhaps we can leave this conversation till later, son,' Mum said. 'When our guests have gone home.'

But Dad wasn't so easily deflected.

'What do you mean! Of course you have a girlfriend. And you'll get married like your sister. And I'll have grandchildren.'

As usual, Dad was trying to make the decisions. If he said something would happen, it would happen.

But I stood my ground.

'There will be no grandchildren. My girlfriend is a boyfriend. Do I have to spell it out?'

There was a moment's silence. Then Mum excused herself and went into the kitchen. Dad's face crimsoned and his fingers tightened on his wine glass. Mr and Mrs Henderson looked at each other. Denise, the groomsmen and bridesmaids started to edge away. Auntie Pat picked up her napkin and patted at her lips.

'Boy oh boy, you sure pick your moment,' she whispered.

--------- 5 ---------

One o'clock in the morning. I sat on the steps of the front verandah. The Hendersons had returned to their motel. Mum had gone to bed, crying. Dad and Auntie Pat were arguing in the sitting room.

I saw headlights coming down the road: Amiria returning from her girls' night out. She stopped the car. Got out. Slammed the door. Leaned against the bonnet, arms folded.

'Did you have to do that?' she asked. 'Why didn't you rain on somebody else's parade.'

'I couldn't take it any longer. All that talk about my girlfriend. It's about time they knew.'

Amiria walked across to me. Sat down. 'Well you sure chose a rotten time to do it. I can just imagine what tomorrow will be like. I'll be standing at the aisle with Tyrone, and the priest will ask that question about anybody having just cause or knowing any impediment about our marriage. And somebody will call out from the back, 'Her brother's gay!'

The idea surprised her into laughter.

'You were always such a drama queen,' I said.

'God! What else is there to do except laugh. And listen to who's calling who a queen. Turning up like the bad fairy to spoil the party. Did you know Denise wasn't going to be a bridesmaid because she didn't like the outfits? Come to think of it, why didn't you lay your egg earlier! I could have given Denise the shove and you could have worn her dress.'

'Pink's not my colour.'

Amiria sighed. She put her arms around me. 'Listen, I'm only trying to humour you — to show you it's okay. This was already turning into the wedding from hell. And we're supposed to be twins. Tell each other everything. I should know when things are happening to you. I never knew anything about this. So how did it all happen!'

'I don't think it happens. It just is. Maybe when we were in the womb together I got a few of your chromosomes and they tipped me over.'

Amiria gave a gasp.

'That means that *I* got some of yours too! Oh my God.'

She got up and gave me a peck on the forehead. 'You're still my twin,' she whispered. 'We're as married to each other as I will be to Tyrone tomorrow. For richer for poorer. In sickness and health. Till death do us part.'

Half an hour later Dad and Auntie Pat stopped yelling and screaming at each other. I sensed that Dad was there, behind me in the doorway. His voice seemed to come from out of the past.

'Can you change?' he asked. 'Can you be fixed?'

Dad always thought you could fix things physically. If you had a puncture, change the tyre and put on the spare.

'No.'

'You don't want to change, is that it?'

'I can't.'

19

Dad's voice spilled over with horror. 'You can't *like* what you do with other men.'

I made it clean, clear and swift. Jason would have been proud of how I did it.

'I do.'

Dad took a step back, as if I had hit him. He searched for words.

'You're supposed to be my son but, so help me, I wish you weren't.'

A star fell from the sky, puncturing the night like a needle piercing your eyeball.

CHAPTER TWO

——— 1 ———

Wellington was picture perfect. The deep distilled blue of the harbour was bisected by the wake of the Interisland ferry as it left the overseas terminal. Every now and then the morning sun on the city's glass towers sent bright flashes across the sea.

I tried the cellphone. At the other end, my own voice on the answerphone clicked on: 'Kia ora. We're not at home right now. Leave a message after the beep.'

Maybe Jason was in the shower.

I aimed the car like a bullet toward the shining city. Today was the beginning of my *real* life. From now on *I* would say who I was, I would tell the narrative of my life as I lived it and not some false history voiced by Mum and Dad. Now the future was all.

I hit the redial. Still no luck. I felt the usual hunger. Floored the accelerator.

'Jason? I'm back.'

I put the key in the door of the flat and opened it. Glanced up the stairs. Raced up, two steps at a time. Put my bag down in the bedroom. Hoped Jason was still here. If he was, perhaps I could persuade him to take the morning off. Ring in sick. Say he had a cold. Celebrate.

I opened the bathroom door. The mirror was still steamed up, a towel lay damp on the floor. The room smelled of him. Must have just missed him.

I caught a sight of myself in the mirror. For a moment I was startled that I had come out of the past few days unmarked.

I peered more closely and saw that something was different in the reflection. At first I thought, 'Yes, there's something changeling about my appearance after all.' Then I realised that it was not my face that was different, but the room itself. Small things were missing. Jason's toiletries. The yellow rubber duck on the rim of the bath. His toothbrush.

I walked into the bedroom, past the unmade bed and opened the wardrobe. Jason's clothes weren't there. Even the hangers were gone. I went out onto the balcony and dialled Jason's direct line.

'Hello?' Jason answered.

'It's me. What's going on.'

'I'll meet you for lunch. The usual place. We'll talk then.'

—————  2  —————

If I was honest with myself, I would have to admit that Jason's leaving the flat didn't really come as a surprise: I had been half expecting it. Over the last seven months we'd begun fighting. Even now I'm not too sure what the fights were about — so many things, not just one. But one theme was common:

'You don't recognise me for the person I am, Michael. You don't recognise us for the couple we're supposed to be. Until you come out to your people, we'll never work.'

I had not expected that my being Maori and his being Pakeha would ever be an issue. I tried to make him understand.

'My people are among the most homophobic in the world,' I told him. 'I'm not supposed to exist.'

'But you do, and *I* do too. It's all a matter of recognition for me. Either you choose to recognise me or you don't. It's up to you.'

'I'm afraid. I'm afraid of the consequences. What might happen —'

It's unbelievable how quickly the fights had escalated. Brooding silences alternated with all-night verbal accusations back and forth, all signalling a relationship in the descendant, a parabolic flaming out. Sometimes at the end of our fighting I would make love to Jason, as if that would solve the differences between us, and he would succumb to my seductions. But afterwards we would argue again and he would accuse

22

me of using lovemaking to deflect his attention from the real issues that faced us both.

Then along had come Amiria's wedding — our most recent battle-ground.

'If you're truly serious about who you are and who I am,' he said, 'you'll tell your parents. You owe it to them, to yourself, to come out. You owe it to me.'

Over the weekend I had made my choice. Now it looked as if I would still end up paying for it.


The traffic around Courtenay Place was so busy that by the time I parked the car I was already a quarter of an hour late. And, of course, when there's something really serious going on in your life, and you need somewhere quiet to find out what's happening, you never get it. The restaurant was crowded, loud, and Jason had chosen the most conspicuous table to sit at. Nor was he alone. When he saw me coming in the door he interrupted his conversation with the person opposite him:

'Michael's arrived.'

At first the expression on Jason's face made me hope. But I realised that it was anxiety written there and that he was afraid of me — and that both surprised and saddened me. Two years ago our relationship had started in such a rush of fun, desire and love. In those days we were lovers rather than Maori and Pakeha, and I hadn't been able to keep my hands off him. After a few months it had seemed entirely logical that he should move in with me and set up house. He'd been happy in the first year and most of the second. How could something which began with so much fun turn into something to be feared?

Jason's nervousness made his companion at the table lean forward and place a reassuring hand on his shoulder. It was Graham, the buddy he had met during his sessions with Margo, his therapist. I waved across the room but just as I approached their table, I heard a shout:

'Michael!'

Rushing towards me, pushing the waiters aside as if they were skittles, was Roimata. Hair a cloud of red. A babe with a figure that looked as if it had been poured into her business suit and was spilling out over the top. High heels that could spike your foot if it was in the way.

Roimata smacked me with her generous lipstick.

Great, just what I needed. Now I'd have greasy lipstick over my face all through lunch. Nor would Jason be pleased that Roimata, of all people, had interposed herself between him and me.

'I've left messages for you,' Roimata said. 'How come you haven't answered them! I need to know how our report's coming along.'

Roimata was CEO of Toi Maori, an indigenous arts organisation that was battling for a share of financial resources captured by symphony orchestras, theatre companies, ballet and modern dance companies, art galleries and publisher organisations. She had commissioned me to write a paper for Toi Maori to use as the basis for a submission seeking direct funding from government.

'I've been out of town. I'll call you tonight. I'm here to have lunch with Jason.'

'Jason? Is he here?'

I gave Roimata a look of scepticism. She and Jason must have seen each other. Why is it that sometimes two people whom you love can never get on together?

'Don't forget,' Roimata said. 'Call me. I must have your report soon. Maori are on the move but there's nowhere for us to go. If the major arts framework won't let us in through the door, we'll just have to go in through the window.'

Roimata always had a flair for the dramatic utterance.

I moved on and joined Jason and Graham.

'I'm sorry about that. I hadn't realised Roimata would be here.'

Jason looked away, unblinking. Graham spoke for him.

'Jason's never come first in your life, has he, Michael?'

So, Graham was doing the talking. It was going to be like that, was it?

I sat opposite Jason. Looked at him. God, he was so damn *cute*. I am not ashamed to admit that when we first met I had been the pursuer and Jason the pursued. Jason used to boast that I couldn't believe my luck when I finally caught him — and it was true. In our circles, his boyish good looks and laughter guaranteed his popularity. Not that there had been much laughter lately.

'Have you ordered?' I asked.

'We've already eaten,' Graham answered, 'and Jason's not staying. He's only come to say one thing to you and then we're leaving.'

I ignored Graham — the buddy had obviously become my enemy.

'Is this arsehole going to say everything for you?' I asked Jason

Graham hissed with anger and Jason put a hand on his shoulder to restrain him.

Then Jason looked at me.

'I'm moving out, Michael. I'll come by to pick up the rest of my things later.'

Graham stood up. 'And now that he's told you,' he said, 'we can leave.'

'Not so fast,' I answered. 'I'm entitled to some time to understand all this. I've told the folks, Jason. They know about me now.'

Jason tried to get away from me but I caught his hands, not letting him go. Sometimes everything you want to say to a person is in the touching. When we had first got together there had been so much physicality, so much fun, so much laughter. So much touching.

'And did you tell them about me too?'

'No, not yet, but —'

Jason shook his head. His smile was bitter and knowing.

'You still don't understand, do you. Anyhow, it's too late.'

He tried to get away from me but I kept holding on to him, not letting him go.

'Speak to me, Jason. It's not too late. Please, I don't want to lose you.'

At my words Jason started on the offensive.

'Michael, you say you don't want to lose me, but it's ownership our relationship is based on. It's dependency. I've always suspected it, but it wasn't until this weekend, after you left for Gisborne, that I had the time to think it all through. I've relinquished the control of my life into your hands. I have to take my life back.'

Jason began to weep and people in the restaurant looked at him, alarmed. Although I reached out to console him, it was to Graham that he turned. I felt the usual sense of helplessness, the usual inability to respond whenever this happened — these tears that came out of nowhere. For the first time I realised that something else was happening to Jason, something more profound than what we were going through. Something bigger than both of us. Why hadn't I seen it before?

After a moment Jason recovered. He turned to me.

'I know I was a coward not to wait until you got home to tell you this,' he said, 'but I had to leave the flat before you got back. Otherwise I would never have had the strength to do it. Even now I can feel myself wanting to go back to you, but I mustn't. If I do, I'll never find myself. I have to find out who I am and what *I* want.'

'Can't we work this out together?'

'No, I have to do it myself. In many respects, this has actually got nothing to do with you or us. What it's got to do with is me. Margo says that what you and I have been going through is only the symptom of the larger problem. There's a lot of identity issues she still has to guide me through before I know what the problem is. Graham's been helping me when we have our group sessions —' Jason paused. His eyes were still shining with tears. 'The thing is that I do think I love you.'

I truly believed Jason. I wanted to believe him. He turned to Graham and indicated that it was time to leave. But not before his parting shot.

'If I do come back to you, it would be nice to know that you'll be waiting.'

He walked away. Long after he had left I sat there, alone at the table, holding that hope of his return in my hands.

Of course I was left to pay the bill.

———— 3 ————

Yes, the irony really was that Jason started it all. But I had no inkling of what was coming, even when I returned to the flat and found a message on the answerphone from Auntie Pat.

'Hello, Nephew. If you have any plans for the weekend, cancel. I'm coming down to see you and I want your undivided attention.'

That's all I needed. I ordered up a pizza, watched a movie on television and tried not to think of Jason. At two in the morning I found myself sitting on the tiles of the shower, the water cascading around me. All I could think of was that I'd come out to my parents, my boyfriend had cleared out, the flat was a mess — my whole life was a mess. And now my aunt was coming to see me when all I really wanted was to be left alone.

How I got through the week, God knows. But, come Friday, Auntie Pat blew in along with the southerly:

'So this is the den of iniquity, is it?'

I gave her the usual minimalist hug, showed her where to dump her suitcase and then took her out to dinner.

'How's the folks?'

'Well, you gave them both barrels last week,' Auntie Pat answered. 'What do you think? How we got through the wedding I'll never know.'

Ah yes, the wedding. The way we played Happy Family should have won an Academy Award. Nobody got up at the ceremony to show just impediment, and I did not disgrace anybody by turning up to the reception in a dress. Immediately after the wedding, however, with Amiria, Tyrone and American in-laws duly despatched to the four corners of the earth, Dad really let me have it. The stone I had thrown at the mirror of my parents' lives cracked the glass apart.

'Setting aside the way the family feels about this, Michael, do you think the iwi will still respect you once they know what kind of pervert you are? They have nurtured you, held you in their cradle of aroha, but what you do is abhorrent to them. It is anathema to their beliefs both as Maori and Christians.'

'Does God have to come into this?' I asked.

'The people have claimed you as one of their own. They have expectations of you because of your Grandfather Arapeta's mana. You have been brought up to have a place in the tribe. People like you are outcasts. They do not belong. If you are a Maori, one of the privileges is that when you die your iwi will honour you by coming for you and bringing you home to be buried. No matter where you are or what you've done — murdered somebody even — they will honour their obligation.'

'So it's better if I am a murderer?'

Mum joined the attack.

'Michael, doesn't your family mean anything to you? You have a proud lineage. Your grandfather was a respected man. You're the only grandson and the only son. Does this mean that we will have no mokopuna? No grandchildren? What will happen to our whakapapa, our genealogy? It will finish with you, Michael. How dare you be so selfish.'

'Amiria can have the children.'

At that, Dad raised his fist. This was the way he always did it. With words, words, always words and, if that didn't work, with fists.

But I didn't back down.

'Why don't you spit it out, Dad? The real reason why you're upset has

27

got nothing to do with me. It's all about this family and its reputation. What you're really angry about is that people will start pointing the finger at you and saying, 'Oh, have you heard? That grandson of Arapeta's, Monty's son, is a faggot.'

Sometimes the threat of violence has as much impact as the act itself. When Dad came for me, Mum screamed — but it was Auntie Pat who stopped him. Quivering, he pointed an accusing finger:

'Nobody in our family has ever been like you, Michael. Nobody.'

'You have to tell me, Nephew,' Auntie Pat asked me over dinner, 'how did all this happen to you?'

I looked at Auntie Pat and thought, 'Why should I be polite any longer?' I decided to be brutal. To her credit she didn't flinch or bat an eyelid.

'Maybe it dates from the time I was molested.'

'By whom?'

Two uncles. Drunk. Coming from a party and stumbling into a room where children slept. Any old bed. Any warm body. Ripping me open like a tin can.

'You don't want to go there, Auntie.'

'Somebody in the tribe?'

'Yes, but if I was you I wouldn't open that door.'

Auntie Pat backed off.

'Your parents are devastated. They thought they had taught you the difference between what was right and what was wrong.'

I lost my temper.

'All this business about what was right and what was wrong. What a man was and wasn't. It never left enough room, Auntie, for the man I was, the man I *am*. You've seen how Dad is. I grew up being told by him how I was supposed to be, what I was supposed to be. I could never live up to what he wanted. Being Maori was so hard! I suppose that's its triumph. But when I left home, to find myself someplace where the prohibitions weren't as strong, I think I failed the test.'

Auntie Pat waited for me to calm down. Then she slipped a question in under my skin and opened me up.

'What matters most to you, Michael? Being Maori, or being gay?'

For a moment I was taken aback. I didn't know how to answer. All my life I had been Maori. Who knows? All my life I had probably been gay as well. One was affirmative, something to be proud about. The other was negative, something to be ashamed of.

'I don't believe any of us should be made to choose, Auntie. So far I've always been what everyone wanted me to be. But there comes a time when you can't lie to yourself. It's not a matter of choice. I am who I am. And because of what I've done I've lost my parents — and I could be losing my boyfriend because I was too scared to do it earlier.'

Auntie Pat paused. Then she took a deep breath.

'Okay, Michael, I'm beginning to understand. And you were right to be afraid. Now, so help me God, show me your world.'

———— 4 ————

Luckily, Roimata was home when I telephoned her.

'Can you come clubbing tonight? I've got a visitor from out of town.'

Roimata laughed. 'Someone for you or someone for me! I was going to wash my hair and go to bed early but for you — let's do it.'

'Good. We'll pick you up in half an hour.'

Auntie Pat and I arrived at Roimata's and found her dressed to kill. She always had great style but going clubbing brought out the wicked in her. She liked to dress in something tight, where you could push things up and squeeze things in, and then perch it all on the highest heels possible. But she didn't seem too pleased when I made the introductions.

'We're going clubbing with your Auntie?'

'Auntie Pat's not that old,' I answered, defensive. 'Fifty, I think.'

'It's not her age that's the problem,' Roimata said. 'Just look at her! Twinset and pearls? We'll have to do something.'

Her face cleared. I knew that look only too well and had learnt to avoid Roimata when she had it. But how was Auntie Pat to know? So that when Roimata asked her brightly, 'Would you like a drink?' and then promptly spilled the lot down the front of the offending cardigan, Auntie Pat really thought it was an accident.

'Oh, my God. I'm so sorry!'

'That's okay,' Auntie Pat said. 'I've got another one back at Michael's flat —'

'Why waste time going back there? I'm sure I've got something that will fit.'

Off came the twinset and pearls and, before Auntie Pat could even move, on went a black crewneck over which Roimata threw *my* leather jacket. Then a fast makeover on Auntie Pat's face, some hair gel and heavy eyeliner, and voila!

'I can't go out looking like this!' Auntie Pat protested. 'If someone from home sees me they'll think I'm butch.'

Roimata pursed her lips.

'Precisely.' She looked at me and jabbed me in the ribs. 'The reason why Michael asked me to come along is so that people will think you belong to me. Isn't it, Michael, dear!'

It took Auntie Pat a while to figure that one out. Then the light dawned.

'Is Roimata the female version of you?'

'A lesbian? Yes.'

Auntie Pat turned to Roimata.

'But, dear, you're so pretty!'

As it happened, the places Roimata and I took Auntie Pat were so dark that it wouldn't have mattered what she wore. At The Hellfire Club the DJ was pumping the volume high, the strobe lights were making laser strikes through the dark and Cher, recently risen like an incredible Lazarus, was singing her heart out. The song was one of Roimata's favourites, and she was eager to get out into the middle of the dance floor.

'You go ahead,' I said. 'I'll get us some drinks.'

'I'll come with you,' Auntie Pat said. She looked like she was ready to bolt and go back to her safe little house in Gisborne.

'Oh, no you don't!' Roimata answered.

Before Auntie Pat could say another word Roimata had pulled her into the seething mass. For a moment I watched, grinning, as a couple of guys, who had taken off their shirts, twirled Auntie Pat around in their arms before releasing her to Roimata. One of them, shaven-headed and with a strong Slavic face, saw me and winked back. He motioned me over to join him and his friend but I put up my hands.

*Thanks, but not tonight.*

He smiled ruefully, then went back to dancing, waving his shirt in the air above the crowd.

I ordered at the bar and worked my way around the dance floor. Far over in one corner I saw Graham, Jason's friend. When he saw me he made a great show of turning his back.

Two can play that game.

Every now and then I caught glimpses of Auntie Pat and Roimata. At first Auntie Pat seemed stunned, as if one of the laser strikes had brought her down. The next time I saw her, it seemed Roimata had persuaded her not to just stand there but, well, to move *something*. She was dancing with what, for her, was considerable abandon.

'Is one of those water?'

A voice yelled in my left ear. I looked around. The shaven-headed guy from the dance floor had joined me. Close up he was taller than I expected. He'd put his shirt back on, using it as a towel and rubbing it against his skin to dry himself off. Compact build. Still boogying to the music.

'Sure.'

I passed the guy the glass. He held it above his head, letting the water trickle over his face and down his neck. The lasers illuminated the water limning his profile with green fire. Some of the water spilled over his lips and he licked the water in with his tongue. Then he looked at me.

'You're usually here with another guy. Is this going to be my lucky night?'

Direct. To the point.

I could have said, Yes, and allowed the exchange to go to the next level. Instead I shook my head.

'I'm with somebody.'

The guy shrugged. Ah well, you win some, you lose some. Then he gave a huge devastating grin.

'The name's Carlos,' he said. He pointed a finger at me and wagged it sternly. 'Remember it!'

Then Carlos was gone, back onto the dance floor, scattering the lights with his exuberance.

Auntie Pat and Roimata appeared.

'Shame on you, Auntie,' I said. 'How dare you enjoy yourself. You'll go straight to Purgatory.'

31

'Oh, leave her alone,' Roimata answered. 'She's having the time of her life.'

'There are men here actually dancing with women!' Auntie Pat said.

'Lots of people come just to dance and have a good time. Here you can do anything you want to do, be anyone you want to be. It's called freedom. Be careful, it can be contagious.'

'Oh, let's not waste any time talking,' Roimata interrupted. She pulled both of us back on the floor. Auntie Pat must have been a rock and roller from way back.

'Go, Girl!' Roimata laughed.

For a brief moment, my eyes connected with Auntie Pat's and I smiled at her.

'Look at *you*! How come it's taken all this time for us to realise that we can have such fun together?'

By three o'clock I was ready to call it a night. We'd gone from The Hellfire Club to Jordan's, where Auntie Pat was introduced to the joys of playing billiards.

'I'm bailing out,' I said.

'Good,' said Roimata, 'because Auntie Pat and I are going on to Girls Only bar. That okay with you, Girl?'

Once Roimata got going she could never stop. Auntie Pat didn't even have the courtesy to look apologetic.

'Sure, Girl,' she said to Roimata. She gave me a hug. 'Don't wait up!'

I caught a taxi, had a shower and put myself to bed. Around dawn I heard a car come to a halt outside the flat and Roimata helping Auntie Pat up the stairs to the spare bedroom. Just before leaving, Roimata came into my bedroom and sat down on the bed beside me. I was half asleep.

'Why didn't you tell me you and Jason had split up!'

'Did Auntie Pat tell you? I was embarrassed. He might come back anyway.'

'God, you men are all the same.'

She kissed me on the cheek.

'Sleep well, Michael.'

I was still asleep when, at midday, Auntie Pat woke me up.

'I have to go,' she said. 'I have to get back to the real world.'

'You haven't had any breakfast. You can't hit the road until you've had something to eat. Let me cook you up some bacon and eggs.'

Auntie Pat was insistent. 'No, stay in bed, Nephew. I'm okay.'

I relaxed, sinking back into the pillows. 'Well, I'm glad you came, Auntie Pat.'

'Thank *you* for showing me Sodom and Gomorrah. All night I was waiting for lightning to strike me dead or to be turned into a pillar of salt!'

To my surprise, Auntie Pat began to stroke my face and to tousle my hair. 'But I didn't just come to dance the night away, Michael,' she said. 'Or understand more about you and your other life. I also came to give you something.'

She reached down to the floor and picked up a large brown package wrapped around with string.

'I've kept this for years and years, not knowing what to do with it. I think I must have been waiting for someone like you to give it to.'

'What is it?'

'Don't read it now. Wait until I've gone.'

Auntie Pat's voice faltered. Then it rose in clarity and strength, as if sunlight had just broken through a clouded sky.

'Your father was wrong to say you were the first gay man in the family. He knows you weren't. He was there when our Dad, your grandfather Arapeta, kicked Sam out. And like you, Sam was afraid to tell Mum and Dad what he was. So I understand you, Nephew.'

'Sam?'

'My brother. Your father's brother.'

'But there's only Dad and you in the family.'

'No,' Auntie Pat said. 'We had an elder brother. His name was Sam.'

Her voice softened. She handed me the package.

'This will explain everything.'

Later, I took Auntie Pat's package out onto the balcony. She had tied the knot so firmly that I had to use scissors to cut through the string. I peeled through the brown paper covering. Within was another layer of packaging, old faded newspapers from 1970. Inside was a book:

SAM'S DIARY.

The diary was charred, as if at some time it had been caught in a fire. I fingered through it gently. The slightest motion caused some of its edges to fray and pages to fly like wings in the wind. Some had been burnt right to the spine. Others were missing.

A scorched and burnt newspaper clipping fell from the diary. It was part of the front page of the *Gisborne Herald*, dated 10 August 1969, and featured a large photograph under the heading: THEY'RE OFF TO VIETNAM. I recognised my grandfather at once, but not the three young men standing with him. Two were staring down at the ground, the third was looking straight ahead. Under the photograph the caption read: 'Poho o Rawiri marae was the venue for the rousing send-off of three young soldiers, the first Maori to volunteer from the district for the New Zealand infantry in Vietnam. Pictured are Mr Sam Mahana, Mr George [the surname was burnt from the clipping] and Mr Turei Johnson. Also pictured is proud elder, Mr Arapeta Mahana, father of Sam Mahana. Mr Mahana Senior served with distinction as a commander in the Maori Battalion during the Second World War, where he was awarded the Military Cross.'

I knew, even before I read the caption, that Sam was the one looking straight at the camera. He had the Mahana way of standing, balancing on both feet, leaning slightly forward, ready to take on the world. The same positioning of the head, slightly tilted to one side, wary but watchful.

Then suddenly it seemed he looked past the camera. By some trick of light he was looking at *me*. His eyes drew me in.

And the past came rushing out.

PART TWO

# Uncle Sam

## CHAPTER THREE

——— 1 ———

'Hei runga, hei raro! Hii haa, hii haa.'

The karanga, the ritual call of the women, came arcing from Poho o Rawiri meeting house to where Sam, George and Turei were waiting at the gateway. George and Turei were so nervous they were looking at their feet.

'Okay, boys,' Arapeta said. 'Time for action. Turei, you and George look up. Your people want to see you the way you will be in Vietnam. Proud. Eager. Men.'

'I'd much rather face the enemy than go through this,' Turei said to Sam. 'I'm used to being around the back digging the hangi, not coming through the front gate.'

'Did you have to do this, Dad?' Sam gestured at the marae and the huge crowd. 'Does everything have to be a big production number?'

'I want them to see what my son has become,' Arapeta answered. 'A soldier going to war, just like his father did.' He grasped Sam's hand in a firm handshake. 'I am very proud of you, Son. This will make you into a man. It is the happiest day of my life.'

Arapeta pulled Sam into a tight embrace. He searched in Sam's eyes for his soul.

'That's the trouble with Dad,' Sam thought. 'Always trying to get into my skin.'

Sam shut Arapeta out. He commanded his soul to hide in the shadows, far away from his father's probing gaze where it could not be seen.

'Toia mai, te waka! Ki te urunga, te waka! Ki te takotoranga i takoto ai, te waka!'

The surging sound of the welcoming haka burst across the air. Arapeta motioned to the black-scarved women in front of him to lead the ope onto the marae. Arapeta had assembled a formidable number of supporters for the occasion: two of his ex-Maori Battalion mates, Claude and Kepa, would help him lead some 50 other men and women from Maori military families of the district. On this day Arapeta would ritually present Sam, George and Turei into the hands of General Collinson, Commander-in-Chief of the Army. Collinson knew a publicity opportunity when he saw one. He had flown up to Gisborne with Army news media to film the occasion.

As the ope moved onto the marae, Sam saw his mother, Florence, and that his sister Patty had wriggled away from her and was running to him. He put his arms around her and ruffled her hair.

'You look so lovely,' Sam said. 'What a pretty dress.'

'I'm wearing this just for you. When are you coming back?'

'Not for a long time, sweetheart. But do you know what I'm going to do? I'm taking a photo of you with me and I'm going to put it in the pocket nearest to my heart. You're my *best* girl.'

At that moment Arapeta looked at Patty. The ritual entry was over and now the speeches would begin.

'Pat,' Dad said, 'go back to your mother and little brother Monty.'

Arapeta began issuing his instructions. A nod of his head here. A look of the eye and a jerk of his head there. The men would be up in the front. The three boys would be with them. The women, children and everybody else would be behind.

Patty gave Sam a quick kiss and was gone.

'This has been how my father has been all his life,' Sam thought. 'Up in the front. Always ordering. Never asking. And this is how I've lived my life, like everybody else, following his orders. But going to Vietnam is something I am doing for myself. I'm going there for *me*, so that I can prove —'

Sam couldn't find the words. Prove what?

The ope took their seats and the speechmaking began. Hemi, the elder for Poho o Rawiri, opened the proceedings, addressing all his remarks to Arapeta and recalling his exploits when he had commanded the 28th

Battalion. Claude, one of the ex-Battalion elders replied, and then came General Collinson. His sentiments were all about the appropriateness of a son of Arapeta Mahana following in his father's footsteps. Sam remembered that General Collinson had been one of Dad's commanding officers during the Second World War; one of the ironies that Dad loved to recount was that Collinson had sired only daughters.

'Blowed if I know why we're here,' Turei said to George. 'Nobody's interested in us. Why don't we sneak off to the pub and let Sam and his Dad hog the limelight.'

'Don't include me in this circus,' said Sam. 'This is Dad's show. It's got nothing to do with me. He's the man in the middle of the ring. We're just his show ponies.'

Some people started to titter and Arapeta made a short snap with his hand: 'Don't spoil it, Son.'

Sam's remark wasn't the only disturbance. There was a commotion in the crowd. George and Turei's mothers had come after all. They were dead against their sons joining up — particularly Lilly, Turei's Mum — and blamed Arapeta for not stopping them. Arapeta looked at them impassively. If they had come to cause trouble, so be it.

Arapeta motioned to his mate, Kepa, that it was his turn to speak. By this time, the day had become overcast. Clouds were advancing across the sky. The last speech was coming from the local people of the marae — next would be Arapeta's turn, and it would be over.

Finally, 'Tihei mauriora!' Arapeta cried. 'I sneeze and it is life!'

He grasped his carved walking stick and levered himself upward. He seemed to lift the sky up with his back.

'Turuki turuki, paneke paneke. Tenei te tangata puhuruhuru.'

Sam watched Arapeta's performance. This was one arena in which nobody could compete with him. When he walked to the centre of the marae, all eyes were on him. He began to speak and his authority hushed the world. He ceased being a man and, instead, became a God incarnate. No wonder men followed him into battle.

'Our ancestors have always been fighters,' Arapeta began. 'The Maori has never been loath to fight. In World War Two our people volunteered to go and fight Hitler, and our contribution was unequalled by any other race or people drawn into the conflict. On 13 March 1940, the 28th

Maori Battalion was given the word that we were on active service. We left Wellington for Europe on the *Aquitania* on 1 May. I will never forget how moving it was. We could still hear the Ngati Poneke girls singing "Now Is the Hour" when we were way out to sea.'

Arapeta pointed his carved drill stick at some of the old men in the crowd.

'We were all boys,' he said. 'Boys from the farms, boys from small maraes all over the country, boys who came out of the scrub and were still learning how to be men. We were all in C Company, weren't we, boys? They called us the Ngati Kaupois, the Cowboys.'

'Ka tika,' the old men called. 'That is true.'

'On 29 November 1940, we were ordered to the Middle East to join the First Echelon. Can you remember? We went via Greece where we had the first taste of battle at Olympus Pass, and had our victory in the sight of the Gods of Greece. After that first battle, we became men.'

Arapeta began to walk back and forward in front of the old soldiers, pausing before Hemi, the elder for Poho o Rawiri. Ribboned medals fluttered in the breeze.

'We tasted battle again at Crete, didn't we, Hemi! You were there! I saw you fighting against the Germans.'

Hemi straightened up. 'Ae,' he answered. 'The Germans had their Air Force above us and their troops on the ground. At Suda Bay we led the bayonet charge which decimated the Germans. We bayoneted over 100 in the kind of close-quarter fighting that comes natural to us. That's where we gained our reputation as fearless in the face of battle. Ae, ae.'

Arapeta moved on quickly, eyeballing another old soldier, pointing his stick at General Collinson.

'But it was in the desert campaign in Egypt and Libya that our Battalion truly made its mark, wasn't it, boys. I was your officer —' Arapeta caught General Collinson's eye. 'I mean no disrespect, Sir, but we did not need Pakeha to lead us. We had our own men, good men, abler men than many Pakeha.'

A murmur of approval ran through the crowd:

'Yes, that's right, Arapeta, stick it to the Pakeha.'

General Collinson remained impassive, though he inclined slightly towards his aide: 'The cheeky old bastard.'

'We had our trial by fire at El Alamein — and survived,' Arapeta continued. 'We fought at Sidi Mgherreb. The Battalion took a total of 1123 prisoners; we lost five killed and eleven wounded. In February 1942, the 28th Battalion was ordered to Syria. While we were there, Rommel attacked the Eighth Army in Libya, so back we went to help those other fellas out. At Mersa Matruh, while all the good guys were moving out, we were moving in. We saw Rommel's columns of German vehicles approaching us and the 21st Panzer Division encircling us. E hika, we were surrounded. But we got out of that little scrape and were soon back on our feet. You remember Munassib, boys, where we killed over 500 Hun? After that came Tripoli, Medenine and Tebaga Gap.'

All his life Sam had heard the old stories of the Maori Battalion's exploits. At every retelling the stories had become more epic — and Sam and his generation had diminished at every telling.

'Then came the battle for Point 209,' Arapeta said.

In the waning day the old soldiers moaned like a desolate wind.

'We were with Pita Awatere and it was he who committed C Company to the attack. The attack started at 5 p.m. that night. Our mate, Moana Ngarimu, lost his life there, clearing the area of two machine-gun posts. The Germans tried to counter-attack, to push us back. We ran out of grenades and picked up stones and used them instead. By 5 o'clock the next day we had won the point. Pita was given his Military Cross there. Moana was awarded, posthumously, the Victoria Cross.'

The marae erupted with calls. 'Ae! Ae! Ka tika!'

Arapeta proceeded quickly, thrusting into the heart of the memories.

'After that was Takrouna. What a battle that was! Our mate, Lance-Corporal Manahi, should have received a Victoria Cross for his work there, but he didn't. However, His Majesty saw fit to award me the Military Cross. After that, I was with Commander Awatere in Europe to continue the fight at the Sangro River and Monte Cassino.'

Skilled soldier and skilled orator, Arapeta paused and looked around the marae. He was accustomed to being listened to. He had learned well how to hold people in the palm of his hand. He did everything with style and with precision. He was used to asserting his mana over the likes, yes, even of General Collinson. The pause, however, allowed George and Turei's mothers to force themselves to the front of the crowd.

'You know we are against this,' Turei's mother, Lilly, called. 'If our boys die in Vietnam, their deaths will be on your head, Arapeta.'

Arapeta looked at her. Of the two mothers Lilly was the one to watch carefully — she could cause trouble, had always been outspoken, and her words came straight from the hip. She was only a woman, and tiny to boot, but Lilly was fearless and her words had a habit of sounding confrontational and had to be parried. Already the crowd were murmuring. Leadership was all about convincing people that you could lead them anywhere and get them there safely — even if you couldn't.

'Your boys will not die,' Arapeta answered. 'How do I know? I know my *son*. Like me, he is a leader, and he will bring your boys back safely to you, just as I brought my men safely back to their mothers. This I promise you.'

There was a gasp as the people on the marae absorbed Arapeta's awesome confidence, his arrogance, his assumption of god-like invincibility. As if he could make promises on behalf of his son.

'Kaati,' Arapeta said. 'Enough.'

He turned to the three boys. With a dramatic gesture, he drew a line in the air with the carved stick, joining them with General Collinson and the Army brass present.

'Ka tuwhera te tawaha o te riri, kaore e titiro ki te ao marama. When the gates of war have been flung open, no man takes notice of the light of reason. This ancient proverb comes alive again today with the decision our three boys have made to fight in Vietnam. It is good to see three of this generation carrying on the tradition of their forebears from the Maori Battalion. Boys, we who are left of the Maori Battalion salute you for your courage and your valour. You, my own son, will maintain the fighting spirit that will ensure that the Maori does not become as weak as women.'

Arapeta held the assembly in the palm of his hand. He encompassed the whole marae in his gaze.

'War parties, before setting off to war, were always made sacred to their mission. I bring you three boys under the tapu of Tumatauenga, the God of War. Fight for the honour of your tribe! Fight until there is no enemy left standing! Go to battle! Go! Go! Go!'

The words barked across the marae and echoed around the surrounding hills. They pulled the storm clouds closer.

With a rhetorical flourish, Arapeta leapt into the air. His eyeballs protruded. Spittle foamed from his mouth. He began a haka, the fierce declamation of Maori men.

'Ka mate, ka mate, ka ora ka ora!'

Immediately, old soldiers leapt to their feet and joined him. Old joints fused. Blood that had been slowed by beer and easy living fired again. The sparks ran like flames, boiling the veins.

'Ka mate, ka mate, ka ora ka ora!'

Sam took his place beside Arapeta and the crowd roared its approval. They believed Sam was supporting his father. He may have been, but he was also asserting his independence from the man who had ruled his life since the day he was born. His fists were bunched. The veins of his neck were taut. His eyes bulged as he looked at Arapeta.

And Arapeta *knew*. He sensed Sam's anger. He roared with laughter.

'So you think you're better than me, son? You'll never be better.'

The two men turned to each other, doing the haka as if they were opponents.

'Tenei te tangata puhuruhuru nana nei whakawhiti te ra!'

The crowd was on its feet, roaring and cheering its approval and, at that moment, the storm burst overhead.

'Aa, haupane, kaupane, haupane kaupane whiti te ra —'

The God of War himself had come to join the haka.

CHAPTER FOUR

——— 1 ———

And then the RNZAF Bristol freighter was flying out of Te Kore, The
Void, and descending through Te Po, the many gradations of The Night.
The night began to be streaked with light, speckled, mottled, fusing and
coalescing one pool of light with another. All of a sudden a blinding *flash*
irradiated the darkness. The sun was there, leaping like an ignited match
to burn a hole in the seam between sea and sky.

'Ara! Ki te ao marama,' Sam whispered to himself. 'Look, the day is
coming.'

No matter how many times he had seen the coming of light, Sam still
felt awed by its relentless majesty. As a young boy, he often sat on the
sacred mountain, Hikurangi, the first place on the earth to be lit by the
sun. There he would raise his face to the sun's, filled with wonder that
all its energy was coming from a molten orb of fire far on the other side
of the universe. He knew that *this* sun had already skimmed Hikurangi,
its beams refracted like a laser to burn its way toward Vietnam.

Other men of Victor Company had woken too, and were looking
below at the South China Sea. The water shimmered vermilion, then
purple, then cerulean blue tinged with crimson until, with a rush, from
out of opalescence came the daylight.

Tuia i runga, tuia i raro.

The world was being constructed again.

Tuia i roto, tuia i waho.

The top and bottom, bound together by the light.

44

Tuia i te here tangata ka rongo te Ao.

Now the outer framework and inner framework. Fixed firmly, the knots soldered by the shafts of the sun.

The promise of life, the impulse of history, was reborn.

Sam woke George and Turei.

'Sarge, I was having such a great dream,' George said. 'She was six foot, a red hot mamma and —'

Turei looked at Sam and yawned. 'Yes, thank you, Sarge, I'll have the chicken not the beef selection, if I may, and could you give me the wine they're serving in First Class?'

Below, like a swimmer rising out of the sea, Vietnam. Ahead, Phuoc Tuy Province, east of Saigon.

The forward doors of the Bristol Freighter opened and the heat of Vietnam poured in. The assault distended veins, popped sweat glands and licked up all the moisture from your skin surfaces. Sam felt his body trying to defend itself: shutting his eyelids, making him hold his breath, sealing itself off. But the heat was patient. It knew that some time he would have to breathe in. When, at last, Sam let out the last cool breath remaining and took another, Vietnam rushed in. Sucked him dry. Propelled its molten pain through every vessel and vein in his body, shredded his eyes and slithered into his scrotum until he was completely possessed.

'From now on,' the heat said, 'you're mine. I'll be in every breath you take and you will never escape from me. Never.'

'Get the men out, Sergeant Mahana,' Lieutenant Haapu ordered.

'You heard the lieutenant,' Sam called.

The company began to disembark, disgorging like fish to flap in the sun.

Sam put a hand up against the glare. The sun was a baleful eye that never blinked. The heat, like the glare, owned him also. His feet touched the tarmac of Vung Tau airbase.

'Holy Hone Hika,' he whispered.

US combat and military aircraft were everywhere. They loomed all around and above him. On either side were serried ranks of the fighter bombers. Armament experts were loading them with Thud missiles. On another runway were F-4C Phantom MiG combat air patrol fighters.

Elsewhere, helicopter squadrons, cargo and transport planes and spotter craft glinted in the sun.

Turei whistled under his breath.

'This must be Vietnam the *movie*. So where's John Wayne?'

At that moment Sam's ears were split by the high-pitched whine of turbines as two Iroquois helicopter gunship convoys took off from the field. One by one the pilots pulled pitch. The choppers shuddered, the noses dropped down then, tails up, began pulling away from the ground. Sam saw a machine-gunner, hunched over his weapon, sitting at an open door, still strapping himself in.

The blades of the gunship slapped the air hard. Pop pop *pop*.

But there was no time to enjoy the view. Immigration procedures had been set up at the American Transit Camp, where companies of Yanks and Aussies were also waiting to go forward into the war zone.

Sam was struck by the sudden quiet. The American boys were confused, disoriented, shit scared. Unlike the Kiwis and Aussies, most of the Americans were conscripts who had been drafted in, straight from civvy street via six weeks of basic training. The US Army made conscripts four promises. They would shave your head, give you a rifle, and send you to Vietnam. The rest was up to you. How you fitted yourself into the infrastructure of your unit was your responsibility. Which part of the battle zone, who you ended up fighting next to and whether or not your relationships would be happy was not part of the contract. Like as not your dope-smoking section commander was somebody who got to that position not because of his abilities but because he had been there a little bit longer than you. Who knows? At some point he might be struck by a bullet through the cranium and you might have to take over from him. Whatever, your experience of Vietnam, its boredom, horror and impact, was in the lap of wilful gods. They might send you out on a patrol that would lead you to My Lai. Or they might send some other bastard on patrol to My Lai.

And the fourth promise? The Army guaranteed that you would be returned home. Whether in one piece or many pieces, alive or dead, that could not be guaranteed. That was up to you. All the American conscript wanted to do was to serve time and, God willing, not return home in a sealed casket draped with the American flag.

Nobody wanted to be the last mother's son killed in Vietnam.

——— 2 ———

'I'm sweating like a fucken pig,' Turei moaned.

At Lieutenant Haapu's order, Sam had mustered the company to meet Major Worsnop, their Commanding Officer, and his Second in Command, Captain Fellowes.

'Company, 'shun!'

Major Worsnop inspected the ranks. Captain Fellowes followed a few steps behind him — and paused in front of Sam.

'You're Arapeta Mahana's son, aren't you?'

'No matter how I try,' Sam thought, 'I will never be able to escape my father.'

'I was present at your farewell on Poho O Rawiri marae,' Captain Fellowes said, 'Your father certainly put us in our place. I'm sure you'll prove to be as good a soldier as he was. Like father, like son.'

'At ease, men,' Major Worsnop said. 'Very soon you'll be moved to our New Zealand and Australian Task Force base at Nui Dat. When we and the Aussies entered the war, the US Commander in Vietnam, General Westmoreland, assigned Phuoc Tuy province as the primary area for our operations against the Vietcong. Vung Tau is the supply base and Nui Dat is the fire base. The command capacity includes three Australian infantry battalions, the Royal Australian Air Force's 9 Squadron — Iroquois helicopters, Caribou and Hercules transport squadrons — and a Canberra bomber squadron. The American backup comprises heavy self-propelled artillery batteries, helicopter units and ground attack aircraft — everything from F-4 Phantom jets and AC47 gunships to OV1 Bird Dog observer aircraft.' Major Worsnop paused, a twinkle in his eye. 'And then there's us.'

A murmur of amusement swept through the room.

'The New Zealand involvement in this war may be small by comparison with our Allies but we play an important part in the overall effort. As you soldiers all know, it's not size that counts but what you do with it.'

The whole company erupted into whistles and cheers. Major Worsnop didn't look the kind of bloke to crack such a funny. He waited for the commotion to die down.

'Men, you are all now part of the ANZAC Battalion. You represent our government's wish to assist the government of South Vietnam against Communist aggression. That is your job. My job, however, is more personal. I want to impress upon you that your command group is here to make sure that we do our job together. None of us is alone. We are all a team. If one of us falls, the rest carry him out. Let's all try to get through this war together. If you can, try to get on with the Australian personnel at Nui Dat.

'Welcome to Vietnam.'

'Okay, boys, saddle up and move out.'

Victor Company boarded a convoy of six trucks, escorted by Australian Army armoured personnel carriers, travelling to Nui Dat. Lieutenant Haapu assigned the last truck to Sam and his men.

'Once you're aboard, Sergeant,' he ordered, 'get your men to load and cock weapons.'

'Already?' George gestured at his rifle.

'Yes,' Sam said, 'and watch where you point that thing. I don't want to start this war with your barrel up my bum.'

The convoy rumbled through the gates and defensive perimeters of the airbase. Away from the port, Vung Tau had a surprising strength and beauty — an arrogance, almost. The French had founded the town as a Customs post, but by the 1890s it had become a prosperous little seaside resort. Bureaucrats and businessmen from Saigon, only 12-kilometres west, recreated the ambience of the French Riviera there; the sprawling villas, palm trees, beaches and bars almost persuaded you that the French still held sway.

George gave a low wolf whistle. 'Sarge, get a look at that.'

A young woman had come out of an office building. She wore the ao dai, a sheath dress over white trousers. Her face was glazed to perfection. If she smiled, it would split and crack.

'I thought you went for bigger women,' Sam said.

'Right now any woman would do.'

'That's not what you felt about my sister when you had your chance with her,' Turei said.

Turei's sister, Emma, was *big*.

'Well,' George pursed his lips, 'actually —'

48

'You bastard,' Turei answered with mock anger. 'I thought that kid of hers looked like you.'

The convoy moved through the more crowded and poverty stricken outskirts of the town. Here the locals seemed to know you were coming and, without even looking behind, stepped neatly to one side as you passed. In this country, the road rules were simple. If you were the big guy you had right of way. Everybody else — motor scooter, rickshaw, pedestrian — gave way. All, that is, except the kids who ran after the trucks.

'Watch that none of them throw you an apple,' Sam said. 'If they do, throw it back. It might look like an apple, might be red and round like an apple, but some of their apples have a habit of going boom.'

The convoy sped into open country, and the temperature soared to 30°C. Soon they left the sealed roads behind, and the red laterite dust swirled in. Sam moved down the truck to see Turei.

'I'll be okay,' Turei said. 'If I don't die of the heat I'll be sure to die of asthma.'

'Count yourselves lucky it's not the monsoon season,' Sam said.

'So my third option is to drown? Oh, great.'

Sam moved back to his seat. He had expected dense jungle terrain — not this. For as far as the eye could see was open landscape which looked as if it had been cracked open by an unforgiving sun. But no ordinary sun had scarred and defoliated this land. It had been ravaged by bombings, chemicals and military firepower.

Half an hour later, the open country gave way to secondary jungle terrain, interspersed with rubber and bamboo. The convoy climbed to 200 metres above sea level. A swampy area of mangroves was coming up. Ahead was a bridge.

Sam's sixth sense was alerted. The roading conditions were slowing the trucks down. The fourth and fifth vehicles in the convoy had lagged, leaving a dangerous gap in the convoy. The cover closed like the fingers of a fist.

'Pick it up,' Sam swore. 'Pick it *up*.'

He watched as the lead armoured vehicle crossed the bridge. The first truck, under Captain Fellowes' command, lumbered over. The second truck approached and negotiated its way across.

The bridge exploded. Isolated from the convoy, the three lead vehicles came under machine-gun fire from a nearby hill.

'Everybody out,' Sam ordered. 'Right side, right side.' He indicated the side of the truck away from the line of fire. He held his rifle high and dived out, hit the ground and rolled.

Tracer bullets ripped into the canvas canopy of the truck. Ahead he heard a boom. Saw an orange ball of fire as Captain Fellowes' truck was hit — but the men had managed to get out first.

There was no cover on the road. Sam kept rolling over the side and into a field of elephant grass. Next minute he felt somebody colliding with him. Turei.

'Can't you find your own cover?' Sam asked.

Another body barrelled into him.

'Is there room for one more?' George asked.

Raising his head, Sam saw Lieutenant Haapu signalling to him.

'Take out that enemy position.'

Sam acknowledged the order. Made the signal to George and Turei to move on his command. Counted one, two, three. Lifted himself off the ground and sprinted through the elephant grass, his body propelled by pure adrenalin. He waited in the lee of the road for George and Turei. They joined him, and all three went up and over, rifles at their shoulders, diving for cover on the other side of the road.

That's when a shadow settled over Sam like a big dark bird.

He looked up. The whole world had changed to whirlwind and deafening thunder. Something with murderous wings was settling, scything the sun, cutting it to shreds.

Slack-mouthed, George mouthed a word of awe. Fu-uck.

Immediately above was a hovering Huey Cobra gunship. It was so close that Sam felt he needed only to extend his hands upward and he would touch it. The turbines were whining, a battle cry, a high pitched scream, the noise driving into Sam's brain. The whole world was vibrating, shattering to pieces.

The gunship dipped, its nose down and tail up. It bristled with an arsenal of miniguns, rocket pods and chin turret guns. The gunners were hanging from the two side doors.

All of a sudden the chopper bucked. Something clicked and dropped from its underbelly and, with a whoosh, a rocket flared away from the gunship. There was another bucking movement and a second rocket was on its way. The rockets trailed blue smoke across the mangroves and up towards the enemy. Then the target area erupted into juddering explosions. The hillside sizzled and smoked.

The enemy fire stopped. With a lazy insolence, the chopper turned at right angles. Its front windscreen flashed. It dipped and sidled off and over the swamp. The gunners strafed the area with tracers. At the last moment the sun glinted off a painting of a cartoon bird: Woody Woodpecker. With a cheeky wag of its tail the chopper lifted away and over the terrain.

Within seconds the convoy secured its position and Captain Fellowes stood the company down. It was almost as if the attack had never happened.


That evening, Victor Company put up its tents in the rubber plantation that was part of Nui Dat. An hour later, Sam sat with George and Turei in the Mess. Kiwis and Diggers ate in rowdy groups, but Aussies with Aussies and Kiwis with Kiwis.

'Even in war time,' Sam thought, 'our friendly rivalry still exists. And if it sometimes boils over into baiting each other and punching each other, hey, that's the way it's always been.'

'Man, Sarge, this food is the best,' George said. 'If I can't have a woman at least food is the next best thing, eh? What do you reckon, Turei?'

But Turei was in the middle of an eyeballing competition with a red-headed Aussie who had taken a dislike to him.

'The bastard's trying to stare me out,' Turei said.

Before he could do anything about it, through the Mess came a group of six airmen. In the middle was a tall, smiling, blond pilot. An Aussie soldier yelled: 'Hey, Harper! Over here!'

The pilot nodded and made his way through the tables. He passed so close to the Kiwis that Sam could have reached out and touched him. Some of the men in the Mess began to whistle and stamp. One of them started to sing: 'Ha-ha-ha haha!' Others join in. 'Ha-ha-ha haha! That's Woody Woodpecker's song!'

The blond pilot bowed low at the waist and pretended to be surprised at such adulation. That's when everybody began to chuck bread rolls at him. Laughing, the pilot put up his hands to protect himself. He caught a roll in mid air and threw it back. As he did so, Sam made out the words USAF and the outline of a pair of wings on his jacket.

# CHAPTER FIVE

—— 1 ——

Victor Company's training cycle started every day at 0500 hours with PT, wrestling and hand-to-hand combat exercises. Rappelling, climbing and classes on Escape and Evasion came next, followed in the afternoons by weapons recognition and drills, demolitions, map reading, compass and night movement. Platoon and section manoeuvres kept the company's field skills honed sharp.

Not that Turei, whose position was grenadier, needed much extra practice. He was quickly an expert on placing claymore mines, and Captain Fellowes couldn't get over his pinpoint targeting.

'If only he knew,' Sam said, 'how much practice you've already had.'

'I'll say,' George laughed. 'All those assaults on police stations when you were a gang member, bro!'

The most important weapon and main fire support at platoon level, however, was the M60 general-purpose machine-gun — and in Sam's platoon the two-man gun team of Mandy Manderson and Jock Johanssen were considered the best. Their skill might mean the difference between winning and losing the close-range fire fights favoured by the Vietcong. Should Manderson become a casualty, Johanssen would take control of the weapon.

'I know you're just a rifleman waiting for your chance to handle this baby,' Manderson would say to him, 'but you've got one hope and that's no hope.'

'Shit. I may have to do the job myself and rig it so you have a little acc-i-dent.'

The physical training was balanced with company and platoon briefings, map reconaissance and other lectures on field operations in Vietnam.

'Gentlemen,' Major Worsnop said, 'Phuoc Tuy is bordered by the South China Sea and Saigon River estuaries. The population is just over 100,000, mainly concentrated along Routes 15, 23 and 44. Baria and Dat Do are the main urban centres but the major part of the population is rural. They are all around us. There are more of them than there are of us. And at least 25 per cent of them have family members on both sides of the conflict. What does this mean to us? It means that someone who looks friendly and acts friendly may not be friendly. One in four people you meet in the civilian population may well be, in fact, the enemy. But you won't know it.'

He waited for this piece of information to sink in.

'Why won't you? Because some of them will appear during the day as simple villagers working in their fields. At night, however, they may become local National Liberation Front militia undertaking guerrilla activities. At the simplest level, they may simply be gathering intelligence on our strength and size to pass on to the professional Communist forces in the area. This is why, unlike the Americans, we do not have local Vietnamese civilians working as cooks and cleaners at Nui Dat. The enemy mortar attacks are close enough as it is.'

The men laughed. Over the last few nights, Nui Dat had been subjected to frequent Vietcong bomb drops.

'The citizenry may be actively laying mines and preparing punji stake traps. Worse still, they may also be acting as local guides for the Communist main force units, allowing them to penetrate throughout our field of operation. Some will be armed.'

Major Worsnop paused. He ratcheted his briefing up a notch.

'I spoke earlier of the professional Communist forces in the area. I repeat, gentlemen, that on this score there are also more of them than there are of us, and they have great cover — at least three quarters of Phuoc Tuy is jungle. Our intelligence tells us that the Communists have two provincial force battalions in the area made up of locally raised soldiers with modern — I repeat, modern — infantry weapons. Don't believe the movies which portray them as some kind of peasant army. They are highly trained, remarkably adaptable to the terrain and extremely mobile.

'As well as these two — D440 and D445 — the Communists have three regular-force CVC regiments in the area. These are the most dangerous of all the Communist forces in Phuoc Tuy. They are primarily professionals, like us: trained soldiers mainly from North Vietnam. They are well equipped and well supported by a rocket battalion. They have air backup from Hanoi. Never forget that we are outnumbered. The Communists are a formidable enemy and it would be a mistake to underestimate them.

'So why are we here, and what can we do against superior numbers? We are here to try to maintain the upper hand. Our strategy is to stay on the defensive but, primarily, to go on planned offensive operations. To maintain unrelenting operations so as to prevent the enemy from even thinking of mounting any major operation against us. How? By blocking their supply routes, their access to Dat Do and Baria. By ambushing them as they move. By mounting major operations against their bases. By ensuring they can't gain even as much as a toehold in this province. Are there any questions?'

There was a silence. Sam put up his hand.

'Sir, the men want to know when they can expect their first operation.'

'It will come soon enough.'

Victor Company's activities escalated to perimeter duty, maintenance of the barbed wire defences and intense patrolling of the immediate vicinity of Nui Dat. Very soon, Second Platoon, under Lieutenant Haapu, also found itself undertaking operational reconnaissance of Phuoc Tuy, maintaining a regular pattern of drive-throughs to establish the Allied presence in villages and towns, and keep the enemy back.

But it wasn't all work. Nui Dat was well set up for sport and recreation and there was an outdoor theatre that Sam thought was surely an open invitation to some Vietcong gunner, if he got close enough, to aim his mortar at the screen. One evening, they even watched *A Yank in Vietnam*. Sam couldn't believe it. It was nuts. There on screen was a helicopter attack, Hollywood style. And there, just beyond the base, a firefight was underway. And he was sitting there with a Coke in his hand and laughing out loud. What he didn't know was that his laughter caught the attention of the blond American chopper pilot. As Harper looked through the crowd, a US Gunship 'Spooky' C47 roared overhead. Its fuselage was mounted with banks of electric powered miniguns that buzzed and poured out lines of tracer across the night sky. Harper saw a dark young guy, trying to stop from laughing so much. By some trick of perspective the tracers illuminated Sam's profile with a halo of fireflies. Something about him touched Harper, so that long after the gunship had swung low and away Sam's image remained on his retina.

———— 2 ————

One morning, Sam was brought face to face with the complex nature of the war and the terror of the local population trapped between opposing armies in a perpetual war zone.

'Get the boys ready,' Leiutenant Haapu said. 'The ARVN Vietnam Army have a search-and-destroy mission taking place at a village on the coast. They've radioed for back-up.'

On the way out to the trucks, Sam saw a shimmering green insect flailing in the dust, desperately trying to escape from attacking scorpions.

Even before the convoy arrived, Sam could smell the violence. At the run, weapon cocked, Sam led the men through the village square. Two of the houses were on fire and some of the villagers were screaming. Sam saw an ARVN soldier lift the butt of his rifle and club an old man with it. The old man fell.

Sam took up a position next to an Aussie veteran.

'What the hell's going on?'

'The ARVN are rockin' and rollin' with the slopes.'

Sam was stunned at the ferocity of the ARVN search. But, after all, they came to war with a history that Sam could not comprehend. They had been fighting the Communists since World War Two. Maybe their fathers had been killed, their brothers and sisters had been killed, perhaps their children had been killed in the bitter battle with the North. Screaming obscenities, they were herding the villagers into the square.

'This village,' the Aussie continued, 'has been resistant to the ARVN for some time now. Ever since their headman was killed' — he looked over at one of the ARVN commanders. 'By that bastard over there, actually. The ARVN doesn't like resistance, even though they may have been the cause of it, so they keep coming back to give these villagers special treatment. This is the third time I've been here and I'm bloody sick of it. I came to Vietnam to protect the locals against the Communists. I didn't think I'd have to watch them being done over by their own.'

Four hours later, the villagers were still confined in the square. The sun was beating down, slashing their faces with heat. The ARVN commander refused them water and food and kept up a constant barrage of physical and verbal harassment. Every now and then, one of the villagers was led off into the surrounding trees. A rifle cracked.

'Scare tactics,' the Aussie veteran said. 'Take somebody away, pretend to shoot them and hope that one of the villagers will break down and admit they're operating a Communist cell. But these people aren't scared by us. Look at their eyes —'

Sam tried to see what the Aussie was seeing. The villagers weren't in fact looking at the ARVN or the cordon of soldiers surrounding them. They were watching the hills. There Sam saw their real fear.

'You catch on quick. The villagers get fucked by us, they get fucked by the Vietcong, they get fucked by anybody who passes through. There they are, trying to get on with their lives, working the paddy fields or looking after their livestock. Next minute we come in, flying our little flags, pretending to be their saviours but roughing them up in the process. If it's not us it's the Americans. We round them up, cordon off their village, search their houses, upset their lives and interrogate them. Our mates, the ARVN over there, kill their cattle or water buffalo to make them talk. Sometimes we imprison them and shoot them if we suspect they're holding out on information. Or some peasant who has a vendetta against another peasant will whisper to the ARVN that his neighbour is a collaborator with the Vietcong. Next minute, *bang*, and Mr Innocent Neighbour is shot in the head and falls down dead.'

The Aussie veteran pulled out a cigarette and lit it. He offered one to Sam. 'The name's Jim.'

'Pleased to meet you. I'm Sam and, thanks, but I don't smoke.'

'We're supposed to be fighting *for* them,' Jim continued, 'but you know what really sucks? We're shit scared of them at the same time. We embark on these search-and-destroy missions, looking for evidence of the enemy, and all the while the villagers are waiting for us to do our job and get out. And who are left in the villages? The policeman is gone. The school teacher is gone. The local priest is gone. All probably executed in the early days by one side or the other for suspected collaboration. Only the old and the very young are left. But we're still scared of them — and you know why? Because it's so difficult to see the difference between a Vietnamese and a Vietcong. Our suspicions feed our fears. Before you know it we start thinking they're shit, they're dogs and we're treating them like that — so don't think it's just the ARVN. Maybe we've just come back from a mission and some of our buddies have been killed. Maybe we've picked up the pieces after they've trodden on a mine. Pushed somebody's brains back into his skull before putting what's left of him into a body bag. So we're all juiced up, hopped up with some kind of rage and need to have revenge. We start thinking, "This boy may be only five years old, but he could kill me." Or, "This old lady looks like a nice friendly grandmother but, who knows, she may have a grenade up her sleeve." So we knock them around and, just to make sure, kick them again. Then somebody gets trigger happy. Some American high on dope happens to let loose with his M16, all because a villager is reaching for something that looks like a grenade. Or some grunt ups his flame-thrower and fries some bystander to hell. Or we see somebody running into his house to protect his family when we arrive and we think, "They must *all* be enemy," and we're firing a 40mm grenade in through the window whether they are or not. Before you know it, the whole platoon is shooting up a village, setting it on fire, killing whoever happens to be in the way.'

Jim took a long draw on his cigarette.

'All this while the Vietcong are watching from the hills. Sure, the ARVN are probably right that there *is* a Commie cell here. When we finally leave, flying our pretty little flags and returning to the safety of our own fucken fortress on the hill, you think it's over for these people? No wonder they've been looking at the hills. After we leave and the twilight comes, the hills start to move and, sure enough, in come the Vietcong and it's *their* turn to fuck these people. With the help of their spies they round everybody up again. You had a conversation with the Australians? Bang, you're dead. You were seen passing something to one of the soldiers. Bang. You smiled? Bang, bang, bang. You say the ARVN took one of your sons to join them? Okay, *we* take your next son to join us. You haven't got another son? Okay, your daughter will do. Say goodbye to your papa, little girl, we're your family now. And, just to teach you villagers all a lesson, we gonna take your head man out into the fields. Oh, look, old man, is that your little granddaughter running towards us to save you? Up comes the rifle and bang. But it's not the head man who falls down dead, it's his granddaughter. That's the lesson. Old man better make sure his village behaves better next time or other grandchildren get the chop.

'On top of all this, all sides are dropping bombs and dumping defoliants on their paddy fields. It's a no-win situation for these villagers, and they know it. That's what we're fighting. A sick, rotten, mean son-of-a-bitch war.'

A few days later, Sam's platoon was assigned another mission, to patrol the 'Fence', a large minefield which ran from Dat Do to the sea, designed to keep the Vietcong away from the population centres and possible sources of weapons supply. It seemed the minefield had also become the source of mines *for* the Vietcong. They dug them up and sneaked away with them under cover of darkness.

On his second morning there, just before light, Sam came across Jim again. Both men were at the end of their patrol.

'Gidday, Kiwi. How goes it?'

'Fine. And you?'

'Me, I'm on the countdown to return to Australia. Only a coupla weeks to go and I'm out of here, mate. Back to the missus and the kids.'

Jim's face wrinkled into a grin. Down by the shore children were playing just beyond the perimeter of the minefield.

'You're one of them Horis, aren't you?' Jim asked. 'If I came up on you in the dark, and if you weren't in uniform, I'd probably mistake you for one of them locals.'

'How would you know I wasn't,' Sam answered. 'The uniform wouldn't guarantee you anything, would it.'

'You *have* learnt fast. That's the trouble with this war. You can't be sure of anything. What the enemy looks like. Who the enemy is —' Jim took out his cigarettes. 'As soon as I get home I'm giving these up.'

Suddenly, there was a small scream. One of the children had fallen.

'Bloody kids! Dong lai! Halt. Get outta here!'

Jim flapped his arms and walked over to where the children were playing. As he approached, they ran away like small black animals scurrying into the dawn. The fallen one remained on the ground, and Sam shouted: 'Jim, *no*.'

He saw that the children hadn't been playing at all. They had been trying to lift mines from the field. One of them, the kid lying on the ground, had messed up.

'Oh, shit,' Jim said.

The mine the kid dropped was only seconds away from detonation. There was nothing else to do except get between him and the mine, and hope he survived the blast.

'There, there, son.'

The mine fragmented, cutting Jim and the kid to shreds.

—————— 3 ——————

The senselessness of it all. Jim's death put Sam into a tailspin. The Aussie veteran was the first soldier Sam had known to die in Vietnam. Now he had dreams about the mine exploding. He had been near enough to see the way in which Jim and the child suddenly disintegrated. One minute they were standing there, silhouetted against the dawn. The next moment they were gone. Chunks of meat and scattered bone on the beach. And he was still standing, in a state of shock, with Jim and the kid's blood falling like rain on his face. What kind of enemy would send kids out to lift their mines for them?

'It could have been me instead of Jim,' Sam realised.

On this occasion death had brushed Sam by. But he had felt the eddy of wind as death passed. The next time he might not be so lucky.

So how did you recover from the death of a friend? You got through it minute by minute, day by day. You tried to put it behind you. You got on with the job. You went forward and before you knew it you were in the clear.

One afternoon, Sam, George and Turei came across some men playing half court basketball at the base: the blond American chopper pilot, his co-pilot and another American airman. The Yanks were making a lot of noise asking for the ball and directing the play, and something about the game made Sam pause – the banter and laughter seemed to come from another world. Just as the three Kiwis were about to pass by, the blond pilot saw Sam, remembered a profile illuminated by tracers and, in a moment of spontaneity, sent the ball spinning over to him. The pilot's grin was free and as wide as Illinois. Somehow it closed the door on Sam's sadness.

'Feel like a game?' the blond pilot asked.

'Us against you? Gee, I dunno.'

'Come on,' the pilot said, 'I know you want to say yes. Don't give me such a hard time. Me, Fox and Seymour could do with some guys to play against.'

Sam pretended to play coy and innocent. In on the pretence, George and Turei tried to keep their faces straight.

'Isn't basketball your national game?' Sam asked, kicking at the dust. 'We don't play much basketball where we come from. We're small town boys and you guys are American city folks.'

'We'll make it fair,' the blond pilot said. 'How about our putting 10 points on the board for you.'

'Make it 14.'

'Twelve.'

'Done,' Sam said, spitting on his hands. He took off his shirt and the greenstone pendant he wore around his neck.

The Americans laughed with surprise but winked at each other. This was going to be a massacre. The blond pilot shook Sam's hand.

'By the way I'm Cliff Harper.'

'You can call me Sam.'

Harper gave Sam the ball. Before he could even draw breath Sam spun the ball over to George, George passed to Turei in the D who twisted, jumped and slam dunked the ball through the hoop.

'What the fuck?' Harper gasped.

'Two points to us,' Sam winked at him. 'Takes us up to 14. You're still to score. Your ball.'

Harper looked at Sam, stunned. 'So you don't play much basketball where you come from? Who taught you guys?'

'Mormon elders from Brigham Young University.'

'And I suppose you small town boys never played professionally?' Harper asked, getting the picture.

'Had you asked I would have told you,' Sam answered. 'We were in our rep team. Can't you cut the talk and get on with the game?'

Harper roared with laughter. 'Oh, you sly piece of shit,' he said.

The game resumed. Harper passed to Seymour but Turei stole the ball from him. Turei was blocked by Fox who passed to Harper who was, Sam had to concede, not a bad player for a Yankee boy. Harper ran the ball into the D. Sam tried to block, there was some jostling —

'Aren't you getting a bit too close and personal?' Harper teased.

Sam stepped back, startled, and Harper pushed past, lifted, and drifted in the ball without touching the hoop.

'Nothing but net,' Harper said to Sam. 'Fourteen to you, two to us.'

The game began again. Sam signed to George and Turei to go man on man. When they scored the next two points, Harper looked at Sam with delight.

'Hey, guys,' he called to his team mates. 'There *is* a God. At last worthy competition.'

Harper hunkered down. It was getting hot, so he pulled off his T-shirt. Sweat was pouring across his pectorals. He pointed at Sam.

'I'm gonna make it rain on you all day. You are my *bitch*.'

The game got serious and had it not been for Harper's schedule, Sam guessed his side would eventually have been outclassed by the Americans. The heat was ferocious and Turei fumbled, letting the Americans even the score.

Sam changed the strategy. He had always been good at long shots at the hoop. Instead of going for the D he kept on lifting, sighting the ball from outside the D and lobbing it in.

'Look at that fucker!' Harper said to Seymour in admiration.

Twenty minutes later, Sam's team was only just ahead. Harper looked at his watch. 'Damn, damn, damn.' He signalled to Fox and Seymour.

'We gotta go,' he said to Sam. 'I'll save you for another day. Be very afraid.'

Sam grinned and they joined the others at the tap, splashing the water over their bodies and rinsing out their mouths.

'So what other games do you play?' Harper asked.

The question was innocent enough but somehow Sam couldn't resist teasing: 'American football.'

'You're kidding!'

'Don't you know? American football, that's a traditional Maori sport.'

With a roar of laughter, Harper lunged for Sam and all of a sudden they were sparring, ducking and weaving just out of each other's reach but sometimes connecting — the warmth of the sun-dried skin grazing the other. Then Sam put up his hands and went to the tap and dashed cold water onto his face. When he turned he saw that Harper had picked up the greenstone pendant.

'What's this?'

'It's a hei tiki. My father gave it to me before I left home. It's been in my family for years. It's supposed to protect me.'

The hei tiki was in the shape of a man. The sun refracted through the whorls and spirals, lit up the face with its wide eyes and protruding tongue.

'A *hay teekee*?' Harper asked. 'I can even see the veins.'

When Arapeta had placed it around Sam's neck, the hei tiki had come alive with his body heat and found a place on his chest where it could settle.

Harper pointed to the penis, curving around the left thigh.

'And what's this? And these?'

There were pale spots in the greenstone spurting from the head of the penis to the hei tiki's shoulders.

'The name of the hei tiki is Tunui a te Ika. The name commemorates Halley's Comet. When people saw it in the sky it reminded them of a man's orgasm when he is making love. As for the pale spots, they're um, stars . . .'

Harper looked at Sam to see if he was kidding or not.

'You're having me on.'

'No, it's true,' Sam said. He tried to keep his face as straight as possible but, in the end, he couldn't help it. He doubled up with laughter, and Harper gave in. Turei, George and the others watched, perplexed. Then:

'I have to go,' Sam said.

He flicked the cord of the hei tiki over his neck. Felt the hei tiki find its home. Extended his hand to Harper.

'Thanks for the game.'

Harper's handshake was firm. 'Affirmative,' he grinned. 'The base is small. Maybe we'll bump into each other again. You owe me a re-match.'

It was a fair enough expectation but it never happened. Then, a week later, Victory Company was given leave in Vung Tau.

# CHAPTER SIX

——— 1 ———

'Time to party,' Turei crowed, rubbing his hands together.

It was four in the afternoon, and Victor Company had just settled into their quarters in Vung Tau. The one thing on everybody's mind was sex and booze — not Captain Fellowes wasting his time with his cautionary briefing:

'I know this will go in one ear and out the other, but don't go anywhere alone, don't spend all your money, stay out of areas that look dangerous, if you want to have sex with the bar girls wear a condom, and get back before curfew.'

Ha. When Sam, George and Turei formed a threesome and headed into town, staying together was the only piece of advice they intended to keep. As for the rest, well, rules were made to be broken, mate, and surely Captain Fellowes knew that Maori never wore condoms.

By five o'clock the three boys from Waituhi hit the shantytown of bars near the port. George was leading and he suggested a shortcut which found then lost in a maze of narrow passageways between bustling market stalls.

'You're supposed to be a scout,' Turei grumbled, 'but you can't even find your way to a fuck.'

The market was filled with flowers for temple offerings, and fruits like pineapples, green papayas, rambutans, mangoes, lychees, breadfruit, guavas, passionfruit, bush limes, custard apples and avocados. Hawkers

63

sold rice, fresh noodles and bean curd. A vendor offered eggs of all kinds: quail eggs, chicken and duck eggs, and preserved eggs covered in a sooty mixture of ash, lime and salt. In another area of the market were baskets crammed with tiny chicks and ducklings, cheeping, wriggling and climbing over each other. Indoors, under a corrugated-iron roof, were fresh fish and meat markets. Fish wriggled and flopped in shallow metal trays. Lobsters with royal blue claws and iridescent purple carapaces lay in heaps. White geese with yellow beaks sat tethered next to black geese with red beaks. There were song birds for sale inside bamboo cages. Clouds of flies rose as customers browsed through lumps of meat. Some looked suspiciously like dog or rat.

George gave a horrified yell as he blundered into a snake pit. The snakes had bright green eyes and shiny green skin. A wizened old man was skinning them. They hissed and struck as he grabbed them and slit them open.

Sam took over the lead as soon as they were through the jumble of stalls. They reached the other marketplace where sex in all its infinite varieties was waiting — a jumble of streets with red-light bars filled with bar girls, pimps and touts. Already trade was brisk, and Sam, George and Turei were just three in a big stream of Yank, Aussie and other soldiers walking through the streets. Girls with big smiles tugged and pulled and called out to them as they passed by.

Some of the girls weren't, well, exactly pretty. It was remarkable what a little darkness and lighting could do; wanting to be laid also helped. There was nothing like a surfeit of raging hormones coupled with the relaxing effect of bad alcohol to make every girl a real doll.

George saw a call girl to his liking. She was built on the big side which was probably why she wasn't as busy as her companions. She eyed George and she knew a sucker when she saw one.

'Whoa up, Neddy,' George said.

'You bastard,' Turei answered. 'She looks like Emma!'

'What can I say? Your sister has ruined skinny women for me —'

George approached the girl and chatted to her. She showed the stamp in her health card, indicating she'd had a check-up.

'You know another two girls for my friends?' George asked.

The girl put two fingers in her mouth and whistled — and she was soon negotiating with other bar girls who had come running at her signal.

'All the girls are ready,' the girl said, 'just for you Kiwis.'

The three girls dragged the boys into the LOVE FOR YOU HERE BAR, just across the street. Very soon they were in separate cubicles with a girl in each. In deference to Sam's rank, George gave him the prettiest one, he held on to the big one and Turei had the third. Sam's girl had him climaxing in seconds.

'Wah,' the bar girl smiled, 'you've been waiting a long time for that, eh, soldier boy!'

Half an hour later, Sam made his way down the stairs. The bar was so crowded and filled with smoke and soldiers that he didn't see Turei until he bumped into him.

'Yo, bro!' Turei grinned. 'Is the Sarge a happy chappie?'

Sam smiled and nodded. 'So where's George?'

'Still upstairs, the bastard,' Turei said. 'But I'm going to have his arse. Look at this —' Turei had been in negotiation with the bar owner and had bought a glass of evil-looking wine.

'What is it?' Sam asked.

The bar owner thought Sam was interested. He showed him a small barrel filled with clear liquid. Coiled in the liquid were several fat snakes, a metre long, with brown backs and bellies striped cream and black.

'Snake wine of course,' the bar owner said. 'Makes your manly weapon big and strong. And after you drink wine you eat snake. No good if manly weapon big and strong but does not go all night long. You want some?'

'No thanks,' Sam said.

At that moment George joined them. 'Oh, mateys, I need a drink.'

Sam saw the gleam in Turei's eye. 'This is not a good idea,' he whispered. George hated snakes. But:

'I'll get you the house special,' Turei said, his eyes mischievous. He signalled to the bar owner and pointed to the barrel. 'Hey, bring us some of your special wine! My pal wants to have a drink.'

The bar owner filled a glass with the snake wine, and George swallowed it down in a second.

'What's it taste like?' Turei asked.

'Isn't it what you guys are having? Isn't it home-made vodka?' George asked. He downed another glass.

Turei gave Sam an evil wink.

'While we're here, we may as well eat,' he said.

Sam went to warn George but Turei kicked him in the shins.

'It's on me,' Turei said.

He ushered George away to a table so that he couldn't see the bar owner taking one of the fat brown snakes from the barrel.

Five minutes later, the bar owner placed a plate in front of George. On it lay chopped chunks of meat, brown on top and striped cream and black underneath, fried and doused in a thick sauce.

'Aren't you guys eating?' George asked.

'We've eaten,' Turei replied quickly.

'You sure you don't want any more? This steak is great.'

'Er, no thanks.'

Sam watched with a queasy stomach as George ate and drank.

'You like?' the bar owner asked. 'You want more?'

'Yeah, sure,' George answered.

The bar owner brought the barrel to the table. Turei started to shake with mirth. The bar owner picked up two snakes.

'Which one? Brown? Or striped?'

'Oh, you bastard,' George said to Turei as he threw up.

---

2

---

By ten, the whole of the red-light district was going up like a rocket. George and Turei were half drunk and singing 'Ten Guitars' and Sam was in the middle, holding both of them up. They joined up with some other Kiwis and headed for MADAME GODZILLA'S. The place was really jumping. There, after a tussle with some Aussies, including the red-headed guy who'd been eyeballing Turei ever since arriving in Vietnam, they scored a table.

'You and me, Hori,' the red-head said, 'one day we'll have a go one on one together.'

'Any time, any place,' Turei replied.

All of a sudden, through the haze, Sam saw Cliff Harper with his chopper colleague, Fox. They were coming with some girls from the back room. As they pushed aside the beaded curtain and returned to the bar, they were greeted with whistles and grunting noises. Laughing, Fox slapped Harper on the back and made him the focus of the applause. Harper grinned.

Some pretty hot sex had been going on in the back room. Even now, two of the girls were fighting for Harper's attention. Good-humouredly, he put up his hands: 'No, ladies, I'll call it a night.'

The girls were persistent. There was a firm glint in Harper's eyes as he tried to underline his answer.

'Then perhaps you want to dance?'

Harper was diplomatic. But after a while, as more girls pressed in on him, frustration showed in his face. He'd had his sex and now he wanted to drink with his pals. And then Sam saw Harper's fingers moving in a strange way.

*Get out of my face, willya?*

Sam was taken aback. Harper was signing, in the language normally used among the deaf. Luckily for Harper, some of his chopper mates were willing to take charge of the girls, who flowed away from him as he slumped down in his chair and put his head in his hands. His fingers moved again in sign.

*God, Johnny, I'm so bored.*

Harper took a swig of his beer. He looked disinterestedly around the bar. Across the room he saw Sam; he squinted his eyes just to make sure, and smiled. He was just about to look away when, impishly, Sam moved his fingers.

*Who's Johnny?*

Beer sprayed from Harper's mouth. He put his glass down in astonishment.

*You can read me?*

*Didn't you know? Sign language, like basketball, is a Maori tradition.*

Harper started to grin.

*Now let me guess. I suppose you were taught it by Mormon missionaries?*

*You got it. Are you with friends?*

*Yes. You too?*

There was a sudden increase in the noise and smoke. Harper gestured helplessly and then made jabbing motions.

*The noise in here is too loud. Meet me outside. I wanna talk.*

Sam nodded. He grabbed his beer and told George he was going for some air. He pushed and shoved through the crowd, getting love pats all the way, and finally broke free into the street. He watched as Harper extricated himself from his friends and joined him. For a moment the two men stood there, looking at the stars. It didn't feel awkward. It felt *right* not to talk. It felt good just to *be*. Sometimes there was no need to fill the air with words.

'So who's Johnny?' Sam began.

'My kid brother,' Harper answered. 'He was born deaf and dumb. Mom and Dad and the rest of us had to learn how to sign so we could talk to him.'

'The rest of us?'

'I'm a mid-Western boy. From Illinois. My Dad has a farm a few hours out of Chicago. I've got two older sisters, Gloria and June, much older than me. But Mum wanted boys, so poor old Dad had to keep on trying until it happened. I came along twelve years after June, and then Johnny a couple of years later to keep me company. I got to know how to sign so well that in the end Mum and Dad gave up on it and whenever they wanted to talk to him they'd say to me, "Cliff, tell your brother this," or "Cliff, tell your brother that." By that stage, however, we were in our teens and he had learnt how to read their lips. But we loved talking together in our own way and it got so bad that it used to annoy the hell out of everyone. "What are you two boys talking about?" Mom would ask. Or June would say, "Are you talking behind my back, Johnny Harper?" I tell you, we had such fun, Johnny and me.' Harper's face creased into an expression halfway between happiness and yearning. 'I miss talking to Johnny. I miss talking to him in our secret language. Sometimes, like back there in the bar, I forget myself and sign as if he's there. Instead, it was *you.*'

Harper ran his fingers through his hair. Gleams of gold scattered through the night.

'I don't usually shoot my mouth off like this,' Harper continued. 'So how about you? How did you learn how to sign?'

'You know those Mormon elders? One of them, Elder Crowe, coached us in basketball *and* American gridiron —'

'You mean you were serious? You're kidding me!'

'Kidding you? Man, if you and your helicopter mates want to try to take me, George and Turei out in football you'll be wasted again — and you'll be *my* bitch.'

Cliff Harper spat on his hands. 'You're on. But what about the signing?'

'Well, Elder Crowe was partially deaf and dumb. You know how it is. His words were sometimes kinda thick and knotted, and difficult for the guys in the team to understand. Because I was captain of the team, I learnt to sign and was able to pass on the instructions. Sometimes, just to get Elder Crowe going, I didn't pass on what he wanted. I remember one game I told the guys what *I* wanted them to do! Only I made out it had come from him. I sure got it in the neck when we lost.'

Cliff Harper roared with laughter. He leaned back and breathed out.

'God it's good to laugh. I mean, really *laugh*. This war takes it all away and before you know it you've forgotten so many things. Like, I've suddenly remembered, you know it'll be the end of Fall right now at Back of the Moon —'

'Back of the Moon?'

'The name of the farm,' Harper answered. 'The trees that were a blaze of orange and red will have lost their leaves. The cold wind will be coming down slow and easy from the north, just cold enough to snap the steam of your breath as it leaves your mouth. My Dad and Johnny will have taken the cattle to their winter feed in the high country. Soon the snow will come and the blizzards and sleet. We had a grizzly killed some of our cattle last year. I had the sights on it but, wouldn't you just know it, the rifle froze up on me and jammed. By the time I got the bolt working again that grizzly had gone. I put the dogs on it, but they couldn't make any headway through the snow. The snow gets to pile up higher than a man. It'll be up to Johnny to get that grizzly if it comes again. Thank God he missed the draft because of his disability —' Harper swallowed hard. 'But there I go again,' he said ruefully, 'talking up a storm.'

There was a loud burst of noise from inside the bar, cheers and whistles, and the sound of applause. Harper turned to Sam.

'Hey! You gotta see this. It's the floorshow. Madame Godzilla.'

Harper put his right arm around Sam's shoulders and began to pull him to a window. It happened so easily, this physical pulling in, the weight of Harper's right arm over Sam's shoulders, that Sam simply allowed his body to flow into the friendliness of the embrace. When they reached the window, because Sam was shorter, Harper pushed him forward and stood behind him so that Sam could get the best view.

'Can you see?'

'Sure.'

The stage was empty, but the pianist was waiting to start up.

'Why is she called Madame Godzilla?' Sam asked.

'You'll see,' Harper said.

Inside the bar the patrons were beginning to thump on the tables, setting up a drumming rhythm that reminded Sam of the natives of Skull Island, calling on King Kong to come for the sacrificial maiden. Except that instead of banging three massive strokes on a moon-sized cymbal, somebody held up a little triangle: *ting, ting, ting*. The deflation of the image made Sam snort with hilarity.

'Here she comes,' Harper said.

The bead curtains parted on the stage. Madame Godzilla appeared. She — or was it he — was a *big* girl. She had poured herself into a black dress way too small and way too high above the knees where a suspicious bunch of coconuts bounced and swung. She was carefully made up and wore an astonishing platinum-blonde wig which obscured one eye. When she smiled several gold teeth flashed inside her betel-stained mouth. She looked vaguely, gruesomely, familiar.

With a kick at the pianist, Madame Godzilla went into her routine.

'You wanna have luv, soldier boy?'

Bump, grind, swing them pearls, bat those eyelids, Girl, and wink.

'Introducing the Marilyn Monroe of Vung Tau,' Cliff said. He was so close, his breath cooled on Sam's neck.

Madame Godzilla stepped off the stage to mingle with the patrons, and four GIs scrambled to get out of her way. No such luck. She hauled them back with her massive arms, sat one of them on her suspiciously bumpy lap and began to sing:

'(You lucky son of a beetch!) I wan' you to luv meee —'

Madame Godzilla was really working her butt, wriggling and rotating and making deep lascivious moans. She dug her fingers, with their three inch nails, into the GI's crutch — and ouch. Yow. He paled as, to great laughter, she pulled a face and made out that what he had was very difficult to find.

'I know a trick I do to your stick (if you got one) —

'I can take you high-ah, fill your desire-ah!'

With a push she sent the GI sprawling and went after bigger fish. But they — bigger or not — weren't having anything to do with her. Disappointed Madame Godzilla finished her song —

'I be the best hot love-ah girl in all Vung Tau!'

She fixed the audience with a beady stare. Nobody dared not clap.

Sam turned to Harper.

'Hey, you were right! I wouldn't have missed that for the world —'

They were like two boys, hip to hip, hugging each other in a paroxysm of mirth. It was as if they had stolen a watermelon out of Farmer Brown's garden and escaped his wrath by jumping over the fence and scooting down the road. Or had managed to sneak past the ticket collector at the circus and were watching the aerialists swinging above the crowd in the big three-ring tent. Or were playing hookey from the war and running up a snowy slope with a sled, ready to come zooming down, the cold snapping their laughter into tiny syllabic fragments.

But somebody, Turei, grabbed Sam and pulled him away.

'There you are, bro! We gotta go!'

'No wait —'

Turei wasn't taking no for an answer.

'C'mon, Sam, you party animal!'

Laughing and protesting at the same time, Sam gestured ruefully at Harper and was gone. He wasn't to know that his departure hit Harper with a deep sense of loss. As if, coming down the slope on the sled, Sam had fallen off and tumbled away into the snow.

———— 3 ————

On Victor Company's return to Nui Dat, Sam was surprised to find Lieutenant Haapu waiting for them.

'Did your men have a good time, Sergeant? Good. Now it's time for work. Assemble the men for an urgent briefing.'

Turei looked excitedly at George.

'Do you think this is what I'm thinking it is?'

Half an hour later, Major Worsnop began the briefing.

'This is it, men,' he began. 'I know you've been waiting patiently. Tomorrow our battalion will join with other Australian and American battalions in a major offensive against the Communists.'

The announcement took Sam's breath away. Some of the men cheered.

'Victor Company is going in the advance group to set up the base camp. Now is the time to put your training to good purpose. Good luck.'

'The code name is Operation Bucephalus.'

The men worked deep into the night, preparing for the operation at company, platoon and section level. Every man prepared himself, making his own check of his personal weapon and equipment: helmet and flak jacket, webbing, harness and belt, butt pack, ammunition pouch, pistol belt, water bottles, bayonet or machete, belted machine-gun ammunition. Lightest of all, NZ freeze-dry rations. Just add water and mix. Then it was a matter of waiting for lights out and hoping you could get some sleep.

Sam spent his time reading letters from Arapeta, his mother Florence and his little sister Patty. His father's letter was formal, expressing the hope that Sam was upholding the mana of the iwi. Florence's letter looked as if it was spotted with her tears. Patty had sent a drawing of her new pony. She complained that little brother Monty always broke things. The letters made Sam sentimental. He put them aside. For some reason — perhaps loneliness or stress — he thought of Harper.

For the rest of the evening, Sam lay in his bunk looking at the moon. Operation Bucephalus was time for payback. For Sam to take utu for Jim's death.

In the quiet of the night George began to strum his guitar and sing:

'E pari ra, nga tai ki te ahau —'

An old World War Two song, the words reminded Sam of his father and Arapeta's war. Would he prove to be as good as his father?

Suddenly George gave a sharp intake of breath, and began to speak.

Intrigued, Sam joined Turei at George's side.

'Who are you talking to?' Sam asked.

George's face was drawn and haunted. He pointed to the trees. At first Sam couldn't see what George was pointing at. Then something moved. Something blinked.

Perched on the branch of one of the trees, maintaining an unwavering stare, was a russet brown owl.

'I've just had a visitor,' George said, laughing. 'See? It spoke my name. I don't think I'm going to get out of this war alive.'

Fearlessly George began to serenade the owl.

'E hotu ra ko taku manawa—'

The owl stared down at George. Screeched. A harsh cry, freezing the blood.

'Don't you like my song?' George asked.

The owl gave him one last look. Blinked again.

One moment it was there. Next moment, with a rustle, like velvet, it was gone, flying up and into the centre of the moon.

CHAPTER SEVEN

———— 1 ————

Four in the morning. Still dark. Sam felt a tap on his shoulder. Lieutenant Haapu, whispering to him.

'Time to go. Rouse the men.'

Sam's feet hit the floor. He was through the tent in a second.

'Get up, guys. Shower and over to the Mess to eat.'

By 5.00, dawn was approaching. Throughout Nui Dat the Australian and New Zealand battalions prepared to move to Luscombe airfield.

'On the double. Pick it up. Pick it up.'

At 5.30, Victor Company took up the all-round defensive harbour position at the airfield. The choppers were firing up.

The gunships left first. Reciprocating engines began to turn. Ignition, blue smoke, the smell of petrol fuel. From dead silence to thundering noise in one second. The helicopters rocked, rolled and shimmied as the blades rotated. The sunlight glinted on the whirling rotors. The lead gunship taxied out.

'Mission control, this is Woody Woodpecker. Radio check over.'

'Woody Woodpecker, I hear you five by.'

'Affirmative. We're lifting off.'

Harper pulled pitch. With a sudden juddering, the nose of the chopper dipped, the tail rose, the rotating blades began to go pop pop pop, and the gunship lifted off the ground. As was his custom, Harper saluted the soldiers below. He promised to do *his* job and keep the enemy pinned down while the troop insertions were underway. He said a prayer for all those poor bastards who would soon be face to face with the enemy.

'Come back in one piece, Sam.'

By 6.00 the Australian companies had left. Now it was time for Victor Company.

'Get ready to move,' Sam called.

Already, the infantrymen were running at speed to board their assigned craft. Sam saw Lieutenant Haapu shepherding the platoon's mortar section, orderly, signaller and medic on board the first chopper. Of all the platoon, the signaller was the one man the enemy snipers tried to take out. Without him to relay orders, and call for backup or a dustoff helicopter to pull out the wounded, you were in big trouble.

'Move, move, move,' Sam called.

The sun leapt into the sky like a chariot. Sam led his men through its spokes, moving swiftly to board their craft. There, the co-pilot acknowledged Sam with a nod. It was Seymour, one of the American basketball players. He and Sam counted in the men: George, Turei, Mandy Manderson, Jock Johanssen, Red Fleming and six riflemen. All were carrying extra pieces of equipment — disposable single-shot anti-tank rocket launchers that were strapped to their packs. If the enemy thought that bunkers would save them, these babies would get them out.

Sam gave Seymour the thumbs-up. The chopper rose, dipped and joined the battle formation. Six hundred metres below, the ground swept past.

Twenty minutes later, the landscape ahead began to explode and erupt.

'It's our artillery,' Sam reassured the men. 'They're giving us cover fire to keep the Vietcong busy while we get in.'

There was a sudden increase in radio traffic, and the clattering air armada began to descend to the landing zone — the most dangerous moment of all for the fleet.

Sam heard the pilot radioing the support gunships.

'One minute to dump time. Negative enemy sighted on LZ. Gunship Leader, I'm making a final approach for insertion. Is it a go, Woody Woodpecker?'

'Roger. It's a go.'

The chopper banked to the left and slid into the side of a dark mountain terrain. In a dizzying rush the ground came up and they were there — hovering above a small patch of barren ground surrounded by

75

jungle. The chopper flared for a stop, swaying six metres off the ground.

Sam caught Red Fleming's eye. 'You okay?' Sam asked.

'I haven't pissed my pants, Sarge, if that's what you mean. Yet.'

Then, as if the pilot had said 'Whoa', the chopper was swaying three feet off the ground right above the landing zone.

'Go go *go*,' Seymour called.

In a second Sam had jumped to the ground. The fine red soil was a whirlwind around him as he ran for the nearest cover and hit the dirt, rifle at the ready, waiting for the bullet that would announce an enemy sniper. His heart was beating so hard it interfered with his hearing.

Sam saw the rest of his men dropping to the ground. The chopper rocked forward. It picked up speed, climbing out over the tree line and away. Attempting to fool the enemy into thinking that a landing hadn't been made. Laying a false trail to some other part of the region.

For the next fifteen minutes, Victor Company kept position as the remaining fleet poured in. At each landing, more troops and supplies. Then it was done — the entire battalion was on the ground.

Everything was quiet. As the last chopper lifted away Sam felt a frightening sense of isolation.

'Holy Hone Hika,' he said to himself. 'This is it. This is really *it*.'

He was in the killing zone.

——— 2 ———

*Day One*

'Let's get the men moving,' Major Worsnop said.

The landing completed, each company of ANZAC Battalion headed out to its assigned operational sector. Sam passed a young Aussie soldier.

'Makes a change from beating up each other at base, eh?' the soldier said. 'Go get 'em, Kiwi.'

'You too, digger.'

Victor Company's destination was two hours' march away in the south-west quadrant. The main distinguishing landmark was Two Horn mountain. The route took them through thick bamboo, then secondary jungle, and finally tall primary jungle. Over to the east, muffled detonations, like distant thunder, indicated that the Americans in Operation Bucephalus hadn't been so lucky in their landing.

By early afternoon, Victor Company reached its position — Two Horn mountain loomed above them — and set up its base camp. Platoons were sent out to clear the area of enemy. By mid-afternoon the base camp's defences had been primed: M60 machine-guns and claymore mines were positioned to ensure interlocking fields of fire. Sentries were posted.

At sundown, Major Worsnop called the company together.

'I have opened our orders and can now tell you why we are here. As you may know, there has been increased enemy activity throughout Phuoc Tuy province. Command have been monitoring it for some time, but our intelligence information has now been able to confirm that enemy activity is being coordinated from a new logistic supply base somewhere here in the vicinity of Two Horn mountain. This base has been supplying Vietcong forces in Long Khanh, Bien Hoa, and Binh Tuy in addition to those in Phuoc Tuy province.

'Up until now, we have been hitting at the enemy wherever they surface. Operation Bucephalus has been mounted to stop them at the source. In particular, the Americans have had intelligence reports that the enemy buildup is preparatory to an attack on the American airbase at Bien Hoa. Our mission is to stop the Vietcong before this happens. Once their base has been located, joint command will manoeuvre to destroy it.'

He handed over to Captain Fellowes, who gave his lieutenants an area of sweep. Lieutenant Haapu's was a delta at the heart of an extended river system. A village further up one of the valleys. A whole system of tracks pushing further into the clouds and up into the mountain.

Lieutenant Haapu turned to Sam:

'You begin patrolling in the morning.'

Sam did not sleep well that night. In this, his platoon's first field action in Vietnam, the pressure was on him to perform. Could he deliver? Could he lead his men into battle and out? When the dawn flared, Sam saw that the sky was like a sea of opalescent waves, tinged with red and stretching to the end of forever. Within it, from east to west, stretched a broad band of cloud, broken into long, thin parallel masses, as if shoals of fish were seething just below its surface.

'The mackerel sky,' Sam whispered.

And he realised that the sky was like a sign — whatever was going to be would be, and whatever was going to happen would happen — and a sense of extraordinary calm came over him. In particular, he remembered the wild-eyed palomino on that day, years ago, when he was in his late teens. Dad and other horsebreakers had mustered a herd of wild mustangs from out of the Rimutaka Ranges. Arapeta was given first pick, and had chosen the palomino. For days he tried to break the stallion in. He used all his resources of wisdom and cunning but, in the end, resorted to the whip. Sam ran out and pulled the whip from him.

'You think you can do a better job than me?' Dad asked. 'If you can tame the horse I will give him to you.'

The next morning, when Sam awoke, he looked up to a mackerel sky. He walked out to the yard where the palomino was corralled.

'You are king of all stallions,' Sam said. 'The world should be your kingdom.'

The stallion's eyes bulged with anger, and it reared as Sam approached. Its mouth was bloodied from the bit. Its back was still moist from the cuts of the whip.

'There, there,' Sam whispered. For over two hours he rubbed ointment into the palomino's wounds. He talked and talked.

The night before, he had twisted an old bed sheet into a soft rope, to use as reins. He wasn't planning to use a saddle. Now he placed the rope in the stallion's mouth and, with a fast leap, mounted.

Dad, Mum, Patty and Monty came to watch the contest.

'Open the gate, Patty,' Sam called.

'What are you doing!' Dad called. 'That horse will have you off its back and be away before you get out.' He tried to stop the gate from opening, but the palomino saw the space, reared, slashing the air with its hooves — and Arapeta cried out and twisted to one side.

With a whinny of passion the stallion charged into the open country. It tried to buck and twist Sam off its back and reach him with its teeth. On and on it ran, thundering across the landscape, making for the hills it so loved. Up the hills it sped, seeking its freedom.

Before Sam knew it, they reached the place where the hills cut sharply into the blue. There in front of them was the mackerel sky.

'Yes, *do* it,' Sam said.

With a hoarse cry the palomino leapt — and was falling into a sky teeming with silvered fish.

Two hours later, Patty saw Sam returning to the farm.

'Sam's back! He's back.'

Sam was walking along the road. He was leading the palomino after him. Arapeta greeted him with pride and delight.

'You did it, son. You did it.'

Arapeta walked out to reclaim the stallion.

With a sudden yell, Sam lashed at the horse.

'*Go*. Get away from here as fast as you can.'

The stallion reared. Turned. Was off and away.

'What did you do that for!' Dad asked.

'You said the horse was mine if I tamed it. Well, I tamed it. I owned it. I let it go.'

Dad had thought he gave the palomino its freedom out of some boyish gesture. Mum, however, knew better. She began to laugh softly.

'The boy's soft in the head, Florence,' Arapeta said. 'Like you.'

The silvered shoal dived into the sky. The memory fell away.

'Time to go find Charlie,' Lieutenant Haapu said.

Sam nodded. Whatever would be would be. He saw that the platoon was ready to move out. The signaller, Zel Flanagan, made a last-minute check on the radio.

'The Americans didn't get any sleep, poor bastards. Twenty casualties from the enemy counter-offensive. The Vietcong were hitting them all night.'

'Nobody said this was going to be a picnic,' Lieutenant Haapu said.

An hour later he nodded to Sam:

'You all know what your job is. Go and do it.'

Sam unrolled the map and showed his men their assigned patrol area, at the farthest extreme of the map.

'All happy? Everybody know what we're doing? From now on we restrict our talking and adopt hand signals as communication. Agreed? Then let's go.'

The patrol drills took over. Scouting in front, George and Red Fleming began to work in tandem, moving and covering each other a short distance ahead of the patrol. Sam followed with Flanagan, the signaller. Mandy Manderson, carrying the M60 machine-gun, and Jock Johanssen came next. Bringing up the rear was Turei, the designated M79-equipped grenadier, and five riflemen under his control — Hempel, Brooks, Jones, Starr and Quincey.

The patrol moved in dispersed formation, five metres or more apart. Three kilometres out, the terrain became close jungle. The temperature rose like an oven. Sunlight pooled and dappled the darkness. The camouflage battledress blended well into the surroundings. Sam checked his map: There should be a track somewhere here. He signalled to George: Here it is.

*One up.*

The patrol slowed and adjusted itself to the new formation. George and Red Fleming moved ahead. The infantrymen split into two groups, three men on either side of the track. They carried their rifles pointed downwards — no jungle ever had right angles.

*We're here.*

The serious business of searching began. Sam did it all by the book. Patrolling to a specific point, stopping, sweeping the area with his binoculars. Setting the next point to patrol to, stopping, using his binoculars, patrolling again to a third point. He kept a tight grid. Forced himself to be patient, not to rush. Took everything easy, 400 metres an hour, looking for any signs of the enemy.

Around three o'clock in the afternoon, George gave a sign:

*Something ahead.*

The section went to ground. Sam crept up to George's side, and took out his binoculars. George pointed above the grass. Sam scanned the area.

Across a sunlit clearing was an old graveyard.

*Go and look?* George signed.

*Yes.*

One minute George was there, next minute he was gone, crawling through the long grass, into the sun, along the southern side of the graveyard and *in.*

Five minutes later, George was back.

*Bingo. A very intuh-resting and very busy cemetery, boss.*

Sam consulted his map. Yes, a village a few kilometres away.

*But two recent graves like I've never seen before, Sir.*

Sam signed for the section to wait, and went with George to investigate. George's instincts were right. When Sam pushed his hands into the loose dirt of the first grave, his fingers went right through a corpse liquifying in a nest of seething maggots. But in the second:

'Hello, hello, what have we here?' He pulled and saw the edge of a canvas sheet. Scrabbling deeper in the dirt: a munitions cache. Grenades, mines, rockets and explosives.

*Pull back.*

Sam and George rejoined the men. The adrenalin was pumping hard.

'Chuck's bound to come back to re-supply from this little lot,' Manderson said.

'We'll be ready for them,' Sam answered. 'Which way will they come?'

'From the hills by the north track.'

'Cover?'

'Optimum. Good elevation above the track. Good concealment. Good sightlines down the track to the next bend. No cover for the enemy.'

Sam took a deep breath. Made the decision.

'Tell the men to rest. At four we go down and set up the ambush.'

Two hours before trigger time. Sam settled the men.

George was lying on his back when Sam came by.

'Thinking about the owl?' Sam asked.

George nodded. His face was shadowed as if by a dark spread of wing.

'Don't let it get you down. We're your mates. We'll cover your arse.'

George jerked his head to the riflemen. 'You've got a bigger problem,' he said. 'We've got virgins.'

Sam swore. *Shit.* He should have thought about it before.

'Call the men together,' Sam said.

The section assembled. Brooks and Quincey were shivering.

How do you tell a boy how to kill a man? How do you tell a boy whose only experience of killing is shooting rabbits that war makes killing a man all right? How do you get him to pull the trigger and feel okay about it?

'Boys, I've never had to talk about this before, so you're going to have to forgive me if I get it wrong. When you signed up, you knew that at some point you might be posted to Vietnam. While you've been in the Army you've had practice on the range aiming at a target. But this is the real thing, not target practice. This time the bullet won't splinter the wood. Wherever it hits it will make an impact, wound and kill. If you aim for the centre of the bullseye, your bullet will go through a man's heart and he will die.'

Hempel blanched and looked as if he was going to be sick.

'I could tell you that you are doing this as your duty to country and to democracy,' Sam continued. 'I will remind you that you are professional soldiers. Neither of those will make killing a man, which is your profession, easy. But he's not only a man. He's the enemy. It's either him or you. And *he's* thinking that way too. If you want to live, and want your mates to live, pull the trigger. As for the rest, living with our conscience, call it what you will, we all have our own ways of dealing with that.'

'What's yours, Sarge?' Quincey asked.

Quincey was quivering. Racked up.

What do I do? Sam thought. Shall I tell him? Instead:

'My advice is for you to remember your training and your rifle drills. Let the procedures take over. Let the rifle do the killing.'

Four o'clock. Sam laid down the ambush. George and Red Fleming were at the top end of the track where the enemy was likely to enter. The rest took up positions overlooking the track. Deliberately, Sam placed Brooks and Quincey as far from the killing area as he could. God willing, if there was any killing to be done this day it would already be done before they were forced to pull the trigger.

Once the ambush was set, Sam primed it. Now it was all a matter of waiting. Of maintaining vigilance and staying so quiet and still that disrupted Nature reasserted itself. So the monkeys skittered and chattered again, the insects chirped and the birds whistled and sang. Somehow, you had to manage absolute stillness, so that snakes, no matter how poisonous, slithered undisturbed across your neck, their weight of coldness and dry scales feathering over your skin.

The sun was spinning in the sky. Suddenly, the birds stopped singing. George signalled.

*Charlie's in the area. Stand to.*

Somebody was coming along the track. The tension was like a tightly coiled spring. George signalled again:

*No, not Charlie.*

An old village woman and her daughter came walking through the sunlight. They passed the hidden infantrymen, entered the cemetery and went to pray at a small shrine. When they returned back past the section, the girl was crying. The woman's face was enigmatic, as if death was merely part of the passage of life.

The jungle stilled again.

An hour later, the sun was burning a hole in the sky. Sweat was pouring into Sam's eyes, stinging them with salt. For a moment he lost his concentration, trying to clear his vision. That's when he sensed that something had changed.

He watched. He listened. Insects were chirping. A small frog: toc toc toc. But the frog was *out*. There should have been a pause between the second and third toc. There wasn't.

Coming down the track, not more than 70 metres away, was the enemy. George and Red Fleming must have given the thumbs-down signal, and Sam had missed it. Two men with AK47s at ready. Was that it? No, wait, wait, Sam thought. Steady your nerves. Don't spring the trap yet.

Now they had passed Sam, so close he could almost sniff their sweat. Couldn't they smell him?

Wait, *wait*. Three more enemy were coming in dispersed formation. Where were the first two? Level with Manderson and Johanssen. Don't get trigger-happy, guys.

*Wait.* Another two Vietcong. Level with George. Would there be any more? Would there? If he left it too late, the first two enemy would be outside the killing ground. Or Brooks and Quincey would be forced to kill.

Make the decision, Sam. Make it. Make it now.

The contact drills took over.

Sam raised the SRL to his shoulder, his right elbow went up, the left hand gripped the woodwork, the thumb slipped off the safety catch, the foresight moved into the centre of the rear sight and then moved up through the centre of the visible mass.

First pressure, squeeze off, follow through.

The SLR kicked. A loud detonation, and Sam could almost see the bullet hurtling towards its target.

The bullet struck. Pierced the cranium, splintered the bone, made a hole. Out came a spurt of rich red blood. The Vietcong soldier crumpled and fell. Did he have time to utter a word? Perhaps a small *oh* of surprise? A moment to think of family, of wife, of children before the terrible pain and collapse into death?

No time to think of that now. Manderson and Johanssen's machine-gun had caught three of the enemy and cut them in two. The rifle group was also active, the deep slow dunk dunk dunk of automatic weapons was close by. Sam saw another enemy go down. Shot in the throat, coughing and gurgling and watching the blood pour out.

But this was too easy. It couldn't be this easy. It never was.

Christ! Another five enemy were coming down the track. Unleashing shots. Screaming. Shouting. George lobbed a grenade. It looked so ordinary, turning in the air. Boom. The Vietcong were retreating, George and Red Fleming in pursuit. Dunk, dunk, *dunk*. After a few minutes, they re-emerged on the track and took up a defensive position.

*All clear*, George signalled.

The section moved onto the track. Already Turei and Mandy Manderson were going through the enemy dead searching them for information. Quincey was vomiting his breakfast. Fox was green around the gills.

*Quincey*, Sam signed, *mop up*.

Best to take Quincey's mind off the killings and get him back on the job. Best to get him handling the dead bodies. The more he looked into the face of Death, the sooner he'd get used to it.

Manderson showed Sam the pickings from the dead. Grenades, packs containing a large quantity of detonators, and documents which indicated that the enemy soldiers were the D440 local battalion.

*No map of the enemy base?* Sam signed.

*No, but one of the dead soldiers is wearing the badge of their 274 regiment.*

274 — one of the professional CVC units.

Sam nodded. They'd already been here too long. Time to get out:

*Back to base.*

Quickly, George led the section out of the area. Turei took Hempel, Brooks and Quincey under his protective wing. Quincey was tear-streaked.

'Oh, sweet Jesus, oh —'

Back at the base, Sam saw that he had blood on his fatigues and on his skin. He whimpered, scrubbing at it, tearing his skin raw. That night the jungle was loud around him, filled with voices, and he curled himself into a ball, trying to protect himself from their accusations. People always said that with your first kill something died within you. Perhaps in the taking of life, watching it depart from a man who was once living, you also gave everything that was your own innocence.

How do you forgive yourself, Sarge? Hempel had asked.

Sam hadn't answered, because he had never killed a man either.

Yes, best to think of the rifle, not yourself, doing the killing.

*Day Two*

The next morning reports came in that the Americans were still pinned down. A number had been killed and many more wounded.

'Let's concentrate on our job,' Captain Fellowes said. 'The best way we can help the Yanks is to find the enemy — and fast — and force their withdrawal. We knew that 275 and 33 were in the area but we didn't know about 274. They'll put up a fight.'

During the night the strategists had considered the evidence of the patrols. No signs of enemy activity or contact had been reported by patrols in the south and east quadrants. Some enemy activity had been found in the far west — but most activity had been reported by Lieutenant Haapu in the north-west quadrant and Sam had been the only one reporting an actual enemy engagement.

Captain Fellowes stabbed the map with a finger:

'Looks like the north-west has the action. Let's get back there and find the enemy before they find us.'

The morning was hot and humid. Clouds blanketed the sky. Heat lightning flared in the distance. Lieutenant Haapu cracked on the pace, keeping the platoon on the run to the Vietnamese graveyard. They hugged the landscape, moving swiftly through the jungle. Basic training kicked in again. Even at speed you didn't fight the jungle. You learnt to glide through so you didn't break branches. You learnt how to walk and how to listen at the same time. To distinguish between the sounds of a two-legged animal and a four-legged animal.

When the squad arrived at the graveyard, Lieutenant Haapu

established a packbase. He marked out Sam's search area.

'I want you to sweep the flats and re-entrants around Two Horn mountain. Report back here at 1300 hours. Good hunting.'

Sam gridded his patch. On the first leg, he found a trail and ordered the men to parallel it. They checked out a small group of hootch complexes, with no result. They crossed another trail, moved off into some thick bush for concealment and monitored movement on the trail. Again, no results. On the second leg, Sam ordered the men to move inland through bamboo two to three metres high. Pushing through bamboo at speed could cut you to ribbons.

Still no sign of Chuck.

'But plenty of bamboo vipers,' Turei teased George.

'Fuck off, you bastard,' George said.

Sam ordered the last leg, a triangulation that led the men through swamp which seethed with leeches. No time to be squeamish. Wait until you get out the other side and then deal to them. Even so, the men shivered with revulsion as, working in pairs, they stripped and zapped the little bastards with glowing cigarettes. Turei yelled with horror when he found one pulsating on his penis.

'It's the only thing that will ever suck on your dick,' George said. 'And don't worry, mate. The taste will probably kill it.'

By midday the sky was overcast. Overhead were vapour trails of high-flying aircraft and, in the distance, the sound of intermittent shelling. The temperature soared and every movement made Sam break into a sweat that was made up of half toil, half fear. Waiting for the enemy to pop you. A sniper in the shadowy treeline, sighting down the barrel and squeezing the trigger —

'Any signs of enemy movements?' Lieutenant Haapu asked when Sam returned to the packbase. 'No? That means we'll all be doing some hiking because the enemy must be up *there*.'

Lieutenant Haapu pointed to Two Horn mountain. He consulted the map. Saw a village marked on the southern flank of the mountain.

'Let's pay a visit.'

The platoon began to climb. A huge cloud front extended across the sky. Just as the platoon entered triple-canopy jungle the air became deathly calm and a breeze began, steady, cool and strong. A smattering of rain fell from the sky, and Sam saw Turei gratefully lift his face and lick the drops into his mouth. The jungle was thick with soaring tree trunks twined with vines. The rain became stronger: birds screeched and flying insects scattered the drops with rainbow wings. A nest of vipers glittered in the rain-stained undergrowth. It was all so beautiful, yet harsh. Halfway up the mountain the jungle thinned out into tall elephant grass. It was astonishing how quickly the sky became pitch black and how strongly the rain fell. The platoon picked its way through a field of green grass. Red flowers opened out like blood-stained hands to catch at the rain. In the middle of war, cruelty and beauty.

*Stop.* Lieutenant Haapu went to ground.

The platoon had reached a stream, swollen and brown with silt. Beside it, a bumpy red dirt track. On the other side of the stream were misty rain-soaked rice paddies and open fields.

*Path to the village?* Sam signed.

*Affirmative,* Lieutenant Haapu returned. 'This is what we're going to do, Sergeant. I want you to wait half an hour while the rest of us go round the flank and take up positions overlooking the village. In half an hour, take your men in. Got that? We'll cover you as necessary and, once you give the all clear, we'll join you.'

Then he was gone, and with him half the squad. As they left, the underbelly of the sky was split with electrical discharges. The ceiling cracked open and a spear of forked lightning plummeted to the ground. The air crackled with ozone.

'Guess who's arrived,' George said.

His eyes were filled with myths and beings of the Maori past.

'Te Uiuira,' Sam answered. The Lightning God.


*Village,* George signed.

It was dusk and the village was a jumble of shabby bamboo-framed hootches. The huts were roofed with palm fronds and raised from the ground, their backs to the sloping mountain. Rainwater urns collected water under their eaves. In front of each hootch was a wooden pedestal set with offerings to the spirits of wind and sky. Most had verandahs and, below them, enclosures for pigs or poultry. But apart from a silky hen and its chicks, there was no sign of livestock.

Sam saw a villager appear and go around to the garden at the back of his hut. A small group of children as thin as rice stalks ran out and began to play around the village dinh, the small concrete shrine in the middle of the square. If children are playing, Sam thought, the village must be safe. He signed to George and Red Fleming:

*Let's go in. Do not fire unless fired upon.*

The section advanced to a cau ki, a monkey bridge with a flimsy handrail. The water in the stream below had a rich smell like damp leaves. As Sam crossed he saw a reflection in the water. His mind flipped to a fairytale about the Little Billy-Goat Gruff clip clopping across a wooden bridge. Underneath the bridge was a troll —

George and Red Fleming went ahead. Cicadas croaked in the water palms, then became silent as the two scouts entered the village. The villager returned from his garden and shouted at the children. Without looking left or right, they ran quickly into their hootches. It was almost as if they had never been there.

Silence descended. Only the rain. Sam always trusted George's gut instincts and, so far, George had not given any sign that there was any danger. But then two black figures ran out. George pointed them out to Sam: *Bring back?*

*No. Leave to Lieutenant Haapu.*

The team patrolled the entire length of the village, alert to every sign that might spell danger. When they reached its northern extremity they patrolled back to the village square where Sam positioned his men defensively in a 360-degree harbour.

He returned to Zel Flanagan: *Send the all clear.*

Five minutes later, Lieutenant Haapu and the rest of the platoon had still not arrived, but Sam was conscious that all around him the villagers were watching.

From the corner of his eye Sam caught a movement. Through the glistening rain he saw that a candle had been lit in one of the huts. It was moving as if someone was signalling.

The candlelight flared and, far away, Sam saw a beautiful chameleon, a creature with an iridescent pale blue body and a yellow throat. As he watched it turned a deep angry blue and then an extraordinary pellucid green. Sam looked through the green of the chameleon's skin. With a sudden flick it disappeared. In its place was an old woman, holding a candle and looking back at him through the open-weave lattice walls of her hut. She put the candle down, pulled and the wall went up. When Sam looked again, she was sitting on the verandah of her hootch like a wizened Queen of Sheba. She motioned to Sam.

*Haere mai. Come.*

'What is this power you have over women?' George asked.

Sam felt himself compelled to approach.

'I'll come with you,' Flanagan said. 'You may need somebody to translate.'

The old woman stood up and greeted Sam. Her voice reminded him of singing. Of an aged grand-aunt who lived long ago. He was taken to her once, to the place where she lived, a hut just like this — except that it was called a whare — and she had welcomed him and his mother in a similar singing language. Later that evening, after dinner, he had traced the moko on her chin and listened as she sung him to sleep with oriori, lullabies for children:

Po! Po! E tangi ana ki te kai mana
Waiho me tiki ake ki te Pou, a hou kai
Hei a mai te pakake ki uta ra —

The rain, the shivering trees and, when Sam blinked, he was back in Vietnam and an old lady was looking quizzically at him. Her hair was scraped into a bun. Her teeth were betel-stained. Behind her was an old man, her husband. He had lost a leg and was standing on a crutch. He had a scar running from his left ear to his chin. From the hut came the aroma of wood smoke and cooked rice.

'What is she saying?' Sam asked Flanagan.

'The old mother says that she has been waiting for us,' Flanagan interpreted.

'How did she know we were coming?'

'The hills have eyes. The birds left their shelter at our approach. The hills have ears too. They sent the vibrations as we trod every blade of grass. The old mother invites you inside to have a meal with her.'

At that, the woman's husband yelled at her.

'The old man doesn't want us to come in,' Flanagan explained, 'but she's insisting on it. She's reminding him that she's the one who wears the pants.'

Sam paused. He felt himself falling, as if he was going through a looking glass, and he remembered again the whare of his grand aunt. Like that house, this one also had mats on the floor, but instead of greenstone and feather cloaks it had an altar with a house God. Placated with offerings, the house God brought good fortune.

The old woman showed Sam the front room. A shrine, with yellowed photographs of loved ones. In front of each, a bowl containing money and tidbits of favourite foods, dedicated to the family's ancestors. Through a window, a small temple in the backyard to appease wandering spirits.

'Pho?' the old woman asked Sam.

She led him into her kitchen. The old man stumped after her. To one side was a cooking area. A large ceramic urn, emblazoned with a dragon and filled with water, sat near the fire.

'The old mother asks if you are hungry,' Flanagan said.

The woman crouched over a charcoal burner. She was so skinny that when she hunched over, folds of loose skin wrinkled around her knees.

'An com?'

She pulled Sam towards a pot that was simmering on the burner, put handfuls of noodles into a couple of bowls, then lifted the lid off one of the pots. Large bones bobbed about in the simmering liquid. Pushing these aside with a ladle, the old woman scooped up broth and poured it over the noodles. Next came handfuls of bean sprouts, slivers of meat and an array of garnishes. The soup looked salty and spicy.

At that moment there was a disturbance. Lieutenant Haapu arrived. When the old woman saw him, she raised a bowl to him. Lieutenant Haapu shot Sam an angry glance. Then he turned to the old woman, and in a gesture that was part tenderness, part sadness, shook his head. He had captured the two black-clad figures who'd run from the village. When they saw that the old woman was offering food, they spat at her. Defiant, she came out of her hut and began to berate them. The two captives retreated as if her anger had become physical and was pushing them back.

'The old mother is telling them,' Flanagan said, 'that they should know she is a supporter of the Vietcong. Didn't her sons and daughters go gladly to fight for them? And her grandchildren? And what is her reward? She knows that one of her daughters is dead but can the Vietcong tell her where she is buried? The old woman wants to know so she can visit her daughter's grave before Tet, and invite her spirit to be at peace. She would offer food and fruit to nourish her daughter's spirit. But she cannot and her daughter has become a wandering soul. She is one for whom no incense burns. There is also a son who is missing. The old mother thinks that he, also, has been hy sinh, sacrificed to death.'

The old woman stopped, exhausted. Her chin came up. She looked to the mountains. She began speaking again.

'While the old mother supports the Communists, she is angry with them at the moment. A few days ago they turned up and, for some reason, they took her prized sow. She wants it back.'

As if that wasn't enough, the old woman looked at Lieutenant Haapu, Sam and the rest of the platoon and began to chastise them too.

'The old mother wants to remind us,' Flanagan said, smiling, 'that she is still our enemy. When the French ruled the country she had no sympathy for them — they killed her father. Neither does she have any sympathy for us.'

'That means that she could poison you with her food,' Turei said. 'Or, at the very least, give you crook guts.'

The old woman must have sensed Turei's concern. She gave a look of contempt. With a theatrical moan, she clutched at her throat and pretended to die. Then, recovering, she pulled Sam, Lieutenant Haapu and Flanagan back into the hut.

Eat! Eat! she motioned.

'I don't understand,' Sam said. 'If we are the enemy, why does the old mother want to feed us? One day we might meet her children in battle and kill them.'

'The old mother asks why you presume you might kill her children?' Flanagan said. 'They might kill *you*.'

The rain began to hammer down.

'We've stayed here long enough,' Lieutenant Haapu said. 'It's time to move out.'

Sam bowed and thanked the old woman for her food. Her face was wan and eternal:

*You are a boy. You were hungry, like all boys, and all boys must eat.*

'Go rejoin your men,' Lieutenant Haapu said to Sam.

His voice hissed out. He could not look Sam in the eye. Halfway across the village square Sam turned back. He saw that the old couple were lighting joss sticks and placing them in the brass incense urn. Cupping her palms like a lotus bud, the old woman began to pray. That's when Lieutenant Haapu grabbed her arm, manhandled her down the steps of her hut and threw her in the mud. The old woman squealed like a bird as she fell. Her husband rushed to protect her. Lieutenant Haapu pushed the old man to the ground and raised the butt of his rifle.

'What the hell,' Sam thought.

Next moment, the hut was on fire. Within a minute it was completely alight. Silhouetted, the old couple cradled themselves, weeping.

Sam grabbed Lieutenant Haapu's arm.

'If I were you,' Lieutenant Haapu said, 'I wouldn't say anything, Sergeant. Now get your men together and let's get the fuck out of here. *Now.*'

Only when the platoon had cleared the village did Lieutenant Haapu pull the men in for a meeting.

'Our mission has always been to find the enemy. He saw us go into the village. He has seen us coming out. He will assume we are returning to home base. He knows we like to be nice and dry, so he'll think it's safe to visit the village after we've cleared the area. Well, he has a surprise waiting for him. We're staying and we're setting up a night ambush.'

'I want to know why you did that back there,' Sam asked. 'That old couple did nothing to us, they —'

Lieutenant Haapu jabbed at Sam, pushing him back.

'Concentrate on the job ahead. There's a crossroad not far from here. That's where we'll lay our ambush. Let's get it done before it gets too dark. And you'd better pray, Sergeant, that we're successful — or, if we aren't, that the Vietcong will be persuaded by the little charade I pulled back there. Can't you see what you did? When you accepted the old woman's hospitality and food you signed her and her husband's death warrant.'

The dark fell quickly, darkness and rain. The jungle closed in, and Sam felt fear setting in. The ambush had been primed and an hour had passed. Although the men were only ten metres apart, all had been swallowed up into the maw of the night.

Sam knew that George was to his left and Flanagan to his right. One second he had seen George raising a hand in a wave and the next second he was gone. Sam strained his eyes to see George again.

'How long have I been lying here?'

He began to feel disoriented. His imagination started to play tricks. Maybe he *was* alone, lying there all by himself and everybody else had gone somewhere else. Or perhaps, right at this very moment, an enemy soldier was sliding snakelike upon George, slitting his throat, and would soon be on his way to despatch Sam. He saw Charlie rearing up out of the wet bushes, bayonet in hand, plunging the bayonet down —

Get a grip on yourself, man.

Sam closed his eyes tightly. He thought of Hempel, Brooks, Jones, Starr and Quincey, all filled with the same fears and hallucinations. He felt ashamed of himself. And he hoped that Lieutenant Haapu was wrong about putting the old woman and her husband at risk of reprisals from the Vietcong. He hugged himself tightly, praying for himself and for the old couple.

'Please God, please God, fix the world firmly again, the top with the bottom, tuia i runga, tuia i raro. Bind it so that it returns to the way it was, tuia i roto, tuia i waho. Let the old mother and her husband be woven within the frame of your protection, please, God, please.'

Then Sam saw Charlie was coming down the track. The prayer remained unfinished, the frame was burst apart.

Sam's body flooded with adrenalin. He felt as if he was drowning. He lifted his head above the waves, gulped for air and reached for his rifle. Lieutenant Haapu had guessed right. The enemy, thinking they had the jungle to themselves, were talking and laughing as they came. Their torchlights stabbed through the darkness. And now the enemy were passing. Some in pairs. Rifles pointing down. Relaxed. Smoking.

A pencil beam flashed in Sam's eyes and he was temporarily blinded.

Sam slipped off the safety catch. The enemy had already passed George to his right, and Sam realised that it was up to Lieutenant Haapu, further down the track, to his left, to spring the ambush.

'Damn, I should be counting. How many have passed?'

Two Charlie, four Charlie, six Charlie, eight Charlie, ten Charlie, twelve Charlie, fourteen Charlie. Hell, how many more before the bag is full?

Come on, Lieutenant, fire the fucken flare.

A distinctive pop and sudden flash, and there it was. The flare turned the jungle a ghastly white. In the blinding light, the enemy were caught like opossums in the headlights of a truck. Caught in mid-stride, grinning. Trapped in mid-conversation, talking of life, love and the whole damn universe. As the flare blossomed around them, they froze in surprise and bewilderment. All hell broke loose as, from Lundigan's direction, heavy firing shattered the night. In the split second that followed, Sam grabbed the claymore clacker, pulled the safety wire, pressed the tit and fired. *Crump*. The jungle erupted in a blinding orange flash and a pall of jet-black smoke. The sudden crash of the exploding claymore mines sprayed the killing zone with thousands of ball bearings. The ground shook with the impact. The air was filled with screaming voices.

Another flare went up. Sam heard Manderson and Johanssen begin their deadly work. Their machine-gun hammered out a steady stream of tracer bullets, and six Vietcong were cut down, throwing up their arms, opening their mouths to take their last breath before falling through the rain. All around him, Sam could hear the dunk dunk dunk as Hempel, Brooks, Jones, Starr and Quincey joined the battle.

'We've got 'em,' Sam thought. 'They're right in the middle of the killing area.'

Sam felt an absurd sense of joy and relief, almost as if he could laugh at the triumph of the attack. But the enemy were reacting now, fighting back, yelling orders to get off the track. They became shadows dancing in and out of the flashfire, taking up positions and returning fire. Somewhere a rocket launcher began its rain of fire.

'Wait for the telltale flash in the darkness', Sam thought. 'Sight it. Squeeze.'

A *crack*, the bullet was on its way, taking an enemy soldier in his face, right behind his left eye, shredding the cornea, coming through the roof of his mouth, the hard palate, through the tongue, hitting the right side of the jaw and blowing it out. The soldier fell, choking.

But Sam had been targeted. Across the track, an enemy soldier stood and screamed, and threw a grenade. Sam watched it as it tumbled towards him — but the grenade fell short, bounced against a tree and fell back on the track. Shrapnel flew; after it came the enemy soldier, bayonet at the ready.

Fuck fire control.

Sam let off one, two, three, four, five shots in quick succession. His rifle recoiled at each delivery. The first shot took the soldier in the arm, spinning him off balance. The second whizzed under his armpit. The third went through his right lung and exited through the right side of his back, blowing out a huge hole. The soldier staggered back. The fourth shot caught him in the face and he spun to the ground.

'Spare me a death like that,' Sam prayed. 'When I go, spare my face. Make it fast and through the heart.'

The enemy was in full retreat. An enemy machine gunner gave covering fire. The tracer bullets, green and white dots in the blackness, floated towards Sam, hypnotising, beautiful. Then with chilling speed they were flashing about him with a *crack*, a *thump*. He hit the mud. Panic overpowered him as green tracers crossed over his face and chest, not more than a few centimetres above him. He breathed in as deep as he could and thought:

'This would be a bad time to get a boner.'

As suddenly as it had begun, the ambush was over. The jungle settled into silence. Sam was panting and dripping with sweat. The area smelt of cordite and burned powder, the sweet copper smell of blood.

Sam heard Flanagan come up beside him. Lieutenant Haapu had radioed:

'Break contact. Secure the area.'

The mop-up was completed by midnight. The platoon had suffered no casualties. Fifteen Vietcong were dead, three had been captured. It was obvious that many more had been wounded but Charlie had managed to carry all except one whose brains had been half shot out.

'When do you think he's going to die?'

'What do you think, Medic?' Lieutenant Haapu asked.

'He's not going to last, Sir.'

Lieutenant Haapu nodded. He gave orders for George to lead the platoon out of the area. He and Sam would stay behind with the dying soldier and catch up.

Sam watched the platoon disappear into the darkness and the rain. The Vietcong soldier knew what was coming and he began to whimper. Lieutenant Haapu knelt beside him and cradled him.

'Don't be afraid,' he said.

The soldier tried to sit up, as if to convince Lieutenant Haapu that he was not dying, but he collapsed again. Blood was forming bubbles of foam at his mouth as he breathed. His eyes started to glass over.

'Hold him tight,' Lieutenant Haapu ordered Sam.

Sam knelt in front of the soldier and embraced him. The soldier looked deeply at Sam — why should he die — and tears spilled from his eyes. He cried for a long time and, then, he sighed and let his head loll against Sam's chest like a lover. One of his hands found Sam's hei tiki and gripped it.

'Yes, that's right. Hold tight.'

Lieutenant Haapu moved behind the soldier. He took out his Bowie knife and said a prayer. He thought back to times when he had been lead man on the chain at the Whakatu Freezing Works. The sheep would come into the killing pens, and he and his mates would walk among them and —

With a quick slash, Lieutenant Haapu slit the soldier's throat.

Sam felt the soldier's fingers unclasp the greenstone.

And all there was, was rain.

## Day Three

The wind and rain squalled and shrieked through the night like banshees. Exhausted Sam tried to sleep. The squad had arrived back at base at midnight and, although they had been lucky, others in Victor Company hadn't. One of the platoon had been crossing a T-junction when the enemy had ambushed them. One man had been killed and two others wounded.

Sam moaned and, finally, entered a world that was not quite sleep, not quite wakefulness. It was like being in twilight limbo. How long would his luck hold? The jungle became jewelled with menace and he heard an owl call out: cu *cu* cu cu. He had a phantom premonition of George falling into a bamboo pit, punji stakes puncturing his chest.

'Oh, God, and we have to go back on patrol again tomorrow. Will that be the day when the owl comes?'

Around 4.00 a.m., Sam was still tossing and turning. The jungle had become truly demonic. Cobras rose, flared their hoods, hissed and struck. They were advancing on him, striking again and again. They struck at his defences, opening him up in all his vulnerability.

And it was as if Arapeta had been waiting for this very moment when his son was vulnerable and susceptible to attack. Through the terrible coil of his nightmares, Sam saw his father loping through the darkness and launching himself at him. Disarmed and defenceless, Sam melted into the embrace.

'Dad!'

Then he saw the obscene smile on Arapeta's face. Before he could stop him, Arapeta had put his fingers into Sam's mouth, as if to prise it open. Sam started to laugh and push Arapeta away. But Arapeta was strong and now had both hands in Sam's mouth, forcing the jaws wider. With mounting terror, Sam heard his jawbone splinter and crack. Eyes bulging, he felt Arapeta's left hand going down past his tongue, around his tonsils and into his throat. Then the right hand, sliding in.

'Open wide, son, and let Daddy in.'

The veins in Sam's neck began to break and shred. Sweat popped like blisters on his skin. He couldn't breathe and his heart was labouring, its pulsations bursting in his ears. He began to choke, and tried to vomit his father out of him. It was all happening so quickly: now Arapeta was up to his armpits in Sam's mouth, the hair of his armpits grazing Sam's lips. And Dad's face was level with his, slick and moist in some unholy kiss. He looked at Sam —

With a cry, Sam fought himself awake. His heart was pumping and he was sucking the air into his lungs. He saw a blood red dawn — the mackerel sky again. And he began to shiver with grief and fear as he remembered what happened a few days after he had let the golden palomino go.

Dad had been acting strangely all that week. He was always absent from the farm, never returning until late at night. Curious, Sam asked Florence:

'Where's Dad?'

'You should know better than to anger your father,' Mum answered. 'Do your chores, Sam. You'll find out soon enough.'

Mum's words made Sam uneasy. One night he stayed up to talk to his father. Dad was buoyant and pleased with himself.

'Where've you been, Dad?'

'Breaking in horses,' Arapeta answered. 'I've got a really good one for myself. I'll show it to you one day. Once I've broken it in. It's a real fighter.' Dad laughed at some private joke and ruffled Sam's hair. 'You'll see, son. Won't be long now.'

Three days later, Sam was doing some repairs on the barn. He was on the roof, and Monty and Patty were on the ground, furious that he wouldn't let them come up on the ladder.

'No, you can't come up. What happens if you fall off?'

'I won't fall,' Monty pleaded. 'Patty might though, because she's a girl and girls are always hopeless and can't do anything.'

At that, of course, a fight broke out between them. Sam, laughing, straightened up. The sun dazzled in his eyes and he put up a hand to shade them. Far off, he saw Dad riding back down the road to the homestead. Monty and Patty saw him too and were off, shouting:

'Daddy! Daddy!'

Sam clambered off the roof and joined Patty as Arapeta reigned up.

He saw that Mum had come onto the verandah and was watching, her arms folded against her chest as she were holding herself in.

'Is this your new horse?' Sam asked.

Arapeta's eyes gleamed under the brim of his hat. 'Yes it is.'

Sam took a step forward. He saw that his father had had to lay the whip to it. 'Wow, he really fought you, didn't he!'

He laid his hands along the horse. Its back was caked with dried blood. Then the horse whinnied and something stabbed at Sam's memory. He looked at the horse again, and stepped back as if he had been struck.

Once, it had been a golden palomino, king of all stallions.

Sam's blood was beating in his temples as he watched his father dismount.

'Bloody useless animal,' Arapeta said. 'I thought he'd be a good horse to keep, but look at him. No good to me at all.'

Arapeta swung his rifle up and, casually, without even sighting, blew the palomino's brains out. The horse crumpled on its front knees. For a moment it panted, then it keeled over into the dust. Somebody was screaming and Sam knew it was Mum. She came running from the verandah and pulled Monty and Patty to her.

Sam took a step towards the palomino. He looked into its eyes and saw a golden sun going down. He knelt there in the dust, bewildered and trying to understand. And he heard his mother cry:

'You had to do that, Arapeta, didn't you?'

'Do what?'

'You had to do that to your son. Catch that stallion again. Break it.

You had to be the king stallion. The black stallion.'

'You never make sense, Florence,' Arapeta said. 'I don't know what you're talking about.'

Sam gave a cry, and backed away from Arapeta. Next moment, he was running. Anywhere, as long as he could get away. Into the open country, across the landscape, making for the hills he loved. Up the hills he ran and, before he knew it, he had reached the place where the hills cut sharply into the blue. There in front of him was the mackerel sky and shoals of silver fish were scattering the light. When he reached the place he jumped and was falling into the sky, the mackerel opening and scattering, flash, flash, *flash* all around him.

'Why did you do it, Dad?'

And now, three hours later, Sam was back on patrol, dazzled by the sun and the silvered sky, climbing Two Horn mountain.

And there it was again, the track to the village.

Sam smiled as, in his mind's eye, he saw the old woman waiting for him on the verandah of her hut. He imagined her shaking her head at all the disturbance the platoon was making in Nature. Hadn't she said the hills had ears? The hills had eyes? Sam could almost hear the slap-slap of her footsteps as she went to the well to fetch water for cooking:

*You are a boy. You are hungry like all boys, and boys must eat.*

Suddenly, George and Red Fleming stopped, raised their hands in warning and went to ground. The platoon hit the deck. Sam low-crawled to George's side. A short moment later he was joined by Lieutenant Haapu.

*Village ahead.* George signed. *Something doesn't match up.*

Sam took out his binoculars and swept the village. It looked exactly like it did yesterday. The same bridge. The same cluster of hootches. The village square and the well. Then he realised that there was no sign of life, either human or beast. Nothing. And he smelt, rather than saw, ash on the air, something still burning.

*Villagers, where are they?*

Lieutenant Haapu looked at Sam. His eyes told Sam that he already knew what had happened. He signalled to George:

*Take Hempel and Brooks. Go forward, investigate and secure village.*

Sam saw images he didn't really want to think about. He started to stand, but Lieutenant Haapu pulled him back. His face was grim.

*Not you, Sergeant Mahana. You stay.*

Helpless, Sam watched as George melted away to the right and up in the direction of the village. The sky filled with dragonflies, their glittering wings whirring like silver knives. They cut the air with foreboding.

Half an hour later, George reported in:

*Come in. Village secured.*

No sooner was Sam in sight of the village than he knew it had been visited by the Vietcong. Even from the small bridge leading to the square, he could smell that some of the hootches had been torched. The paths between some of the huts were strewn with litter, as if each hut had been searched and vandalised. The most chilling aspect, however, was the silence and stillness. Nothing moved. Not even a chicken scratching the dust.

Ahead, George was waiting. His face was waxen. Hempel was retching. Brooks was sitting on the ground, staring at nothing.

'I'll have your report,' Lieutenant Haapu said.

'The villagers are dead, Sir. Men, women and the children. Even the animals have been slaughtered. It must have happened either last night or this morning. They were beaten and then shot. Their bodies are all in a field at the back.'

'Nobody left at all?'

George looked at Sam — and in that moment, Sam *knew*.

'Two, Sir, but —'

In the distance, Sam saw that the platoon's medic, Vickers, was ministering to two old people, who sat opposite each other, tied to two stakes under the hot sun.

'No, merciful God —'

George tried to stop him: 'Sam, matey, they're not a pretty sight.'

'Take your hands off me.'

Sam ran across the sunlight. As he ran he saw the old woman lifting her head to him. He fell on his knees before her. In one horrifying second he saw her blood splattered dress and knew what the enemy had done to her. They had cut her stomach open. Her intestines had spilled out and every time she breathed or swallowed they flipped and moved around like earthworms. Black flies buzzed angrily around her head. They swooped at Sam, angry that he had interrupted their feasting. Already, their eggs were pupating, hatching in the raw slit of her skin.

Even so, it was not her own condition the old woman was worried about. She motioned to her husband. He, also, had been gutted. Vickers had tried as best he could to minimise the pain, and was wrapping triangular bandages around the old man's stomach to contain the guts. As he moved to help the woman she whimpered and motioned to Sam.

*Look what they did to my husband.*

'I've given them both shots against the pain,' Vickers said. 'How they've endured so long I do not know. The old woman wanted me to work on her husband first. But she's the one whose condition is worst. There's nothing much I can do except make them as comfortable as I can. God, I wish they'd just die. But, apparently, they've been arguing over who should go first.'

Vickers's lips creased into a sad grin. Sam could see he was simply at a loss as to what to do. He kept looking at the woman's entrails.

'It's no use,' Vickers said.

The old woman must have understood. Her face was laced with the fine cobwebs of pain. She put a hand on the medic's left arm to comfort him and thank him. Sam began to moan, rocking backwards and forwards. Spittle formed on his lips.

'It's my fault, oh Jesus,' he cried.

'How did this happen?' Lieutenant Haapu asked.

He motioned to Flanagan to speak with her.

'The old mother says the Vietcong came this morning,' Flanagan said. They were angry that we had ambushed their men and killed them. They set fire to the whole village. They shot everything that moved. They took the villagers out the back and executed them. The Vietcong were told that the old mother and her husband had given us a meal. For this, they made the old couple watch the executions. Then they did *this* to them. This is the slow way of dying. Not so easy and as painless as a bullet through the head. The enemy wanted them to really suffer for having offered us food.'

The old woman lapsed into silence. The effort of talking had exhausted her. She looked at her husband and murmured to Flanagan.

'She wants me to tell her husband to hurry up and die.'

The old mother started to cough. Her intestines danced in the dust.

Sam ran to an urn, cupped his hands in the water and returned with it. He smeared the water on the old woman's lips. She opened her mouth and sucked on his fingers.

*Ah, rainwater. It is always so cool.*

Sam dripped water over the old woman's forehead. She lifted her face gratefully to the sparkling drops.

'I caused this,' Sam said. 'I caused this to happen. Your village to be destroyed. You and your husband to die —'

'No, it was me,' Lieutenant Haapu said.

The old woman looked at them both.

*You must bear your pain. I must bear mine.*

She motioned to Sam to come closer. Their noses and foreheads touched. The blue mist of age edged her eyes. She whispered to him.

'She is telling you not to be sad,' Flanagan said. 'The day before we entered the village she consulted her lunar calendar and it told her that that day would be unlucky, the next would be unlucky but — ah — the third day would be a lucky day.'

'Why lucky?'

'Can't you see? Today is the day on which she will die.'

At that moment the woman's husband began to shout and yell.

'The old father wants us to shoot them,' Flanagan told Lieutenant Haapu. 'He's asking us why we're waiting. Do we relish their pain? Why can't we be merciful and rid them of this miserable existence. He wants us to shoot the old mother first.'

The old woman started yelling back. Flanagan's lips creased with the humour of it.

'The old mother is saying "Oh no you don't!" to her husband. She doesn't trust him one bit. For all she knows he might recover once she's dead and he'll go over to his old girlfriend's village and set up house with her. And now *he's* saying he just wants to make sure she's dead because he's sick and tired of always listening to her.'

Lieutenant Haapu turned to Sam. 'I want you to take the platoon out of the village. Wait for me by the bridge.'

'No.'

'That's an order, Sergeant.'

Sam felt tears spring to his eyes. 'No, Lieutenant. I am responsible for this. Let me do the job.'

Lieutenant Haapu hesitated, then nodded.

'Before you go, the old mother wants to leave you two gifts,' Flanagan told Lieutenant Haapu. 'The first is the whereabouts of the enemy base. It is up there between the twin peaks. They have tunnelled into the mountain. The second gift is to tell you that to live you need two things — rice and clean water. But if you want to live well you need three more — a garden, a pigsty and a fishpond.'

Lieutenant Haapu saluted the old woman and moved toward the waiting platoon. 'Okay, everybody, grab your shit. We're out of here.'

Sam watched as the men retreated. The seconds passed. He took out his pistol. The old woman saw it and sighed with gladness. She asserted her strength, indicating with an insistent motion towards her husband:

*Him first, do you hear? He is not as strong as I am. It would be easier for me to look upon his face in death than for him to look on mine in death. It would break his heart.*

Sam looked away. The old woman's voice rose in anger.

*Please, women are stronger than men. They have stronger bodies. They have stronger hearts. Let me give my husband this last gift of my strength and my love.*

Sam paused and nodded. The man started to protest, then threw up his hands in exasperation.

Sam shot him. The old man slumped in his arms.

Sam turned to the old woman. She smiled a serene smile.

*I used to wash my prized sow three times a day.*

She took Sam's pistol hand and pushed the nozzle against her temple.

*Quick. My husband is already too far along the path and I must catch up with him.*

The sound of the pistol cracked across the hills.

Utu. There must be revenge.

An hour later, Lieutenant Haapu signalled for a halt. The thick, jungled mountain looked immense, the twin peaks like horns. Clouds draped the peaks like dark veils.

'Time to split up,' Lieutenant Haapu said. 'Sergeant Mahana, you take the right spur, search, but do not make contact. I'll take the left spur. We rendezvous at the top at 1600.' Lieutenant Haapu paused, then smiled at Sam. 'I know you're still hurting for what happened to the old woman

103

and her husband.'

'It was my fault.'

'It was as much mine as yours. I didn't have to order an overnight ambush. But I did. I'm supposed to make the hard choices. That's what I'm paid for. It's my job.'

Sam turned to his team, who were champing at the bit.

'Ready to go, Sarge.'

'Okay,' Sam nodded. Diamond.'

George and Red Fleming led the team out and up the side of the valley. In a horizontal line, on the cross, came Sam, Flanagan, Manderson and Johanssen. Turei and the rifle group covered the rear. Soon they were clawing through huge trees and up rugged, boulder-strewn terrain towards the twin peaks where the ridge split and formed another valley with its own drainage system.

Ahead, George was waiting for Sam's instructions.

*Take the left ridge,* Sam signed.

Suddenly, Red Fleming put up his hand and knelt, weapon at ready. He motioned to Sam.

*Come see.*

Fleming had stumbled on a trail, zig-zagging through head-high shrubbery and bush, which showed signs of recent movement. Sam signalled to his men to get off the track and follow at single file, parallel to it. The men dropped down from the track some ten metres and resumed their search. It was hard to keep sight of the track, but even harder to keep the intervals between the men. The switchbacks were so tight that often they were forced to bunch up.

Half an hour later, Sam signalled for the team to take a break. George slumped to the ground, rolling his eyes with gratitude.

'Phew. Hard work, boss.'

Suddenly Sam felt a tug at his elbow. It was Flanagan, and his eyes were as round as saucers. He put his finger to his lips and pointed towards the flank.

'What the hell?'

Manderson was sitting on the ground with his feet out in front of him and he had laid his rifle across his ankles so he could slip out of his machine-gun harness. The shoulder pads were off his shoulders and he had become rigid. Johanssen, off Manderson's right, had laid his weapon against Manderson's ankle. The riflemen were playing at being statues, immobile, in whatever position they were in.

Turei, who had been assigned to pull drag, was waving furiously.

*Freeze. Enemy in sight.*

It was uncanny. The entire group had become motionless, as if freeze-framed.

Sam turned his head. Slowly. A millimetre at a time, until he could see what Turei had picked up. On the other side of the cover the track doglegged up to the top of the ridge. There was a hole in the green bush in front of him. A VC — and he was looking through the hole!

For a moment Sam panicked. The enemy platoon must have been only a few minutes behind them on the track. Following? No. Then what were they doing? His heart was beating so fast he couldn't believe that the Vietcong soldier couldn't hear it. Nor could he believe that the soldier could not see him. It was like playing a game of hide and seek. The Chuck was going to laugh soon: 'Peekaboo! I can see you!'

Sam realised it was his face camouflage that was saving him. The enemy soldier was moving his head back and forth, trying to look past all the leaves to see what was on Sam's side of the bush. Then he continued on.

There was no time for relief. Another Charlie had stepped up. Sam froze again, staring back, trying to squint his eyes so that the whites weren't showing. The Vietcong soldier seemed to connect.

'If he puts his gun up,' Sam thought, 'I've got to roll, grab my rifle and fire.'

The enemy soldier bopped on by.

Sam signed to the team:

*Good boys. Keep laying dog.*

An entire Vietcong platoon passed on the track.

Five minutes later, when the last Charlie had disappeared over the ridge, Sam signed again:

*All clear.*

The team collapsed to the ground.

'This time, I really pissed my pants,' Turei said.

Quincey and Hempel were doubled up, trying not to laugh. Jones was on his back, his feet waggling in the air. Sam let them release their tensions. Then the thought struck him:

'They must be going back to base.'

Sam and George scrambled up onto the ridge. There, they low-crawled to the top, and Sam tracked the Vietcong patrol with his binoculars as they entered the treeline. All of a sudden, they were gone. The track was empty.

'Where did they go?'

The sweat was pouring down Sam's forehead as he tried to find the enemy patrol again. There they were, hugging the slopes and moving further down the mountain and between the twin peaks.

'Shouldn't we follow?' George asked. 'Play tag?'

Sam shook his head. 'We might get too close.'

Almost as if on cue, one of the Vietcong soldiers looked back and seemed to see a flash from Sam's binoculars. All Sam's nerves screamed in his head. But the soldier had seen something much closer by — monkeys began to screech and yell and move like a river away from the enemy platoon.

Sam and George went back to the section.

'George and I are going ahead to follow the enemy. Hempel, you come too. The rest of you, wait here. Flanagan, radio Lieutenant Haapu and tell him we have an enemy sighting and probability of the base not far from here.'

He signalled to George to lead the way. They moved swiftly, keeping to the track. The monkeys were still screaming and chattering and racing in the treetops above them like disturbed dreams. The Vietcong flitted through the vegetation.

*Stop*, George signalled.

The enemy had totally disappeared, swallowed up as if they had never been there at all. The track ahead was clear of footprints. George, Sam and Hempel backtracked. George sniffed the air. His head swivelled and he signed:

*They went down there.*

Swiftly, George left the track. His head bobbed only a few metres ahead of Sam and Hempel. All of a sudden, he was in the middle of a group of wild pigs, snuffling around in the bush. With a gasp, George put up his arms, stepped sideways and fell. And Sam looked for the owl:

'No, you can't have him.'

106

In a panic, Sam ran to see where George had fallen. His friend looked up at him:

*Sam, don't come any closer.*

George was in a pit of decomposing bodies. The pigs had been feeding off them. The corpses wore the uniforms of American soldiers. They were crawling with maggots, and George's fall had thrown up a cloud of stench and gas. With his left hand, George pointed something out to Sam. A trip wire was connected to one of the bodies. Three other bodies were lined up in a perfect row and wired to blow. Behind the bodies was a black ditch.

A concealed tunnel.

Sam's mind tracked past the tunnel. Behind it there would be tunnel-like bunkers dug into the side of the bank, the outworks of a defensive system of tunnels going down into the valley.

'This is it,' he thought. 'We've found the outer defensive perimeter of the enemy base.'

Sam heard Hempel coming up beside him. Hempel took one look at George and the pit of decomposing bodies and, next moment, was turning and retching and —

*Stop him, Sarge*, George signed. *The whole place is booby-trapped.*

It was too late.

'Oh shit —'

A hole opened up under Hempel. The grass was falling into it. With a gesture of resignation, Hempel fell.

Silence.

When Sam went to look he saw Hempel in the middle of a carefully laid tiger pit. It was lined with metre-high punji stakes of fire-hardened bamboo, sharpened to a point and smeared with human faeces. Hempel lay skewered. One stake had pierced his throat. Another punctured his left shoulder. Still another was protruding from his stomach. The wounds were spilling with blood. His eyes looked up at Sam, bewildered, like a fawn's. Then they rolled up into white. Hempel opened his mouth and blood fountained out.

'Oh no,' Sam thought. 'Not one of my virgins —'

Quickly Sam helped George out of the tiger pit and then down to Hempel.

'He's dead. Sarge, the sonofabitch is dead.'

George was shivering and shaking as Sam let down a rope to pull Hempel's body up. For a stunned moment both men sat there, looking at him.

'Jeez, Sarge, close his eyes willya?'

And, oh, Hempel's body was still warm and the blood was still so red, so red.

More minutes went by. 'I've lost a man. I'm a man down.'

Then Sam motioned to George: 'Come on.'

'Are we taking Hempel back?'

Sam's face was grim but determined. 'Let's find the enemy base first, for Hempel's sake. He's not going to die for nothing.'

George helped Sam lift Hempel's body into the low branches where pigs couldn't reach him. They entered the concealed tunnel and followed it as it sloped underground. All of a sudden there was an opening ahead. When Sam crept up to the opening the dirt started to crumble and he almost fell.

He was at the top of a cliff. Below was a hidden valley, and towering above it were the twin horns of the mountain. In the middle of the valley was the enemy base.

'This is for you, Hempel.'

Sam took down the details — the sitings of defence positions, possible minefields, gun emplacements, concealed bunkers interconnected with tunnels, camouflaged fighting pits and spider holes. He looked for the likely command post. Then, once it was done, Sam signed to George that they should return to the patrol. When Quincey saw Hempel's blood-stained body he began to sob.

'Quincey,' Sam said through gritted teeth. 'Stop it man.'

'It's all right for you, you bastard,' Quincey said, 'but Hempel was my mate.'

'Well Hempel's gone, and we're here, and the best thing you can do as his mate is to do your job.'

Sam turned to Flanagan: 'Get me Lieutenant Haapu on the radio.'

The radio clicked and buzzed.

'Sir, we've found it.'

The platoon returned to the village. The battalion had begun to reposition there and gunship convoys were landing men and military supplies.

Sam stood alone in the field behind the village where his men had buried the old woman and her husband.

The sun slipped away. The sky turned shades of purple, pink and gold. The trees of the jungle rapidly darkened into shadow. The moon, pale and round, had come up, although it was still not yet dark. Sam had heard that in Vietnam the moon was very beautiful, but he had not expected it to be so wan and luminous. Wild dogs were baying and, in that time between light and darkness, Sam could hear the spirits moving, whispering in the rivers and washing in the sea. They were sighing all around him in the stones and whistling in the trees, as if glad to have dominion. This was the time when Maori believed that the spirits of the dead began their long voyage to Te Reinga. There, at the northernmost tip of Aotearoa, they waited for the sun to go down. Already, perhaps, the old father had reached that promontory overlooking the sea where the spirits leapt from this world into the next. Had the old mother reached him in time?

Sam's eyes prickled with tears.

'I hope you caught up with your husband, old mother.'

Then he turned on his heel and returned to his men. They were waiting at the landing zone. All around them choppers were spinning, darting, their blades glistening like the wings of iridescent fireflies. Hempel's body lay waiting to be flown back to Nui Dat.

'Are you all set, Sergeant?' Lieutenant Haapu asked.

Sam nodded. He saw that Major Worsnop, Captain Fellowes and all Victor Company had mustered. He also saw Cliff Harper was there. In the rush and the roar of the world —

*Hello, Sam.* Cliff signed.

Sam lifted his face. *God, I feel so alone —*

*I'm here for you.*

Major Worsnop turned to the platoon.

'It is never easy to lose a friend,' he said. 'It is never easy to lose a good soldier. We ask the Lord to take John Hempel into his care. Hempel, you are going home now.'

Major Worsnop led the salute. A guard of honour let off a rifle volley as Sam, George, Quincey, Brooks, Jones and Starr picked up Hempel's poor broken body and lifted it into the chopper. Harper slipped into the pilot's seat. The engine started up, the rotors whined. All the ihi, the mana, the wehi and sorrow flooded into Sam and before he knew it he was leading George and Turei in a haka to Hempel.

'Ka mate, ka mate, ka ora, ka ora —'

Feet stamping. Eyes bulging. Crouched and slapping thighs with hands.

'It is death, it is death, it is life, it is life —'

Spittle arcing out, sweat far flung into the air.

Harper felt the grief of the moment.

'Ker-rist! Why am I crying for some soldier I don't even know.'

Harper looked down at Sam and saluted. The chopper lifted, turning the landing zone into a place of whirlwinds.


*Day Four*

By sun-up the battalion was in position for the attack on the enemy base. They had deployed on the ridge facing the twin horns, looking down into the valley. Major Worsnop looked at his watch. Okay, let's get the show underway. He ordered the two-battery artillery barrage assault to soften up the enemy before his boys went in.

'Box grid and column fire,' he commanded.

There was half a minute's silence as the message was radioed. Then:

'On the way over.'

Overhead, Sam heard the rounds approaching. The barrage hit the south side of the enemy base in one big twelve-round orange *crruump*. More rounds followed, whistling overhead, working from south to north, the shells impacting on the enemy position. A few seconds later the detonations reached Sam and the ground lurched.

'How can the enemy survive all this?'

The barrage was devastating to watch. It seemed to go on for hours. Then the last rounds impacted. The roar of the detonations receded. The smoke drifted away from the killing ground.

Suddenly there was a lull. The sun burnt off the clouds — an astonishing interlude of beauty and radiance. And Sam remembered when he had a chorus part in a high school musical put on by those Mormon elders from Brigham Young University:

Mine eyes have seen the glory
of the coming of the Lord,

he is trampling out the vintage
where the grapes of wrath are stored!

As if they had been waiting in the wings to join the chorus, an air strike of F-4 Phantom jets descended, whistling down on the wind.

'Wow, Sarge,' Turei whispered, 'just look at those beauties —'

From his grand-tier cinemascope seat, Sam watched the jets as they made their approach. They came screaming towards the twin peaks and through the gap between the horns. As they swooped over the ridge they released their rockets — so close that Sam could see the stabilising fins pop out. He followed their trails as they tracked down towards their target.

A whistling sound was followed by the thunk, thunk, *thunk* as the rockets hit the enemy base in splendid stereophonic sound. Concentric rings emanated from the explosion. The Phantoms increased power, fighting against the G-forces as they sought the sky.

A second later came the boom, boom, *boom* of the explosions. The earth heaved and swayed.

A second strike was ordered in. It carried bombs and napalm — called *bom bi* by the Vietnamese because when the mother *bom* detonated it spawned 600 baby bombs.

The enemy base brought in its ground-to-air defences. One of the jets, levelled into its bombing run, was hit. It just managed to clear the ridge, its slipstream parting Sam's hair, trailing smoke. Sam saw the pilot struggling to eject.

'Come on, man. Get out. Get —'

The Phantom exploded, raining the sky with burning debris.

But now helicopter gunships had swooped down from the north-west. They flew in a daisy chain, like the corps of an American ballet. Their movements were choreographed with skill and beauty as they bled off elevation. For a moment they disappeared before popping up over the ridge, black carapaced flying gun platforms, their front windows flashing in the sunlight.

'Hey,' George called. 'I see an old friend.'

Woody Woodpecker was on the case again. As he passed overhead Sam saw the gunners so near, leaning out of their doors, that he could reach out and shake hands with them. Down into the valley of Death rode Woody Woodpecker. As Harper swung in low over the contact zone, the gunners opened up:

Glory, glory hallelujah
glory, glory hallelujah
glory, glory hallelujah
God's truth is marching on!

'Now it's our turn,' Sam said.

He saw it was almost time for Victor Company to go in. 'Come on Captain Fellowes, give the order to engage.'

At that moment, Sam saw the tarantula. He picked it up. The spider had always been an important symbol to the Mahana family. It was a kaitiaki. A protecter. The spider evoked memories of Riripeti, the spider woman of Waituhi, whom some had called Artemis.

'E Riripeti, kia ora,' Sam said.

The spider seemed to be smelling him. Sam brought it up to his face. The spider touched him gently with its legs. In a sudden movement it turned and faced the enemy base. It reared, taking up the attack position.

This was it. This was the moment.

Sam took a deep breath. With all his power he invoked Tumatauenga, God of War, Tu, the eater of man, to come to the battle. It was time for reprisal, for utu to be exacted. Sam's breath hissed out. He hurled his words across the twin peaks.

'Contact *front.*'

Sam sprinted forward. He let the M79 fall under his arm, supported by its strap, so he could use his rifle and bayonet more easily in the close contact with the enemy. His gut was in a knot, and steady breathing had become hard labour, but he felt no fear. He remembered that whoever got the most punch out the fastest got the upper hand. Wax the enemy before he waxed you. He touched his greenstone pendant. It leapt in his hands, searing him with its heat.

'I refuse to die today.'

Sam led his platoon down the slope towards the enemy base. He could see the enemy fire patterns, the interlocking fields of automatic weapon fire sweeping at ground level. He wanted to cry out a warning to the

112

company, 'Don't get trapped.' All he could hope for was that the gunners, jet fighters and gunships had knocked most of the defences out. Across the contact zone, firefights were breaking out like displays of violently beautiful fireworks. Tracers flowed back and forth. The air was filled with the noise of the ground attack, pops and cracks like popcorn popping and, every now and then, a puff and an orange mushroom explosion.

Why does war always look so beautiful?

Suddenly, Sam looked up and saw that a gunship had been hit by an enemy B-40 rocket in the tail section. Hydraulic fluid was spraying everywhere. And the enemy gunner had the chopper in his sights and was following it down. Sam's heart lurched. Was it Woody Woodpecker? No, it was Harper's mate, Fox, who was in trouble.

Fox's voice came over Harper's headphones.

'We've been zeroed —'

A 12.7 round hit the doorframe above Fox's head. The next round hit the forward post near the starboard door gunner. Another hit right next to Fox. The rest of the rounds were smacking into the engine cowlings.

'They're going down,' Harper whispered.

Fox's gunship started shuddering and losing height. It drifted away from the battle zone towards the jungle, the props chewing the shit out of the treetops.

'Pull up, Fox, pull *up*.'

It was too late. Fox's helicopter erupted into an instantaneous sheet of flame.

And that glorious *Battle Hymn of the Republic* came booming into Cliff Harper's head, a patriotic hymn filled with the valor of martyrdom, swelling out on the wings of angels from all the wars that Americans had ever been involved in:

In the beauty of the lilies
Christ was born across the sea,
as he died to make men holy,
let us die to make men free!

The gunship fell from the sky to Sam's left, but there was no time to take a look. His men were running into trouble.

'Make smoke,' Sam commanded.

He heard the plop and whine of smoke canisters, but the enemy had already zeroed him. Through the smoke came the unmistakable sound of enemy rounds breaking the sound barrier. The rounds clapped around his head. He felt a hot crack close to his right cheek and ear, then several others like a string of cracks together. Then a bomb went off and the soldier who detonated it virtually disappeared. One of the men near him had both his head and helmet taken off but his heart kept pumping, spraying blood through the air. Others near him were blown into the air the way they are in cartoons, legs still running. Sam felt a wet rain lick across his face. Tasted someone's blood on his lips.

There were booby traps everywhere. A big-ditch bank was ahead and, to the left, barbed wire in rolls. Some of the advance team had been caught up in it or had tried to evade the wire by running down lanes where fire was targeted.

'Turei!' Sam called. He saw that George was caught in the wire. 'Don't let the owl get him.'

Turei nodded. He saw the enemy machine-gun team manning the lane. Up went the rocket launcher to his shoulder and —

'Bye bye Charlie.'

Sam helped George out of the barbed wire.

'Thanks, Sarge.' They began to run again. Bullets were cracking around them.

There were tripwires all over the place. It was all a matter of luck. If it wasn't your day you ran into the wire and *boom* you were blown to bits. Or looking at a smoking stump where your leg had been.

Stumbling, Sam looked down and saw a man's head, eyes still open, rolling in the red dust. Another soldier, coming up from behind, kicked at the head and it sailed above the ground like a bizarre football.

Sam dropped to one knee. For a moment he was disoriented by a shell grazing his head. A lane of fire opened up before him. George, beside him, was covering off his left rear shoulder. Then Turei was there at his right.

'Er, boss,' Turei said, 'I don't like this movie. Let's go next door and see something that isn't so noisy.'

They were really going through their ammunition, spraying the area in front of them, peppering and stitching up the base — and it really *was* like movie time, when the good guys came riding into the sleepy town and helped the defenceless villagers against the bad gringo guys.

Sam placed his rifle beside him, swung the M79 into his right shoulder and fired. Six grenades soared and exploded, showering the Vietcong with metal shrapnel. Then he was up and running again, George and Turei with him all the way. Ahead the grenades were going off like fireworks in the air, Roman candles, golden showers, Fourth of July, Guy Fawke's Day —

All around Sam, the troops of Victor Company were advancing.

A line of little spouts tracked towards Sam in the red dust. Jesus! Transfixed, paralysed, he watched as rounds went right around him.

'Oh, you are one lucky son of a bitch.'

He raised his rifle and let a whole magazine fly towards the bullets' source. Empty magazines were scattered where soldiers had been reaching and slamming them in, emptying one and reaching for another, slamming it in and emptying it — just letting the rounds fly. By return, a ferocious barrage of enemy machine-gun fire erupted from the front, red-hot slithers of metal and B-40 rockets. The soldier next to Sam was cut in half at the waist. No time to think about that. Just keep moving. Fire from the hip, keep firing, and change magazines.

'Was it like this for Dad, when he was in the Maori Battalion?'

All of a sudden, Sam was through the base's defensive perimeter and in among the bunker system. Charlie was popping up everywhere.

Aim, squeeze the trigger, let off the shot. Aim, squeeze, and another Chuck goes to Vietnam Heaven. Take down as many enemy as you could before they hugged you by your belt.

All around him, other soldiers were engaging in hand to hand combat.

Magazine empty. Ahead an enemy soldier was charging him. Sam reached for a new magazine and hit the release on the bolt receiver. Oh, shit. His rifle had jammed.

The enemy soldier raised his rifle. Incredibly, it jammed too.

With a cry, Sam launched himself at the man. The stench of the soldier overpowered him as they grappled at close quarters. Then the concussion from an exploding bomb kicked them and hurled them into the air. Dazed, Sam sat up. The Vietcong was crawling towards him, knife in hand. He raised it and —

George was there, shooting the enemy soldier in the mouth, unclipping a grenade, pulling out its pin and throwing it into a Vietcong bunker.

Boom, and smoke exploded out of the opening.

Sin loi, enemy soldiers. Too bad.

Sam rolled and dived for the rifle that still smoked in the hands of a dead comrade. Ahead, the enemy were beating feet, breaking contact, spilling out of the bunkers and running before the assault. An image came into Sam's mind of having jumped into a chicken coop: All those chickens.

Men were firing, firing, firing. One of the chickens sprayed blood and lost a wing. Another had its head shot off and was flapping around, a headless chicken, running off into the distance.

And Sam was in among the bunkers, lifting his bullet stream and directing it down into the enemy who cowered there. He saw the pleading look as he blew a Vietcong soldier out of his Ho Chi Minh sandals. Twisting to his right, he fired into another bunker where three of the enemy had thrown themselves together to protect each other. All around him, Sam's team was in a feeding frenzy. Throwing grenades like lethal fruit. Moving through the smoke and destruction and firing at anything at all. If it moves, fuck it.

There was no concept of time. It was winding up before him and unwinding behind him. He was running to breast some finishing tape and Dad was cheering: Go, son!

He was tired, sucking massive air, and the adrenalin was absolutely coming through his ears. He was living a lifetime of stark terror. He kept firing and firing. An infantryman near him had a flame thrower, but he was shot in the face as he lifted it. Another bullet, *crack*, and his spinal cord was severed.

Enraged, Sam picked up the flame thrower, flicked the switch and sent the flame into the enemy foxhole. Take that, arseholes.

Five screaming figures, human torches, spilled up and over the lip of the hole. Their bodies danced like candles. Sam saw his mother putting her hands to her eyes. She didn't want to look. And the tape was in front of him and —

'You did it, Sam, you won!'

Sam heard somebody screaming. Out of control, Quincey was running amok through the enemy base, laughing his head off. The sound was like a buzzsaw and it cut through Sam's bloodlust.

OhmyGod.

He looked around him. The sheer lunacy. The sheer madness. And all of a sudden silence fell. All except Quincey, still laughing, gun spent, but still pressing the trigger.

> Glory, glory hallelujah
> glory, glory hallelujah
> glory, glory hallelujah
> His truth is marching on!

———— 3 ————

After the battle, there was a cloudy cooling breeze. It was mop-up time. The attack had reaped a bitter harvest.

'If I ever wanted to picture Hell, this must be what it's like,' Sam thought.

Everything moved into slow motion. Rapid casualty evacuations were occurring. Dust, grass and other debris swirled in the air as choppers ferried the wounded back to Vung Tau. On the ground medics rushed to administer morphine, to stabilise the wounds, stem the bleeding or resuscitate hearts. Men shook and screamed. There was blood every-where, and the powerful stench of open wounds. One man's flesh had been fireballed off his face, neck and shoulders. Another looked as if his torso was a leg of pork, filleted open. His bicep muscle was visible and yellow sinews poked out from his wounds.

Sam saw Lieutenant Haapu beside one of the wounded who was making a hacking sound and dribbling blood from his mouth. The soldier had been smacked hard and his chest had been turned to mush. Lying next to him was a soldier who had his back blown out. He was dying.

'Mum, have you come to get me? Is it time to go home now?'

Further along, a priest administered last rites to another soldier.

'Please don't talk to me, Padre,' the soldier whimpered. 'I'm not dying, I'm not dying, please, I'm not —'

The dead lay waiting in baskets covered with blood-splattered ponchos. Soldiers on detail loaded the bodies into a Chinook. Sam saw a head fall from a basket and roll like a melon in the dust. Turning away, he tripped over a boot and saw a foot in it. For a moment he had the absurd notion that he should take the foot with him and ask if anybody wanted it.

Lost a foot? Will this one do?

His thoughts were interrupted by the whining of another Chinook as it worked with rigging straps to ferry away one of the downed gunships. He heard a voice shrieking above the thunder of the chopper:

'Lai dai! Lai dai! Come here, you Charlie bastards, and lie the fuck down.'

Enemy prisoners were being herded brutally into a makeshift compound. Some had half their clothes blown off. Others had suffered grievous wounds.

Sam moved on towards the enemy bunkers. In some of them the bodies were so mangled they didn't look human at all. Some had been fused together, monstrous creations of war with three heads and flame-soldered tentacles for arms. How many enemy were dead? Sam didn't know. He saw drag marks where some had tried to carry their friends in the headlong escape from the attack.

In a daze, Sam moved to the lip of a foxhole and sat down. He bowed his head in his hands. Then, across the sunlight, he saw Turei advancing on George with a small snake, waggling it furiously.

In the middle of all this — an absurdity.

'Come on, George, you're not afraid of a liddle wee baby snake, are you?'

'Get away from me, Turei.'

Turei lifted the snake to his eyes and looked sadly at it. 'Did you hear that little wee baby snake?' He looked deep into the snake's eyes and then threw it.

With a yelp, George stepped back. The snake fell through the open neck of his shirt.

George gave an unearthly scream. 'I've been bitten.'

He yanked off his shirt and the snake fell out. Turei was apoplectic with mirth.

'Stop acting like a baby. Can't you see it's dead?'

George's breathing slowed. He looked at the snake. Then rounded on Turei and socked him in the mouth.

'I go through a battle and I don't have one mark on me,' Turei said. 'The only wound I have is when my best pal hits me in the jaw.'

Sam smiled, ruefully. In war there were no winners or losers. There were only the living and the dead.

And he was jolted straight back to the battle — he saw a discarded flame thrower and realised the foxhole looked familiar. He had picked that very flame thrower up, flicked the switch and sent flames into the foxhole. Five screaming figures had spilled out, their bodies burning, burning, burning, their flesh sizzling and flaming as he watched.

Five may have died on the open ground but another five had been incinerated where they lay. With mounting horror, Sam saw all of the burnt soldiers were Vietnamese women.

'Oh, no. Oh, no, please, no.'

Sam remembered the old mother and an appalling possibility came to him that one of these girls might have been her daughter. He had already killed the old mother. Had he also killed her daughter? With a cry he jumped into the foxhole.

'I'm so sorry, oh, I am so sorry.'

He cradled the charred bodies, pulling them over him. One of the girls had averted her face from the flames, perfect amid the carnage. In her hands she held a letter.

Flanagan was there, calming Sam down. Sam gave him the letter.

'It's to her boyfriend,' Flanagan said. He began to read it:

'My love, there is a plate of perfect roundness. The plate has a Chinese pattern etched in shades of blue. It shows two lovers pursued through a glade of drifting willows. The brushstrokes are delicate like eyelashes. The lovers look so strange, so remote and, if you turn the rim you can follow their flight across river, mountain and bridge. They are running away hand in hand, unlike you and I my love, separated by this war. But I think of you as I turn the plate and watch the two lovers running away across bridge, river and mountain. Perhaps, when the war is over we will be like them at the end of their journey because — there they are! Two birds released from an outstretched hand, flung into the sky, free! Free! *Free* —'

With despair, Sam realised the place had become a black cloud and the air was filled with buzzing.

Where do the flies come from? How do they know?

Before Sam knew what he was doing he was striking out at the seething cloud. It re-formed around him, angry, bloated and crazed with blood.

'No, you can't have them yet. I won't let you have them.'

His face was streaming with tears.

'Sarge, snap out of it,' Flanagan said. 'This is war, Sarge. War.'

Three hours later, Major Worsnop ordered the destruction of the enemy base and its ammunition supply.

'The place is tripwired and booby-trapped and enough men have already been killed this day. Let's send it back to Hell where it belongs.'

The detonation, when it came, was like an eruption. By the time it was finished, night had fallen. Phosphorus flares were lit at the landing zone. The choppers flew in to pick up the battalion for return to Nui Dat. Dozens of them sat there, like horses champing at the bit.

The men sprinted through the dust. The gunships lifted off into the setting sun. Sam looked down at the mangled mess that had been the enemy base. He should have felt elation. He saw that Flanagan had taken a small book from his shirt pocket and was reading it intently. When he was finished, he handed the book to Sam.

Pity them, the souls of the lost thousands
They must set forth for unknown shores.
They are the ones for whom no incense burns
Desolate, they wander night after night.

PART THREE

George's Story

CHAPTER EIGHT

———— 1 ————

The photograph fell out of Uncle Sam's diary:

SAM WITH CLIFF HARPER, VIETNAM, 1969.

In it, Uncle Sam and Cliff Harper look as if they've just come up from the beach after a swim. It must have been taken when they were on leave in Vung Tau, some time after Operation Bucephalus.

Harper is sitting on the sand. Uncle Sam, in the middle of the photo, is resting in the harbour of his arms. Uncle Sam's upper body is strongly developed. Around his neck is a greenstone hei tiki. His right arm is up in protest, as if he doesn't want the photograph to be taken. He is laughing and his lips are curved in a resisting, 'No.' But the one who really draws the attention is Harper, who looks directly into the camera. With his boyish grin and half smile he traps you in his gaze. He seems to absorb the light. Wherever there are shadows — on his shoulders, in the definition of his back muscles as he encloses Uncle Sam in his arms — they serve only to highlight his skin's extraordinary translucence.

Some men are lookers, but Cliff Harper is something else. His looks transcend time. Blond, clean cut and devastatingly handsome, he is breathtaking — yet, in his unswerving gaze is a mixture of innocence and knowing. He seems to come wrapped in a shyness and modesty that makes him the boy next door or the brother you wish you had. Or the boyfriend you dream about.

123

'Michael? I know you're there.' My sister Amiria's voice. 'Pick up the phone, pick it up right *now*.'

I put Uncle Sam's diary, and the photograph, aside.

'Hello, Amiria, How was the honeymoon?'

'I knew you were there, I'm your twin, you can't hide from me. The honeymoon was great but —' Amiria wailed, 'I'm pregnant.'

'Already? Nobody gets pregnant on their honeymoon.'

'You know what they say about the Mahana family.' Amiria didn't sound too happy about it. 'The women are always so fertile. A man only has to look at one of us and she gets pregnant — though I guess a woman wouldn't have to worry in your case! But that's not the reason why I'm ringing. Tyrone and I are leaving from Auckland by United Airlines for Texas this weekend. His Dad wants him to start work at the casino immediately, and I'm starting to get cold feet. I may be leaving New Zealand for good.'

Amiria was sounding tearful. At that moment I felt the same sadness. My twin was going to the other side of the world.

'Will you come up and say goodbye to me?'

'I don't know whether that's wise. Mum and Dad will be there. I don't want to start World War Three.'

'Please, Michael. We might never see each other again.'

I caught the afternoon flight from Wellington to Auckland where the international terminal was crowded with Cook Islanders returning to Raratonga. Bedecked with flowers, they looked so festive and relaxed. Across the sea of flowers I saw Mum and Dad with Auntie Pat. For a moment I considered backing away. Perhaps I could pretend I hadn't come, ring Amiria in Texas and give some excuse about work or fully booked flights. But Auntie Pat saw me and pulled me towards Mum and Dad.

'Now, Monty,' Auntie Pat said to Dad, 'we're all adults —'

Dad's face went red with anger and Auntie Pat had to intercede again.

'You've already spoilt Amiria's wedding. Let's try not to spoil her going away, shall we?'

Dad glared and said nothing. Mum looked awkward, as if she wanted to hug me but was being restrained by her loyalty to Dad. For a while we just stood there, a silent knot in that singing crowd. What can you say to a father who has made it quite clear that you don't belong in his life any longer?

Amiria and Tyrone joined us. They had been doing some last-minute duty-free shopping. As soon as she saw me, Amiria began to cry. When we had been small children we were always trying to push each other out of the pram. As teenagers, there had been times when we wanted to throttle each other. The gap in her teeth was bigger than mine. How would we get on at opposite ends of the world?

Auntie Pat started the conversation.

'I suppose your sister's told you that she's pregnant?'

Amiria sniffled and glared at Tyrone.

'I told you to keep on using your condoms.'

Mum gave a nervous laugh, and Dad tried a different track. 'Better start thinking about buying that double pram for the twins,' he said.

Tyrone blanched, Amiria started to wail, and you could count on Mum to make things worse.

'What did you two get married for? To have children of course!'

Another family argument began. Dad apologised to Amiria that he had only been joking. Mum folded her arms and said she didn't know what the fuss was all about. Tyrone tried to hug Amiria and reassure her that he didn't mind that she was pregnant.

In the middle of all of it, Auntie Pat pulled me away. 'They won't miss us,' she said.

But I saw the look Dad gave her, as if she was doing something he disapproved of. Despite the fact that she was older than Dad, he was head of the family. Auntie Pat had always been somebody who said yes to him, a sister he had sometimes gently ridiculed because of her submissive nature and her spinsterhood.

'Am I causing trouble for you, Auntie Pat?'

She stared at Dad and then turned to me — and I sensed that the relationship between her and my father was changing.

'Yes,' she answered. 'Your father doesn't like me taking your side. He's used to me being the kind of girl I was when Dad had us under his thumb, and the kind of sister I've been — up until now. He doesn't like it when I argue with him or speak against him. He's not used to it.'

We went to find some of the stuff that passes for coffee at an airport.

Auntie Pat was tense — but for another reason. I guessed it was the diary.

'I've begun reading Sam's story,' I said.

She sighed and took both my hands in hers and held them tight. I was surprised at the intensity of the gesture and the force she put into it. Any further pressure and her grip would have hurt.

'I never realised how much of a relief it would be to share his story with someone else. To share it with you —'

I knew what she meant. Once, I had simply been her nephew and she had been my aunt. My coming out had led to a particular act of trust — the giving to me of the diary. And like Auntie Pat's relationship with Dad, hers and mine was changing. I liked this new Auntie Pat, this spirited woman whom I was becoming close friends with. Our alliance was shifting the shapes of both our lives.

Then Auntie Pat said something strange, as if speaking to herself. 'And now that the lid is off Pandora's Box, I guess whatever is in there, for good or ill, will come flying out —'

She closed her eyes and sighed.

'When you get back to Wellington I want you to go out and talk to George.'

For a moment I didn't know who she was talking about. Then it clicked:

'George? So he didn't die in Vietnam?'

'No. What makes you think that! I haven't seen him in many years but I rang Emma —'

'Turei's sister?'

'You know about her? She gave me George's number in Porirua, just outside Wellington. I told him you might want to talk to him about Sam. He's expecting you at the Porirua Tavern eight o'clock Friday night, next weekend.'

'Can he tell me about Cliff Harper too?'

A look of fear crossed Auntie Pat's face. 'How much do you need to know about Cliff Harper?' she asked. Her expression was angry, almost bitter.

We rejoined Mum and Dad just as Amiria and Tyrone's final boarding call was made.

It was obvious that Mum would cry. But none of us was prepared for Dad's sudden grief.

'Amiria,' he burst out. Tears were rushing down his cheeks like a river.

At the sight of Dad's sorrow, tears sprang to my eyes too. Part of it was because of the emotion of the moment. Another part of it was because here was my father, weeping for Amiria who was only going to America; and here I was, his son whom he had thrown out of the family. Had there been any tears for me? No. None. Even so I tried to close the gap between us.

When Amiria and Tyrone went through Customs, Dad was still weeping. I went to offer support. He looked at me, dabbing at his tears with a handkerchief, and turned his back on me.

'Your mother and I have decided,' he said. 'Don't come home for Christmas.'

Auntie Pat began to argue with him: 'Now, Monty, that's a stupid thing to say.' But he was already walking away with Mum through that roistering Polynesian crowd.

My anger made me walk after him and force him to turn and look me in the eyes.

'Dad, why do you think I stayed away from home? Why do you think I live in Wellington? It makes no difference to me.'

Did I mean it? Yes. No. Yes —

'Then don't come back at all,' Dad said. 'Ever.'

——— 3 ———

It was raining when I returned to Wellington. I was depressed and angry with myself for having pushed Dad too far, for mishandling the situation. But there was no use crying over spilt milk.

What's done was done. The gloves were back on.

The taxi queue was chaos, with men in business suits jumping the queue and grabbing taxis without apology. A guy carrying a large, bulky canvas bag over his shoulder bumped into me, and for a minute I was on the defensive. Bloody idiot. Why didn't he look . . .

But I was drained by the altercation with Dad and by Amiria's departure. So I let the moment go — until he bumped into me again.

'Remember me?' the culprit said, laughing.

Shaven head. Taller than I had expected. Lasers had limned his profile with green fire. 'Carlos.'

'Good boy! You've passed Go and been given a hotel on Mayfair. Why didn't you tell me that the person you were with at the club was your Auntie! I met your girlfriend, and she told me. I thought you were with another guy. Are you available?'

His boldness took my breath away.

'I'm in a relationship right now, but it's rocky. I'm not right for anybody. I don't want to get involved.'

'Damn,' Carlos answered, making a teasing gesture. 'Here I was hoping we'd do the wild thing! Look, I'd give you a lift but I've got to get this gear back —' Apart from his canvas bag, he had a pile of aqualung equipment on a trolley. 'I've been doing some diving up around the Hen and Chickens.' He took out a piece of paper, and scribbled his telephone number on it. With another grin he pretended to throw dice.

'If you don't call me soon you lose your hotels on Mayfair and go straight to jail, you hear?'

Back at the flat, I dumped my bags and opened a can of beer. Life was changing all around me and it was happening so fast. In less than a month I had come out to my parents, my boyfriend had walked out, and my sister was now on her way to live in America. My parents no longer talked to me, and my aunt had given me the diary of an uncle who I had never known existed. A history which once I had been part of and belonged to was disappearing as surely as if somebody had pressed the *Delete* button on a document named Michael Mahana. Correction. *I*, Michael, had pressed the button and consigned the file to the Recycle Bin. By my own act I had rendered myself a man without a history. And now a guy named Carlos had given me a hotel on Mayfair.

Later that night, however, my thoughts turned to Jason.

'The thing is that I do think I love you,' he'd said. 'If I do come back to you it would be nice to know that you will be waiting.'

I truly believed Jason. I wanted to believe him. Love was always the problem. Before you knew it you could only think of one person to the exclusion of any others. I had to admit to myself that I loved Jason. Although I was now writing myself a new history, I wanted to include him in it. I wanted a partner to walk with me into that brave new world. Too much time had passed already. There was a shapeshifter at work in my life, shifting the shapes according to forces I had myself set in motion.

The shapes were out of control now, and I was afraid if too much time went past they would move Jason and me further apart. And I needed him. Physically as well as emotionally.

The next morning I telephoned Jason at work. I was so confident. I felt that all I had to do was talk to him and he would melt. That all I had to do was to say 'I miss you', and he would come running back.

But Jason wasn't in. 'Sorry, Michael, nobody knows when he'll be back. Do you want to leave a message? All right, I'll tell Jason you called.'

I put the receiver down. I was frustrated. I replayed the conversation I'd just had back in my head. You know what it's like. You start becoming suspicious. You begin to imagine a hidden, unspoken text:

Sorry, Michael, Jason isn't in, *not to you.* No, nobody knows when he'll be back, *but even if he was he wouldn't talk to you anyway.* Do you want to leave a message? *You can if you like, but it'll end up in the trash can.* All right, I'll tell Jason you called, *but quite frankly, Michael, can't you take a hint and take a hike?*

I was really spinning out of control. I needed somebody to talk my anxieties out with. Who better than Margo, Jason's analyst? I decide to telephone her.

'I'll see if Margo can talk to you,' her secretary said. 'Yes, she's just finished with a client. I'll put you through.'

The phone clicked and buzzed, and Margo's voice came down the line. 'Hello, Michael, how lovely to hear from you.' She sounded warm, reassuring, like a soft couch you could sink into.

'Margo, I need your help. Jason's left me and I haven't heard from him since. Do you know where he is?'

'You don't know where he is?'

'No, and I'm going out of my mind with worry. When he first started to go to you I thought it was for simple issues. Like why is he unhappy? Or what he wanted out of life.'

'You thought those were simple issues?'

'I never anticipated that they would escalate like this. Three months down the track and he's questioning everything and everybody. What's happening to him, Margo? How can I help him?'

'You don't know what's happening to him? You want to help him?'

I began to feel my temperature rising. Sometimes, talking to Margo was like listening to an echo or having a talking parrot in the room.

'Michael, there are two issues here. One of them is what Jason wants and the other is what *you* want. Are you sure you're ringing because of your concern for Jason — or is it because you're really concerned about yourself? Have you considered that the reason Jason hasn't let you know his address is because he doesn't want to be found? He needs time to think these things out. He's given himself permission to explore who he is, what he wants and where he wants to be —'

I listened as Margo put it all on the line for me. She was right: I *was* concerned for myself. Secretly I had hoped to hear her say that Jason had spoken about me, that he had told her he loved me and that he wanted us to be back together. Instead:

'I have had to guide him through some very serious matters. While this might mean that some of us might not be happy with the outcome, what is more important is that Jason defines the outcome for himself. So if he chooses not to be in touch with anyone, we have to respect that choice.'

It all sounded so reasonable. And, obviously, if Margo knew where he was staying, she wasn't telling. I tried another tack:

'In that case, Margo, can you give me Graham's telephone number?'

A pause. 'You know about Graham?'

'Yes.' Her intonation had risen a few decibels. Why?

'Well, I suppose it will be all right.'

A few moments later, I was talking to Graham, the buddy who had become Jason's closest friend.

'You've got a nerve ringing me,' he said. 'But if you want to know, Jason's moved in with me.'

Moved in?

Graham went for the jugular.

'Why don't you leave him alone, Michael. Why don't you admit that all he ever was to you was another scalp you could hang on your belt.'

Later that day Roimata asked me to meet her for lunch to talk about the submission I had written for Toi Maori — her Board was delighted with it. As usual she had chosen a restaurant where we would stand out: the only brown people in the room. She liked to make visual her political position — that Maori were a minority but, dammit, we could still walk through the front door and play with the family silver.

'So things look really bad for you and Jason, right?'

'You don't have to sound so pleased.'

'Well, you know how I feel about Jason. We've never liked each other.'

'Can you blame him?' I reminded her. 'Who was that certain Maori maiden who tried to break us up by introducing me to an alternative candidate!'

'He wasn't only an alternative,' Roimata said. 'Don was Maori, he had mana and, from what I've heard, he wasn't called Long Dong Silver for nothing. He was totally suitable but what did you do? You rejected him and became a — a potato queen.'

'Look,' I answered. 'I like white boys. When I put my brown hands on them it makes me feel so dirty.'

Roimata knew I was joking. Even so, she couldn't resist pushing home her point.

'I only wish, Michael, dear, that you would see that you've been colonised twice over. First, by the Pakeha. Second by the *gay* Pakeha. Even in the gay world the White majority holds the power, the money, the decision making power — and it is their images which tell you what is desirable, what you should be like and what you shouldn't be like.'

Roimata always had a particular strength, a particular vision. It came from her university training in Maori studies, women's studies and art history — a potent combination that had turned her into an outspoken Maori activist. Add to this her lesbian identity and world, watch out.

'Take, for instance, the Pakeha gay attitude to family,' Roimata continued, warming to her subject and talking academic-speak. 'The Western model de-privileges any notions that gay men or women might have children. Therefore, the White gay species is the only one which doesn't replicate itself. But our Maori model is a tribal one. It should therefore include the possibility of growing a tribe. Of having children.'

Roimata's passion was overwhelming, pouring out of her, and her eyes were glowing and luminous.

'Don't you understand, Michael? The issues of identity and space — of sovereignty, of tino rangatiratanga — that our people have been fighting for within Pakeha society are the same issues for gay Maori within Pakeha gay society! That gay tribe that your Auntie Pat asked about won't just happen — it will have to be created, God dammit —'

Sometimes Roimata's words weren't expressive enough for her and, before you knew it, you became the target of her spontaneous passions. This time, she reached over the table, grasped my head in both hands and kissed me. Roimata was always helping herself to my body, leaving lipstick all over my face, so I wasn't surprised. However, this wasn't just a kiss. It was strong. Deep. Long.

'Why did you do that?' I asked. I had the feeling another shape was shifting in my life.

Roimata tried to hide her emotions with flippancy.

'Well it works in films and in television ads,' she said.

She looked at me, as if trying to decide whether to push her point or not. Then decided that the meter had gone too far into the danger zone, so backed off — for now.

'But that isn't why I asked you for coffee. Are you able to come to Canada? Next month?'

'Canada?'

'There's a big indigenous arts conference being held in Ottawa. The First Nations people of Canada are hosting it and they've invited indigenous representatives from all around the world — Black Africa, the Caribbean, Asia, Europe and, of course, Polynesia. The conference will consider the models available for indigenous cultures in terms of setting up our own network. I've already been asked to go but last week, you lucky boy, I emailed them a copy of the submission you wrote for me. They want you to come with me. They're paying all travel and expenses. Will you?'

'If the dates work out, yes.'

'Great.'

'Now,' I said gently, 'that kiss —'

Roimata was silent for a moment. She hated being cornered. She nodded to herself and there was both sadness and acceptance in her eyes.

'I know you're gay,' she began, 'and you know I'm lesbian. But I love you, Michael, and I wanted you to know it.'

I took Roimata's hand and kissed it. I was surprised to see tears welling in her eyes. Our relationship had always been unspoken. Amiria was my twin but Roimata and I shared something else. Amiria was part of the old world; with Roimata there was a promise of the new.

The moment grew dangerous. Then:

'What a pity you're not a woman,' Roimata smiled.

'What a pity you're not a man,' I answered.

In every other respect we knew we were made for each other.

At that moment the waiter arrived. 'More coffee?' he asked.

'Yes,' Roimata said. Her voice was strong and thrilling. 'He'll have a tall basketball player —'

'A long black.'

'And I'll have —'

'A flat white?' I laughed.

'Yes,' she nodded. 'A dead Pakeha.'

──────  4  ──────

In the evening there was a knock on the door. I went down the stairs to answer it.

'Jason.'

My heart leapt in my chest at the sight of him. He was looking stunning, and absence only made him look more desirable. Without thinking I went to embrace him but he took a step back.

'No.'

I stood there looking at him, panicking that I could not touch him. How can you turn something around when the other person won't let it happen? Jason was trembling, but there was a firm look on his face. I didn't realise how much courage it had taken him to park his car outside the house that he once lived in and to knock on the door as if he was a stranger.

'I hear you've been looking for me,' he said. 'I don't want you ringing Margo or Graham. The reason why I've come is to demand that you don't do it again.'

Demand? I acknowledged what he was saying with a nod.

'Won't you come in?'

'No,' said Jason. 'Now that I've said what I want to say, I'll go.'

Jason started to walk away. Ultimatums have always been to me like a red rag to a bull. I remembered that Jason had always been good at making statements and walking away before I could reply. As if I had no right of reply or that my reply wasn't of any relevance. There was only so much of that I had ever taken and, as for playing the forlorn lover, it wasn't a look that I liked. Before I knew it, I was walking after him and getting between him and his car. I wasn't about to be rejected without a fight.

'I wish you had told me to stay out of your life before I went to Amiria's wedding. It would have saved me the bother of coming out to my folks.'

Jason pushed past me. Whatever Margo's therapy was doing for him, he was certainly not taking anything lying down.

'I won't take physical intimidation,' he said, 'and I won't be made responsible for what you said to your parents.'

'You were the one who wanted me to do it!'

Before either of us could prevent it, we were arguing again, our voices echoing along the street, going over all that stuff, raking it back up.

'I may have suggested it,' Jason said, 'but the decision was yours, not mine, and it was time you came out of the closet. Margo was always saying in our sessions you can't live a life of freedom until you come out; by doing so, you also come out to yourself, not just to the world. As far as you're concerned, I was only trying to provide you with an example of how you denied me. In all the time we were together you never put me first. Whenever we walked down the street and saw any of your family, your Maori relatives or friends, you always seemed embarrassed I was with you. I got sick and tired of answering the phone and pretending I was your — your room mate.'

'That's unfair,' I answered. 'I was never embarrassed. Don't try to palm off your feelings of embarrassment on me. If you felt that way it wasn't my fault.'

'How was I expected to feel? Listen to your message on the answerphone. What does it say? Not "Jason and I are not in right now" but "*We're* not in right now." Your voice is giving the message. You never ever considered what this made me look like. Not a partner. Just an anonymous somebody else who lived in the flat.'

I thought about that and conceded. However:

'You could have changed the message,' I said. 'Why didn't you?'

'The flat's in your name and you never gave me permission.'

It was beginning again, the descent into accusations and recriminations where guilt was situational, something unthought of until pointed out. I tried again.

'We've talked about all of this before, and it was the reason why I came out to Mum and Dad. To make legitimate what we were to each other. I

134

know there were times when I didn't realise how you felt —'

'Whenever you had to meet clients, did you ever introduce me as your lover?'

'Did *you*?'

'I'm not the one answering the questions, Michael, so don't try to change the subject. Well, I can tell you the answer. No, you never did. You preferred, in fact, to take your girlfriend, Roimata, rather than me.'

I felt helpless. I was always having to provide proof, proof and more proof, more and more signs that I loved him. When would I ever find the holy grail?

Jason stared at me. He wrenched away, opened the door of his car and stepped in.

'You've never understood me, Michael. Never.'

The line between us snapped and I could see him spinning away, spinning, spinning, and I reached out to grab him before it was too late —

'I don't want to lose you,' I said.

Tears began to stream down Jason's eyes. 'When I'm with you, all my old feelings for you come back. But I have to figure out whether that's because I really want to come back or if I'm doing it only because it's what you want. I'm all mixed up, Michael, and talking to you only confuses me more. Did I get into my relationship with you because I needed to be loved? I've never really known what my needs are. As I said before, this has got nothing to do with you. It's about who *I* am and what *I* want. Margo says I have to find the child in me. I have to touch him. Nurture him. Once I have found him, then I can begin to heal myself. I asked you to wait for me. Please be here when I come back.'

He started the car. Burnt rubber as he put his foot on the accelerator.

'Jason? Jason —'

———— 5 ————

I was still depressed by my argument with Jason when Friday come around. That evening I was to drive out to Porirua to meet a man named George. Of course Auntie Pat had assumed that I knew George's surname, which I didn't, and when I'd rung her to ask her, she was either out or watching one of her beloved old movies on Sky's Turner Classic Movies network. She'd had a satellite dish put on her roof just so she could tune in. Not even the telephone could take her away from all those melodramatic scenes with their sweeping violins when the hero kissed the heroine. Her favourite star was an actor called Guy Madison, who appeared in *Till the End of Time*. She had a whole scrapbook of photographs and clippings about him.

On a wing and a prayer I arrived at the Porirua Tavern. The bar was big and brash, dating back to the days when drinking yourself stupid was the name of the game — and bar owners provided carparks that took up to a thousand cars to enable you to do it. Carpet deodorant could not mask the overriding smell of cigarette smoke and spilt beer. One look at the roistering, carousing crowd in the public bar — wall to wall Maori and Pacific Islanders — and I knew there was only one hope of finding a man named George, one of the most common names of Maori men, and that was no hope. To make matters worse, I arrived right on show time. The lights went down just as I had paid for my beer at the bar.

Great. Now I'd be stumbling around looking for somebody I didn't know in the dark.

A spotlight came up on a small stage at floor level. A fifty-ish singer came forward. A good-humoured cheer went up.

'Hey,' the singer grinned, 'you can do better than that!'

This time he was rewarded with a bigger roar of welcome, and this seemed to please him. He was wearing a very bad wig, sunglasses, a dreadful white retro suit with bell bottoms, and a wide-collar half-unbuttoned disco shirt. With a gold chain around his neck, he was a throwback to the disco dinosaur days of the 1970s.

'Thank you, folks, and thank you all my loyal fans —' The crowd started to laugh. '— for coming along for this little stroll down Memory Lane.'

The band started to play, the singer took the microphone in his hands and began to sing that great Maori anthem to Mum, Dad, the Maori flag and puha pie, 'Ten Guitars'. Once upon a very long time ago, the singer must have had a pretty good voice. All the bass notes were there. Trouble was, whenever he tried to reach for the high ones his voice wobbled like a train going off the rails and his suit split open, exposing a startlingly white and gruesome beer gut. But he was obviously a local favourite, and the punters sang along in the chorus — and they sang the high notes for him.

The song concluded with whistles, applause and stamping feet. The singer bowed, wiped the sweat off his brow and, to much laughter, took off his toupee and began to fan himself with it.

'Thanks, folks,' he said, 'but now we'll leave the singing to the younger fellas, eh? Put your hands together, because here they are, the ones you've really been waiting for, the Porirua Punishers!'

The atmosphere immediately changed. Black and Polynesian rhythms crisscrossed the bar room. From out of nowhere dry ice started to drift across the stage. Laser beams started to strike through the blackness. Two hip men and two girl singers strode out into the light.

'Oh, wahine, haere mai ki au,' the boys sang.

'Oh, taku tane, let the good lovin' flow,' sang the girls.

'Let's do it! Get down to it! Arohaina mai —'

The audience roared. There was nothing like being in a bar filled with Maori and Pacific Islanders on a night when the music was cool, sweet and moaning with love, sex and wild dreams. A few minutes into their bracket, though, I checked my watch. I was supposed to meet George at eight and it was already half past. I walked through the crowd, targeting every fifty-ish man who looked like he could have been a Vietnam Vet. The only Vietnam soldier I had ever seen was Sylvester Stallone in the *Rambo* movies, so I looked for an older version of Sly. Somebody who once could have worn a red bandanna and, bare-chested, operated a machine gun with one hand and shot down a helicopter with it.

No such luck.

I decided to call it a night. I walked to the bar, intending to put my glass down and leave. The singer had divested himself of his white suit and was pulling handles. The lights blazed on his bald head. One of the patrons called to him:

'Pae kare, George, you can still show those young fellas a thing or two.'

George grinned. Our eyes connected. For a second I saw surprise in his eyes. He nodded and reached across the bar to shake my hand.

'You must be Michael. Patty told me you'd be coming tonight.'

George led me into another bar, empty because it was being renovated. 'It'll be quieter in here,' he said. Gib board was stacked against the walls. Bags of cement, flooring materials and timber was strewn around the room. Muttering to himself, George kicked away some planks, found a couple of chairs, motioned me to take a seat and cracked open two beers.

We sat drinking, the thump thump thump of the band coming through the walls. Neither of us said anything for a while and, as a way of beginning, I showed him the photograph of Uncle Sam with Cliff Harper. His hands trembled as he looked at it. He must have registered Harper but, if so, he pretended not to notice him. Instead, he pointed at Sam:

'Yeah, that's my mate. That's the bastard. You want to know about him, right?'

'As much as you can tell me,' I answered.

He nodded. He went quiet for a moment. He looked at me, as if wondering how much he should say.

'We must have been a bit younger than you — Sam, Turei and me — when we joined up to fight in Vietnam. God we were young. We were two years out of school and the war had been going on for about four years. Sam was our leader and we were his followers. Sam grew up hearing about his Dad's exploits in war. You know about Arapeta, don't you.'

'He died before I was nine,' I answered, 'but I've heard the stories.'

'Arapeta was the *man*,' George said. 'Some people thought he was more formidable than his older brother, Bulibasha. Strong as an ox. Never gave up. Stubborn as. Fast with his fists. I've heard he was a hard husband and a hard father. He wasn't a person to cross but you have to hand it to him. He knew what was right and what was wrong, and very few people challenged him. He had guts. Anyway, Arapeta was about 24 when he married Auntie Florence. Sam was born two years later, and me and him are cousins on Auntie Florence's side. We're the same age, so that must mean Sam was born in 1948. Turei was a year younger.'

George chuckled to himself.

'You know, they tell a story about Sam when he was born. When he came out of Auntie Florence's womb, his hands were bunched up into tiny fists and the first thing he did was to poke Arapeta in the eye. Apparently, Arapeta poked him back: 'You want to fight me, eh?' The hospital had never seen such a sight as that — a proud father, skipping and boxing with his newborn son in his arms. From that time onwards, Arapeta was inseparable from Sam. When Sam was two, Arapeta bought him some boxing gloves. Sam liked nothing better than to box with his Dad. The trouble was that Arapeta always won. You'd think a father might pretend to lose some fights to his son, but Arapeta never did. Ever. By the time we were all at high school, it was still the same. Sam was a

138

high flier. In the fifth form he was a prefect. He was Most Popular Boy and vice captain of the First Fifteen. But you know what his Dad used to say to him? "Only a prefect? I was head prefect! Only vice captain? I was captain!" Arapeta loved raising the bar to another rung, and that used to make Sam mad.'

George paused. Leaned forward. Took a sip of his beer.

'I think, in the end, that's why Sam joined up. I think he realised if he didn't get away from his dad and make his own way in life, Arapeta would break him as surely as if he was one of his horses. Arapeta would have a stallion on the end of a rope and in his other hand he held the bullwhip. Every now and then he cracked the whip over the stallion's head. It was his way of showing who was the master. Well, you can do that to horses, but it shouldn't be done to a man.

'Throughout Sam's teens, his father was always cracking the whip at him. Letting it sing just above his head, when Sam was least expecting it. Just to make him remember who was boss.

'Well, we were all in the Upper Sixth at high school when Sam started to talk about joining the Army. The next year we went out shearing in the Mahana Number Two gang. The following May, 1967, the news came that a rifle company of 121 from the First Battalion in Malaysia was going to Vietnam. Sam was sick of shearing, and he told us he was going into Gisborne to sign up. I decided to join him, and so did Turei. Our mothers, especially Turei's Mum, Lilly, hated the idea but by that time it was too late. We went to Burnham Camp for basic all arms training, then we were shipped off to Malaysia for further training. From there we went with Victor Company to Nui Dat.'

George's voice drifted into silence. He looked at me to provide another cue. I confronted him with Harper.

'Can you tell me anything about the guy who's with Uncle Sam?'

George lifted the photograph to the light. I watched his eyes crinkle and clear with recognition. His gaze went right through me.

'What do you want to know?'

'His name. Anything.'

George didn't even blink.

'Are you playing with me, son?' he asked gently. 'You know who he is — Woody Woodpecker, the American chopper pilot at Nui Dat.'

It was obvious George didn't want to say more, but I pressed on.

139

'I'm not playing with you. I'm just trying to understand their story. How they became —'

George's eyes narrowed. The question hung in the air and I thought I had blown it.

'Well, I guess it must have happened straight after Operation Bucephalus while we were on our second leave in Vung Tau —'

And suddenly the blades of a gunship were slapping the air hard, pop, pop, pop. It was late evening. Three young men were watching a helicopter making its way northwards across the town towards the dark Vietnam horizon.

# CHAPTER NINE

## 1

'Go, cowboys, go!'

The chopper convoy was wheeling through the air. In the street below, soldiers and civilians were cheering and waving. The noise was shattering as the convoy lifted up and over and away into the night. Sam was aware of the heat again. Yes, it had kept its promise:

'I'm in every breath you take. You'll never escape me. Never.'

Sam looked across at George and Turei, and grinned. They'd started at a popular Steam and Clean massage parlour where the girls had been playful and sexy — and when Sam had climaxed, his laughter following the release of tension had ricocheted through the walls setting everybody else off. From there they'd gone on to the LOVE FOR YOU HERE BAR where George had avoided the steak but had shouted Sam and Turei another round of sex; hey, that was the great thing about Vietnam. Sex was easy. All you had to do was pass over your money and you got laid. Now they were on their way to another bar where Turei had been told the action was supposed to be hot and the beer the coldest in Vung Tau. After half an hour's searching, however, they still hadn't found it.

'Are you sure you got the name right?' Sam asked.

'I tell you,' Turei insisted, 'the bar's called The Cock Door. We're supposed to look for a sign of a naked woman. It must be around here somewhere.'

When at last they found the place, Sam let out a sigh of amused exasperation.

'God, you're dumb,' he said to Turei. 'Not only did you get the sign wrong. You got the language wrong too.'

The bar was called Le Coq D'or and the sign was a golden rooster.

'C'mon,' George said. 'We've already wasted good boozing time.'

Inside, the bar looked like a packing crate. The walls were framed with whatever wood the proprietor had been able to scrounge, and covered with large sheets of the thin metal that beer cans were stamped from. Thousands of Carling and Falstaff labels on top of the sheets gave the place a certain atmosphere.

'Hey, Kiwis!' The patrons were full of drunken exhilaration, shooting the bull, excited and happy to be alive and having a good time. The Vietnamese scrambled to service the orders of beer. The barmaids and whores cracked the air with shrill laughter.

'There's sure a lot of Aussies here,' Sam said.

He jerked his head at a tableful of Australian soldiers. One of them was the red-haired bastard from the base and, as usual, he was eyeballing Turei.

'Good,' Turei said, staring back. 'I feel like getting physical. I've had some sex, some drink, and now all that's left to do is take out a certain red-headed cunt.'

He called for some beer. He paid the barman 50 piastres extra to spin the bottles on ice to get them really cold. Then, wiping the top of the bottle — not to mention the rust on the bottle rim — Turei offered a toast in the direction of the soldier.

'Fuck all Aussies.'

To be fair, the baiting between the sides had started long before Sam, George and Turei arrived. There'd been some pushing and jostling, beer guzzling contests, and lots of macho crushing of empty beer cans. An Aussie and Kiwi soldier had done the Dance of the Flaming Arseholes standing butt-arse naked on a table, with two-metre lengths of toilet paper trailing from their bums. Bets had been taken as to who would do the dance first, someone had tossed a coin and, to much groaning from the Aussie side, the Kiwi soldier won first opportunity to set his competitor's toilet roll on fire. But you can never trust the Aussies to play by the rules — when nobody was looking, someone in the crowd lit the toilet roll of the Kiwi soldier halfway along the roll.

Now there was no doubting the mood among the Kiwis — 'Let's get the bastards'. So that when the red-haired Aussie started to hassle Turei, everybody was primed.

There was deadly quiet as the bar patrons collected into three groups. The Aussies. The Kiwis. Everybody Else.

'No, no!' the bar owner remonstrated. 'No fighting! No fighting!'

Turei patted him on the head and smiled benignly.

'Okay, chief,' he said. 'How's about another bet instead?'

'What the bet? No more fire in arsehole. Something else.'

Turei turned to the red-haired Aussie.

'Feel like taking me on, cobber? The guy who pisses the farthest wins.'

'Not in bar! Not in bar!' the bar owner yelled frantically.

But it was too late. The Aussie had jumped on the table, chugged as many jugs as he could, burped and pulled down his trou. Around him odds were being laid and bets exchanged. The bar girls giggled as they caught sight of the Aussie's red bush and bloated pink dick.

'Oh, he win for sure!' they laughed. 'And after you win, cobber boy, you spend money on us, we show you good time-ah?'

The Aussie soldier burped again, winked and nodded. He pointed himself towards the open door.

'Clear the way,' he called.

Everyone scattered.

'On the count of five! One! Two! Three! Four —'

'Five!' the patrons in the bar roared.

For a moment nothing happened. Then something began to dribble from the end of the Aussie's dick. Gradually the stream thickened and arched upward. Very soon it was fountaining higher, flowing and splashing across the floor. As it did so, everyone began to cheer. Onward and upward went the stream of piss — right to the threshold of the door.

'You pay! You pay for pissing on floor of bar!' the bar owner cried.

Shaking himself dry, the red-haired Aussie jumped down from the table.

'All yours, Hori,' he said to Turei.

Bad move that, calling Turei a *Hori*. Turei masked his anger and stepped nonchalantly on the table. He was always a showman and he knew how to play the crowd. He knelt down, as if making mental calculations: if x equals urine and y equals volume and you added z to represent distance then —

'Come on, Kiwi,' the red-haired soldier called. 'You're wasting time.'

'Patience!' Turei smiled as he wet a finger and put it in the air as if to test which way the wind was blowing. He shook his head sadly at the audience, and winked at Sam.

'I'm going to have to up the stakes to make this all worth while,' he said. 'See that door? And the road outside? And the other side of the road? It's double or nothing that I can piss that far.'

The audience cheered wildly. The Kiwis looked at each other nervously. There was no way Turei could do it.

'You're on!' the red-haired Aussie called.

'Okay,' Turei answered. 'In that case, you and your mates can go out there to make sure I reach the kerb and, by the time you're there, I'll be ready.'

With that, Turei asked Sam and George to get him some jugs. He downed the lot. Then, he pretended to do a strip on the table and dropped his jungle utilities.

'Holy Hone Hika,' Sam thought as Turei mooned everybody with a very dark and pimply set of buns.

The bar girls shrieked with laughter.

'It's not what you see that counts,' Turei said, offended. 'It's what you do with it.'

He turned toward the door. Far beyond it was the red-haired Aussie and his mates. Then Turei showed everybody his cannon — and the Kiwis in the crowd groaned because, compared to the Aussie's dick, Turei's was short, stubby and uncircumcised. What they didn't know, however, was that Turei's was a grower not a shower.

Turei applied himself to a quiet and fierce concentration. He chug-a-lugged several more beers as he scoped out the problem, finalising his mathematical assumptions about the arc of fire and the velocity needed to piss across the road.

'You really think you can do it, bro?' Sam asked.

Turei nodded. He had finally concluded he was ready. 'Stay right where you are, cobbers,' he yelled to the Australians. Then he turned to Sam: 'When you're ready, my good man.'

Sam waved for silence:

'Ready!' he called.

Turei massaged his dick a few times, and it began to grow. He pinched his uncircumcised foreskin closed with his fingers. He began to piss and piss and piss. A gasp went up in the room as Turei's foreskin ballooned outward.

'Aim!'

With a loud grunt and strain, Turei sighted through the doorway of the bar. He put all the force of muscle into his thighs, elevated onto his toes, brought his balls and dick into a 90-degree position, let go his foreskin, flexed —

'Fire!'

With a huge monstrous fart, which sent everyone coughing for fresh air, Turei sent a big yellow water ball of piss sailing through the bar. It was an astonishing and beautiful sight as it rose to the ceiling and over the heads of the patrons. On it went, reaching its zenith — and then it began its downward trajectory. Everybody — except the red-haired Aussie and his mates — fled for shelter.

*This couldn't be happening! This wasn't possible!*

Oh yes it was. Splash. The ball of piss hit the target.

The whole bar erupted into whoops of astonishment and laughter. Turei rolled his eyes as if there'd been nothing to it. George began to collect on the bet.

'How he do that?' the bar owner asked.

'Mormon elders taught us applied science,' Sam said.

A beer bottle came flying through the air. With a roar, the red-haired Aussie launched himself at Turei.

'You black bastard —' If there was another word that Turei disliked it was *bastard*.

'Didn't your mother ever tell you not to swear?'

With the sound like a crack of a bat hitting home, Turei let fly with his fists. Next minute the fight was on. Beer cans, Ba Muoi Ba bottles and other assorted articles rained across the room.

'No fight! No fight!' the bar owner cried.

But this was what life was all about, wasn't it? Kiwis against the Aussies. The sheer exhilaration of physical contact. Even the bar girls got into the act, head butting and groin kicking for all they were worth. And right in the middle of it were Sam and George, laughing their heads off and drinking a toast to Turei.

'Oh, you are one truly foul dude,' Sam called.

The riot rolled into the alley, attracting more and more people.

'Hey, boys! Fight! Fight!'

Within minutes, soldiers were leaping into the battle and it didn't matter which side you were on. Then there were whistles as the Military Police arrived to break everything up, but they only made matters worse because they were White Mice — South Vietnamese police in white helmets, gloves and shirts — and, man, they were so clean.

Not for long. 'Enjoying yourself?' George asked Sam.

'Yup,' Sam laughed. 'It's just like Saturday night at home.'

More whistles sounded, and this time American Military Police arrived in jeeps from all directions.

'Time to bail out,' Sam yelled.

'Damn,' Turei said, and he smiled at the red-haired Aussie. 'I'm going to have to make this short.' With that, he let fly with an upper cut, and the Aussie was down for the count.

Sam grabbed George and Turei and they were out the door and running together with the rest of the crowd down the street. Next moment Sam tripped and took a dive. When he picked himself up, his mates were gone, not realising he was not following them. Panting, he saw blood on his hand and gingerly inspected his forehead: ouch. He must have been grazed during the fight. He pushed through the crowd and, as he passed an alley, he saw the sea, just on the other side of a strand of beach. He headed for the waves, where at least he could wash off the blood. He took off his boots and socks, and started to laugh when he thought of Turei's pissing act.

By chance, Sam looked up and saw three other soldiers staggering about further along the beach. Two of them were trying to get the third to stand. Sam was about to leave but blood was still dripping from his forehead. He was splashing his face with sea water, the salt stinging the wound. He looked again at the three soldiers and he took in the situation for what it really was.

Only one of the three men was a soldier. The other two were local Vietnamese, probably friendly to the enemy, and they were beating the soldier up.

'Hey —'

Immediately Sam was up and running, running along the beach to the rescue. One of the attackers turned. A knife flashed in his hand. Sam kicked, the knife went spinning, and the attacker went down. The other attacker whirled into the fight, leaping at Sam neck. Sam blocked, stepped to one side, brought his elbow up into the attacker's face, and kicked again. Next moment, the two assailants were fleeing the beach.

Sam knelt beside the soldier, who was spitting and coughing and nursing his jaw. 'Are you all right?'

The soldier looked up. He was paralytically drunk and his attackers had found it easy to lure him to the beach. His eyes were unfocussed.

It was Cliff Harper.

## 2

Harper gave Sam a shove that sent him sprawling.

'Leave me alone, willya, just leave me alone.'

Next minute, disorientated, he was up and stumbling into the sea, wading, falling, advancing further and further in. Sam waded in after him, tackled and brought him down. They were chest deep in the water and, immediately, they were fighting.

'I told you, leave me alone —'

Harper was swinging, ineffectually, his movements uncoordinated. He was half whimpering, half crying. He gave a mighty left hook which didn't connect and, spun around by his own momentum, fell again into the water.

Sam waited for Harper to re-surface, but he only flailed wretchedly before going down again. Sam stroked out to where Harper had disappeared, took a breath, and dived. A few seconds later he felt something in his hand, pulled, and dragged Harper back up into the air. Together, the two splashed into shallow water.

'How come you can't swim!' Sam asked. 'Everybody can swim.'

'Not if you come from Illinois you don't. All we've got there are the great lakes and you have to crack the ice to get in. No *way*.'

Harper floundered up to the beach and fell down.

'Oh Christ —'

He sat there, his elbows on his knees, cradling his face. He was panting with exhaustion. Sam sat beside him. Harper's mind had flipped completely away from the attack. It was somewhere else. Somewhere darker.

'What's up with you?' Sam asked.

Cliff Harper was up again, trying to find something, anything, to hurl at the sea. A rock. Another rock. And another.

'This fucken war, that's what's up with me. I've lost some good pals to this war. Fox is gone now, God dammit, Why didn't he bail out, man? And I keep taking soldiers to the front and they count on me to get them there alive and get them back alive. I've seen their eyes, how they trust me. They see me as some kind of god. When they're stuck in some shithole of a situation they're saying to each other, "Good old Cliff, he'll get through. He'll get us out of here to safety." But there are times when I can't deliver.'

Harper looked across at Sam. 'Have you ever had a man die in your arms? Have you ever seen his eyes roll up and into white and felt the warmth draining away from his body? Have you? Every time I go out, every time I take grunts to the front, I know some of them won't come back. When they come piling back into the chopper, you know what I see? I see the gaps where somebody's supposed to be. During the medevacs after Bucephalus, for instance, there was this cute kid, couldn't have been more than twenty for God's sake. He kept saying, "Please don't leave me. If you stay with me I know I'll be okay. Please." So I rode with him to the base hospital.'

Harper looked at his hands. 'When we got to the hospital, the kid begged me to stay with him. He held my hands and he pleaded with me as if I was his saviour. But I didn't listen to him. I said, "You'll be okay, kid." I was tired, I was exhausted, I just didn't have anything left over to give to him. When I left him he was okay. But he up and died on me. I feel angry at myself for not being there for him. This war's getting to me. I can't keep on doing this. I can't.'

Harper began to shiver. Next minute he was puking his guts out.

'I'd better take you home,' Sam said. 'Get you out of those clothes. Get you to bed. Where are you staying?'

'The Flags.'

Sam hoisted Harper to his feet. Together, with Sam shouldering Harper, they made their way to the soldiers' club. Harper threw up a couple more times and, when they arrived, the sergeant on the desk didn't want to know. He backed away from the wet, blood-spattered pair and threw the keys of Harper's room to Sam.

'If you're planning to get back to your own quarters before curfew,' he said to Sam, 'you're out of luck.'

'Looks like you're staying the night with me then,' Harper said.

Once they were in the room, Sam propped Harper against the wall. Harper was still drunk and kept on sliding down. Sam lifted him up again and, to keep him upright, put a knee between his thighs. He started to take off Harper's shirt and Harper came over all coy, buttoning up all the buttons Sam had unbuttoned.

'For Christ's sake, stop that willya?' Sam said, slapping Harper's hands away from the shirt.

'Don't get any ideas,' Harper answered, wagging a finger, and giving Sam a blast of his acrid breath. 'I'm heterosexual and I never kiss on a first date.'

Harper gave a drunken giggle, yawned and, next minute, his head came forward onto Sam's shoulder as he fainted. Out like a light. Just like that.

'Great,' Sam said to himself.

It took Sam quite a while to wrestle Harper's shirt off. He finally got it unbuttoned and pulled the tails out of the pants. He opened one flap and then the other. The wet shirt clung to Harper's ratty T-shirt and skin, so that unclothing him was like ripping off a band aid. Harper's dead weight didn't help matters either. Sam placed his head in the middle of Harper's chest and wrestled Harper's arms out of the sleeves.

The T-shirt came next. Harper was struggling so much there was nothing else to do except take it in two hands and rip. The pressure of Harper's chest did the rest, causing the T-shirt to break across his nipples. Sam reached behind Harper and ripped the back of the shirt. Harper made a murmur of complaint — and then surrendered. Exposed, his upper body was an artist's dream. He was like a nude model in a drawing class, breaking out of the shreds and tatters of the shirt. His shoulders were wide and his chest was smooth and hard. His pectorals were well defined and his abs rippled in the light. Harper's chest hair sprang in tight curls against Sam's skin. His dogtags clinked within the clavicle of his breast. The scent of Harper's armpits was like sea water.

Hard against Harper, Sam moved his hands down past Harper's navel and started to undo Cliff Harper's belt. Harper began to rotate his pelvis and murmur to himself.

'Oh, baby, yeah baby —'

149

Harper's penis pulsed against Sam's thighs, and he began to butt against Sam's pelvis.

'Oh, boy,' Sam said to himself between clenched teeth.

The pants dropped to the floor. Underneath, Harper was wearing Army regulation boxer shorts.

'Okay, chopper boy,' Sam said. 'Let's be having you.'

Sam bent, let Harper fall over him, flexed, and took him in a fireman's lift. He kicked the door open. The dogtags waggled in his face as he carried Harper to the showers. He sat Harper in one of the stalls and turned on the taps.

'Daddy, Daddy, the water's too cold,' Harper complained in a small boy's voice.

Sam adjusted the temperature and Harper began to sigh. He curled himself up within the water, lifted his head to the flow, and started to snore. Leaving Harper there, Sam went back to the room and collected Harper's puke-stained clothes. He returned to the showers and threw the clothes in the next-door stall. He stripped off and stepped into it himself.

Five minutes later, Sam switched Harper's shower off. Harper protested as Sam pulled him out.

'You're not making this easy for me, are you!' Sam said as he tried to get Harper dry with a towel.

Harper opened his glazed eyes and tried to focus them. He looked at Sam closely, gave up, and snuggled into Sam's arms.

'Tickles,' Harper giggled as Sam dried his hair and under his armpits.

'Okay,' Sam said to himself, 'here comes the moment of truth.'

With a quick motion Sam gathered Harper's shorts in his hands and gave another rip. Harper sucked in his stomach in a deep indrawn gasp, clenched his buttocks, and the fly buttons went popping across the shower room floor. Unleashed, his penis stirred strong, and wedge-shaped, thick-rooted, in a grove of golden pubic hair. Cliff Harper was a *big* boy.

Sam towelled Harper briskly. For the sake of modesty he knotted the towel at Harper's waist.

'Alley-oop!'

Lifting Harper in his arms, Sam took him back to his room, put him to bed and pulled the sheet over him.

'Night Mommy, night Daddy, night John-Boy,' Harper whispered.

He turned into the sheets and began to hump them in a movement that Sam didn't even want to think about.

Sam turned out the light and went back to the shower room, washed his and Harper's clothes and strung them out to dry. When he returned to the room the moonlight was flooding in the window. Harper had turned onto his front, pushed the sheets down and released the towel. His right arm was flung across the bed and his head nestled on his left arm. One leg was pulled up, the towel tangled around it. As Sam watched, Harper moved, and the towel slid away. He began to breathe deeply. Sam grabbed a blanket and wrapped it around himself. He arranged himself as comfortably as he could in a chair at the foot of the bed.

'Oh, what a night,' Sam said to himself.

———— 3 ————

But it was not over. No sooner had Sam drifted off to sleep than Harper began to toss and turn in a terrible dream. Harper dreamt he was flying in a gunship convoy through a red sky filled with flames and showering sparks. All of a sudden, to his left, his friend Fox's chopper was hit. Harper screamed. He followed Fox down through the fiery sky and saw Fox's gunship explode on the ground. He managed to touch down and saw that the land had been napalmed to death and was writhing with agony. But Fox was walking out of the explosion. Only, something was wrong with Fox and he was not alone. Walking with him was a whole battalion of soldiers and, silently, they all began to pile into Harper's chopper. But each soldier was Fox and he kept saying *Don't leave me*, his fingers like talons on Harper's arm. The chopper became filled with soldiers, and still they kept coming and wanting to board. *I can't take any more of you*, Harper said. Before his eyes, all the men metamorphosed into masses of seething maggots — and Harper woke up screaming.

Dazed, Sam heard Harper's scream and saw Harper was standing on the bed, backing away, making wiping motions, as if he was trying to brush something off his body. The entire gunship was filled with rotting corpses crawling with maggots, and each liquifying corpse was shouting *Please don't leave me*. Then the nightmare changed, and the corpses transformed themselves into Vietcong soldiers, jabbing at Harper with bayonets and —

151

'Harper —'

He saw Sam and gave an unearthly yell:

'Keep away from me.'

He was going up the wall and straight over the cliff into hysteria. As Sam approached he lashed out and reached for Sam's throat, as if he wanted to rip his windpipe out.

'I'm not the enemy,' Sam cried.

Harper whimpered and scrambled out of the bed, onto the floor and towards the wardrobe. He reached for something inside and then leapt back on the bed. Sam froze as Harper levelled a Colt .45 at his head.

'Then who the hell are you?' Harper hissed.

He pulled the trigger. The chamber revolved. Sam's heart stopped. Click. The chamber was empty.

Harper pulled again. Click.

'Bang. You're supposed to be dead,' Harper said.

His gun arm wavered. His sanity returned as he *pushed* against the nightmare and started to lift his gunship out of it. He cleared the battle zone, blinked, and saw Sam — and he looked down and saw the gun he held in his hand.

'I could have killed you —'

The Colt fell to the floor with a thud. Sam was just in time to catch Harper as he collapsed, limp, into his arms.

'Oh God . . . Fox, *Fox*, where are you, man . . . How long will my own luck hold, how long can I stay up there . . . How long before I go down . . .'

Harper began to shiver uncontrollably. He pulled Sam's arms around him and whispered, horrified, into Sam's face.

'I can't keep doing this . . . Flying backwards and forwards every day . . . Taking guys to the front and bringing them back dead . . . Day after day . . .'

Sam held Harper tight. He began to stroke him, and he thought of the golden palomino and a mackerel sky.

'Harper, you have to find a place where you can put all this stuff you're talking about, all these fears and nightmares. A place where you can throw it all. Then you have to lock it up there, and walk away from it without looking back.'

'Without looking back? But they follow me —'

Sam waited a few moments for Harper to calm down. Then gently, he tried to free himself from Harper's arms.

'You should try to get some sleep now,' Sam said.

Harper held on tight.

'Please don't leave me. If you stay with me I know I'll be okay.'

For a moment, Sam hesitated. Then he nodded and lay down. Harper turned on his side away from Sam.

Sam didn't know how long they stayed like that. But, just before sleep sneaked up, Harper's voice curled across to him.

'Was that you down there at the beach?'

'Yes.'

Harper was silent. Then:

'So you came for me when *I* went down?'

'It was a small thing.'

Harper reached back for Sam's right arm, pulled it underneath his armpit and across his heart.

'Don't let go,' Harper said. 'Please —'


And it was still not over. When the dawn came Sam was aware of a sudden stillness. His left arm was numb and he could feel Harper's head nestling in the harbour of his upper arm and neck. He realised that at some time during the night Harper had turned in his arms and was now facing him. Something about the moment made Sam realise that Harper was awake.

Sam opened his eyes. As soon as he saw Harper's dark green eyes staring at him and the double rows of blond eyelashes that framed them, he knew he was gone, gone, gone forever. His mouth was dry and his heart began to pound. Even so, he tried to escape.

'I hate people watching me when I'm asleep,' Sam said.

He pushed Harper roughly in the chest and tried to get up. As he moved he realised that Harper had an erection, his penis rock hard against his stomach. He heard Harper's groan — or was it his own — and he gasped as *he* became drenched with sexual arousal, his own cock pulsating and lengthening.

'No, this mustn't happen,' he said to himself.

He looked into Harper's eyes and saw what must have been in

153

his own eyes — the sheer incomprehension and horror that this could be happening with another man.

'No,' Harper said. 'Don't move —'

It was a plea for help. *I'm heterosexual*, Harper had said, *and I never kiss on a first date*. Harper was almost there, almost ready to climax. Sam saw he was fighting the moment, hoping that his insane desire would disappear. But Sam could feel Harper's heart fluttering against his chest and the way in which Harper's penis was pulsing. He was gasping, out of control, past the point of no return. And Sam found that the force of Harper's lust was taking him with it.

'No —' Sam said.

It happened so quickly. Everything in him told him this was wrong. Maybe he'd been made vulnerable by Hempel's death. Maybe it was living all this time taking orders. Then Sam looked into Harper's eyes again and realised no, it was the reality of Harper himself. It was all mixed up with sympathy and passion and physical yearning — and he felt himself yielding.

Harper's arms tightened around Sam. Propelled by desire, Harper began to turn Sam onto his back. He was whimpering, his penis trying to find a sheath. As he turned, Sam saw Harper's eyes, clouded with a terrible look of fear and lust, and gladness too that Sam was capitulating. When the kiss came, Sam felt the electric shock of it go right through his body and somebody said *Yes* inside him, somebody who had been locked up all his life in a room with a closed door.

The touch of Harper's lips was dry, firm, taking full possession of Sam's mouth. The pressure increased, and Sam felt the full erotic force of the kiss begin to flood through him.

Suddenly Sam heard laughter. It was only soldiers going down the corridor but it was enough for him to wrench away from the kiss.

'No,' Sam said again.

Sam leapt up from the bed. His heart was pounding. He wanted to stay. He wanted to go. He didn't know what he wanted. He pulled on his clothes. Quickly. Desperately. He turned to Harper. The blond American was sitting up in bed, a horrified look on his face. He looked at Sam and there was fear written in his glance.

Sam went to the door. He managed a smile.

'You were drunk. All the bars were closed. We were both feeling horny.

I was there. You were there. That's all it was, right?'

Cliff Harper's lips quivered. 'Right.'

———— 4 ————

But that wasn't all it was. When Sam got back to the Peter Badcoe Club, no amount of ribbing from George and Turei — 'Where were you last night?' 'Was she hot?' — could dispel his sense of regret about what had happened, or what had *not* happened, between him and Cliff Harper. Throughout the day, the touch of Harper's lips, the smell of him, the feel of him, remained. He excused himself from his mates, needing time to himself, and made his way to Roches Noires Beach. When he was a teenager and wanted to be alone he would go down to the Waipaoa River. There, beside the deepest waterhole, he would take a heavy boulder, dive, and let the stone pull him down to the bottom. Anchored there, amid the swirling mud and sunken logs, the eels nipping at his body, he would sit looking up at the surface of the water. What bliss it had been to be alone in that glowing green world. To watch the bubbles streaming up from his lips — until, inevitably, the pressure to breathe would build, and he would kick himself from the bottom and soar towards the light. His first gasp of breath was both a victory and a defeat.

Sam swam as far out as he could, and lay on his back, looking up at the sky. He thought about Harper and searched his past to see if there was anything there which predisposed him towards men. Nothing. But, somehow or other, Harper had got through to him.

'So why didn't you let it happen, Sam?' he asked himself.

This was why. The *mana* of a man, his value in Maori culture, was in his fighting power and his warrior tradition. It was all symbolised in a man's cock. It, as much as the fighting club, personified all that a man was. With both, man was made sacred and women profane. This had been the way since the beginning of Time when Ranginui, the Sky Father above, was set apart from Papatuanuku, the Earth Mother below. Ever since, the roles of men and women had been preordained. Indeed, all the Gods were male until Tane decided to make a woman out of the red dust and mated with her. Male to female union was therefore sanctified by the gods. Any other kind of union could never be countenanced; it transgressed the order of the Maori world, it transgressed the *tapu* nature

155

of man. The consequences were too fearful to contemplate. You relinquished the mana, the tapu, the ihi or life force and the wehi or dread that the dynamic of being a man depended on, to maintain your power relationships with the world. You brought noa upon yourself, the loss of sacredness, and, without sacredness, you were prone to punishment, dishonour, banishment and death. You also brought this on your partner.

In the evening, trying to drink himself out of his sadness, Sam sat in yet another Vung Tau bar with George and Turei. He called for another round and, from the corner of his eye, saw Cliff Harper. Immediately Sam's heart lifted. He grinned, and Harper grinned back. His smile lit up the whole room. But Sam suddenly felt slashed by lightning, and he turned away.

'I can take my punishment, Harper,' he thought to himself, 'but I won't allow you to be punished.'

When he looked back, he saw that Harper was still looking, and his fingers were moving.

*Hi, Sam.*

The message was filled with loneliness and need, as if Harper was the only one left in the world. Across the crowded bar it came: 'Is anybody there? Can anybody hear me?' Sam put up his hands and deflected it.

*Sam, I know you can hear me. Please talk to me.*

Harper was standing, working his fingers with furious speed. All around, people were looking at him, curious. The words started to come out too fast, losing all sense, desperate.

*Talk to me talktome pleasetalk . . .*

Sam turned to George and Turei. 'Let's get out of here,' he said.

The next day, George and Turei were sleeping off a hangover. Sam had been told about a Buddhist temple on the outskirts of Vung Tau. For some reason he felt he should go there. He borrowed a bike from the Club and negotiated his way out. For a while, Sam was escorted by a pack of laughing young boys. They zoomed around him like butterflies, shouting out: 'Hey! Kiwi! Can you fly?'

At the outskirts the boys dropped behind, shimmering, settling in the dust. Sam found himself biking through another country. This was a country that breathed. At every inhalation the trees, grasses and rice shoots bent down as if bowing to the wind. At every breathing out, the soft warm breeze brought with it the tintinnabulation and tinkling of a thousand temple bells.

'One small piece of land,' Sam thought, 'and so much blood spilled for it.'

The sun was at its apex in the blue-hot sky, and very soon Sam found himself sweating. But he didn't care. The oxygen breathed through him, making him at one with the breath of the land, and he began to smile at his sense of unity with God's creation. The sun was shimmering. The paddy fields stretched away into the haze. Raised dykes criss-crossed them like a chequer board. Family tombs popped up here and there. In some of the fields women were cutting the rice with sickles, feeding the stalks into threshers worked by fast pedals, stacking up the straw like conical hats. In other fields the women bent over, uprooting seedlings, gathering them into bundles and carefully placing them into sacks. Some walked along the dykes with heavily laden shoulder poles. In adjoining fields, men guided harrows yoked to plodding water buffalo. In the calm, almost soporific surroundings, Sam was reminded of his own people of Waituhi, his aunts, his uncles, his kaumatua and kuia. They lived like this too. Substitute maize and kumara for rice and they could be bending in these fields.

An hour later Sam, perspiring heavily, stopped to rest. Opposite him workers were shifting water from an irrigation channel to a field, using a conical basket sealed with lacquer and attached to a double rope. Standing either side of the channel, they dropped the basket into the water, then stepped back and tightened the ropes, swinging the brimming basket up into the air and dumping the water into the field. Nearby, an old man was sitting beside the road. He was dipping a ladle into an urn and drinking from it. When he saw Sam he gestured to him.

*Water? The drink to give you life?*

Sam nodded.

'Yes. Wai ora. Yes.'

The man watched with approval as Sam drank. When Sam was finished he made questioning motions.

*Are you going far?*

Sam nodded and put his hands together, signifying prayer.

The old man nodded, frowned and then pointed to the sky. Sam was surprised to see that clouds had begun to gather. Even as he stood a gust of wind swirled through the green rice shoots.

*Go fast!* the old man motioned.

He made a rising and dipping motion with his hands.

*Get to temple just before the rain, just over the next hill.*

Sam smiled as the old man hastened him to his bike and, with a strong push, sent him on his way. At the top of the rise, Sam could see the rain falling across the landscape, like cobwebs from the sky. The wind was rippling the water in the irrigation channels. Workers were moving quickly along the banks of the rice paddies, heading for shelter.

Ahead was the Buddhist temple. Sam let the bike freewheel down the slope. The exhilaration bubbled within him and he began to laugh. Then the rainstorm was all around him, pelting him. Staining the red dust and turning it into mud. Quickly, he dismounted and ran towards the temple. As soon as he reached the threshold, he felt a sudden fear:

'No, I can't go in.'

All around him were carved figures, forbidding in their strangeness. He stepped back and turned to leave. Better to face the rain than to continue inside. There, he would have to confront the temple's holiness. There, he would be unmasked, unclothed in the sight of God. He took one step away from the temple and then another. And at that point, Buddha exhaled and breathed upon the rain. And every raindrop from Heaven held within it a tinkling bell, so that the entire landscape resounded with the harmonics of life.

Sam felt awe overwhelm him, as if the pavilion were calling to him. He knew it was only the austere voices of chanting monks but it sounded like a karanga, reaching out and around him, calling:

*Haramai, Sam.*

So it was that Sam turned and confronted his fears. He saw before him a pavilion gate, blue, the colour of Heaven. Stretching ahead was a court-yard of tiles, green, the colour of humanity. He sensed the imminence of a kind of peace that was also a mystery. He took a step over the threshold — the paepae — and the pavilion opened like a meeting house and welcomed him in.

Before him was a large inner courtyard, open to the elements. Around the pavilion was a portico coloured with a pale green wash. Ornately carved wooden pillars marked the perimeter, and at the foot of each pillar were pots of flowers. Two dragons, yellow and red, stood on a pair of tigers. The dragons faced each other with snarls and curling tails. Sam remembered that the Vietnamese believed they were descended from a dragon king who mated with the queen of the fairies to produce a hundred sons, one of whom became the first leader of Vietnam. Dragons were lucky and protective.

But what drew Sam's attention was a pagoda at the far end. Within was a huge altar dominated by a golden Buddha.

*Come to me, Sam.*

Sam walked across the courtyard. He was drawn along a centre line of white marble, the path of Immortals. As he entered the depths of the temple he noticed little details. Elaborate ceramic friezes; wood, metal and ceramic sculptures; numerous drums, gongs, urns and other Buddhist relics. Diagonally across from him he saw saffron-robed monks in processional along one side of the pavilion. They were walking, shaven heads bowed, through a gateway to some outer temple garden. One of the monks looked up, saw Sam, and paused.

Sam approached the pagoda. The roof was sustained on thick hardwood columns carved with ancient inscriptions. The gilded Buddha was sitting within on an inverted gold lotus throne. Buddha's hands, with their stylised fingers, were resting on his knees. His eyes were open, and his face had an expression of total peace, of extraordinary serenity. Its majesty and permanence transcended all.

Scattered on the altar were offerings of food and flowers. Incense spirals, each more than two metres long, hung from the gilded ceiling. Below them were large brass urns filled with sand and bristling with incense sticks. Sam stood there for a moment, looking up into the face of the Buddha. He saw that a monk had come to his side. He lit a candle and took a package of lit incense sticks and held them over his head. The monk closed his eyes and said a long mantra. Then he knelt, continuing to intone the mantra. The incense wafted around him as he held the incense sticks above his head.

Sam knelt to pray.

*I need your help.*

He closed his eyes, and a feeling of vertigo overwhelmed him, sweeping him off his feet and, before he knew it, he was tumbling through Te Po, the Night. Down, down, down he plummeted. Was this his punishment? He felt Harper's kiss, and his heart was pounding with fear. He saw Harper's face above him, heard himself whimpering, caught between desire and self loathing. He saw that they were both tumbling through the darkness, sending ripples that disturbed the entire universe.

Time stretched and expanded, and Sam knew that they had fallen through thousands of years. Sam cried out to Harper:

*Go back, damn you, let go.*

But Harper looked at Sam and shook his head. They kept falling, like two astronauts whose lifelines had snapped, their oxygen leaking away from the trailing cord.

*Oh, God, then breathe, Harper, breathe in deep.*

A black hole was opening below them and stars were cascading into it: the entrance to Te Kore, The Void. Once through its gateway there would be no return. And Harper thought Sam had accepted him but with one quick surge of strength Sam kicked at Harper and sent him spinning away.

*No,* Harper cried.

Alone, Sam fell through the black hole. Punishment was for him alone to take. Sacrifice was for him alone to make. The sin was his and his alone. His lungs began to burn and he fought against opening his mouth, because he knew that there was no air to breathe and that he would surely die. He felt his heart beating in his brain, and, all of a sudden, four words formed on his lips.

*Please, not eternal darkness.*

With a start, Sam opened his eyes. His heart was thundering, almost breaking out of his chest. He grasped the altar, steadying his terror. How long he knelt there, he never knew. Perhaps it was another thousand years. He looked up again at the face of the Buddha and made an obeisance to the figure. All the world seemed to recede around him and away from him. More years passed by, the rain tinkling down like a gentle benediction. Mist surrounded the head of the Buddha, refracting the light. A patch of light, a golden glow, opened above him and Buddha's aura came streaming down. It was like an absolution.

Suddenly Sam saw that something was moving in the stillness. From the corner of his eye he saw it. Something dislodged by the torrent of rain coursing down the pitched roof, sliding down the pillars of the temple, coiling wet and glistening, slipping downward through the rich red and gold figurines. A cobra, dusky and dark in colour, almost two metres long, with a diamond-shaped head. Ferocious. Deadly. One bite and you were gone in a few minutes, foaming at the mouth and screaming in hideous death.

Mesmerised, Sam watched as the cobra slithered to the floor. There it paused, saw the patch of sunlight glowing where Sam was sitting. It began to slide towards the sunlight, scraping the cobbles like dry leaves falling. At the last moment it sniffed Sam and reared, its hood flaring, ready to strike, its black tongue a piece of lethal licorice, feathering in and out. It stood over Sam, crowding him, and when it hissed, its hood flared again.

Without realising what he was doing, Sam also began to feather *his* tongue in and out in the action that Maori call the pukana. The cobra reared even higher, and so did Sam. For a moment both Sam and cobra eyed each other.

Then Sam stopped. Relaxed. The cobra imitated his movements. Lowered its head from the strike position. Feathered water from a small puddle among the cobbles and without a look at Sam, coiled itself in the sun, resting itself like he was, waiting for the rain to stop.

'You and me, snake,' Sam thought. 'You are hated and reviled, and men would wish only to stamp on your head and crush you beneath them. If they knew about me they would do the same. Our paths have crossed. Let us enjoy our brief friendship in the sun.'

Sam closed his eyes. He wasn't sure for how long; perhaps he dozed. One minute. Ten minutes. The sun was so warm on his face. A shadow awakened him. The saffron-robed monk was kneeling beside him. The cobra had gone. But the monk was looking at Sam in a quizzical manner. He cocked his head to one side. His tongue began to feather in and out.

It was so comical that Sam felt the urge to laugh. Soon his laughter was uncontrollable — and the monk joined him, laughing and laughing. Then, in a quick movement, the monk pressed his hands together and bowed. He motioned with his hands, and Sam saw that the world had changed. Although drops were still falling like a beaded curtain from the perimeter of the temple, the storm itself was over. When Sam stepped into the sunlight, it was as if the whole landscape was holding its breath.

The world seemed to stop, to glow, to find serenity. With a sigh, a deep exhalation, the world began to renew itself. The sky was a sumptuous blue, unrolling clear to the other end of the universe. The rich rays of the sun were transforming the landscape into a place of glowing beauty. Wild swans flew overhead like a glissando, their wings describing arabesques in the light. Where the rain continued to fall was a soft shimmering curtain. More birds flew homeward, this time starlings and swallows, swooping and circling towards far distant trees. They piped the world with glorious song, and some spun songs of delight above Sam as they found roost in the temple's eaves.

Sam mounted his bike. He ascended the rise. When he looked back at the temple it had been spun into gold by the sun. All around it, the paddy fields had turned into emeralds. The dykes were silvered filigree. Arching above was the rainbow.

And Sam was laughing and crying at the same time. His life had reached a point of perfection. A kind of understanding. A moment of revelation. He felt more open to life than he ever had before. He closed his eyes and breathed deep. It was as if he had disappeared into the landscape, become transparent, and was watching all the molecules that made up man, leaf, snake, bird of sky, river, mountain, sun stream through himself like glowing lights.

It was going to be *okay*. When he next saw Harper he would explain and maybe Harper would understand and, if there was a God of second chances —

The wind breathed through Sam, in, out, in, out.

He heard the universe singing.

# CHAPTER TEN

————— 1 —————

If there was a God of second chances . . .

No sooner had Victor Company returned to Nui Dat than they were called to a briefing. Sam had no time to talk to Cliff Harper, to move his fingers: *Hi Cliff. Yes, let's talk please, let's talk* in that secret language that had become their own.

'The American's have called us in to help them,' Major Worsnop reported. 'We took out the enemy base, but there's still a large battalion out there. They were found yesterday and now the Americans have begun Operation Roundup. They've already begun to drive the enemy towards the corral here —'

Major Worsnop pointed to a semi-circular valley with an opening, the gate, at one end.

'Once they're in, our job is to close the gate.'

At 1400 hours, the choppers began to ferry Victor Company to the operational zone. An hour later, they were on the ground and had dispersed into their assigned formation. But Intelligence had under-estimated the enemy strength, and the gate was exposed to open ground.

'This smells bad,' Lieutenant Haapu said.

The platoon entered a deep ravine. There was no cover and nowhere to go except forward or back. The only concealment was in the creek bed, and there the vegetation was sparse.

This was Vietcong terrain. Like a trapped scorpion the enemy would already be waiting, sting curved and ready to strike.

Sam signed to his section to spread out:

*Open formation, one up.*

He was working on instinct, just in case they were hit.

Suddenly, something flowered and fizzed from the right.

'Hit the ground!'

Sam rolled to his left — and the hillside opened up with enemy firepower. The first rocket hit. An orange ball of flame erupted. A second enemy rocket exploded in the creek bed, sending up mud and water like a fountain. Then came the automatic heavy machine-gun fire.

'Fall back. Fall back!' Lieutenant Haapu called. 'Everybody get the Hell out —'

There was a hail of bullets, like a swarm of angry bees, and Lieutenant Haapu was down with a round through his chest.

Sam waited for a lull as the enemy finished their first magazines, then he was up and over to the lieutenant, repeating his order:

'Fall back, you bastards! Turei, get a line on that rocket launcher.'

Lieutenant Haapu was sitting now, looking at his wounds.

'Fuck, fucken bast-ard.'

Sam grabbed an arm and hoisted Lieutenant Haapu up. Turei had managed a lucky shot and had taken the rocket launcher out.

'Medic!' Sam called.

Vickers arrived and started to work on Lieutenant Haapu. His left lung had collapsed and he was having trouble breathing. Vickers tore open a compress bandage, split the plastic in half, and began a patch up job on him.

Sam turned to George. 'Go to Turei. Both of you give us cover while I get the lieutenant out of here.'

George nodded and began wriggling quickly through the elephant grass to Turei.

'Sir,' Sam said to Lieutenant Haapu. 'We've got to go.'

Lieutenant Haapu nodded. He took a quick look at the situation. The men were moving fluidly in retreat but the enemy was picking them off.

'You've got to make smoke,' he said. 'Put up a screen to hide everyone.'

Sam understood. But the wind was capricious, opening up holes in the smoke. All of a sudden there was a yell as Flanagan, the radio operator, took two rounds in the back and two rounds in his right leg.

'Get the radio! Get the radio!' Sam called to Red Fleming.

Over to the side, there was another cry as Manderson was hit.

'Goody goody,' Johanssen said to his stricken colleague. 'Now I get the chance to fire the big gun.'

He began to lay down fire as fast as he could.

Trying to gain an edge, Sam speed-crawled after Red Fleming to the radio operator. Flanagan was drooling, spitting blood, but trying to keep breathing. His eyes were wide, staring up at the blue sky with terror. As soon as Sam reached the radio he grabbed the handset and gave the platoon's coordinates:

'We're pinned down. We have dead and wounded. Request gunships, reaction force and extraction.'

The enemy started up again. Sam watched as a grenade came sailing into the area. He scrambled on top of Flanagan and rolled with him away from the grenade. Whaaam. The concussion slammed him and he felt a hot stinging in his crotch and legs.

'I can't get hurt,' he thought. 'I've got to get the men out.'

Sam pulled out one of his own grenades, popped the handle off, counted a couple of seconds and threw it in the direction of the hillside. With relief he saw that his men were halfway out of the enemy's killing zone, firing and moving as they retreated, pulling their wounded comrades with them. Red Fleming was lobbing grenades and firing his M-79, trying to get air bursts on the trees. Johanssen managed to find good cover and was hitting the enemy with all he could give. Machine-gun chatter filled the ravine. With every burst the belt lashed like an angry snake. Johanssen grabbed and hooked a second belt. The spent cartridge cases spilled out of the weapon as if they were the shells of peas. Raising his head, Sam saw that his men were in the clear. But George and Turei were still out there.

Sam tapped Lieutenant Haapu on the shoulder. 'Sir, I have to leave you a moment.' Sam made his way over to Johanssen: 'Can you keep the enemy's heads down? I'm going to get those two dumb Horis out.'

Sam crawled over to the dry creek bed and rolled into it. Enemy bullets whizzed over his head and kicked up small puffs of dust. Five minutes later he hauled himself up beside George and Turei. The two were talking dirty.

'Did I ever tell you that your sister was a great lay?' George asked Turei. Squeeze the trigger. Bang.

'Not as good as your mama, you bastard,' Turei answered. Line up the sights. Squeeze.

'I heard about that. Mum told me you got a tiny one.'

Enemy fire. Duck your head.

'Is that so? Well, my sister said that you were all blow and no go.'

Turei saw Sam and, at the same time, heard the thunder of gunships approaching from the north.

'Oh, hi Sarge,' Turei smiled. 'Hey! Isn't that the cavalry?'

Sam grinned and remembered all those bad B-grade Westerns Mum had taken him to at the Majestic in Gisborne. Sometimes Turei or George would come too. The wagon train was surrounded. Those Redskin Injuns were riding their horses around and around it, picking off the poor defenceless settlers. You could never trust them, those mean snakes-in-the-grass varmints. The settlers were down to their last bullets and were getting ready to go to Heaven. The heroine, either Rhonda Fleming or Joanne Dru, was trying to look brave and resolute. Whaddyknow, on the soundtrack came the strains of 'Oh! Susannah' and, yippee, the cavalry arrived, their horses high-stepping onto the battle scene. Then, it was Guy Madison, Ronald Reagan, John Wayne, Randolph Scott, Joel McCrae or Errol Flynn crying, 'Lower sabers!', 'Charge!'

The reaction force was landing, giving cover fire.

'Time to go, my beauties,' Sam said.

'You said it, Sarge.'

Turei stood up. He walked a few steps.

All of a sudden there was a shift in the air, as if something was approaching. A sense of whirring wings as something which had called out a name on a long-forgotten evening came flying into the valley.

The owl, uttering a harsh hunting cry.

George looked up, his face blanched, and he put up his arms to protect himself.

'No—' Sam roared.

Turei looked back. He began to run towards George. But the owl beat past George, so close — and that's when Sam realised:

'Turei.'

Somewhere on the hillside, an enemy machine gunner zeroed in on a standing soldier. He sighted. Tracer began to flow, so beautiful, so mesmeric, floating like wings down and around its target.

And Turei fell.

'Hey, you bastard,' George yelled at the owl. His eyes were raging and the hupe was flowing. 'You were supposed to come for *me*. It's me you want. Me.'

He stumbled to where Sam was already crouched beside their wounded companion. The blood was spilling out, everywhere. Every time Turei moved it spurted like a fountain.

'Jeez,' Turei said.

His eyes rolled up, he began to shudder, his mouth pouring blood. Then he was gone. And, as he held his friend, Sam began to break apart with the horror of it all. Even though there had been no physical transgression, it was already happening.

'This is all my fault,' he thought. 'I caused this. Everyone around me will be punished.'

<hr /> 2 <hr />

The company was in shock when it returned to Nui Dat. Sam made his report to Major Worsnop, and Captain Fellowes telephoned Army Headquarters in New Zealand to tell them about Turei's death. The news would be delivered to Lilly, through official channels but:

'I'll do it,' Sam said. 'Turei was my responsibility. It will be better for Auntie Lilly to hear the news from me.'

When the connection was made Sam, devastated, was already weeping, and Lilly knew straight away what had happened.

'I blame your father for this,' Lilly said.

She was already screaming with grief and, in the background, Sam could hear others of Turei's family yelling and screaming with her.

'I want Turei returned to me immediately, do you hear? I don't want my son to stay a minute longer among the people who killed him.'

Lieutenant Haapu was the one who should have accompanied Turei's body back to New Zealand, but he was still in a critical condition. Sam pleaded with Captain Fellowes on his and George's behalf.

'Sir,' he said firmly. 'It's our job. We came together. Turei was George's best mate. As for me, I failed to look after him. I have to front up to the iwi — and to my father.'

'Okay, Sergeant,' Captain Fellowes said. 'I understand. I'll do my best.'

Spent and exhausted with grief, Sam was walking back to his tent when Cliff Harper stopped him.

'Hey! Sam —'

Harper looked so wonderful, his blond hair glowing in the moon's light. He was the only person that Sam would have wanted to see at that moment. But then Sam thought of Turei's death — and he knew what he had to do.

'Harper, I know what you've come about, but I don't want to hear it. I want you to turn around and walk away.'

Harper's face was set with determination.

'You're not getting away as easy as that. I'm a stubborn Illinois boy and I confront everything that happens to me. I don't walk away from anything.'

'In that case,' Sam said, 'I'll do the walking.'

He went to pass by, but Harper pulled him back.

All Sam wanted to do was to take a stone, dive into the river and stay down there forever.

'No you don't,' Harper said. 'I want to have it out with you. I thought I could get over what happened the other night, but I can't. So I'm going to put it on the line for you, Sam. Something happened to me—'

'Put it out of your mind, chopper boy,' Sam answered, brutally. 'Whatever you thought happened, didn't happen. Okay? Now let me pass.'

He pushed past Harper. He was three steps away, his heart thudding, when Harper's voice stopped him in his tracks.

'Listen,' Harper shouted. 'All I want to know is: did it happen to you? If it didn't, fine, you go your way and I'll go mine. But if it did —'

Sam turned. Harper was standing in the moonlight, his fists clenched, his arms outstretched in a gesture of helplessness.

'Sam, do you think I want to admit to myself something that would disgust me?' Harper was flailing to explain himself. 'But what do you do when something big hits you between the eyes? I'm in big trouble and I'm burning up inside. You know what I did last night? Me and Seymour went into Vung Tau and had us three women apiece, but something's happened to me in here.' Harper jabbed at his heart. 'I keep thinking of you.'

With a cry of anger, Sam launched himself at Harper and they were sparring with each other.

'Listen, you bastard,' Sam said, 'you're a handsome heterosexual son of a bitch and you like to fuck girls. Stay that way. End of story. It was just a kiss, damn you, just a kiss —'

With that, Sam let Harper have it between the eyes, and Harper fell to the ground. But Harper grabbed him and, rapidly began to sign:

*Was that all it was? Just a goddam kiss?*

Harper held on to Sam and looked into his eyes and made Sam confront himself. When Sam's eyes flickered with evasion, Harper knew without needing to be told.

'So I was right.'

'Even if you were, I can close the door —'

'I knew something was happening between us,' Harper said, running his fingers through his hair. His voice lightened up with incredulity and relief. 'From the first time I saw you I *knew*. Jumping Jehosophat, Sam —'

'Stay away from me,' Sam warned. His voice was rising with fear. 'I told you I can close the door and I can keep it shut. It's Pandora's Box. Who knows what might be in it?'

The two men were panting as they faced each other. Then, slowly, Harper began to spell out his feelings again in sign:

*So, you're scared, right?*

'Yes, aren't you?'

Harper nodded. He lifted his face to the light and his voice cut through the darkness.

'You gotta talk to me, Sam —'

'Talk?' Sam asked.

He was fearful. This thing Harper was wanting had to be stopped before it got out of hand.

'Talk about what? There's nothing to talk about! Hey, I can be your friend, your brother, your father if you like. Let's keep it like that, eh? Buddies? Good friends?'

For a moment, Sam thought he had won and that Harper would agree: Yes, good friends. But he should have known better, and when Harper answered him, the words leaned so hard on the walls of Sam's world that he could feel them collapsing around him.

'Sam, the box is already open. You know what was in it? A grenade. It has already exploded in my face.'

Harper turned on his heel. He walked away into the darkness.

'Haramai ki o tatou mate e, haramai, haramai, haramai.'

The sound of the karanga came across Poho o Rawiri marae like a spear. Sam and George and other Army pallbearers waited at the gateway. In front of him, Sam felt the rage of the iwi that one of their sons was being returned not in glory but in death. The old women of the village had now begun to cry out their distress.

'What is the sign in our hands? They are the kawakawa leaves of mourning. You ask again what is the sign in our hands? I tell you, kawakawa leaves! Alas, lower them to the waist and let them fall! Death alights —'

Beside him, Sam heard George in agony. George had sobbed all the way from Vietnam. All through the night flight to Singapore, then all day down from Singapore on an RNZAF Hercules, George had not left the side of Turei's coffin. The sound of George crying among the Army equipment and supplies struck Sam as the loneliest he had ever heard. And he was still crying as they waited for the karanga to end.

'Turei! Turei, you got in the way of the owl,' George cried. 'It was coming for me. Why did you do it, you bastard?'

Sam saw his father leading the men in a haka powhiri. 'Toia mai, te waka! Ki te urunga, te waka —'

Old men with Maori Battalion medals and ribbons, stamping their feet and slamming their chests with their fists.

'Bring our son back to us! Bring him among us —'

Sam signalled the pallbearers to lift — and they had Turei's casket on their shoulders. Boy, was Turei heavy? Was he *what*.

The pallbearers slow stepped their way through the gate and onto the marae. Behind them General Collinson, other Army brass and supporters followed, heads bowed.

'Return in spirit, son, return to your birthplace —'

The old women completed their welcome to Turei. Their calling drifted into silence. Sam signalled to the pallbearers to lower the casket onto the marae. He saw Lilly on the porch of the meeting house, being comforted by her daughter Emma and other female relatives and friends. Among them was his mother, Florence — and was that Patty? Yes, it was. She smiled across the marae at Sam and waved to him.

Arapeta stood to speak. He strode purposefully backwards and forwards across the marae. His glance flicked across General Collinson — and then across Sam. There was no sign of recognition.

Arapeta pointed his walking stick at the casket.

'He was not supposed to come back like this,' Arapeta thundered. 'Why has he come back before his time? Why has he not come walking back so that we may greet him with our pride and in joy? Why has he come back, sealed away so that we are not able to cry over him as is our custom? Why?'

Arapeta's walking stick slashed its anger and accusations across the marae. At every outburst the grief of the mourners escalated. Lilly was screaming for her son, and the women surrounding her were having trouble restraining her. With a sudden determined movement she pushed them away and, crying, went stumbling through the crowd.

General Collinson spoke nervously to his Maori adjutant.

'I hope Arapeta is not blaming the Army for this.'

'No,' the adjutant said. 'The protocol of the tangihanga demands such rhetoric. It is our way of appeasing all the conflicting thoughts of the mourners.'

Sam knew otherwise. He knew that his father's words were obliquely referring to him: Why, son, did you not save your mate?

'There is not one old man here,' Arapeta continued, 'who would gladly give up his life if he could so that this young son of ours could walk again among us. We have had our lives, we have had our battles —'

'Ah, ka tika,' the old men murmured, 'that is true, indeed you speak truly.'

'But we cannot, for he has already been taken by the man-eating insect. Yet —'

Oh, Arapeta was so good at korero. With skill he modulated his voice and turned the thoughts of the mourners to the ideals of heroism and personal sacrifice.

'By being taken unto death, Turei has brought honour to his iwi. There was no greater accolade for a warrior consecrated to Tumatauenga, the God of War, than to die in battle. For all of us who are here today, that was not our honour or privilege. And so we are belittled, made lesser men in the face of this young son of ours who did what we didn't do — gave up his life in the service of his people and his country.'

The mourners began to sigh at Arapeta's words. A hush came over the marae.

Suddenly, screams started to come from the crowd.

'No, Lilly, don't.'

Lilly reappeared. Her eyes were streaming with tears. In her hands was an axe. Before anybody could stop her, she strode across the marae to the coffin and struck it with the axe.

'Turei! *My son!*'

The whole assembly began to moan and weep as the sounds of the axe reverberated across the marae. General Collinson blanched. Sam felt a tremendous pain in his heart and turned to George.

'Come on,' he said. 'We have to finish the job.'

Sam walked over to Lilly. When she saw him, she swayed and collapsed in his arms.

'I can't let Turei go,' Lilly said, 'without seeing his beloved face —'

Sam nodded. 'Give me the axe, Auntie.'

Sam struck at the lid. At every blow the wailing escalated, a wild, demonic sound that could have split the sky apart. But when it was done, and Turei's face appeared, the keening subsided into a soft sighing sound. Lilly leaned and stroked Turei's face and she nodded at Sam and George.

'Thank you, boys,' she said. 'Once there were three of you. Now there are only two —'

She motioned for them to take the coffin onto the porch and lay it to rest among the women.

'Savages,' General Collinson muttered.

Angrily, Arapeta pointed his walking stick at him.

'Ka mate, ka mate! It is life, it is life, it is death, it is death! You must understand, Sir, that our people have never been afraid to look upon the face of Death. Our boy once belonged to the army. Your right to him ends here —'

Arapeta pointed to the gateway.

'He is ours now.'

Later in the afternoon, Sam, George and other young men of the village carried Turei up to the village graveyard. The hills echoed with the sounds of rifle shots from the Army's guard of honour. The bugler sounded the Last Post.

At the graveside Florence, Patty and Monty stood beside Sam. On the other side, George was standing with Lilly and Emma — and Emma's baby boy. Already George was taking Turei's place as surrogate son.

Sam felt Florence press his arm.

'It's so good to see you, Sam,' she said. 'Are you well? Are you staying home for a while?'

'No, Mum,' Sam answered. 'Just tonight. George and I return to Vietnam tomorrow.'

'Did you bring me a present?' Patty asked.

Sam gave her a smile. 'Yes, one for you and one for Monty.'

Sam's heart was aching, but the ceremony was almost over. The clouds were lowering.

The wind brought the promise of rain. As Turei was laid to rest, Lilly came forward and threw the first handful of dirt upon his coffin.

'Farewell, son! Go to the threshold of the Pleiades. To Antares, farewell —'

In the evening, Sam sat with his father on the verandah of the homestead. The silence between them was forbidding, punitive. When Arapeta spoke, his voice curled out of Te Kore, The Void.

'I promised Lilly that Turei would come back alive. Instead, he came back in a coffin. It was up to you to ensure that my promise was kept. You should have looked after him. You didn't. The sperm that was in him from his father has died with him, and there will be no further issue. The whakapapa from his father to him is now terminated. Because of this, I have lost mana. You have let me down. The only way you can redeem yourself is to avenge his death. When you return to Vietnam, you must take utu against those who killed him.'

———— 4 ————

Back in Vietnam, Sam immediately went to Captain Fellowes to ask him when the next company manoeuvre might be ordered.

'There's nothing planned right now,' Captain Fellowes said. 'What's the rush, Sergeant?'

'I've gotta get back in there. For Turei —'

Captain Fellowes understood. 'Listen, your mate's gone and nothing will bring him back.' But Sam wasn't listening. 'Okay,' Captain Fellowes continued. 'The best I can do is to put you on the roster whenever a spare man is required by the Aussies or the Yanks.'

'Sir,' Sam saluted. 'I'll take anything you can get.'

He wanted to get out, find some action, go anywhere — and hope the guilt of Turei's death wouldn't follow him.

The guilt was everywhere. Worse, it lay between Sam and George like a living thing. Instead of bringing them closer together, it pushed them apart.

'Has he guessed?' Sam wondered, 'that I'm to blame?'

But George was on another track altogether, blaming himself and ashamed to look at Sam.

Over the next weeks Sam was called to complement an Aussie patrol on perimeter duty of the horseshoe minefield. An attachment to a local ARVN South Vietnamese unit followed. Then came a mission to search a village reported to be hostile to the Allied command. Exhausted by his grief and driven by his need for some kind of release, Sam was already juiced up and trigger happy. The hot sun was burning his skin off and the heat was like a hot oven coil frying his guts. He lost all perspective, all sense of who was the enemy and who wasn't. When he glimpsed a movement at the corner of his eyes he was already swinging his rifle, his finger pressing the trigger — and the only thing that stopped him was hearing a baby cry as the young girl he had aimed at fell to the ground, protecting the baby as she fell. Sam remembered Jim, the Australian veteran:

'Before you know it, the whole platoon is shooting up the village, setting it on fire, killing whatever happens to be in the way.'

The incident sounded warning bells for Sam. 'What's happening to me?'

The only person who got anywhere near explaining it to him was Cliff Harper when he happened across Sam at the base. Harper was still in his flying kit, having just come back from a mission. He was battle weary but:

'That last time we talked was bad timing, right? I didn't know then about your pal. I know what it's like —'

'You know nothing about what it's like.'

'Hey,' said Harper. 'I lost Fox, remember?'

Harper took a deep breath and spelt it out again.

'I'm in trouble here, Sam. Doing my nut —'

Sam gave Harper an angry stare.

'But I've been thinking this through,' Harper continued. 'Maybe you're not just another guy. You're Sam. People make these other categories, but maybe you and I don't fit, maybe they don't apply to us.'

Sam was in turmoil.

'I'm a soldier, you're a flier,' Sam said. 'I'm a Maori, you're a Yank. We come from different places, different cultures. Let's keep it that way.'

Harper's face grew still. Then, 'Okay, you arsehole,' he said. 'I've admitted I'm wide open for you but you can't do that for me. I could have been the best thing for you but you haven't got the guts to admit it. Somebody should give you a medal for being the chickenshit coward you are.'

They split up, and Sam wanted to say: 'No don't go away.' He went back to his tent and for a long while lay on his bunk staring at nothing.

Meanwhile, drama was unfolding in the skies above him.

Deep into enemy territory an American bombing strike was on its way to Hanoi. The bombers were escorted by a Phantom F-4 defence wing. One of the F-4s was being piloted by the two-man crew of Riccardo 'Speedy' Gonzalez and Johnny Johnson. They were keeping a look-out for enemy aircraft above and any surface-to-air missiles from below. Gonzalez heard Adams in an F-4 to the left of him:

'Two MiGs at ten o'clock, another two bogies at six o'clock high. Okay, fellas, intercept and engage —'

With that, Gonzalez put his F-4 into a turn — and was into a dogfight with one of the enemy MiGs. The dual was a hair-raising series of spins, loops and other acrobatics in which each craft tried to get the other into their firing envelope. Gonzalez had a lucky break. He was on the MiG's tail, trying to outguess the enemy pilot, when the MIG broke left. Gonzalez had chosen to go left also — and the MiG was right there in the middle of his sights. He got a rocket away and, next moment, the MiG exploded. However, Bailey was calling:

'Gonzalez, another bogey coming at ya.'

It was a classic attack straight out of the sun. In a matter of seconds the MiG had Gonzalez in the middle of his firing envelope and had sent his missile, tracking it for a hit. Over the radio, Gonzalez heard Bailey yelling out, 'Break right and roll,' so he pressed the F-4 into an escape maneuvre to shake the MiG off his arse. The missile exploded just above the F-4 and the concussion threw the aircraft into a wild spin. Gonzalez corrected and managed to put the F-4 into a descending seven-G turn. Before he knew it, the MiG had the F-4 in its sights again. Its cannons raked the F-4's underbelly. There was a sickening lurch, the red warning lights started to flash — and Gonzalez heard the telltale warbling sound which warned that the F-4 was on fire. Next moment, black smoke started to fill the cockpit and they were flaming down like a torch.

Gonzalez tried to get the F-4 backup flight control system operational. But the MiG had done its stuff and the F-4 fell through 2500 metres, through 1800 metres and all of a sudden they were at 1200 metres.

Gonzalez yelled to Johnny Johnson: 'Eject, bail out *now.*'

There was no answer. Johnson was dead, peppered with enemy cannon shots.

Gonzalez realised he was getting pretty close to riding the F-4 into the ground. He pulled the ejection ring. The canopy flew off and the ejection sequence kicked in — and he was clear. His chute opened at under 600 metres and before he could utter a prayer he was hurtling into the jungle canopy, crashing through the branches like a rag doll. The ground hit him and he felt every bone in his body jolt and crack. But he was alive and, although dazed, had his wits about him. He remembered his training and activated the beeper which would let his buddies know he was still alive and where to find him — and waited.

When Sam got the call he was on his feet in an instant, and on the run down to Nui Dat's airbase. Even before he reported to the duty officer he knew there was a problem: there were only two helicopters on the field, and one — Harper's — was being serviced. In the adjoining crewroom he heard Harper's voice raised in argument with his fellow airmen. He walked to the door in time to see Seymour remonstrating with Harper.

'Sir, let some other squadron do the rescue.'

'We're the closest. That's why we got asked,' Harper said.

One of the other men, Tom Pike, groaned. 'We're whacked, Sir.'

'Come on, guys,' Harper pleaded. He turned to Prick Preston. 'You've got a full tank, Preston.'

'Listen,' said Preston, 'we don't owe nobody anything and neither do you. You've done your job. Forget it. Seymour's right — there must be someone else to do the pick-up. Live to fly another day.'

Sam saw the look on Harper's face. He watched as Harper picked up a chair and hurled it across the room. Before Preston could move, Harper had him by the collar of his flying jacket.

'Give me your keys, Preston. Give me the goddam keys. And *you* —' he pointed angrily at Frank Seymour, 'you get saddled up. We've got a job to do.'

Harper was off at a fast walk. When he came through the door and saw Sam standing there he came to a standstill. His eyes narrowed.

'You're not going to tell me that you're the spare?'

'I'm here to do a job. That's all you need to know.'

'Well, don't get under my feet, that's all I've got to say to you, Kiwi.'

As they left, Sam heard someone swearing and shouting. He looked back and saw that two of the other men, led by Pike, were shambling after Harper.

'Do you always have to show you've got big nuts?' Pike said to Harper. 'Do you always have to be a hero, you *fuck*!'

In the chopper Harper hit the trigger. A high-pitched whine began. He fuelled the igniters and the engine wound up to a start. Two minutes later, he put the chopper into fast idle, warming up. He did the usual radio check.

'Tower, this is Woody Woodpecker. We're lifting off.'

The engines roared. The chopper lifted off the ground. Above, two Skyraiders cruised in from their orbit to join the mission.

Seymour had his headset on.

'Uh-oh,' he said. 'Sir, the odds have just gone up. One of the F-4s is standing by and can see the enemy advancing on the ground, but he's only got air-to-air missiles on board. They know we've got a man down. The enemy must have fixed his position from the emergency transmission.'

Sam watched as Harper nodded.

'Tell that F-4 to confirm to Gonzalez that a search and rescue is in progress. Get in touch with those Skyraiders and request fire support. What's their call sign?'

Seymour laughed. 'MacDuff. And they have confirmed they will suppress any enemy ground fire at the rescue site.'

'ETA 30 minutes,' Harper said.

Twenty minutes later the two Skyraiders arrived at the crash site. Moose Bailey, in the F-4 circling above, heaved a sigh of relief. He'd stayed behind to ensure that Gonzalez's position was pinpointed. Now he vamoosed for a rendezvous with a tanker before his fuel ran out.

Ten minutes later, Seymour turned to Harper.

'MacDuff has made contact with Gonzalez. He's guiding them to him. He can hear their propellers west of his position, but he can't see them.' A pause. 'Sir, they're now initiating authentication procedure.'

Pike burst into laughter.

'MacDuff has just copied Gonzalez's question. Who was the girl of his dreams and did she come across? His answer is — Wanda Rodriguez and, no, she didn't, so he fucked her big sister. He's our man.'

Sam looked down at the jungle. The canopy was impenetrable. No *way* would you be able to see one downed man. A needle in a green haystack.

'Sir,' Seymour interrupted again. 'MacDuff reports bad guys moving into the area, ten minutes from where they think Gonzalez is.'

Cliff Harper nodded. 'Confirm ETA five minutes. Are we close enough now to be in direct contact with Gonzalez?'

Seymour tried for a frequency. Secured it.

'Copy,' he said. 'Damn, Gonzalez only has visibility straight up. Can't see the Skyraiders but he can hear them. They're trying to get him to fix his location with his compass. *Got* him!'

Quickly, Seymour worked out the coordinates. They were three minutes out. Then Harper got the news:

'Woody Woodpecker, bad guys closing in. MacDuff will decoy them to where Gonzalez's F-4 went down. Maybe they'll take the bait. No, bad guys have split up. Small party still heading for Gonzalez.'

The noose was closing.

'Copy. Tell MacDuff to buy me time. Tell Gonzalez: sit tight, friend. Pop the flare at my command.'

One minute later, Harper made the command.

'Where the hell is he?' he yelled. 'Can you see him?'

The chopper was skimming across the jungle. Sam was looking out one side of the chopper. Pike was looking out the other.

'*There!*'

Coloured smoke, drifting straight up through the jungle canopy. One and a half minutes out.

Harper pointed to the sky. The Skyraiders were moving in perfect coordination to straddle the chopper as it made its final approach towards Gonzalez. Thirty seconds out, they crossed over a vertiginous river valley that had what looked like a derelict swingbridge connecting one side to the other. Harper pointed it out to Sam. On one side was a steep ridge. The coloured smoke was coming up from the valley behind it.

'He can't see us,' Seymour said. 'But we're right on top of him.'

The chopper was hovering over the trees.

'Let down the rescue cable,' Harper answered.

'Sir, Gonzalez says he needs help for the ride up. He's injured.'

At that moment the chopper came under attack. From out of the jungle came a small *puff* and a rocket sizzled through the air and whooshed past the front windscreen.

'Fuck,' Harper swore. 'They've got a rocket launcher —'

He held the chopper steady. He radioed to MacDuff to take the rocket launcher out. Sam looked at Pike and nodded:

'I'm the spare,' Sam said. 'I'll go.'

Harper didn't even know what Sam was doing until after he had clipped himself onto the rescue cable and stepped out of the chopper. When Harper looked back and saw Sam motioning to begin letting him down it was too late to stop him. The hydraulic winch began to whirr and whine, and Sam was swinging like Tarzan. Thirty metres below, the jungle waited to claim him.

He was twenty metres down when he began hearing the crack and pop of rifle fire. He heard the clinking sound as bullets hit the chopper. His left trouser leg tore with the impact from a near-hit. Then he was down among the foliage, trying to steer the rescue cable through the branches to the ground.

Gonzalez lay in a sitting position, frantic with fear. 'My leg's broken —'

'It's okay, buddy,' Sam said. 'No time to talk.' He buckled the safety strap around Gonzalez's chest. Yelled instructions into the emergency radio: 'Gonzalez secured. Take him up.'

Sam felt the upward force of the chopper's hydraulic winch as it reeled in the cable. Gonzalez was spinning through the foliage, smashing through the branches, trying to protect his head. Then, all of a sudden, there was a whump, the chopper juddered in the air and Gonzalez was spinning back to the ground.

'We've sustained a hit,' Seymour yelled. 'Hydraulic winch malfunction.'

Harper heard Seymour yelling in panic. His body flooded with adrenalin. 'God, don't let me go down like Fox.' He was checking the gauges, his training automatically initiating the procedures to ensure damage control. To his right he heard the Skyraiders coming in again with high-speed strafing of the area from which the rocket had been launched. They walked their incendiary shells down the slope, and the forest flamed and smoked; and Seymour yelled:

'They've got the fucker! But, Sir, MacDuff, advise enemy moving fast towards us. They estimate we have only five minutes to exit area.'

There was a moment's silence. Then MacDuff radioed:

'Your call, Woody Woodpecker.'

Harper's heart was racing but his body was ice.

'I'm not leaving them.'

On the ground, Sam could hear the enemy shouting, approaching, and the chatter of gunfire. He realised the odds had just stacked up, too high, and fallen on top of him and Gonzalez. He reached for the emergency radio. He knew he had to give Harper permission to leave.

'Hey, Harper! Do you know what haere ra means?'

In the chopper, Harper couldn't respond.

'It means goodbye. So get out of here.'

Seymour was listening in and looked at Harper.

'No,' Harper said.

He worked the controls and the chopper started descending into the foliage.

'What are ya?' Seymour yelled. 'Are you crazy?'

Harper was seesawing the chopper back and forth across the top of the trees, cutting down the treetops with the rotor blades, mowing through the upper density. Startled, Sam scrambled away as branches and leaves began to fall like an avalanche around him.

180

'I want to *see* him,' Harper said.

He lifted the chopper. Peered down.

A sunlit space. Sam stepping into the space. The chopper was stationary, in a holding position, its rotors seeming to slice at the sun. Leaves and branches were whirling to the ground. Sam knew that Harper could see him. The situation was hopeless. Ah well. With a shrug of his shoulders, Sam motioned Harper to climb. He made a sweeping gesture with both hands:

*Go.*

Harper looked down. His eyes unseen behind dark glasses. His face impassive. Coming into the trees were the enemy soldiers.

*I said, Go, damn you,* Sam signalled again. 'Can't you take orders you crazy gringo American? For God's sake, go!'

The motor of the chopper roared. But Harper wasn't leaving. He was making jabbing motions to Sam.

*Look left. Go left. I'll decoy the enemy, make him think the chopper is going down. If I succeed they'll come after me.*

Harper put up his hand and showed four fingers.

*Four minutes. Go. Rendezvous.*

And Sam remembered: the derelict swingbridge.


The chopper dipped and left. Sam knelt beside Gonzalez.

'Okay, Gonzalez, the enemy have shot up Plan A. We have to go to Plan B.'

'What's Plan B!'

'We've got to get over that ridge. Can you walk?'

'I'll try.'

'Then lean on me.'

Meantime, Harper put the chopper into a steep turn, orbited, and did a fast series of 360 degree spins. He saw the astonished faces of the Vietcong as he spun over them. Next moment the belly of the chopper was raked with bullets.

Sam hoisted Gonzalez up. They were in luck. Harper's ruse had worked. He heard the enemy moving off to the right, in pursuit of a chopper that they thought was going down.

'Let's go,' Sam said.

He hauled Gonzalez through the jungle. He followed the contours of

181

a slope and began to climb. His lungs were burning by the time he stumbled across the old track which must have been used when the swingbridge was still functioning. He ran, pulling Gonzalez with him, as fast as he could along the track.

As for Harper, he had bought Sam as much time as he could, and it was time to make the pick-up. He went flying back with the wind, losing altitude, dropping down to tree-top level, balls to the wall. The gunners portside and starboard were blazing away, pow pow pow. Tracer whizzed through one door of the chopper and out the other.

Sam heard the shouts of the enemy as they returned to the chase. Suddenly he was clear — and almost falling from the sheer cliff into the river far below. For a moment he swayed there, the edge crumbling away from beneath his feet. He paused. Immediately in front of him was the swingbridge.

'Holy Hone Hika —'

The swingbridge hung by a thread — one long span of what looked like No.8 wire. The rest of it, a series of broken planks, dangled from the wire. So near and so far.

Gonzalez began to gibber.

'We're never going to get out. We're going to die in this stinkin' country.'

'Shut up, Gonzalez,' Sam said.

Sam looked at his watch. He had 65 seconds to position himself and Gonzalez on the bridge. Ah well, they'd have to do it the hard way.

'Belt yourself on and hold me tight.'

Sam made a jump for the wire. Grabbed and pulled himself up so that his legs were also gripping the wire. The dead weight of Gonzalez was pulling at his grip as he began to work himself and Gonzalez along. Halfway across, streaming with sweat and exhausted, he stopped. Waited.

Ten seconds. Where was Harper?

'Come on, Harper, I can't hold on much longer.'

Sam heard the sound of the chopper approaching. The steady whop-whop-whop of the rotor blades was the most wonderful sound he had ever heard. He began to laugh and grinned at Gonzalez.

'So what did I tell you?'

The chopper roared over the ridge and filled the ravine with its clatter. Harper heard Pike drawl out:

'Looks like there's two lucky sons of a bitch waiting to hitch a ride.'

The chopper dropped into the narrow corridor of jungle, its engine sending explosive echoes down the gap, and then rose like an angel, sideways on to the bridge.

Harper took off his sunglasses. Grinned.

*What are you waiting for fellas?*

Suddenly the tree canopy off to Sam's right erupted with tracers. A bone-shuddering whoosh enveloped him. It was now or never. He jumped — Gonzalez screaming — and caught one of the landing skids. Dangled for a moment. Bullets zinged past him and bounced off the underside armour plate of the helicopter. He reached in panic for the entry door. Missed. But rough hands were around his and Gonzalez's shoulders, pulling them in. The chopper banked.

'Men aboard. Woody Woodpecker moving out.'

The chopper moved away quickly out of the ravine, heading fast out of the area. When they crossed back into South Vietnam, Seymour gave a joyful whoop and holler. Harper radioed to the Skyraiders:

'Thanks for the help, MacDuff.'

'Pleasure to be of service, Woody Woodpecker. Over and out.'

Back at the base Sam watched as the chopper team slapped each other and congratulated themselves on the rescue. Seymour had extra reason to be joyful. When he lifted his canteen from his web gear to take a drink, there was nothing in it but a bullet hole.

'I've been shot!' Seymour laughed as he kissed the canteen.

Sam went to find Harper. He saw him stoically flushing out the chopper. Dusk had turned the landscape into a charcoal-grey haze.

'Thanks,' Sam said.

'All in the line of duty,' Harper answered.

His glasses glinted in the sun.

——— 5 ———

Two days later Sam heard that Harper had been medevaced to a hospital for wounds sustained by automatic enemy fire during the rescue operation. He had five wire sutures attaching his two bottom ribs to his ribcage.

When Sam walked into the hospital, Harper turned and looked out the window.

'You didn't have to come,' he said.

Sam tried to make conversation.

'Now I know why you rescue pilots are the most decorated combatants of the war. It takes guts to hover over the jungle like that. To sustain all that enemy fire and hold on. You could have left me out there —'

'And risk the wrath of your tribe, let alone the New Zealand Government? I've heard all about you Kiwis and you Maoris and the revenge you take. No, it was better to bring you back alive. All part of the service.'

Cliff paused, a wan smile on his face. Then:

*What happened to us, Sam? We got so close to making it.*

Sam looked into Harper's eyes and knew he had to explain.

'I'm no good for people, Harper,' he said. 'My mate, Turei, I think I'm to blame for his death. I don't want *you* on my conscience. I'm here for one reason and that's to fight this war and get out in one piece and go home.'

Harper sighed and leaned back into the pillow.

'Is *that* what happened? Well, I'm not letting you off the hook so easy. Sometimes, when I talk, I know too much of me falls out. But that's the way I am and I'm not about to change.'

Sam stared at Harper. He stood up quickly.

'Back off. Back off me. Leave me alone.'

'Answer me one question. Do you think about me?'

'No.'

'So you still want to give me the flick?'

'Yes.'

'You are one fucken liar, Mahana. May you fry in hell.'

Sam stood up. His voice was firm.

'I've already told you, I can't have you on my conscience. Goodbye, Harper.'

Sam was halfway down the ward when he heard a shout.

'Wait!'

Harper was struggling out of bed. His bandages were flying all over the place.

'You can't leave like that, you arsehole.'

Harper grabbed his crutches and came limping toward Sam. When

184

he got close enough he threw one of them at Sam.

'You want to know why I didn't leave you back there when you were down with Gonzalez? I never leave anybody behind, but you're not just anybody. I didn't want to lose you. You talk about conscience. Put that on your damn conscience.'

Sam felt all the walls crumbling around him.

'You're in my heart, and I can't get you out —'

'Haven't you been listening to me, Harper? I said no to you —'

'Look, don't I have a say in your decision? I don't *care*. I'm prepared to take the *risks*. Don't you understand? We were meant to be. We owe it to ourselves to see this thing through.'

Sam took a step back. He began to sign:

*We can't. It will never work.*

'God, Sam, this is your last chance. Face up to yourself. For once in your life, let somebody in. Let *me* in.'

At that moment two nurses, attracted by the commotion, came rushing towards Harper.

'This man should be in bed,' one of them said crossly. 'Whatever he wants, say yes so that we can get him back there.'

It was said in innocence, but the shock of it made Harper and Sam look at each other, their jaws open. Sam started to laugh, and so did Harper. Next moment they were holding each other, doubling up with tears of laughter.

'Oh, what the hell,' Sam said. 'All right then, yes.'


Sam ended his tour of duty in Vietnam three weeks after Harper was released from hospital. They were able to get a day's leave in Vung Tau. A photograph was taken of them at the beach.

'I want you to have this,' Sam said. He took Tunui a te Ika from his neck and placed it over Harper's head. 'It looks better on you than on me!'

He looked deep into Harper's eyes.

'It will keep you safe. I want you to bring it back to me. In New Zealand.'

'You want me to come to New Zealand?' Harper asked. His eyes were shining.

'Yes.'

185

At Vung Tau airbase, just as Sam was about to board the freighter back to Singapore, there was a shattering sound. Harper's helicopter was there, hovering. He dipped the rotors. His face was serious. He made hand movements.

He pointed to Sam. *You.*

He pointed at himself. *Me.*

He made a thumbs-up signal.

*Love you.*

He saluted, and the gunship was wheeling away and thundering into the sun.

CHAPTER ELEVEN

————— 1 —————

The gunship was lifting and wheeling back into the past. Thirty years later it had all come to this: me and a Vietnam Vet named George, sitting in a pub in Porirua on a cold, rainy night, talking about Uncle Sam.

George looked up. A clock on the wall ticked its way to closing time at the Porirua Tavern. The regular thump thump thump of the band reverberated through the night.

'Sam and I ended our tour of duty in Vietnam in late 1970. We finished our time with the Army in Singapore, and when we arrived home we had a big welcome on the marae. That welcome was different from the one we got from everyone else where the hostility really brought us down to earth. We had no formal recognition from government. We were humiliated by the protest groups. Some of us began to die from the chemicals. Sam's Dad wanted him to stay in Waituhi, but I decided to come down to Wellington. I managed to get a job as an Army instructor at Trentham. I got married twice. The first time was a mistake. The second time was to a nice girl from the South Island and we had four kids. I didn't treat her too well and she took off. Around ten years ago I bought this pub. It's been my life. I get the cough now and then. Cancer. Yeah, it got me too — Agent Orange. I'm up and down. Right now I'm up. I still see a few of the old mates at Company reunions, RSAs and so on. There are fewer of us every year. Time is passing. Very soon nobody will remember us.'

George's voice trailed into silence. Then:

'I'd better get back to the bar. Help the boys out before we close for the night. But thanks for coming out. I've enjoyed talking about my mate.' He looked at me with rough admiration. 'Do you realise how much you look like Sam? It's like looking at a bloody ghost. You're about his size, maybe a little thinner. You have his eyes and, from the looks of you, his stubborn streak. He was a great mate. You could trust in him. Rely on him. There was something fearless about him. In a scrape he never let you down.'

George saw me to the door.

'Sam will always remain young in my mind. It's only the rest of us who get old and develop beer guts so that we can't see what's down below — if there's anything still there.'

Smiling ruefully, he shook my hand. His eyes were moist and I realised he was still thinking about old times and people who had gone from his life.

'Tell Patty that it was really nice to hear from her. If she's ever down this way, tell her to call in, okay?'


I arrived home just after midnight. I couldn't sleep, so I took Uncle Sam's diary and finished it just before dawn. I found some ash-edged remnants of letters Uncle Sam and Cliff Harper had written to each other while Uncle Sam was in Singapore and Harper was still in Vietnam:

'. . . happened, yesterday. It made me realise how precious life is and that you have to hold on to what it is that you . . .'

'I often think of you and . . . (Hell, do you think some censor is reading this stuff?) Well, if he is, enjoy it pal because . . .'

Whatever else was in the letters, the fragments confirm that the attraction (or was it love?) that Uncle Sam and Cliff Harper felt for each other had deepened. They would see each other, war or no war.

Uncle Sam must have returned to New Zealand some time in January 1971. Cliff Harper's own tour of duty in Vietnam ended two months later, in March. The last entry in Uncle Sam's diary was dated 7 March:

'Cliff hitched a ride via Singapore on one of the American military aircraft doing the weekly hop to Australia. He telephoned from Sydney last night to say he gets in to Auckland tomorrow morning. It's been almost two years since I last saw him. We've defied the gods so far.

He'll get to Gisborne by bus tomorrow afternoon.'

The final words in Uncle Sam's diary, however, were not written by him. You can tell because they are scrawled with a different pen.

*May God have mercy.*

# PART FOUR

# Auntie Pat

## CHAPTER TWELVE

—— 1 ——

Tuia i runga, tuia i raro.

The world was being constructed again.

Tuia i roto, tuia i waho.

The top and bottom bound together by the light.

Tuia i te here tangata ka rongo te Ao.

Now the outer framework and inner framework. Fixed firmly, the knots soldered by the shafts of the sun.

The promise of life, the impulse of history, was reborn.


I made a cup of coffee and watched the dawn rising. Impishly I decided to ring Auntie Pat.

'You're lucky some of us don't need our beauty sleep,' she said. 'What's up?'

'I've seen George and I've finished reading the diary.'

'Good,' she said. 'I've never liked this conspiracy of silence, this secret about Sam. I was too much of a coward to do anything about it while Dad was alive. Monty and I kept the secret by remaining silent. It's a great weight off my conscience knowing that you are now aware of him.'

'Why didn't you tell me I looked like him?'

'Who told you that?'

'George remarked on it. You can see it in the photograph.'

Auntie Pat thought about that for a moment.

'Yes, I suppose I can understand why George would think that. He always had a sentimental streak and would have wanted to see Sam in you. But Sam was much handsomer.'

'Gee, thanks, Auntie.'

'So I guess you'll be wanting to know what happened when Cliff Harper came to New Zealand. You know I don't really want to talk about him, don't you? But I suppose I have to. Are you still making a lot of money? Fly up and see me at the end of the week. You can stay at my house in Gisborne. Don't worry, I won't let your folks know you're coming. We'll talk then. Can you do it? You're not otherwise occupied?'

'If you're asking if Jason and I are back together, no.'

'No other boyfriend? Goodness, that must mean you're still celibate. You better watch out. Your gears might rust up.'

'Do you want me to come or don't you!'

'Yes of course I do, Nephew. I'll see you soon then.'

———— 2 ————

All that week I was working at Toi Maori finishing off another commission for Roimata. Two days before leaving for Gisborne, Roimata came in waving a fax and smiling with satisfaction.

'This is it!' she said. 'This is the official invitation for you and me to go to Canada! They want us there next month, all expenses paid. So who's a clever girl?'

I grinned at her. 'That's abso-bloody-lutely fantastic.'

The idea of getting out of the country and away from all the stuff I was dealing with sounded wonderful.

Roimata took a deep breath and then said lightly, in a way that made me suspicious, 'Let's go out and celebrate. I have a cousin in town. I told him I'd meet him at Jordan's bar.'

'If this is one of your schemes to hitch me up with somebody, I've already met Long Dong Silver.'

'No, it's not him. It's somebody else and, anyway, you owe me for the night out with Auntie Pat.'

'Look, I can find my own dates. I don't need you to pimp for me.'

Roimata grabbed my arm and pulled me after her into the street.

'Tane's nothing like that,' she said, laughing.

As it happened the cousin wasn't a blind date, and he was somebody

I had long admired but never met. His real name was Tane Mahuta, but a national magazine had profiled him with the headline 'The Noble Savage', and the nickname stuck.

'Kia ora, Michael. Roimata's told me a lot about you,' Tane said as we shook hands. He turned to Roimata: 'Listen, cousin, I can't stay long, but —'

I watched as Tane and Roimata continued their conversation. In the 1980s Tane had been a popular male prostitute. He'd become politicised when, during the Great Epidemic, all the health funding went to Pakeha organisations for the simple reason that there weren't any Maori ones. Maori themselves, with their heads in the flax, pretended there wasn't a problem because Maori gay men didn't exist — except for transvestites like Carmen and they weren't men — and there were no Maori gay leaders in the community. But Tane knew Maori were dying of Aids in Auckland, the largest Polynesian city in the world. Every month more Polynesians became statistics, crawling into holes like animals to give their last gasp rather than to go home and shame parents who would have hidden them away anyway. The job chose *him*, and so Tane left his beat on Karangahape Road. He came out publicly, was vilified for it, but an extraordinary thing happened. He was one person standing up, and the next moment, others started to join him. Te Waka Awhina Tane, the first gay organisation to support the needs of Maori and Polynesian young gay men, was born.

'You know,' Tane said, 'the funny thing was that our Maori people felt it was bad enough my working the streets, but when I came out as a gay leader that was far worse. You know how our people are.'

Tane's eyes were glowing and his smile was as bright as the sun. In his emerald-coloured pareu, and with a whalebone neckpiece against his bronzed skin, he looked as if he had been born with the dawn.

'You've just come out, right?' he asked.

'Yes. It hasn't been easy.'

'You may think it's the end of your life, but it isn't. It's just the beginning. It takes guts. Too many people associate being gay with being weak. It isn't a weakness, it's a strength.'

'I know,' I said. 'What brings you to Wellington?'

Roimata answered for Tane, and he looked at her with amusement. 'Tane's setting up a branch of Te Waka Awhina Tane down here. Gay men and women are strong, but we need to be stronger. We need to become more visible. You know, the problem is that our lives are controlled by the white heterosexual culture —'

Tane looked at me — and interrupted Roimata with a laugh.

'Does she do this to you too?' he asked me.

'All the time,' I said, sighing, and Roimata poked me crossly.

'You guys need me,' she said, 'and don't you forget it.'

Tane hugged her and then looked at his watch. Roimata gave him a glance and he nodded and turned to me.

'Perhaps next time I'm in Wellington we could have a talk about how you can get involved with what we're doing down here. As well, Roimata had hoped there'd be time for me to ask you about —'

Roimata didn't think I saw her give him a quick kick on the shin.

'Yes, well, we *will* leave it for next time. Obviously I need to be properly briefed.'

He kissed Roimata and shook my hand.

'And now I really have to go. Ma te Atua koe e manaaki.'

---

3

---

Friday came around and it was time to fly to Gisborne to see Auntie Pat. Another week had gone by — and still no sign of Jason. Every evening I arrived home full of hope that he'd rung. I sometimes imagined him waiting for me, saying, 'Forgive me, I'm sorry.' I saw myself kissing him and replying, 'No, it was my fault.' And all the while we were pulling off each other's clothes because, God, it had been such a long time since we had made love. There were never any messages and Jason was never waiting. I couldn't go on living with all this indecision. I telephoned him at work — and he answered.

'Oh, it's you,' he said. His voice was cold, dismissive.

'Can you spare me half an hour?' I asked. 'I'd really like to see you,'

'Yes, it's time we talked. The Angel Bar in an hour? Good.'

I took a seat by the window and watched Jason as he approached the bar. As soon as I saw him I knew this was a different Jason. You know how it is — you live with someone, you love someone, you get to know everything about him — and then one day, you see him on the street and it's not him any longer. Sure, it looks like him, talks like him, but it isn't him at all. He's gone, and another person has slipped like a thief into the place where he once used to be.

'Do you want a beer?' I asked.

Jason nodded. There was no smile as he took the seat opposite me.

'How much time are you able to give me?' he asked, scarcely able to hide his sarcasm.

'I can take a later flight,' I answered.

'Oh, I wouldn't want you to do that,' he mocked. 'Anyhow, the shorter our conversation the better.'

I tried to look into Jason's eyes. Once, I'd been able to see straight into his heart. Now there was a mirror there, and it deflected everything.

Jason's beer arrived and he took a couple of gulps. Then:

'I've made my decision about us,' he said. 'I'm calling it quits. I'm leaving you for good.'

I felt a deep sense of loss. No longer would I have this wonderful companion. A sudden memory flashed in front of me — of tussling for the Sunday paper in bed while we had breakfast — and tears welled into my eyes. But damned if I was going to let him see them.

'So all this stuff about wanting me to be there for you when you get back. You don't want that, is that what you're saying?'

Jason spoke his words like spears.

'I know I said that, but I was only saying what I thought you wanted to hear, not what I really wanted to say. You forced me to say it. Well, it's all very clear to me now. I know now from my sessions with Margo that you haven't been feeding me.'

The accusation flared across the table, and I flinched. I thought to myself how much I would miss making love to him. I had once assumed that in any relationship it was the top partner who held the power. Jason had never been the active partner but there was no doubt that he held the power now. Perhaps there was potency in vulnerability after all.

But where was he getting all this stuff from? Of course I had 'fed' him! Sometimes love that is thwarted never plays fair. I went on the offensive.

'So who's feeding you then?' I asked. 'Margo? Graham?'

Jason coloured. 'Who told you about Graham?'

One look at Jason and I knew that Graham had become Jason's new lover. The minder who had been conveniently provided him by Margo's encounter classes had become the shoulder to cry on and the new fuck. My head began to spin with anger and Jason saw the signs. He put down his glass and took a few steps back.

'I always did what you wanted me to do,' Jason said. 'I never did what *I* wanted to do. Well, now I'm going out and doing it — and Graham is helping me to explore who I am. I never really liked having sex with you, Michael. And you have to pay for what you've done to me.'

It sounded like a threat. It *was* a threat.

'Pay? For what! For loving you? If you want to play hardball, Jason, you're on the wrong court.'

He stood his ground.

'I once said to you that what I'm going through had nothing to do with you. But it does. I do have to deal with you, Michael. You've got to be made to face up to what you've done to me. And you do have to pay.'

I was still very angry when I checked in for my flight. I was angry with Jason, I was angry with Margo and I was angry with Graham. Somehow I had the feeling that all this stuff with Jason had been cooked up secretly behind my back. There's nothing worse than thinking you look like a fool. Everybody had been in on the secret that Jason was leaving me — 'Come on, Jason, you can do it' — and no doubt there'd be hugs and congratulations from his cheerleading team at his next therapy session.

As for me, I was left sitting in a locker room by myself. Who was on my team?

As I handed over my ticket at the check-in counter, I saw Carlos's business card. So Jason wanted to play hardball, did he? Well, two could play the same game — and I'd already gone long enough without having sex. My brain began to fill with images of Jason and Graham together — and I was quivering with rage by the time I rang Carlos's number. When he answered I got straight down to it:

'How about a date?'

'Now let me just see,' he teased. 'Wow, wouldn't you know it, I've just had somebody ring in a cancellation! How about Saturday night?'

'Sorry, I'm on my way to Gisborne. How about when I get back?'

He sounded disappointed. 'I can do Tuesday —'

'Not Monday?'

'Okay,' he laughed. 'I'll have to shift a few things around, so you better take me somewhere really good!'

A quarter of an hour into the flight to Gisborne, I was still trying to calm myself. How could I have been such a stupid fool as to hope that Jason would come back? Why hadn't I read the signs? Ah well, so it was over. Where to from here? I settled into the seat and tried to read a magazine. But that wasn't helping me. My eyes flicked over to a young high school boy just a few rows in front. I noticed that there were other boys with him and that they all came from my old school, Gisborne Boys' High. And I remembered that I must have been about their age when I made my own first trip to Wellington during a similar school visit. New Zealand from the air had looked amazing. The country riffed with thousands of jagged valleys, ziggurats spilling from the backbone of the fish that Maui pulled from the sea. His brothers, growing hungry, had attacked the fish, tearing its flesh and stuffing their ravenous mouths.

On that first visit the plane flew through a rainbow, the symbol of our tribe's protective deity, Kahukura. On the other side was Wellington, a place wrapped around with squalls and a strange luminosity compounded out of sleet and wintry light. In those days I saw Wellington as a place in another land. I saw Waituhi as some country left behind in the past.

Since that time I had flown backwards and forwards countless times. I went to Wellington to play sport. I did my university degree there, escaping the constraints of Waituhi for the seductive pleasures the city had to offer. Although I grew up in Waituhi I became a man in Wellington. I worked hard, played hard, partied hard, and had lots of sex. The longer I stayed, the more I exulted in the freedom. And Wellington offered other infinite possibilities.

Like my life.

Looking out of the plane window some ten years later, I was conscious yet again of going back, of returning through the rainbow to Waituhi. It was a transition not only from city back to country but also from present to the past where the land of being Maori was. That Maori land was the land of boyhood. Once upon a time I had been happy there. I had belonged. My valley was called the Waituhi. At one end there was a palisaded fort. In the middle stood the meeting house, Rongopai, surrounded by the villagers of Te Whanau A Kai. At the other end of the valley was Maunga Haumia, the sacred mountain. A river called the Waipaoa ran through the valley.

Once I was lucky enough to have a people and a valley to come home to.

But that was then, when I had been a dutiful son. This was now.

———— 4 ————

The flight arrived on the icy wing of a southerly. The passengers ran into the air terminal. Auntie Pat was wearing a hat, a thick overcoat with the collar turned up, a hat and, somewhat out of place, huge dark glasses that covered most of her face.

'Are you expecting sunshine?' I asked her.

She pushed the glasses down her nose and, looking over their rims, said, 'I thought I'd better dress incognito, just in case somebody sees me with you.'

She laughed, took me by the arm and hurried me out to the car. 'Dinner's already on and we have to get back because it might be burnt.'

I put my overnight bag into the boot and, out of habit, walked around to the driver's side.

'I like it when you're masterful,' Auntie Pat sighed, giving me the keys.

We drove through the suburbs of Gisborne City. The main shopping centre had been turned into an obstacle course, thanks to all the palm trees and other so-called visual improvements by which Gisborne had been accessorised for the Millennium celebrations. But the streets were deserted except for the occasional shell-shocked Swedish backpacker looking vainly for something that spelt either entertainment or food. Through the first set of lights we went, past the hideous bicentennial memorial, across Kaiti Bridge and around the harbour to Auntie Pat's house in Crawford Road. All I could think of was that I had foregone a night out in Wellington for this?

Auntie Pat went ahead of me, hurrying into the kitchen to check the stove. Habit made me head for the bedroom where I slept whenever I visited. I threw my bag on the bed and then went to join her.

'Can you open a bottle of wine for us?' Auntie Pat asked. 'We could drink one of your father's if you like.'

'Might as well,' I answered. 'Looks like I'll be buying my own from now on.'

'You and me. He's hated me bringing up Sam after all these years. When I mentioned to him I had given you Sam's diary, he hit the roof. He hadn't wanted you to know. And he hadn't known that I had Sam's diary. He thought everything of Sam's had been burnt in the fire.'

'So there was a fire?'

Auntie Pat paused and shivered.

'Yes, but we'll talk about that later. Meantime, why don't you go into the dining room? I'll bring our dinner in soon. It's pork bones and puha.'

As it turned out, dinner was actually a mussel bisque, followed by swordfish steaks broiled with olivada and rouille. Dessert was poached apples with gorgonzola. As well as being a fan of Hollywood movies of the 1940s, Auntie Pat loved cooking. She always made light of her culinary accomplishment, as if Maori weren't supposed to know how to cook à la cordon bleu.

'Those were the best pork bones I've ever had, ' I said.

'It was nothing,' she answered. 'They only took me a few minutes.'

With dinner over, we moved to the comfort of the living room. Auntie Pat had lit the fire. I couldn't remember when I had ever been so relaxed with her. At least that was a plus of coming out. It had brought me and my spinster Aunt closer together.

'Anything happening between you and Jason?' Auntie Pat asked.

'I saw him just before I came up,' I said. 'We're finished. I only wish I didn't love him, but I do. If you were ever in love, then you'll know how I feel.'

I kicked myself as soon as I said it.

'No, it's okay, Nephew,' Auntie Pat smiled. 'After all, you've only known me as your spinster Auntie and I've never made a habit of talking about myself. But there were boyfriends, nothing serious, and—'

Auntie Pat paused, choosing her words carefully.

'Yes, there was a man I loved but, at the time, he belonged to somebody else. The usual story. So, yes, I think I do know what you mean about love. And I wasn't always like this —'

She stood up and went to her dressing table. When she came back she had a photograph album in her hand. She flicked through the pages.

'Here we are,' Auntie Pat said. 'This is me with Mum and Dad when I was twelve. It was taken just before Sam went to Vietnam. Probably at Poho o Rawiri marae, from the look of the surroundings. I hated it when he left.'

'You were twelve? I always thought of you as being much younger.'

'I guess you get that idea from Sam's diary,' Auntie Pat nodded. 'Sam always thought of me as being his little kid sister. I think he preferred it that way. When he was in Vietnam I used to write to him every week, did you know that? Even after he returned to Waituhi he never saw me as I really was —'

Auntie Pat paused at a page in the photograph album.

'This is what I was looking for,' she said. 'I was fifteen.'

I had forgotten how pretty Auntie Pat had been. If photographs tell the truth, three years had changed the young skinny kid, tightly holding her mother's hand, into a young vivacious girl with long curly hair and a wide flirtatious grin.

'This was my boyfriend Charlie,' Auntie Pat said, pointing to the boy with her. 'Look at what we wore in those days! If you saw Charlie now you wouldn't believe that he'd ever managed to fit into those pants. As for me, well, I was trying to be so California.'

Auntie Pat and her boyfriend Charlie were mugging for the camera. Charlie was pretending to be like Fabian or James Darren. Not to be outdone, Auntie Pat was posing like a Hollywood ingenue, one arm behind her head, mouth pursed in a kiss, and the other hand on her hips. She had a beautiful bust and small waist, and was wearing a white blouse and hip hugging blue jeans.

'Whatever happened to you, Auntie Pat?' I wondered. The physical person was still there, but it was almost as if someone else was now in that body. Some person or some event had altered the destiny that seemed to be ahead of that laughing young girl who posed one sunny day long ago with a boy named Charlie. The girl in the photograph looked as if she had all the world at her feet and loved being touched. The woman next to me disliked the idea of physical contact, and lived hermetically sealed away from life in a small house surrounded by old movies and cordon bleu cooking. Who did it? What was it —

All of a sudden a gust of wind came down the chimney and Auntie Pat leaned back from the momentary increase of heat. She looked at me with terror and made as if to get up, to take a runner from the story she knew she had to tell. But the flames, fuelled by the burst of oxygen, leapt like tongues and began to talk to her.

*Tell him, Patty. Before you change your mind, tell him. Now.*

Auntie Pat sighed. She traced the photograph of herself tenderly, almost caressing it as if the girl in the photograph was a living person.

'I was this age, fifteen, when Cliff Harper came to New Zealand. All that Sam had ever told us about him was that he was his American friend. I went with Sam to the bus station in Gisborne to wait for Cliff. I loved my brother and, because he was happy that his friend was coming, I was happy too. More than that I was just happy to be with Sam. We were so close. Sometimes people used to take us for boyfriend and girlfriend because we were always kidding around. I loved it when he put his arm over my shoulders to pull me into him.

'Anyway, the bus was late, it always was. It was the early afternoon bus and it finally got in at three o'clock. At last all the passengers got off, and there was no Cliff. I said to Sam, 'Maybe he'll be on the next bus.' I mean, *I* didn't care! But I could see that my brother was disappointed so I put my arms around him to make him feel better. I had my face tight against his chest and I felt and heard his heart beating. Incredible, really, to remember that after all these years. It was going der *der* der *der* der *der*, and it was like a little bird beating its wings in there. Then all of a sudden the heartbeat changed. It went *der* der *der* der *der* der. That's when I heard somebody laughing behind me and felt Sam push me away. When I turned around to see who it was, a man was standing on the step of the bus in an American airforce uniform. 'Looking for me?'

The next moment Cliff jumped down and he and Sam were slapping each other on the back and laughing. They kept turning and turning and Cliff's hands were on the skin of Sam's neck. I felt closed out and jealous and angry, and Cliff must have noticed because he broke the embrace with Sam.

'So you're little Patty —'

Auntie Pat gave a nervous laugh.

'Well that made me feel even angrier, being called 'Little Patty'. Cliff followed it up by hugging me and I was so shocked at being hugged like that by somebody I didn't know. I turned to Sam for help. He was busy hoisting Cliff's flight bag over his shoulder and didn't realise I needed him to rescue me. Then it was over, and I was gasping for breath. I was angry and afraid, and then we were walking to the car and Cliff's right arm was around my waist. When we reached the car Cliff assumed that I was sitting in the back. I looked at Sam, because he knew I always sat up front with him. But when Cliff opened the passenger door and stepped in, all Sam said was: 'You'll be all right in the back, won't you, Patty?'

Auntie Pat's words were on fire, so I tried to stop her mounting anger. 'Did Harper look like his photograph, Auntie Pat?'

She stared at me. She seemed to be struggling against her reply. When it came it was like a release. An admission.

'I know that beauty is not a word you normally associate with men,' she said, 'but when I saw Cliff Harper I thought he was the most beautiful man I had ever seen.'

## CHAPTER THIRTEEN

——— 1 ———

Der *der* der *der* der *der*.

Sam's heart was beating fast. After all this time and, at last, Cliff had arrived. And the feeling was still *there*.

Cliff gave a devastating wink.

*You and me against the world, right?*

Cliff saw that Patty was glowering at them both.

*Uh oh*, he signed, *your little sister is not very happy*.

In an attempt to make her feel comfortable, Cliff put his arm around her shoulder as they walked towards the car.

'You're travelling light,' Sam said. 'Only the Army bag?'

'I've left my stuff up in Auckland at the airport,' Cliff answered. 'I didn't think I'd be wearing much.'

He grinned and let Sam figure that one out.

'Okay,' Sam said as he started the car. 'Are you all right back there, Patty? Then let's go.' He turned to Cliff. 'I'm sorry, Sir, but the guided tour of Gisborne and the district has been postponed —'

'Can I have my money back?'

Sam laughed. 'Dad wants me at the farm as soon as possible,' he explained. 'He's gathered some of the other farmers together for a cull of wild mustangs up in the hills. Every spare man is needed to help get them across the Waipaoa River.'

The car reached the outskirts of Gisborne. Ahead, the mountains were

205

rising fast. Sam put his foot on the accelerator. Soon they were at the Matawhero crossroads.

'You don't mind, do you?' Sam asked Cliff. 'I thought I'd drop you at home where Mum and Patty can look after you?'

'No way,' Cliff answered, shaking his head. 'I came all this way to spend time with *you*. You said you needed every man.'

'Can you ride a horse?'

'I'm an Illinois country boy. I was born in the saddle.'

'There's the river to ford and you can't swim.'

'In that case, you'd better give me a horse that can do freestyle,' Cliff said. 'Or breaststroke. As long as it floats.'

Half an hour later, they arrived at the farm. Florence was waiting on the verandah.

'You'd better hurry, son. Your father will be at the river soon.'

Sam nodded. 'This is Cliff,' he said. 'He's coming with me.'

Florence only had time to shake Cliff's hand.

'Okay, Illinois boy,' Sam continued. 'No time to talk. Let's go.'

Patty joined her mother on the verandah and watched as Sam and Cliff headed to the barn. Florence became aware of Patty's silence.

'What's wrong, Patty?'

'Nothing.'

--------- 2 ---------

Sam and Cliff left the farm at a gallop, following the contours of the land. For a while they rode abreast as Sam checked out Cliff's equestrian skills.

'How long has it been since you were in the saddle?' Sam asked.

'Give me a break,' Cliff answered. 'I'm still used to helicopters.'

'Well,' Sam grinned, 'this should be easier. You kick to go and you pull on the reins to stop.' Then he looked at his watch. 'We've got no time to waste.'

Sam urged his stallion, Czar, ahead, and cracked on the pace. When he came to the foothills, he broke left up a small river tributary. Cliff, on Honcho, had lagged behind, but he waved him on.

'I'll catch up. You go ahead —'

Sam spurred Czar onward. Soon, he heard the sound of the rushing river. The bush opened up and he was there, at the T-junction where the tributary forked from the river. Two of the local wranglers, Jake and Jimbo, were waiting on the sandspit at the junction.

'You made it just in time,' Jake said. 'They're on the way down.'

Jake pointed up the river valley. Sam looked ahead. At the bend of the river was a track winding down from a steep ravine. His eyes followed the track to the top. The sun dazzled. Dust swirled against the sky. He could hear voices, whistles, shouting.

Cliff arrived. 'I want my helicopter back,' he said.

Sam introduced Cliff to Jake and Jimbo.

'I'm glad you brought a mate,' Jake said. 'There's no way we could have set up the block with just the three of us, and I don't know what side of the river they'll come down. How about splitting the difference? Two of us on this side and two on the other? As long as we head them off, force them into the tributary and down to the lowlands. Who's going to get wet?'

'Heads you and Jimbo go to the other side,' Sam answered. 'Tails we go.'

The coin flipped and flashed in the air.

'Tails,' Jake said. 'Enjoy the swim, boys.'

Sam saw Cliff's face blanch at the thought of riding through all that rushing water. Before he could protest Sam had taken his bullwhip from the pommel and stung Cliff's horse on the flank. Honcho, bawling with surprise, leapt into the water — and Cliff gave an unearthly scream.

'Ride him, Cliff!' Sam yelled.

He put the spurs into Czar and plunged in after Cliff. The water rushed against Czar, and Sam was surprised it was so strong. He'd crossed nearly to halfway before drawing abreast of Cliff.

'How you doing?'

'Remind me to kill you when we get to the other side,' Cliff spluttered.

He had stopped screaming and yelling, and was actually enjoying himself. The water had soaked his shirt so that it was plastered tight against his skin. His hair, slicked back by the currents, had become dark brown, the curls tightening on his scalp. He grinned at Sam and made a thumbs-up sign. Honcho, then Czar, found the bottom, and with a clattering on the river stones they heaved themselves up and out of the water.

Sam and Cliff had positioned themselves none too soon. Down the track came a lone rider. 'They're on their way —'

The rider was Bully, who came splashing along and reined in beside Sam. 'That father of yours,' Bully said admiringly. 'There's about eighty head coming down —'

'*Eighty* —'

'He wouldn't leave any behind. He told me to come ahead to give you the numbers and to help turn them when they arrive. Here they come!'

From far up the river valley came the thunder of hooves. The high whinnying of the wild mustangs. The crack of the bullwhips as the wranglers chased the herd down. The thunder bounced down the valley and, when it reached the five horsemen waiting there, sounded like an advancing avalanche. All of a sudden Honcho was up on his hind legs and Cliff had to fight the reins to keep him from bolting.

Sam saw the first mustang. He was a beauty, as black as sin, and he was leading the herd, coming down their side of the river. The herd was moving too fast. At this pace, they would overrun the three men. Sam signed to Bully to follow him.

'We can't wait here. We've got to try to turn them before they reach this T-junction.' He turned to Cliff: 'Stay here.'

Sam and Bully were off, advancing on the approaching herd, swinging their bullwhips and making the air sing with the lash.

With a shrill whinny the black mustang reared, its hooves flashing. Sam pulled Czar away just in time — but Czar was from wild horse stock himself and turned back to face the black mustang. The two horses began fighting, bawling their rage at each other.

'Get back!' Sam yelled. 'Get back, you black bastard!'

The mustang herd milled around the two fighting horses in confusion. Next moment Sam was able to crack the black mustang across the shoulders with his bullwhip — and it turned from its attack and leapt into the river. The herd followed, and Bully whooped in elation.

'We've done it!'

But the black mustang saw Jake and Jimbo on the other side. Bully's cry of triumph turned to a groan when it turned away from the shore and set its course midstream, swimming strongly through the block.

'What the hell,' Arapeta reigned in beside Sam. 'You haven't done your job, son. Dammit, it'll take us hours to get the herd back here again.'

'I did my best, Dad,' Sam answered.

'Well it wasn't good enough.'

That's when Bully gave a laugh, interrupting the argument.

'Hey, Sam, who's your mate?'

Sam's heart stopped. Cliff had taken to the water on Honcho, arrowing into mid-stream. He was trying to head off the black mustang.

'Crazy Yankee son of a bitch —'

Kicking his horse into action, Sam galloped back along the river.

'Give it up, Cliff,' he shouted. 'Let them go.'

But Cliff was yelling at the black mustang, whistling and waving his hands. Then the mustang was on top of Honcho, biting, slashing, fighting. Whether by luck or by accident, Honcho managed to get his forefeet on the mustang's back. Half out of the air, Cliff teetered and fell.

Immediately, Sam urged Czar into the river.

'Hang on, Cliff! Hang on —'

He saw that Jake and Jimbo had also swum their horses out to help. The black mustang saw them and turned. Made for the shore. Ascended onto the sandspit. For one suspenseful moment, the mustang halted. Sniffed the air. Shook itself dry of the water. Then it turned down the tributary — and the rest of the herd followed.

'Well, if that doesn't beat everything,' Arapeta laughed.

He reined up beside Sam as he pulled Cliff out of the water. He looked down at Cliff and put out his hand. Cliff's eyes looked straight into his.

'Kia ora, Pakeha. So you're Sam's friend. Welcome —'

A firm handshake. A puzzled look on Arapeta's face.

'This boy is without fear,' Arapeta thought. 'I do not intimidate him.'

Cliff's eyes blazed in the sun and Arapeta, blinded, put up an arm as if to protect himself. He turned to the other horsemen and jerked his head after the herd:

'Let's get after them, boys.'

It took another two hours before the herd was corralled. Patty and Monty came down to the yards to watch the wranglers at their work. Patty's gaze kept shifting between Sam and Cliff Harper. Love for her brother kept bursting inside her as, following Arapeta's directions, Sam separated the herd, the older horses from the younger colts. Sam's work was so fluid. A slight pressure on Czar's flank, and Czar would neatly sidestep between two mustangs. With a quick flick of the reins, Sam would make another separation. It was so beautiful to watch, and the wranglers, standing against the rails, murmured their approval.

'Nice work, Sam. Watch the piebald! Watch the black. Get in between there, Sam! Good —'

By the time the work was over, the day was cooling and the sun was going down.

'Hot work,' Sam said. 'Time to cool off and get rid of the dust, eh, boys?' He turned to Cliff. His hair and skin were brown with dust. 'How about it, Yank? Feel like getting wet again?'

'I'd better,' Cliff answered. 'Somewhere there's a white boy under all this.'

The men laughed, and Sam was pleased at how quickly Cliff had been accepted by them. He saw Patty staring with hooded eyes at Cliff.

'What's up with her?' he wondered. Then Dad interrupted his thoughts.

'You boys go down to the river,' Arapeta said. 'A shower will do me.'

He walked up the steps, past Florence on the verandah and into the house. Quickly, Patty seized the opportunity.

'Can me and Monty go for a swim too?' she asked Florence.

'Sure,' Sam intervened. 'There's bound to be some of the girls swimming further upstream.'

'Yeah,' Monty said. 'Patty can go up with the girls and I can stay downstream with the men.'

With a laugh Cliff picked up Monty.

'So you're a man, right?'

'Dinner will be at nine,' Florence said.

The men started to scramble for their trucks. Cliff, with Monty on his shoulders, followed Sam to the car.

'Do you have something for me to swim in? Don't we need towels?'

'You won't need either,' Sam said.

'So I do what the natives do, is that it?'

'Yes,' Sam answered.

Ten minutes later, Sam parked the car on a small bluff overlooking the swimming hole on the Waipaoa River.

'Popular place,' Cliff said when he saw other cars and trucks parked along the roadside.

'They must have known you were coming,' Sam answered dryly.

He led Cliff along a dirt track through willows where it forked, one track going upstream and one going downstream. From there they could hear the giggles of women bathing upstream.

'Good*bye* Patty,' Cliff said gently.

With a flounce, Patty was running through the dappled sunlight. Meantime, Monty was off running in the opposite direction with Sam in hot pursuit. Cliff trailed. Even as they were running Sam and Monty were throwing off their clothes so that by the time they arrived at the bluff they were both completely naked. Then both of them jumped —

Cliff reached the jumping point just in time to see Sam and Monty let go of the ropes that were dangling from the branches of the overhanging willows.

'Bombs away!' Monty said.

Below, Jake, Jimbo, Bully and other men were trying to swim out of the way. Next minute, the water erupted as Sam and Monty belly-flopped into it. Sam swam to the surface, spouting the water from his mouth. The sun-stars rippled around him. He waved Cliff to come and join them.

'Come on, Cliff. Come and get wet!'

Cliff shrugged his shoulders, took off his clothes, disappeared down the track to make his run for the rope and, next moment, was a shape blurring through the sky.

'Yee-*haa*!' Cliff leapt for a rope, swinging back and forth as if afraid to let go, and everybody started to laugh and —

'Oh shit,' Sam yelled, remembering. 'He can't swim!'

Sam watched Cliff plummet down into the water. With quick strokes he made his way to the middle of the swimming hole and dived. All around him other men were diving. Beneath the surface Sam saw a trail of bubbles and felt the pulse of disturbed water. He saw an underwater world of sunken logs and then a flash of sunlight against something spectral white in the luminous green of the river.

Cliff, sitting there, at the bottom of the river.

*Hello. Fancy meeting you here.*

Cliff's hair was flowing around his face. The sunlight rippled across his body, dappling it with extraordinary sensuality. Sam signed to him.

*What are you doing, you stupid Yank?*

Cliff shrugged his shoulders.

*Waiting for you. I think this is called drowning.*

All of a sudden Cliff belched and the air that he had taken into his lungs ascended in a huge glassy bubble. Quickly, Sam grabbed Cliff, propelled himself from the river bottom and shot them both to the surface. When Cliff broached the surface his first intake of breath gulped in the entire air of the universe.

Sam pushed Cliff to the bank of the river. All around, Jake, Jimbo, Bully and the other men were laughing.

'From now on,' Sam said, 'you stay here and paddle in the shallows.'

Sam was half lying on Cliff, wagging his finger in Cliff's face as if he were a naughty boy.

He started to slide back into the water. He heard Cliff gasp.

Unseen by the other men, Cliff's penis was stirring. Helpless, he looked into Sam's eyes.

'God dammit.'

With a smile, Sam pulled Cliff a little further down from the bank to where the water covered him from the waist.

'Try not to frighten the fish,' he said.

Then he broke away to clamber up the bank, run at the rope and swing out again into mid-river. There, just as the sun flamed across the water, he let go and was suddenly made molten as he arrowed into a crucible of gold.

With the sun off the river, the night began to cool. Some of the men, led by Bully, snuck off to have another look at the women upriver. The rest stopped swimming and sat on the riverbank, quizzing Cliff about being a helicopter pilot. Sam could hear the skill in Cliff's responses. He gave them what they wanted to hear, the stories of bravery that would affirm the experience. Nobody wanted to know about the darkness and terror that was at the heart of every soldier's experience in Vietnam.

'I'll tell you what, though,' Cliff said, 'you guys were fortunate to have such good camaraderie between Maoris and whites.'

'Yeah, well, whites are almost as good as us,' Sam quipped.

'No, seriously, in the American Army, it wasn't the same for American blacks. They often fought a different war. Do you think the racial discrimination stopped because we were fighting on the same side? I heard talk that blacks were regarded as cannon fodder and often pushed to the front of American attacks on the enemy — and they knew it.'

Cliff was interrupted by the return of Bully and his raiding party — and they were chortling with glee. They'd come across some of the women's clothing and stolen it. They sat waiting for the fireworks, and sure enough an outraged voice boomed out from upstream:

'Okay, Bully. We know it was you who pinched our clothes. You just give them back!'

'Who, me?' Bully yelled back, all innocent. He was showing the boys a bra. 'It must be Anita's,' he said.

'No, Anita has bigger tits,' Jimbo replied loudly. 'I think it's Kara's.'

A furious squeal came from Kara, because the bra concerned was, well, of ample dimensions.

'I heard that, Jimbo! How dare you go looking through Anita's window at night!'

Jimbo flushed, and the men ribbed him — and because the conversation had taken something of a sexual turn, he coughed and asked Sam:

'Ah, Sam, what did you say your mate's nickname was?'

'You should ask him yourself.'

'Hey, Yank, why do they call you Woody?'

'All the guys have nicknames.'

Cliff was noncommittal, but the telltale crimsoning of his neck gave him away.

'Do you have a cartoon character by the name of Woody Woodpecker down here?'

'Yes.'

'I'm named after him.'

Jimbo looked at Sam and grinned. 'I reckon it's also got something to do with *that*,' he whispered, motioning to Cliff's penis. 'That is some pecker, huh, Woody?'

Until that moment, Sam had not made any sexual connection. When he did, he couldn't help it. He lifted his throat and:

'Ha-ha-ha, ha-ha! Ha-ha-ha, ha-ha! That's the Woody Woodpecker song!'

While Sam was singing, Cliff stood up and began to make mock poses, flexing his biceps, sucking in his stomach and making all the men laugh. He was right in the middle of the routine when Anita and Kara, supported by Patty and a few other women, marched up to get their clothes back. What they saw was a buck naked American boy with green eyes like the river whose hair had been set on fire by the sun and whose pellucid body was jewelled from the water. They saw it all — and there was a lot to see.

Sam heard the girls scream with laughter. Patty seemed totally shocked. Next moment, cowpats and clumps of mud rained around Cliff and the men. Kara, arms akimbo, yelled to Bully:

'You know very well that wasn't my bra!'

Sam turned to his mates. 'Let's get out of here.' He dived for cover back into the river, and the others followed.

'What about me?' Cliff called to Sam.

'You're on your own,' Sam called as he saw Cliff run for shelter behind some bushes.

'That's not going to do you any good,' Anita shouted after him. 'You need trees!'

Kara nodded in agreement. 'Lots and *lots* of trees!'

Gales of laughter rang across the swimming hole. The sun winked out.

———— 4 ————

Sam was nervous at family dinner that evening. He wanted everything to be right. He wanted his family to like Cliff; he wanted Cliff to like his family. Just before sitting down he whispered to Cliff:

'Look, Dad likes dinner to be formal. He'll say grace —'

'I'm accustomed to that.'

Cliff had changed into a red-checked lumberjacket shirt and rolled up jeans.

'And I'm on to your father. Head of the household, right?'

'Mum's been worried all day about whether you'll like the food —'

Cliff's eyes crinkled into a grin. 'They're worried? Hell, I'm the one who's worried!'

For the first quarter of an hour, everybody was on their best behaviour. The men seated themselves and Arapeta said grace. He gave the briefest nod to Florence and Patty, as if they were personal kitchen staff. Immediately, the two women began to bring the meat, potatoes and vegetables to the table, serving the men before they sat down. Arapeta picked up his knife and fork and at this signal the family followed suit.

'What about some wine for our guest?' Arapeta asked.

'I'll do that,' Sam said.

'No,' Arapeta answered. 'Let your mother do it.'

Florence was rising from her chair when Arapeta turned to Cliff:

'Are your lamb chops all right? Not overdone? And the kumara?'

Sam saw Mum give Cliff a stricken look. Sometimes, Dad's questions often sounded like a death sentence.

'They're the best I've ever had,' Cliff said.

He turned to Florence and made a gesture to the table. It was overbrimming with farm fare: bowls of peas and beans, dumplings, pork chops as well as lamb chops and bread freshly baked from the oven.

'You are a fine cook, ma'am, and I congratulate you on the beautiful meal we're having here.'

Florence blushed at the compliment. She went to the scullery and returned with a bottle of wine.

'I've only just begun to make wine,' Arapeta said. 'I hope this chardonnay will be to your liking.' He raised his glass. 'Welcome, Sir,' he said to Cliff. 'The hospitalities of the house are yours. Nothing is good enough for the man who saved my son's life and —' Arapeta's eyes twinkled '— was bold enough to stop my horses going down that river!'

Cliff made a gesture with his hands. He returned to the food.

'Well, it's certainly a pleasure to have some real home cooking. Beats the Army Mess at Nui Dat doesn't it, Sam?'

Sam smiled a silent thanks to Cliff for diverting attention from his mother and on to the middle ground of man-to-man talk. He saw that Florence had noticed Cliff's skill. A look of tenderness came over her. The evening progressed and, following a second bottle of wine, Arapeta relaxed. Sam knew that his father always prided himself on being a generous host; having a guest in the house brought out the best in him. Even better, Cliff kept asking the kinds of questions which played to his

215

vanity, allowing him to recall story after story about his exploits during the Second World War.

'The desert campaign? Yes, I was there when Kippenburger decided to use the Maori Battalion at Munassib. That was in August 1942, and he wanted us to take a pre-emptive strike and thwart an anticipated German attack. "Go in with bayonets," he said, "and take prisoners and not scalps." He also ordered Reta Keiha and Ngati Porou's C Company to throw a screen across the front of the entire battalion. Although we struck opposition we continued to attack. Ben Porter was with A Company. Pita Awatere was with D Company. After the withdrawal had been ordered, and the body count taken, it was reckoned that 500 enemy soldiers had been killed. Later, Rommel accused us of massacring prisoners and the wounded because very few prisoners or wounded were found.'

Arapeta chopped the air with his left hand to make his point.

'All the combat was hand to hand,' he said. 'Little quarter was asked. Little quarter was given.'

'Were you also at Monte Cassino?' Cliff asked.

'Yes,' Arapeta answered. 'That was two years later, in January 1944. The Germans had a garrison there, the Fourteenth Panzer Corps of the Tenth Army, and they brought the American Second Corps to a standstill. Your 36th Texan Division lost more than 1500 men on their assault but you gained a foothold on the mountain. That's when the Maori Battalion was ordered forward to help you out. We were assigned to assault across the Rapido River, along the railway line, and to capture the railway station. The plan was that we would use the station to launch a further assault on Cassino. The Germans threw everything they had at us. Then on 15 February the monastery was bombed. Three days later we attacked.'

Sam stole a glance across the table at Cliff and tapped out a message on his fingers.

*God, you're a charmer, you Illinois boy, you!*

Without breaking his attention to Arapeta, Cliff signed back.

*I love your Dad's stories. And I love the fact that I'm with you in your house and —*

Suddenly, Cliff stopped signing. Momentarily, he paled. Sam waited for Cliff to resume signing. He saw Cliff make a pointing motion:

*Someone's eavesdropping.*

Sam was immediately alert. What was Cliff on about? He looked around the table. He looked at Patty. He caught a quick glance from Cliff.

*No. Your mother —*

Mum had been in the kitchen preparing pudding. She was standing behind Arapeta, waiting for him to finish his story before she put the plates on the table. Her eyes had caught the silent conversation between Sam and Cliff. She was frowning. She glanced at Sam. She glanced at Cliff. She gave a small intake of breath. Her eyes dilated.

'I was with Colonel Awatere in that attack,' Arapeta continued. 'Men began to fall to the fire and the mines. B Company lost 128 men on their attack on the railway station —'

*What do we do?* Cliff signed.

Florence was trembling, almost spilling the plates. She was trying to hold herself together.

*I think she's guessed about us*, Sam answered.

He was panicking. Quickly, he got up from his chair and walked towards Mum.

'But on the next attack on the station,' Arapeta said, 'we did not fail. We hunted the Germans through the rubble and debris of Cassino until every one of them was down.'

'Utu,' Cliff murmured.

But his eyes were on Sam as he approached Florence.

'Can I help you, Mum?' Sam asked.

Florence looked into his eyes. Her face trembled. Then she smiled, a deep sad smile.

'No, I'll be all right, son. You go and sit down.'

Sam knew that smile well. It was one that Mum always used whenever she was sorry for herself. It was as if she knew her son and this American were in love with each other. But she recognised it only because it was something she had never had.

Meantime, 'You know about utu?' Arapeta asked Cliff.

He saw Florence putting the pudding plates onto the table.

'But here I've been talking all night! Let's finish dinner and then — is our guest's bed made up, Florence?'

'Yes.' Florence nodded at Cliff. *Be careful of my husband.*

'Good,' Arapeta continued. 'We have a busy day ahead. Sam's got his work to do in the morning before he goes into Gisborne to get the rental car —'

'Rental car?' Cliff enquired.

His heart was thudding as he watched Florence, eyes downcast, resume her seat.

'I forgot to tell you,' Sam said. 'You're coming with us to a wedding. It's at Tolaga Bay, about three hours' drive away. Did you bring a tux? The family's staying there for the night, but Dad wants me to come back to look after the horses. That's why the rental car. Would you mind coming back with me?'

Cliff's eyes danced, 'Sure.'

He looked again at Florence. She was deadly still. The game of double conversation was not over.

It was time for bed.

'It's been a great day, Sam. Thank you.'

Sam and Cliff stood close together on the verandah. The sky was spilling over with stars. Dad had retired and Mum and Patty were doing the dishes.

'I'm glad you're here,' Sam said. 'I'm sorry we didn't have any time alone today. Perhaps tomorrow.'

The two men stood like that for a long time. A star fell.

'I have your greenstone pendant. I brought it back to you,' Cliff said.

'You should keep wearing it until you leave,' Sam answered. 'There's time enough to return it.'

He wanted to stay out here forever with Cliff. He wondered how he would get through the night, knowing that Cliff was only down the corridor. He needed him.

'So what do we do about your mother?' Cliff said.

'I don't know,' Sam began.

For some reason he remembered an old Maori myth. At the very beginning, all the gods were male. Desiring to have offspring, Tane went to his mother, Papatuanuku, and asked her advice. She told him to make a woman from the red earth which he would find on her mount. Tane did this, fashioning Hine ahu one, but when he wanted to enter her, he didn't know which orifice to use. He tried her mouth, her nose, her armpits, her ears, her eyes and even her anus, and this is why all humans have secretions from these places. Finally, he found her female opening and sanctified it with the full inward thrust of his penis. Some variations of the myth told that it wasn't only Tane who did this but all his brothers also.

As Sam remembered this he shivered. The male was high and sanctified. Woman was low and common. How much lower were men who loved men —

Sam turned to Cliff. He put his hand up to touch his face, to draw him closer. But he heard a noise, turned, and saw Patty shadowed in the doorway. She had come to show Cliff to his bedroom.

'You'd better go,' Sam said. 'I'll see you in the morning.'

For a while Sam stood there, and a pang of loneliness hit him. He looked at the night sky, the Southern Cross turning on its axis, and its immensity surrounded him.

'Where does love come from? Why has this happened?'

He felt someone slipping an arm around his waist. For a moment he thought Cliff had returned. It was Patty, and she was trying to nestle in under his shoulders, pulling his arms around her.

'Are you cold?' he asked.

Patty nodded her head. Then, 'I love you, Sam,' she said.

'I know,' Sam answered. 'Do you like Cliff?'

'I think so. I'm not sure. I know he's your best friend.'

'Yes, he is.'

'But I'm afraid —' Patty burrowed in further.

'Of Cliff?' Sam asked, surprised.

'No,' she began. Then, 'Yes,' and she nodded. But she was still unsure. 'I don't know,' she concluded. Patty sounded as if she was lost somewhere in a black hole in space. She was shivering, uncertain. Then she whirled out of Sam's embrace and ran into the house.

CHAPTER FOURTEEN

———— 1 ————

Sam was up with the dawn. He opened his window, and he laughed with surprise when he saw the mackerel sky. The clouds were tinged with red, stretching to the end of forever. For a moment he stood there, his elbows on the window sill, watching the mackerel as they swirled and teemed around the rising sun. As if they sensed some disturbance, the mackerel were jumping, splitting into shoals, showering the sky with silver.

Quickly, Sam dressed. There was a lot to do today before leaving for the wedding. He looked in on Cliff, but he was still sleeping. The rest of the house was quiet as he tiptoed out, put on his boots and strode down to the barn. There, the wranglers had divided the mustangs between them, leaving twenty to Dad. The horses were still spooked. It was the black mustang who was doing it, so Sam decided to isolate him with five or six others in an enclosure — and let the rest of the herd out into a larger paddock with some of the farm horses. He saddled Czar and, surprisingly, it was easier than he had expected to back the black mustang and some mares into a special corral. Before he let the others loose, he decided to check the paddock fencing. He rode out along the fencelines. On his way back in he saw a figure waving to him from the barn.

'Mum!'

'Do you want me to open the gate?' she asked.

'Okay,' he answered.

Florence undid the latch and the herd sprang through. Watching, the black mustang put on a show of anger, snorting and kicking.

Sam dismounted. 'Is Cliff up yet?'

'Yes. He wanted to come down to help you, but your father told him you'd be back soon. I left them talking on the verandah.'

Sam slapped Czar's haunches. With a whinny he was off, streaking through the sunlight.

'We'd better get back to the house,' Sam said.

'No, not yet,' Florence said, putting a hand out to restrain him. 'There's something I want to talk to you about.'

Immediately, Sam was wary. If Mum asked him about Cliff, what should he say? He looked at Florence and saw she was biting her bottom lip. When she started to speak, however, it wasn't about Sam and Cliff at all.

'I want to tell you about me and your father,' she began. 'And why you must be careful.'

'About Dad?'

Florence nodded. She leaned against the railings.

'How much do you know about how I came to marry your father?'

'I know some,' Sam answered.

'Did you know he was actually supposed to marry my older sister? Madeleine was the beauty of the family, and the plan was that she marry Arapeta after his return from the war. But she met another man, your Uncle Pera, and before anybody could stop them they eloped. To salvage your father's pride, and his mana — his prestige — *I* was offered to Arapeta. All of the negotiations were done around me. I had no say. Your father and I never even courted. They sent him a photograph of me while he was still in Europe, he said 'Yes', and the first time I laid eyes on him was when I walked down the aisle and saw him waiting for me.'

'Why are you telling me this, Mum?'

Sam saw that his mother's eyes were wide open and staring, as if she was walking in her sleep.

'So that you can forgive me for not defending you against your father,' she said.

Sam went to embrace Florence but she moved away.

'As soon as I saw him I knew there would never be any love between us. I lifted the veil from my eyes, expecting to see a man who would be thankful for my sacrifice. But for him I was utu, payment. Something owed him in lieu of something that had been promised. I was good for only one thing — to bear him a son. All those months I was pregnant I feared you might

221

be a girl. My life would have been worth nothing if that had happened. When you were born I cried with relief. After you were born I was nothing to him. I never did the things he was used to getting. He found me unimaginative. I was glad when he turned from me to you.'

'I don't understand what you mean —'

'Your father lives for you and through you. He expects a lot of you, more than anybody can humanly be expected to fulfil. That's why he rides you so hard. He has never forgiven you any weakness, any failing in the past. So do not expect him to forgive you for any weakness or failing now or in the future. If he discovers your secret, his rage will know no bounds.'

Sam's heart stopped. He looked at Florence. Behind her he could see a huge spider's web, shivering in the rain.

'You know my secret?'

'Every mother knows her son's secrets and his desires. If your father finds out what they are, he will be unforgiving. He will consider you an unworthy vessel for his hopes and his ambitions. You are his eldest son. You're supposed to succeed him tribally and personally. If you deny him this he will give you no quarter.'

Florence began to cry.

'The reason why I am telling you this is because you must not expect me to help you. Where your father is concerned, I am a weak person. I can't stand pain. I hate being shouted at and told I am useless. All I can do is warn you. Be careful of him. Don't let him in. Otherwise he'll sneak like a thief through your bloodstream, and enter your soul and your heart. And if he does that, he will indeed find out your secret.'

There was a noise in the trees. Florence looked into the shadows, startled. Sam had seen that look so many times. It was the look his mother gave whenever Dad came through the door.

'We'd better get back. Forgive me, Sam, for being a coward. I like your friend Cliff, but if anything happens, I will not be able to intervene against your father. You will be on your own.'

---

2

---

'Come on, everybody, move. Florence, what's taking everyone so long?'

By mid-morning everyone was rushing. Arapeta was in command and Mum was hastily packing two suitcases for the overnight stay: formal clothes for Arapeta, herself and the children, and bedding for the meeting house. Sam and Cliff were well out of the way, ready and waiting at the car.

'Is your father always like this?' Cliff asked as yet another outburst came from the house:

'Don't forget my medals, Florence! This is not just a wedding. All the Maori Battalion will be there and General Collinson from the Army in Wellington. I won't allow him to upstage me.'

At last the family came hurrying out.

'It'll be a bit of a squeeze, but you won't mind, will you?' Sam asked Cliff.

'Not at all,' Cliff answered as they all piled into the car. Monty was sitting on Florence in the front, and Patty was in the back between Sam and Cliff. Whatever had been bothering Patty was apparently over. She was animated and bright-eyed. Sam had never seen her looking so pretty, especially with her hair now curly instead of straight. How long it would last was anyone's guess.

'She's got a boyfriend,' Sam told Cliff. 'What's his name, Patty? Frankie, Harry? Blackie?'

'You know very well his name's Charlie.'

She turned to Cliff with stars in her eyes.

'He isn't my boyfriend. He *was* my boyfriend or at least he thought he was my boyfriend but —'

Mum laughed. 'Goodness me, Patty, all this chatter! What on earth has got into you this morning?' She turned to Cliff apologetically. 'She's not usually like this. She's normally very quiet.'

Patty coloured and cuddled into Sam. He exchanged a glance with Cliff who said to Patty:

'Hey, that's okay, babe.'

At the word 'babe', Patty blushed even redder. Sam sighed — sometimes you could never tell what to say or do with Patty. She was silent for a while, and then she looked at Cliff and gave a gasp.

'I've been trying to think who you remind me of,' she squealed, 'and now I remember!'

Patty leaned forward and tapped Florence on the shoulder.

'You remember that old movie you took me to, Mummy? The one about a young soldier who comes back from World War Two? Don't you think Cliff looks like Guy Madison?'

Sam caught Mum's face in the mirror. Mum was laughing.

'I'm sure I don't know what you're talking about!'

'There's a scene where he returns home on the bus and —' Patty's eyes were shining as she turned to Cliff. 'Do you know any movie stars, Cliff?' Patty was off, asking question after question. Sam relaxed. By the time they arrived in Gisborne it looked as if she liked Cliff after all.

'Don't forget,' Dad said as Sam and Cliff got out, 'the wedding starts on the dot of 1500 hours.'

He made it sound like a military manoeuvre.

'Seeing as you're the best man,' Mum reminded Sam, 'you'd better not be too late. No sightseeing on the way.'

Then Patty started up.

'Can I come up with you and Cliff in your car, Sam?'

'No,' Mum said. 'You'll just be a nuisance.'

Cliff leaned against the window. 'Tell you what, babe, let's have a dance tonight, how's that?'

Patty was still thinking how to reply when Arapeta spun the car out into the traffic and away.

'You Yankee sweet-talker,' Sam said. 'Calling my sister a babe when she's only a kid.'

'A kid? You'd better open your eyes. Patty's dynamite. You don't know it and it's just as well she doesn't.'


Sam signed for the rental car and took Cliff to the menswear shop where he'd previously been measured for a hired black tux. While Sam paid, Cliff wandered around looking at the clothes.

'Who's the blond bombshell?' the menswear assistant asked. He had been staring at Cliff from the moment he had walked into the shop.

'He's a friend from America,' Sam said, trying not to laugh. 'We need a tux for him too. Do you have one?'

'We've had a run on our formal wear this weekend,' the assistant said, 'but I think I can rustle up something.' He fussed around Cliff with his measuring tape, and by the time he was finished was positively salivating. 'You just wait right here. I think I've got just the thing.'

He went into the dressing room and, in a mirror, Sam saw him opening up a box marked THE ROBERTSON-CARLISLE WEDDING and taking out a white dinner jacket. He crooked his finger at Cliff.

'Would you come into the dressing room, Sir?'

Cliff looked uneasily at Sam. 'Will you come with me?'

'You survived enemy fire in Vietnam,' Sam laughed. 'Don't tell me you're frightened of a menswear assistant. Go on, be brave — and give him a thrill!'

Two minutes later, after a lot of oohing and aahing, Cliff reappeared. The effect of white jacket and blond good looks was devastating. Cliff was pleased.

'Give me a pink carnation, and I'll be all dressed up for the prom. All I need now is a date.'

The menswear assistant looked at Sam

'If you get a cold and can't go, I'll take him.'

Half an hour later, when they were on the Coast Road to Tolaga Bay, Sam and Cliff were still poking fun at the menswear assistant.

'What was he doing with you in the dressing room?' Sam joked.

'Measuring and stuff —'

'And stuff?' Sam arched an eyebrow.

'Waal,' Cliff drawled, 'he wanted to take some measurements of my thighs and, even though we were only there to get a jacket, I let him!'

'Do you think he knew about us?' Sam asked.

'Yes. I told him.'

The openness of Cliff's admission took Sam's breath away. Here was a man who was setting the pace. Prepared to tell strangers. And when Cliff put his arm around Sam's shoulders as he drove, all Sam could think of was the rightness of it all. It didn't matter where they were going as long as it was together.

'Another person knows,' Sam said. 'Mum. But I think it's okay with her. She's had a hard time with Dad. I'm pretty sure all she wants is for me to be happy.'

'I'm glad she knows,' Cliff answered.

Ahead on the road Sam saw a beat-up truck with a Maori family on the back deck. It was going very slowly — and Cliff said:

'If this was Vietnam, we'd have the right of way.'

It all happened so quickly. All of a sudden the landscape changed, and Sam was back in Phuoc Tuy province. The sun was a malevolent eye over a red landscape wasted by military strikes and defoliants. In the air, helicopter gunships buzzed like hungry bottleflies. Vietnam villagers ran like tiny insects trying to find some place to hide. One of them, an old woman with her entrails pulsing in the red dust, smiled at Sam:

*You were a boy. You were hungry like all boys. You had to eat.*

Then somebody with a flame thrower was burning her to a crisp. She fell into a nest of flame-charred bodies, huddling to protect each other. And a flying owl was screeching out of a virulent sky, and Turei —

Before he knew what was happening, Sam was wrenching the wheel, trying to avoid the memories. The car swerved across the highway and careered into the sand dunes. Sam was out of the car, leaning forward, balancing on his feet and punching the air as if he wanted to take the whole world on.

'Oh, God. Oh, *God* —'

Sam looked at Cliff, his eyes wide open: and when Sam started to weep, a sea of pain and guilt spilling out of him, Cliff opened his arms and took Sam into them. He held Sam close, feeling tears on his neck, and love overwhelmed him for the vulnerability of this man who was sobbing on his shoulders.

'Oh, *fuck*,' Sam said. 'That hasn't happened for a while. I'm sorry.'

'Don't be sorry. Vietnam's not something you can leave behind. Its memories can come on you at any time of the day or night. I still wake up screaming sometimes.'

Sam wandered down the beach, with Cliff following him.

'Were we right, Cliff?' Sam asked. 'Or were we wrong to be there in Vietnam? I know that when I went I thought God was on our side.'

'God and the American flag.'

'But what did we achieve, Cliff? We fucked the people up so bad that it's going to take them years to recover. We napalmed the shit out of that country. We went there, did our war thing and then got out scot free. But they had to stay there and live in the shit we left behind. Were we right, or were we wrong?'

Cliff looked confused for a moment. When he looked at Sam he was frightened.

'You know, when I was drafted I went to fight in something called the Vietnam War. But do you know what the Vietnamese called it? They called it the American War. So I guess your question depends on which side you were on.'

Cliff walked down to the sea, as if hoping that the surging waves would help him to give Sam his answer.

'All I know is that war is war and those kind of questions about whether we were right or wrong get suspended when you're there, in the middle of it all. I'm an American boy through and through. I believe in my country and I would fight to the death for it. But, in my heart of hearts, I think we were wrong to be in Vietnam. Knowing it doesn't make it any better for my conscience to cope with. But pretending that those moral issues shouldn't be dealt with is condoning what happened.'

Sam sighed, and relaxed against Cliff.

'Thank you for saying it wasn't right. And for telling me the truth.'

'The truth?' Cliff answered. 'The truth is, I'm scared too. I've come through a war and now I have to find my way through peace. I thought that after Vietnam I'd go back to the States, meet a nice girl, settle down and get married. I thought I was regular like the other guys: I fucked girls and they loved it. Then you happened to me. Maybe the war does this to people. Changes them. But when I was in that bar in Vung Tau, surrounded by all those girls and soldiers, I was so weary. I thought of my brother and started to sign —'

'God, Johnny, I'm so bored,' Sam remembered.

'When I saw you signing back to me, it was like I wasn't alone any longer — that there was somebody in the world who could hear me.'

The sea was rolling in. The waves were sucking at the hot sand.

'Love happened to me in Vietnam, Sam, and I wasn't expecting it — but it was the only good thing to come out of my war and I'm going to trust in it.

'Sometimes I feel shit scared about what has happened to us. What *is* happening to us. I know it's the same with you and we're both terrified of where we go from here. I never ever wanted a complicated life. I think I'm still basically heterosexual, but that's had to go on hold too. Since that first night in Vung Tau we've avoided talking about the physical stuff. But one of these days we're going to have to bite on that bullet —'

'It might explode in our faces —'

'We've got to take the risk,' Cliff said. 'If we don't, we'll never know.'

'What happens if it doesn't work out?'

'You go back to your life and I go back to mine.'

Sam turned and looked at Cliff. 'And if it does work out?'

227

Cliff's eyes crinkled into a grin. He was looking sexy as hell.

'What do you mean *if*!'

——— 3 ———

By the time Sam and Cliff got to Tolaga Bay they were really running close to time — and the town was packed to the gills.

'Holy Hone Hika,' Sam said as he negotiated the traffic and sped towards the marae. There, cars were packed in like sardines.

'This must be some wedding,' Cliff said.

'Yes, it's a special one. My father always puts on a good show. He's made sure everybody has pulled out all the stops. A lot of important people are coming.'

Sam grabbed up his gear and led Cliff into the meeting house where wedding guests were changing into their flash clothes. Until Sam and Cliff's arrival everybody had been carrying on as if they were in the changing sheds at the public baths. Old kuia were putting dresses over slips. Men were hitching up pants over longjohns.

'Hey, Milly! You better stop feeding your man! Jumping Jack's getting so fat he can't keep up his pants anymore.'

'Oh, don't worry about him, Whina. It gives Jack his excuse to flash.'

'Flash? What? I didn't see a thing, Milly! Did any of you other girls see anything?'

The other 'girls' looked at each other blankly.

'Us? No, it must have happened when we were looking!'

When Sam walked in with Cliff, everyone went silent. As Sam made the introductions he could see the women coyly reaching for sheets under which to continue dressing. And did their language change? Did it *what*.

'Oh, Whina, dear, do you happen to have a spare comb?'

'No, Milly, darling, but I think I have a hairbrush! Yes, here it is.'

'Oh, thank you, Whina.'

Sam smiled at Cliff and shrugged his shoulders.

'They're embarrassed because you're a Pakeha.'

'So I should do as the natives do?' Cliff asked.

With that he dropped his trousers. There was a gasp — and a groan of disappointment as everyone realised Cliff was wearing underpants. An old woman's voice floated across the meeting house:

228

'Now I know I saw nothing, but give me that any day to Jumping Jack's *flash*.'

Everybody roared with laughter and normal misbehaviour resumed. Across the room, Sam saw Patty waving furiously — she had already linked up with Kara and Anita — and Florence pointing at her watch.

'Hurry up and get to the hotel! Your father's already gone to collect the bride. You better get George down to the church quick and smart.'

'George?' Cliff asked. 'Your mate in Vietnam?'

'Yes.'

Five minutes later, Sam and Cliff were running into the hotel where George was waiting with his two groomsmen, Red Fleming and Zel Flanagan.

'Hey! Woody!' Red called. 'I didn't know you were in town.'

Cliff made the rounds. Meanwhile, Sam was trying to put George at ease. He was pale and sweating with nervousness.

'Gee, Sam, I was hoping you wouldn't arrive so that the wedding could be called off. Couldn't you have had a little acc-i-dent?'

The two friends gripped each other tightly. When Cliff came up to shake George's hand, George couldn't let go.

'This is worse than Vietnam, mate,' George moaned. 'The whole thing's turned into a circus. Do you know how many guests at last count? Over eight hundred. At least in Vietnam the only thing I had to worry about was a battalion of Vietcong. Here, it's the whole of the East Coast and Sam's father!' He turned to Sam. 'Can you remember when you, Turei and I were being farewelled from Poho o Rawiri and how we wanted to get the hell out of there and leave you and your Dad to it?'

'The man needs another beer,' Zel Flanagan said.

'No,' Sam said, 'we want him to walk to his wedding, not to be carried to it.'

'What about you, Woody!' George said. 'Maybe you could rescue me! Is your chopper handy? Feel like doing a medevac?'

'Listen, George,' Sam said, taking him to one side. 'There's still time to get out of this. If you're really serious we can still get a message to Emma. Call the whole thing off —'

'No, I have to go through with it. First of all, your father would hound me forever if I didn't. More important, I owe it to Turei.'

229

'Owe him? By marrying his sister?'

'He was my mate, Sam. The owl was supposed to come for me. Emma is a fine woman. That kid of hers could be mine. She says it is.'

'But do you love her?'

George shrugged his shoulders.

'Does everything have to be done for love?'


'Okay, *two up*.'

Sam gave a patrol movement order and the boys, all except George, laughed. They pushed George down to the car and were soon on their way to the church. As they sped along the highway a shadow settled.

'What's that?' George asked.

It was General Collinson flying in from Wellington in an Army helicopter.

'Oh no,' George agonised. 'This was supposed to be a small wedding.'

The helicopter clattered across Tolaga Bay, making it a war zone, and little boys came out of their houses, pretending to fire at it with water pistols and ray guns.

'Here we are,' Sam said at last. Ahead, he saw the General and his entourage shaking the vicar's hand. A guard of honour, made up of returned veterans including Jock Johanssen and Mandy Manderson, saluted the General as he went into the church.

A huge crowd had gathered. Arapeta had made sure of that. The guest list read like a Who's Who of the East Coast district, and especially of the East Coast military families. Still, despite the high tone of the occasion, there were still some cheeky buggers around. As George stepped out of the car one of them called out:

'Still time to cut and run, George!'

George shrugged his shoulders helplessly as he took in the crowd.

'Trust your father to want to make a circus of all this,' he said, turning to Sam. 'Why couldn't he wait until you got married? Why did he have to pick on me?'

'You know what Dad's like. He told you it was going to be the wedding of the year and he meant it.'

The guard of honour snapped George a salute. George paused as he went past Mandy Manderson:

'I'd much rather be on platoon, mate. It's good to see you and Jock.'

The vicar, looking harassed, greeted him at the doorway.

'I suggest we go straight in. The bride is due any moment.'

Sam, Cliff, George and the groomsmen walked into the church. Sam saw Florence, Patty and Monty sitting in the pews on the bride's side, and he took Cliff across to them before rejoining the boys at the altar. George looked as if he was having a heart attack.

'Oh, Jeez,' George said. 'Tell me, Sarge, tell me what I should do —'

Not Sam. Sarge.

It was too late. Sam was watching the door and, outside the church, Emma had arrived. She was radiant. When she stepped out of the car, on the arm of Arapeta, who was giving her away on behalf of the family, even those who had known her as Big Emma were made speechless by her beauty. Moved by the occasion, some of the old women began to call Emma into the church.

'Haramai, e hine, haramai, haramai, haramai —'

Emma's mother, Lilly, who had once seen her son Turei go off to war, replied on her daughter's behalf. She who had taken the axe to her son's coffin lifted her face to the sun and cried out:

'Karanga mai ra koutou ki a matou —'

Call us in, you who wait, call my daughter and let it be the call of love, oh let it be the call of man to woman.

Sam stole a quick glance at Cliff to see that he was all right. Cliff's face was like a pale star, and Sam knew he was feeling the emotion of the moment. He saw Patty come to the rescue and take Cliff's hand in hers. Throughout the church wedding guests were sighing, remembering Turei.

All of a sudden, Sam heard George moan. Sam looked at him questioningly, and George recovered.

'It's all right, Sarge. I know I'm doing the right thing —'

Sam pressed George's shoulders reassuringly. Yes, something was being put right today. Some attempt was being made to close the gap where once a laughing soldier had been. Out of this marriage would come a son — not Turei's own, but he would be of Turei's spirit, coming out of his proxy, his good friend, George.

'She's almost here,' Sam said.

He saw a blur of white and the scent of a bridal bouquet as Emma moved down the aisle on Arapeta's arm. A gleam as sun glowed on

Arapeta's medals. The organ was playing and the old women were still calling, calling, calling.

'Come forth, come forward, beloved, and come to your husband.'

Then Arapeta and Emma were beside George. Arapeta was so splendid and handsome in his military regalia, and everybody knew what a father he had been to Emma after her own Dad had died. Sam, watching it all, felt again the formidable nature of his father's charisma, and the force of his authority. You think that the guests had come just for George and Emma? No, they had also come because Arapeta, their leader, had called them. Godlike, he was, in all respects, invincible, and Sam remembered Mum's words:

'If anything happens, Son, I will not be able to intervene. You will be on your own.'

Arapeta snapped a salute at George, and there was a murmur of laughter as he whispered in George's ear, no doubt to give him manly advice. Then Arapeta turned to the audience. His eyes skimmed above General Collinson and the Army brass, as if they weren't there.

'Cheeky old bastard,' General Collinson muttered.

Instead, Arapeta sought the faces of his old Battalion mates, Claude, Kepa and Hemi among them. With great dignity he saluted them before taking his place beside Emma's mother. Florence, watching, felt herself trembling as she remembered her own wedding day. Something strong and good had died in her that day, and later, that night, when Arapeta had abusively thrust his penis into her every opening as if she was made of dirt.

Sam smiled at Emma. George was trembling so violently that Sam thought he would crack apart. Emma slipped her right hand into George's. For a moment, George's hand remained open. Hesitantly, as if unsure, it closed on Emma's. Then George stopped shivering and his fingers interlocked with hers.

------ 4 ------

'Haramai ki te kai.'

The call came from the dining room for the guests to come and eat. Sam was relaxed now that he'd managed to get George through the ceremony. On his part, once he'd said 'Yes', George had seemed happier. Sam tried to persuade himself that his friend's whole problem had been simply last-minute nerves. He made a silent prayer that the marriage would be happy. He set about looking for Cliff.

'I wouldn't worry too much about your mate,' Arapeta said, amused. 'Ever since he got here he's been surrounded!'

Indeed, Sam saw that Cliff's presence was causing a sensation among the teenage girls — not to mention some of the older women, unattached and attached. He was American, he was drop-dead gorgeous and he'd been a heroic chopper pilot to boot. Not only that, but Anita and Kara had been gossiping about the manly attributes they had glimpsed down at the waterhole. The consequence was that girls were bumping into Cliff accidentally on purpose from all directions.

'I think you need rescuing,' Sam said. 'What is this power you have over women?'

He pointed to yet another group of starstruck girls who were hanging out with Patty, quizzing her on Cliff.

'I've never understood it,' Cliff answered, pretending wide-eyed innocence. 'Sometimes it gets so bad that girls all over the place are walking into lamp posts.'

Laughing, Sam shepherded Cliff to the back of the cookhouse. There, Jake, Jimbo and Bully were drinking beer with other local boys while waiting for the hangi to cook.

'You'd better watch out,' Bully winked at Cliff. 'Maori women are sweet loving women. If they want you they'll get you. Before you know it you'll have a kid on the way and you won't be needing that airline ticket back to the States.'

'Gee, guys,' Cliff responded. 'I better radio a chopper team to pull me out.'

'You think you'll get away that easily?' Jimbo asked. 'If there's any blond kids born here nine months from now, there'll be a war party coming over to the States to bring you back.'

'Er,' Cliff said. 'Is that dead or alive?'

The boys roared with laughter and slapped Cliff on the back. He was like one of them, all right, a real good bloke.

'Hey, Cliff! Come and sit by us!'

As soon as Cliff walked into the dining room girls were calling him.

'You're on your own, Illinois boy,' Sam said. 'I'm compére as well as

233

George's best man. I have to sit at the top table with the wedding party.'

'Can't I come with you?'

'Tell you what,' Sam said. 'I'll sit you next to the prettiest girl here.' He plonked Cliff in the seat beside Grand-Auntie Annie, eighty if she was a day, and browned to perfection by the sun.

'Yeth,' Auntie Annie said because she hadn't any teeth, 'you thit right nextht to me and I'll look after you.'

Sam made his way towards the top table. Mum, Dad, Lilly and General Collinson were already at their seats. Sam got a nod from the boy at the door. He took the microphone.

'Ladies and gentlemen, please stand for the bride and groom.'

George and Emma entered with Emma's son. The boy's presence caused one wag to whisper in a loud voice: 'Boy, that was quick.'

Sam signed to the vicar, who stood up and began to intone the prayer for grace: 'Whakapaingia enei kai —'

Before the pastor could draw another breath —

'Amen,' someone said.

The serious business of eating began. The kitchen doors burst open and in came the servers with bowls of seafood — crayfish, paua, mussels, oysters, all the bounty of the sea. At Arapeta's command, the boys of the village had been diving for two days to bring such a rich harvest to the wedding. General Collinson's mouth dropped open in amazement.

Sam couldn't stop himself. He took the microphone again.

'Hey! All you people, send your oysters over here! George will need all he can get. I understand that Emma has certain plans about what to do with his manly body tonight.'

George fixed Sam with a steely grin. Emma pretended to be virginal.

And what was this? Pots of kina swimming in cream were coming out of the kitchen. The guests began to hoe in.

'I'm sure glad I'm not sleeping in the meeting house tonight,' Sam said. 'And don't say I didn't warn you. Tonight you'd better make sure the windows and doors are wide open —'

Everybody started to guffaw. Kina are an epicurean delight, but have one unfortunate side-effect. Before long, your bowels are ballooning with the foulest stench on earth.

'In fact,' Sam continued, 'if any of you other guys want to seduce Emma, send your kina over to George as well! If he eats enough she's

234

bound to kick him out of bed and you can sneak in just like Kahungunu, our revered ancestor, when he wanted to sleep with the beautiful chieftainess Rongomai wahine.'

'But she was beautiful,' somebody yelled out. 'And Kahungunu was biiiigg!'

Everybody laughed again. Sam took his seat. He leaned over to George. 'So how are you feeling?'

'I think I need some oysters,' George answered. Emma's fingers were already wandering south. 'Lots and lots of oysters.'

The feasting and drinking, hard talking and laughing continued for a long time. Occasionally Sam searched out Patty, and he frowned as he saw her drinking with Kara and Anita. She was too young to be drinking beer. He also sought out Cliff. It was hard to avoid him in that sea of beautiful brown faces.

*Kia ora, Illinois boy. How're you doing with Auntie Annie?*

*She's a great gal. I'm having the time of my life. And Sam —*

*Yes?*

*You're the best looking guy here, you know that?*

The feast was abating when Arapeta, with a cough, rose from his chair. Immediately people stopped eating and talking, and Sam wondered again at the strength of his father's personal mana. Unlike Joshua at the battle of Jericho, Dad wouldn't need rams' horns to bring those walls down. All he'd need to do was to cough.

'Ladies and gentlemen,' Arapeta began, 'and distinguished guests —' He nodded to General Collinson. 'When a man takes a woman to be his wife he is re-enacting a tradition that goes back to the very first woman, Hine ahu one, she who was made from red earth. Through his woman, a man achieves his immortality. He has a son —' A son. Not a daughter. 'And in this manner he conquers the formidable Goddess of Death herself. This is the achievement of George tonight.'

Around the dining hall came murmurs of approval.

'Ka tika,' some of the men said. 'Yes, that is right.'

'I made a promise to Turei's mother,' Arapeta said. 'I told her that her son, my son and George would all come back from Vietnam. I said that my son would ensure this.'

He turned to Lilly. 'Lilly, if I could, I would trade my son for your son, and it would be my son who would have gone to Death and

235

your son who was alive today.'

Sam knew his father's words were rhetorical, ritual. But God, it hurt to hear them hurled at him.

Some in the audience began to weep. Others grew silent. None of it had anything to do with Sam. They were simply remembering Turei as he had been. The hardcase, always ready with a joke, the lovely boy who had once lived among them. Alone among them, only Cliff saw the impact on Sam and he began to sign across the room.

*Sam, can you hear me?*

'However, we cannot change the past,' Arapeta went on. 'We must continue with living, and tonight we can begin again with this marriage of Turei's sister, Emma, to Turei's best friend, George.'

The dining room burst with thunderous applause. Arapeta took up a glass and called for a waiter to fill it. Everyone was standing and raising their glasses.

*Sam, I'm here for you, Sam.*

'George,' Arapeta said, 'I drink a toast to you and I congratulate you. *You* have brought Turei back to us.'

Arapeta lifted his glass and quaffed the wine in a single gulp. He put the glass down and, with great deliberation, saluted George. All eyes were turned to the bridegroom — and, at that moment Sam looked across at Cliff. He was gasping with sorrow.

*Just keep your eyes on me, Sam. The rest of the world doesn't matter. I'm here for you, Sam.*

Sam tried to smile. Slowly he replied.

*You'll rescue me and take me away from here?*

*With guns blazing. Against all comers.*

Throughout the dining hall old men were standing and saluting. They were jostling against Cliff and making it difficult for him to keep his line of sight on Sam. Desperately, Cliff moved to one side. Saw Sam looking for him.

'Ka mate, ka mate!' Arapeta roared. 'It is death, it is death!'

*Sam, look at me, Sam.*

All around, old men were joining in the haka. Eyes bulging. Spittle flying. Crouched into a semi-fighting stance. Slapping at their haunches.

Across that sea of faces two stars lifted.

*I've never left anybody behind, Sam. Never.*

236

By early evening the feast was over and the wedding guests were making their way in the dark down to the War Memorial Hall. The celebration dance was in full disco swing. Up on the marae, however, the official wedding party and local elders had been detained farewelling General Collinson and his aides.

'Until we meet next time,' Arapeta said.

The dislike was palpable between him and General Collinson. All those old wounds, from a time long ago when Pakeha commanded and Maori took the orders, had never healed, never closed.

'Yes, until next time,' General Collinson replied.

The universe shattered to pieces as his helicopter lifted off, circled the marae and, red lights winking, headed north across Tolaga Bay township for Wellington. For a moment there was silence, as if the party was waiting for Arapeta to give the movement order.

'Now that he's gone,' Arapeta said, 'let's go down to the hall and really let our hair down.'

He turned to Sam. Saw the haunted look in his son's face. Remembered what he had said in his speech.

'You know why I had to say what I did in the dining hall, son.'

'I know, Dad.'

'I had to appease everyone and to finally make it right. For Lilly. For George. For all those who loved Turei. So that everyone could put the past behind them and get on with life.'

'I know.'


But all the way to the hall, Sam felt himself dying inside. He remembered the golden palomino and how Dad had suddenly lifted his rifle and shot it. The palomino was still alive when Sam ran to it. He looked into the golden iris and saw himself reflected there — and then the golden light began to go out.

The wedding party arrived at the doorway to the hall. Inside, the guests had cleared a space in front of the band to welcome them:

'Karangatia ra! Karangatia ra! Powhiritia ra!

Nga iwi o te motu, kei runga te marae,

Haere mai —'

The music was so joyous, but all Sam wanted to do was to find Cliff. It was peace time, but he felt he was still living in a war zone. He searched the hall for Cliff but it was so crowded and filled with cigarette smoke. Meantime, the women were swinging their hips, the men were stamping their feet with the pleasure of living. Eyes were wide and bright, and emotions were open as the group poured out their aroha to the bride and groom.

'You have called us and we have come,
all the people of Aotearoa to this marae,
where we celebrate with you —'

Somebody bumped into Sam. It was Patty with Anita, Kara and a gaggle of other girls. Patty giggled and swooned over him:

'Hullo, Sam —'

Sam smelled the beer on her breath.

'What's got into you, Patty? No more drinking, you hear?'

Patty giggled and gave a mock salute. Anita gave a small scream and pointed across the floor — and the girls were off to where Cliff was standing with Bully and Jimbo. For a moment, Sam remembered Madame Godzilla's bar. He caught Cliff's attention and signed to him:

*Haven't we met before?*

Cliff grinned back.

*Are you coming on to me? If you are, I warn you, I never kiss on a first date.*

The action song ended and there was loud applause. Sam realised that all attention was on Arapeta as he turned to George:

'May I have your leave to have the first dance with your wife?'

Arapeta bowed to Emma and took her hand. He led her into the middle of the floor. The band began to play the 'Fascination' waltz, and, with a dignified gesture, Arapeta put his arms around Emma and swept her around the room. Immediately there was scattered applause, and Cliff was able to escape from Patty and the girls to join Sam. Together they watched Arapeta, medals resplendent, as much in command on the dance floor as he was in battle. Sam heard Cliff say to him:

'Are you and your Dad okay?'

'Yes. He didn't really mean what he said back there in the dining hall.'

Cliff paused. Then:

'Whether he did or not, Sam, I don't like what he said — and I don't like him. He uses fear to make people do what he wants. You, your mother, your whole family. Even though he's your father, I'll fight him if I have to. He's a bully.'

'Let's not talk about Dad,' Sam answered. His face was set with determination. 'Let's think about us —'

The waltz was over. Arapeta took Emma back to George, and with a sigh of relief the band started up again: this time, a hot rock 'n' roll number. The women were kicking off their high heels, tucking their dresses into their pants and taking to the floor. Sam's eyes were turbulent, smouldering.

'Will you be ready to leave in, say, five minutes?' he asked Cliff.

'Leave?' Cliff was trying not to swallow.

'Yes,' Sam said. 'It's time —'

Cliff stared at Sam.

'Yahoo!'

But Patty was there, screaming above the melee.

'Come and dance with me, Cliff! You promised me a dance —'

Cliff gestured helplessly at Sam.

'Don't you move! I'll be back!'

He followed Patty onto the dance floor. He was in such a mood of elation that he couldn't help it — from out of nowhere he conjured up a spin that made everyone yell with surprise.

'Look at that Pakeha boy move!'

Next minute, Cliff was dancing so cool that everybody moved aside to watch him. Patty was obviously way drunk but Cliff made her look as if she was the greatest dancer on the floor. He spun her, controlled her and made her into a star. At the end of the bracket there were whistles and shouts, and Patty was over the moon with excitement.

'Wow,' Sam laughed when Cliff returned. 'Who taught you to dance like that?'

Cliff exaggerated a yawn.

'Mormon elders from Brigham Young University — and you've had your five minutes, so let's get out of here.'

It was too late. Without Sam and Cliff knowing, Patty had run to the bandleader and whispered something in his ear. He took up the microphone.

'Okay, everybody, we're going to have a change of programme. Instead of another boring action song for George and Emma —'

People in the hall laughed and pretended to be insulted.

'We're going to have an item from our special guest from America. Put your hands together for Mr Cliff Harper!'

'Oh, no,' Cliff groaned. 'What can I do?'

'Can you sing a song? "Yankee Doodle Dandy" or something? How about the "Battle Hymn of the Republic". Anything!'

All around the hall people were chanting, 'Cliff, Cliff, we want Cliff!'

A gleam came into Cliff's eyes. 'Okay, I've remembered something I worked up at Junior College. Can you wait a few more minutes?'

'I might start without you —'

Cliff was shy and handsome and he knew he couldn't get out of it. He gave a gesture of good humour, walked over to the band and started to talk to them. The bandleader nodded and began to instruct his drummer and lead guitarist. Cliff took the floor.

'You know, I'd much rather be flying a helicopter than doing something for you all,' he began. 'Flying a helicopter is something I know how to do well. However, seeing as I'm forced to do something, and thank you, Patty —' Patty blushed and giggled '— there is a traditional American folk song that we like to sing at home in the States, something nice and slow. Lucky for me the band knows it, so —'

Cliff gave the nod to the lead guitarist who strummed a mean chord. With a sudden gesture, Cliff ran his fingers through his hair, releasing crackles and sparks of golden light. Then, with a hip-swivelling motion that sent everybody rolling as if they were skittles, he began:

'Since my baby left me —'

Whop. Swivel. Hold that pose.

'I found a new place to dwell —'

Bump. Grind. Swivel. Smile.

'Down the end of Lonely Street
at Heartbreak Hotel —'

And all of a sudden the girls were screaming and the older generation were watching, mouths open, as Cliff swung into a routine that would have left Elvis for dead.

'I'm so lonely, buh-huh-by —'

Crouch, shake, rattle, hiccup, rock.

'I'm so loh-honh-nely —'

Playing up to Auntie Annie, pulling her onto the floor. Auntie Annie pretended to faint in his arms.

'I'm so loh-honh-nely, I could die —'

Stunned, Sam watched as Cliff suddenly unbuttoned his white jacket and began to swing it in the air. When he let go of the coat it flew toward Patty and her friends — but it was Anita who caught it in a swoon. Winking at Sam, Cliff started taking off his bowtie, teasing the girls with it, and then throwing it at Patty — but this time Kara caught it. Slowly he began to unbutton his shirt.

'Oh shit,' Sam thought. He closed his eyes. 'He's not going to strip, is he?'

Sam peeked through his fingers. What a relief. It seemed Cliff had decided to unbutton only to the navel. He put his knees together, splayed his feet out as far as they could go, and was hip-hopping his way across to where Sam was.

'Although it's always crowded —'

Cliff's voice was mean, raunchy and filled with sex. He was teasing Sam, playing with him.

'You still can find some room —'

He spun away towards Florence and Arapeta, who were laughing at Cliff's antics.

Suddenly, Arapeta's face froze.

He saw a cord around Cliff's neck. He caught a glimpse of something attached to it. The boy was wearing —

'For broken-hearted lovers

to cry there in the gloom —'

Arapeta looked at Florence to ask if she had seen the hei tiki. Her eyes were wide with terror and she stepped back from him. Without thinking, she glanced across at Sam, as if to warn him.

'Oh, you fool, Sam. You fool —'

In that single glance, Arapeta saw Sam's secret.

'They're so lonely buh-huh-by, so lonely —'

Sam roared with the crowd as Cliff, with a run, went down on his knees and slid all the way back across the floor to Patty, pretending to sob. Sam saw his mother's face and it was wan and frightened. She was

241

making pointing movements and, when he followed them, he saw Dad moving through the crowd as if he was stalking something. Or somebody.

'So loh-honh-nely, they could die —'

The band went into an orchestral riff. All around, people were screaming and laughing. God, that was a white boy out there and he could sure sing!

Sam saw Dad pushing to the front, to where Patty was. Arapeta's eyes were bulging, and the veins were standing out from his neck. Sam didn't know what was happening — that Arapeta had seen a hei tiki ablaze on Cliff's chest:

'Yes, it was Tunui a te Ika. What was it doing around this American boy's neck?'

Arapeta looked at Sam. Disarmed by love, Sam was defenceless. Arapeta saw into his soul.

George turned to Sam: 'Did you know he could do this?'

'No,' Sam answered. His face was alight. He watched as Cliff wound his act to full lift-off and pulled Patty squealing onto the floor.

'So if your baby leaves you —'

He had her in his arms. Leaning over her. Dropping her to the floor. He didn't see Arapeta trying to push through to him.

'And you've got a tale to tell —'

Now it was Anita's turn. Clutch, pelvic grind, lay her down, yeah, baby. Arapeta was closed out behind a wall of cheering onlookers.

'Just take a walk down Lonely Street
to Heartbreak Hotel —'

Cliff signed to Sam:

*Meet me at the doorway and let's get out of here.*

Grinning, Sam signed back:

*You betcha, Illinois boy.*

He started to move towards the door. At that moment Arapeta forced his way to the front of the crowd, grabbed for Cliff — and missed.

Cliff made an exit to bring the house down. He pulled out all the stops. Sam had lit the fuse and Cliff exploded.

'And you'll be so lonely buh-huh-by —'

Sam waved to George and indicated to Florence that they were going now.

'So loh-honh-nely —'

242

One last swivel and a groan of desire. The girls yelled out to him, 'Don't go, Cliff, don't go!' But a sneer, a bop and a pelvic thrust, and he left them crying for more.

'You'll be so lonely you could die!'

And Sam and Cliff were away, running out of there, making for the car. Patty and the girls crowded the door, yelling 'Cliff!', and Patty stumbled after him. Cliff slipped in the dark and Sam, laughing, found himself rolling down a small bank. Cliff embraced him, and wouldn't let go, drawing him into a kiss that took Sam's breath away. Then they were up and off again, into the car. Roaring away.

Arapeta reached the doorway of the hall just as the car turned out of the gateway. His blood was pounding with anger and fear. The girls were waving. He heard somebody vomiting in the bushes and saw that it was Patty. The beer had finally got the better of her. Her eyes were red, and she moaned as she brushed past her father and went back into the hall. He held her and wouldn't let her get away.

Far in the distance, Arapeta saw the lights of Sam's car as it braked at the corner.

'Go and get your mother,' Arapeta said to Patty.

He had bitten into his lip and blood was welling from it.

'We're going back to the farm. Tonight.'

--- 6 ---

Sam sped fast through Tolaga Bay. Soon they were on the coast road back to Gisborne. The road was a ribbon of moonlight curving through shadowed valleys. They were still laughing hysterically when, all of a sudden, something swooped, beating its wings against the windscreen. Sam caught a glimpse of hooded eyes and velvet wings and —

'Sam, watch out!' Cliff yelled.

Sam wrenched the wheel to the left, as if trying to avoid something. He slammed on the brakes and, next moment, was out of the car, staring into the sky, into the trees. He was on the balls of his feet, leaning forward with clenched fists.

This should have been the happiest night of his life. But on the branch of a tree was a visitor. It glared at Sam, extended its pinions

243

and called out a name — but the name was indistinct.

'Which one have you come for?' Sam yelled. 'Call the name again. Say it —'

Cliff joined Sam on the roadside. 'What's up?'

Above him, in the trees, an owl screeched, lifted, and disappeared into the night.

Sam put his hands up to his head, trying to figure it out. He was reeling about, terrified.

It was happening. The owl that George had seen in Vietnam had followed him home. Why? He should have known he couldn't spit in the face of the gods and get away with it. He was to be punished, and all those around him were being punished too.

Sam turned to Cliff to explain. But what could he say? He saw that Cliff's shirt was unbuttoned and Tunui a te Ika was against his chest — and something else clicked in:

Mum, pointing at Dad, and Dad moving through the crowd as if he was stalking something. Dad must have seen the hei tiki and —

'You okay, Sam?' Cliff asked.

Sam tried to get a hold on himself. He looked back down the road towards the marae and the War Memorial Hall. It wouldn't be long before Dad came after them. 'There's nothing I can do about it,' he thought. 'Nothing. Whatever is going to happen will happen.' Sam turned to Cliff and smiled. With great defiance, he sought Cliff's mouth. When he broke the kiss, he looked across Cliff's shoulder at nothing — and everything.

'We haven't much time,' he said.

Ninety minutes later, the car sped through Gisborne. In another thirty minutes they would be home.

And it seemed to Sam that he was racing against Time. The clouds were storming through the night sky, shredding the moon, ripping it to pieces. But the faster he sped, the slower Time became. The clock ticked past the minutes, but every minute became an hour. The closer they came to the farm, the further away it seemed. By the time they reached the homestead, Sam's heart was thundering with desire and fear.

Then Cliff turned to him with a moan and Sam realised that Fate had closed the door behind him. There was no going back. He had to keep on going forward and hope against hope that there was a way of escape from whatever destiny lay in front of him. And, if there wasn't —

'Come with me,' Sam said.

He took Cliff's hand and led him away from the homestead. His senses were magnified. He seemed to be both inside and outside his body. Inside was molten carnality. Outside, he could see himself stumbling with Cliff down the track towards the barn. The strong wind eddied among the trees, causing branches and leaves to fall around them. Far off, the wild horses were whinnying. They were uneasy, stamping the ground, trying to find a way out of their enclosure.

The barn door was swinging in the wind. Sam went to close it, to buy them more time, but Cliff couldn't wait. He was following behind Sam, pulling at Sam's clothes, ripping them off. By the time Sam reached the ladder into the hayloft his shirt was half off his shoulders. He was climbing the ladder when Cliff reached around his waist and unbuckled his belt.

'Don't move,' Cliff hissed.

Sam groaned and arched and stretched both arms, reaching for the rung above his head. Standing behind him, one rung below, Cliff stared mesmerised with wonder as Sam's shoulder muscles rippled with light. Sam turned, as if to escape, and Cliff saw that dark nipples spiked the hair of his chest. The light showered like a waterfall into his groin.

Pinned there, Sam felt Cliff's lips on his neck. Cliff's hands were around his waist and one of them was sliding under the waistband of Sam's pants and underpants. Whimpering, Sam felt his trousers falling to his knees.

'No,' Sam said.

He clenched his buttocks. Tried to push Cliff away but it was too late. Cliff was undressing on the ladder. His shirt fell away, and Sam gasped at the feel of Cliff's chest against his back. He made one last attempt to get away, lifting his right leg onto the next highest rung, but Cliff held him tight.

'God, Sam, your skin is so soft.'

And Sam was gone, gone, gone beyond the point of no return.

With his free hand, Cliff released his belt and Sam felt the rough fabric rasping his skin as Cliff's trousers and boxers fell to his boots. Cliff's cock, strong and smooth, jabbing blindly against his inner thighs, trying to find a way in. Cliff's hands joined his on the rung above Sam's head, fingers interlocking. Pressed up hard against Sam's back, Cliff was whimpering with need.

'Open your legs, Sam,' Cliff pleaded. 'Oh, please —'

Sam obeyed, arched his back and let the breath hiss out between his teeth. Cliff hung over Sam like a God. He positioned himself, saw his cock glistening with lubrication. Let it slide between Sam's buttocks, stilled, and *lifted*.

'Oh, God —' The pain, he hadn't known about the pain.

Sam felt beads of sweat pop on his brow. He tried to wrest free of Cliff but Cliff was too far along to be stopped. Cliff was holding Sam tight, keeping up the pressure, easing in, sliding in until he was up to the hilt.

'No,' Sam said. 'Wait —'

Cliff had his teeth in Sam's shoulder and he was growling with lust. He began to move, thrusting, thrusting, twisting this way and that way, up and down, side to side, up and down. Every thrust was so painful, but Cliff was oblivious as Sam began to cry out. Sam was breathing short and fast, flexing his muscles and biting back on the sheer agony of the act. He closed his eyes. Vertigo overwhelmed him.

And he was tumbling through Te Po, The Night, and falling through Te Kore, The Void. He felt himself nearing unconsciousness. Took a deep breath.

*Please, not eternal darkness.*

A thousand years passed. Then, across the Void, a pinpoint of light. Something began to build in Sam, something made up of Cliff's rhythmic movements. He opened his eyes and saw that Time had stretched and expanded. *Go fast,* the old man motioned, *before the rains come.* In front of him was a temple, and voices were calling, *Haramai, Sam.* His heart was thundering, almost breaking out of his chest.

'Oh, Sam —'

Harper was lunging now. Going deeper.

Sam saw something sliding down the pillars of the temple, coiling wet and glistening. *You and me, cobra, let us enjoy our brief moment in the sun.* A saffron-robed monk was kneeling before Sam and suddenly Sam began to feel a sun exploding within him, showering Te Kore with light.

Cliff was in orgasm, his body shuddering and spilling over. The shock of it forced Sam to breathe out, let go — and he reached a kind of understanding. A moment of revelation. He opened himself up, made himself vulnerable. With a groan he too was pulsing a river.

'Sam, yes —'

They were both laughing and crying at the same time. Nothing else mattered, past, present or future. All there was, was *now*.

This was the secret embrace at the end of the day.

And they had found it.

# CHAPTER FIFTEEN

———— 1 ————

Auntie Pat gave a deep groan. She grasped the arms of the chair, leant forward, her eyes staring into the past.

'Sam!' she cried. 'Daddy's coming —'

Then she closed her eyes and, exhausted, seemed to fall into unconsciousness.

'Auntie Pat,' I whispered.

I was concerned for her but I also knew I might not get another chance to hear her story about Uncle Sam. It was coming at a cost. At every disclosure she was diminished, as if the telling was draining her of life.

My mind went to Uncle Sam, and I thought of him with Cliff holding him after they had made love. I thought of him in surrender, in all his vulnerability. I was above him and Cliff, looking down at them. I imagined him wide-eyed, his face drawn and enigmatic. I conjured up a single tear, welling up and out from his left eye, glistening in the moonlight. I willed him to look into my eyes and share his silent grief with me.

In the old world of the Greeks, a man was still considered a man when he was the active partner. He remained himself, maintaining his masculinity. He could shower, put on his clothes and walk away, back into his own life. But it was different if you were the passive partner. There was no going back. Having a man inside you changed you. It was as if the penetration reached not only some physical centre but also some small room within which your identity lay. The masculine identity of the man inside the room had been constructed by his society. His very being had been imprinted with codes which guided him and said, 'This is what a man does and this is what a man does not do.'

Being made love to by a man was, I knew from my own first experience, a kind of crucifixion of all those hopes and dreams of living as others live. Whoever you were, it shattered your room like an eggshell. All the king's horses and all the king's men could never put you together again.

Auntie Pat began to stir. As she moved, my attention was drawn to the movie poster just behind her — of the old RKO movie called *Till The End of Time*, the one with Guy Madison in it. When I was younger, and Auntie Pat was my reluctant babysitter, her idea of entertaining me was to take me to the matinee where they showed such movies at the Majestic. While other boys played rugby with their friends, I spent my afternoons with Auntie Pat, eating popcorn and licking a chocolate cone upstairs in the balcony. When I grew up and blamed my own taste in movies on her, she confessed to me that it was the only way she knew of to keep me occupied without having to do anything or to talk. When I was much older, and had my first sex in the balcony with Jimmy Whelan, I kept thinking of Auntie Pat and whether she knew how much more exciting going to the movies could be.

'I hate it when people watch me while I'm asleep,' Auntie Pat said.

She stared at me and there was such hostility in her glance. I knew she was always so careful about how she presented herself, and it suddenly struck me that I really had no idea which was the real Auntie Pat and which was the false. I suspected I didn't know her at all, just as she hadn't known the real Michael either.

'I didn't know George's first wife was Turei's sister,' I said.

'It didn't work out,' Auntie Pat answered. 'Those marriages that are made because of sentimental obligation, never do. As I said, George was always a sentimental person. Don't be taken in by him.'

Auntie Pat lapsed into silence.

'Do you want to go on?' I asked.

She nodded. Then:

'Sam and Cliff didn't have long together,' she said. 'Perhaps an hour at the most.' Sam looked up and, through the window where the hay bales

249

were pulled by winch, he saw our headlights. He heard the warning cry of the wild horses. He knew we had arrived.'

———— 2 ————

'Cliff, wake up.'

The headlights swung, dazzling, through the window of the barn. Cliff was still sleeping. Sam wanted to memorise the smell, taste and touch of him. He breathed Cliff in. He held Cliff forehead to forehead, mourning and keening over all that they had been to each other.

Cliff started awake. He looked at Sam, his eyes trying to focus, and almost fell off the ladder. He remembered where he was and, with a sexy smile, he began to nuzzle Sam's neck, his lust rising again.

'Well, what do you expect?' he said cheekily. 'After all, I'm a healthy mid-Western boy —'

Sam quivered with emotion.

'We have to get dressed,' he said. 'My father's coming.'

Arapeta was out of the car and snapping his orders.

'Florence? You, Patty and Monty stay in the house.'

Florence went up the steps without looking backward. She could have gathered Patty and Monty with her, but she didn't have enough strength for them or for Sam. They would have to fend for themselves. All she wanted to do was get as far away as she could from Arapeta and what he was going to do. Humming to herself, her eyes glazing over, she entered the house. It was better to go into the bedroom, shut the door and wait until it was all over.

Patty took Monty's hand. Her heart was overflowing with regret, and she turned to Arapeta.

'Daddy, please don't hurt Sam.'

'Go inside, Patty. Now.'

Patty began to scream and scream, as if wanting to warn Sam.

'What's that?' Cliff asked. Something was wailing in the wind. Then, nearer at hand, the wild horses were panicking in their enclosure.

Sam switched on the outside lights. The black mustang, seeking a way out, had come with the wild horses to the gate. It reared up, battering its hooves against the gate. All of a sudden it was down, bawling in pain, its right foreleg caught between two bars.

'You wait here,' Sam said to Cliff.

In an instant, he was running past the stables towards the fallen horse. As he approached, the animal began to struggle, its eyes wide with fear, its mouth filled with foam.

'Easy, boy, easy.'

Back at the barn, Cliff saw someone approaching.

Arapeta.

And Auntie Pat was gripping the arms of the chair so hard that her knuckles showed white. She was staring into her memories, trying to break the constraints holding her to the present and to go, willingly, into the past.

'Dad had ordered me to stay in the house but I couldn't. I waited until Mum and Monty were inside and then I ran. I ran as fast as I could. All I could think of was my brother and Cliff, and I was afraid of what Dad would do to them. I loved my brother. When he'd been away in Vietnam I wrote to him every day. I kept calling his name, "Sam, Sam, Sam," hoping he would hear me and get away. I came to the barn and I saw Dad. I saw Cliff. But Sam wasn't there. I crouched down in the dark and looked between two bars of the fence, and I heard Dad talking to Cliff Harper —'

Across the yard, Patty saw Arapeta closing in on Cliff. Arapeta feinted to the left. He feinted to the right. At each feint Arapeta was watching, trying to search out any weakness in Cliff's defence. It came to him again that this boy was fearless, and he nodded in acknowledgement. He laughed in a humourless fashion.

'Mr Harper, when Germany finally surrendered, I was with Colonel Awatere's staff. I was there at the Allied action which took Ravenscrag, Hitler's secret mountain command post. I was there at the kill.'

Two men looking at each other. One the father. The other the lover.

'Colonel Awatere was there with other generals of the Allied forces. You know what he did? He unbuttoned his fly and began to urinate on the carpet. Others tried to physically restrain him and some of the generals cried out, "You can't do that." Colonel Awatere answered, "Watch me." When he was finished he said, "When a Maori goes into battle all he has in mind as the final outcome is that he will be able to eat his enemy's head. If he is unable to be found, then what I have done is an alternative expression of the sweetness we feel, the contempt we feel for the enemy we have conquered."'

The full force of Arapeta's words, veiled though they were, hit Cliff in the solar plexus. He stood his ground.

'You're not afraid?' Arapeta asked. 'You should be. You have been my guest, Sir, and you have betrayed the hospitality of my house. Before this night is done I will eat your head.'

Auntie Pat put an arm up to her mouth. She was oscillating between past and present, the terror of her memories shaking her apart. Her eyes were wide, blinking rapidly, as she tried to recapture that night for me in the way she wished to remember it.

'They began to fight, Michael. And although Cliff was the younger, I don't think he realised how strong Dad was. When Dad came out on the balls of his feet and made his first jab, his second with his left fist, and then followed through with his right fist, only then did Cliff realise Dad's boxing skills. He put up his left elbow, blocking the punch. Before Dad could get under his guard, he had moved out of range. They were circling each other, taunting each other —'

Cliff moved away from Arapeta, averting his face, moving lightly and balancing on his toes. His arms were up and he was moving constantly, his eyes on Arapeta. He saw Arapeta's nostrils flare, signalling a second sequence of jabs. He blocked them all, and with a quick flurry of his own — one, two, three —caught Arapeta on the chin. Rocked off his heels, Arapeta fell back.

'Your threats don't bother me,' Cliff said. 'I don't care if you're Sam's father, you're only a man as far as I'm concerned.'

Cliff saw that he had drawn first blood and Arapeta, surprised, tasted blood on his lips. He closed quickly again with Cliff, weaving fast, feinting, jabbing, trying to get past Cliff's defences. Cliff laughed at him.

'Not only are you just a man,' Cliff taunted. 'You're an old man. You're so up yourself you can't really see *me*. All you think you see is weakness because I am a man who is in love with your son. But you've lost the advantage. I was trained by bigger men than you'll ever be. You think becoming a helicopter pilot is something that just happens? I earned it, Arapeta, and my training, boxing included, has put me beyond your understanding. You can't cut it with me, Arapeta. You've been boss for so long, you think you're invincible. Well you're not, you son of a fucken bitch. You're a tyrant, and a bully. You'll eat my head? Your time's over, old man.'

With that, Cliff moved the fight from the defensive to the offensive. Leading with his left he established a rhythm. One and two and punch. One and two and guard. He saw an opening, took Arapeta off guard and let fly with a straight left. The blow caught Arapeta on his right cheekbone and cracked against his nose.

Arapeta staggered back. Shock showed in his eyes. All his life he had been the king, he had been the man, and he had laid claim to the title by virtue of his physical prowess.

Cliff felt a moment of regret. But this had to be done. Arapeta, the patriarch, had to be knocked off his perch. He had to be shown up for what he was. It was the only way to free Sam. Then all the mind games Arapeta had played with Sam would be over.

Cliff closed again on the old man, ready this time to knock him senseless and blow all he represented to kingdom come.

At that moment, with a quick wrench of the fence bars, Sam set the black mustang free. It leapt to its feet and crashed through the gate. The herd followed, running past Sam and towards Arapeta and Cliff. Before Arapeta could get away the mustang was upon him, up on its hind legs, and he had to twist aside to escape its hooves. The mustang slammed past Arapeta, and he fell to the ground.

'All I could think of,' Auntie Pat said, 'was that my father was lying on the ground. I ran across to him, screaming. Cliff was standing there and I can still feel now what I felt then. I hated him. I hated him so much. I hated him for coming and destroying our lives. I hated him for what he had done to Sam —'

With alarm, Sam saw Patty running out of the shadows towards his father. She bent down to Arapeta and then, fiercely, leapt to her feet and started to push Cliff Harper back. When Sam, on the run, reached them, Arapeta spoke one word:

'Son —'

'Sam, it's over for you here,' Cliff cut in. 'You belong with me now.'

Blood was spilling out of Arapeta's lips, and his face was bruised and swollen, and Patty was screaming:

'Don't listen to him, Sam. We love you, you can't leave us.'

Patty was up and throwing her hands against Cliff.

Arapeta spoke again:

'I am your father, Sam.'

Cliff watched Sam struggling, trying to choose between him and Arapeta. It seemed that a thousand years went past before Sam finally sighed and began to stroke his father's head.

'No, Sam —'

But all his life Sam had been obedient. All his life the one thing he had wanted was for his father to love him. No matter what his father was like, the template of his authority could not be broken. No matter what his people were like, he was, after all, Maori.

And Cliff saw that he and Sam were in Te Po, tumbling through the darkness. He heard Sam cry out, *You must go back. Let go, damn you.* Ahead was the entrance to Te Kore, The Void. It was a black hole and stars were showering into it. And Sam was calling to any gods who were listening: *The price is mine alone to pay. If there is any sacrifice to be made, then I will make it.* With one quick surge of strength he kicked at Cliff and sent him spinning away — and passed alone through the gateway.

And Cliff knew that he had lost.

'I want you to leave,' Sam said.

'Don't listen to Arapeta,' Cliff answered. 'He's fucked you in the head. He's playing mind games with you.'

Sam knew he had to give Cliff permission to leave:

*Hey, Harper! Do you know what haere ra means?*

Cliff remembered the chopper rescue, when Sam was down on the ground with Gonzalez and the Vietcong were closing in. He had seesawed back and forth across the treetops, moving through the upper foliage. All he had wanted to do was to see Sam.

'Take the rental car. Go,' Sam said.

Cliff made one last effort.

'You can't ask that of me. You know I've never left anybody behind. Never. I'll carry you out of here, Sam. Please come with me. Now.'

254

'I'll follow as soon as I can.'

Sam tried to put as much conviction into his words as he could. He had to get Cliff to go.

'You'll follow?'

Cliff's face was blanched with doubt and fear.

'I can't leave Dad like this,' Sam answered.

He tried to make it sound plausible, to work on an Illinois boy's sense of duty, of the right thing to do. Why did Cliff always have to be so stubborn?

'Okay, Sam. I'm leaving Auckland on Friday, two days from now. I have to check in at the airport at 8.30. My flight leaves at ten. I'll wait for you, and you better be there, you hear me? You hear me?'

Cliff's words were wild with passion, stormy with frustration. His eyes were glowing with rage and helplessness and, all of a sudden, he was punching at the air, punching at himself, whirling like a cornered animal, punching at whoever or whatever was out there in the darkness.

'Oh Jesus —'

Across the light he made a gesture of longing, of yearning.

Sam knew he had to be strong. He began talking to Cliff.

*Please don't cry, Cliff. We've got the rest of our days to be together. Just let me sort things out here and I'll be on my way to you.*

Cliff's fingers were a whirl of movement. He still wasn't convinced.

*I don't believe you, you bastard.*

*You have to believe me. You have to believe what I want to say to you now.*

Sam put all his heart into his words.

*I love you, Cliff.*

Cliff looked at Sam. His hair was spun with gold.

*You love me?*

Sam began to comfort him.

*From the first moment I saw you I loved you. I love all there is about you. Yours eyes, your laughter, your sexiness, the way you care for me, the way you are, everything. We've come too far together to let anything stop us now.*

Cliff began to sigh and nod his head. He wiped at his tears with his left sleeve. Looked in his pockets for a handkerchief. Couldn't find one, so blew his nose on the tail of his shirt. Looked at Sam again.

*I want you to promise me that you'll come to me.*

His finger movements were stubborn, insistent.

*Okay, damn you, I promise. But don't you understand? You're in my heart and nobody will be able to take you out. You're there forever.*

Still Cliff wasn't budging. With frustration, Sam began picking up stones from the roadway, hurling them at Cliff.

'Go, you stubborn Yankee arsehole.'

Cliff began to back away, shocked. He made an angry gesture of acceptance. With a cry he reached his hands around his neck and broke the cord from Tunui a te Ika. He threw the greenstone towards Sam. It twisted and tumbled, catching fire and turning into a flaming bird.

Sam caught the pounamu. He looked dully at it.

'Bring it back to me, Sam,' Cliff ordered. 'You son of a bitch, you bring it back to me. You hear? Bring it back.'

He pointed at Sam. *You.*

The sound of a helicopter gunship hovering.

Cliff pointed at himself. *Me.*

The rotors slicing at the sun.

Cliff put his two thumbs together, thumbs up. *Love you.*

Then he saluted and was gone.

--------- 3 ---------

Auntie Pat sighed and closed her eyes.

'Cliff was right, of course. Sam should have gone with him right then. But after the fight with Dad, I think Sam made up his mind not to join him.'

'Why not?' I asked.

'It all goes back to the question I asked you when I came to Wellington,' Auntie Pat answered. 'What matters most, Michael, being Maori or being gay?'

'I can remember replying nobody should be made to choose —'

Auntie Pat pointed a finger at me.

'But you did choose, Michael. You ran away. You went to Wellington. As for Sam, he stayed. By staying he elected to honour his father and his culture. I think it was only during the whipping that Sam began to change his mind —'

My blood ran cold. 'The whipping?'

'I told you once,' Auntie Pat continued, angry that I had not picked up on the point, 'that your grandfather was worse, much worse than your father. For him, everything was absolute. Either black or white. The truth or a lie. Right or wrong. And if you had done wrong, justice demanded that you be punished —'

The whipping began the day after Cliff left the farm. Throughout the day, Dad acted as if nothing had happened down at the barn — as if Cliff Harper had never been. He and Sam got up as usual in the morning and had breakfast. Jake, Jimbo and Bully came over to help brand the wild horses. With every hiss of the branding iron, Sam felt that Dad was as surely branding him as he was the mustangs. When night descended, so did Arapeta's wrath.

Florence was clearing the table when Arapeta made his move. He motioned her to sit down. He looked across at Sam.

'In traditional times, son, people like you never existed,' Arapeta said. 'They would have taken you outside, gutted you and left your head on a post for the birds to eat. Men like you abuse the sperm which is given to man for only one purpose. The very sperm that died inside my mates when they were killed on the battlefield. The sperm that is for the procreation of children. Don't you know that the sperm is sacred?'

Sam bowed his head. It always started like this. Ever since he'd been a boy, Dad had always begun his punishments here, at the dinner table, in front of Mum, Patty and Monty.

Arapeta banged on the table with so much force that some of the glasses fell to the floor, and the cutlery and dinner plates cracked against each other. Mum gave a small cry as Dad stood up and jabbed his finger at Sam.

'You are an affront to your iwi. You are an affront to all that I and my Maori Battalion mates fought for.'

His hurled accusations were like blows to Sam's head.

'Your ancestors are crying in their graves. Can you hear them, son? You are supposed to be a warrior. Instead, you are a woman. You deny yourself the rights, the mana, the sacredness of man. You also deny yourself all those privileges that come to a son born of rank. I am ashamed of you. I am disgusted with you.'

His spittle sprayed through the air. Yes, it always started like this. First the abusive words. And then —

Arapeta came around the table and jerked Sam's chair from beneath him. Sam fell. Arapeta pulled him up, made him stand straight — and kissed him.

'I love you, son, but I have to give you your punishment.'

Sam had been expecting to be punished. Now that the prospect was here, he was relieved — as long as it was done quickly. It was easier all round to get it over and done with. Then everything could get back to normal.

Sam walked out of the house and onto the verandah. He waited for Dad to tell Mum to stay in the house and then to follow him.

But this time it was different.

'Florence, I want you and the kids to come with me,' Dad said.

Mum began to plead, 'No.'

'They don't need to see this,' Sam said. 'It's always been just between you and me.'

Dad shook his head. That's when Sam felt a surge of rebellion.

The family walked down to the barn. The dogs began to bark and, in the paddock, the mustang herd started up a soft whinnying like the wind. The moon was bloated, full.

Dad stopped at the yards where, earlier that day, the horses had been broken in.

'Haramai e tama,' he said.

Sam stepped forward.

'Strip to the waist.'

Sam took off his shirt. His skin gleamed with the moon. Dad pushed him towards the gate. Made him turn. His back to the gate. His face looking forward. Sam's heart began to race with anxiety because this, again, was different. In the past, Dad always positioned him with his back to the whip. Before he could protest, Dad had tied ropes to his wrists and splayed him across the gate.

'What are you going to do, Daddy?' Patty cried out.

'Sam has been bad,' Florence said.

She watched as Arapeta went into the shed to get the bullwhip.

Sam shouted at them both. 'Mum, go now, take the kids with you. Mum?' But it was too late, because Dad was back.

With desperation, Sam called out again.

'Mum, all of you, turn around so you won't see. Put your hands over your eyes, okay? Dad, this has got nothing to do with them. Let them go.'

Dad's voice came out of some dark hole in space. 'They must stay.'

All of a sudden, Sam began to fight. When Arapeta came up to him and whispered into his left ear, 'Have you asked God's forgiveness?' Sam answered:

'Look, Dad, I chose to stay because you're my father. I choose to stay because I realise I have obligations to you and the iwi. Do what you have to do, but don't bring God into this.'

'So you don't want his forgiveness?'

'I've done what I've done, and you can punish me for that. But as for how I feel about what I've done —' The words slipped out so freely that they surprised Sam. 'How can I ask God's forgiveness for something that doesn't feel wrong?'

'It was a sin, son,' Dad answered. 'You feel no remorse? No shame?'

With a gasp of wonder, Sam realised that no, he didn't feel sorry. He didn't feel ashamed.

'But I haven't sinned,' he said.

It was the first time he had stood up for who he was and for what he had become — and he began to laugh. He was still laughing while Dad was laying out the whip, tracking its length across the ground. A snake, ready to strike.

'So you will not repent of your sin?' Arapeta asked.

Arapeta's eyes were popping with rage. He felt that Sam was not only laughing at God, but also at him.

'If there is one thing I will do tonight, it will be to whip that laughter out of you and teach you obedience.'

Once started, Arapeta could never be stopped. Once begun, whatever he had decided to do was done until it was over. Despite Sam's protestations he sent the lash to flick diagonally across Sam's chest. He sent it again to curl around Sam's neck like a lover's embrace. Once more he sent it, and Sam hissed as he felt its cool touch across his stomach.

'I am to be punished,' Sam realised, 'regardless of whether I am right or wrong, guilty or innocent.'

He called out to Arapeta.

'Dad, can't you see that I've stayed? I've stayed out of love for you —'

With a cry, Arapeta drew back his whip hand, and the whip began to sing its song.

'You say you love me when you have abused everything that I have given you? Your manhood, your tribe, your history? You disgust me, Son, you make me wish you had never been born.'

The whip arced through the air and sliced the moon in half. The second cut criss-crossed the night, pulling in meteors. The third added the upper horizon, shredding the night and letting the blood of Heaven spill out. At the fourth cut, the blood was trickling like crimson comets. By the fifth, it was running across the moon like a river.

'Oh, Holy Hone Hika . . .'

The whip opened Sam's skin and the pain arrested his body with shock. Florence was wailing. Patty and Monty were watching with horror.

Ten lashes — and at every lash, the rebellion in Sam rose until all he felt was a seething rage against Arapeta and all he represented. Then Arapeta put the whip down and Sam thought the punishment was over. Patty brought some water from the pump, and Mum began to untie the ropes.

'Leave him there,' Arapeta ordered. 'He still hasn't asked God's forgiveness.'

Mum began to wail.

'Sam, tell your father you're sorry. Tell him, and all this will be over. Lie if you have to.'

Sam smiled at her.

'I can't, Mum, I can't. Dad won't ever let me be who I want to be, I realise that now.'

He looked across the distance and held Arapeta's glance.

'I should have gone with Cliff.'

'You turn away from me, your own father? You still won't repent. So be it.'

No quarter asked. No quarter given. Ten more lashes. In the paddock the horses were racing in circles. The dogs had stopped barking and were whimpering, pulling at their chains, trying to huddle in the furthest corner of their kennels. As he was wavering between consciousness and unconsciousness, Sam remembered a story from his days at Bible Class. It was about the great battle in Heaven between God and the Archangel Satan. God's angels had won the battle and, at the peace talks, God said to Satan, 'If you will bow down to me, I will forgive you and you may stay. But if you will not, you will be banished to Hell —'

Arapeta was there once more.

'Will you give me obedience, Son. Will you repent?'

Sam shook his head. He had his answer ready.

'I won't bow down to you,' he said. 'I would rather rule in Hell than serve you in Heaven.'

He fainted. For how long, he didn't know. But through the haze of pain and sadness, he hear Mum shouting:

'No, Arapeta. No more. No more.'

'Get out of the way, Florence. You too, Patty —'

'No,' Mum said again. 'You'll have to kill me first —'

Sam saw Mum fighting with Dad. But he must have been imagining it because Mum never ever fought with . . .

Sam felt something like soft warm rain splashing on his face. He sighed because it must all be over, and it was so warm, so warm.

But Mum was still screaming and Sam realised something was terribly wrong. He shook himself awake and put his left arm to shield himself against the rain to see what was happening. He started to shiver with grief.

*This can't be happening. Please let it be just a dream.*

Dad was standing above him. He had unbuttoned his trousers. With a cry of horror, Sam was rolling out from beneath the arc of Arapeta's piss.

'You animal,' Florence said to Arapeta.

Her eyes were filled with loathing.

Disbelievingly, Sam wiped his face clean. The world had tipped over into insanity.

'Dad, what have you done to me?'

Arapeta buttoned up his trousers.

'You are no longer my son or a man,' he said. 'It should have been you, not Turei, who came back in that lead-lined coffin.'

He sighed and, in a moment of tenderness, kissed Sam on both cheeks.

'Go now, Sam. May God have mercy —'

Auntie Pat's mouth was open in a soundless scream.

'For thirty years,' she said, 'I have lived with that night on my conscience. When Dad did that to Sam he exiled him, banished him forever. Sam was moaning, almost driven mad. We took him back to the house and bathed him and put ointment on his wounds. But the punishment had gone far deeper than skin. Sam said to us, 'I have to go, Mum, I have to go, Patty. Dad's left me without a country. I haven't a place here anymore. I'm going to meet up with Cliff.'

'It was Mum who organised everything. On the day that Cliff was due to leave Auckland she rang George and told him to lend Sam his car. She took Sam into town to collect it. As he left I flung my arms around him and told him I loved him.'

Auntie Pat's eyes were streaming with tears.

'I think it happened about five in the evening. Sam was two hours out of Auckland. He had almost reached the intersection where the Tauranga highway connects with Highway One at the bottom of the Bombay Hills. It was Friday night and traffic was heavy — people wanting to get home, big trucks from the port of Tauranga trying to get to Auckland during the rush hour. There was an accident involving a truck and another car — and Sam. A really bad pile-up. And Sam . . . Sam . . . was killed.'

Auntie Pat has always disliked close physical contact. But she was crying so much that I had to put my arms around her. She started screaming and screaming.

'Leave me alone. It wasn't my fault, I didn't mean to do it —'

Over and over again.

———— 4 ————

That evening, sleeping at Auntie Pat's, I dreamed the dream that always had me waking up screaming. But something was different about it. I was an onlooker and not involved in the dream. I saw a young man stumbling along a never-ending road. There was a thrumming sound. Something was coming from out of the darkness behind him. The young man stopped. He looked back down the road. I knew what it was. I cried out to the young man:

*Run.*

You know what it's like in recurring nightmares. The adrenalin starts to pump. The fear turns your blood to ice. You moan and thresh. Did you really think that the nightmare had ended? Foolish, oh you were so foolish! Yet again the nightmare has pounced on you when you were least expecting it.

The young man began to run but he could only move in slow motion. I tried to help him, crying out to him, *Come on, come on.* Faster. Faster. I heard myself moaning with helplessness, my pores popping with explosions of fear.

I saw the stallion. Eyes of fire. Hooves arcing showers of sparks like flints. Then it was no longer coming down the road but circling him with tight rings of flame like a noose being tightened. Thrum, thrum, thrum. Suddenly it was there, in front of the young man. It reared on its hind legs and plunged down on him.

Only it wasn't the stallion. It was a truck speeding through the night.

I woke up crying out the young man's name:

'Uncle Sam, *no.*'

The next morning, Auntie Pat took me to Gisborne Airport to catch my plane back to Wellington. Her face was calm and I thought I had never seen her look so beautiful. In telling Uncle Sam's story, she had delivered herself of thirty years of guilt, denial and pain.

The boarding call was made. I kissed Auntie Pat on the cheek. She smiled at me.

'Yes,' she said, 'you do look like him.'

It was then that I decided:

'Auntie, I'm going to Canada soon. I think I'll stop off in Chicago —'

'You'll try to find Cliff Harper?'

'Yes.'

Auntie Pat flung herself into my arms.

'Thank you, Michael,' she said. 'That's the final thing to do, isn't it? Find Cliff, find him. Even after all these years you know what still haunts me? That Cliff didn't know Sam was on his way to the airport. We must make up for what happened to Sam and set everything right.'

I walked to the plane. I heard Auntie Pat calling to me.

'Cliff has to know. Find him. Tell him.'

# PART FIVE

# Finding Cliff Harper

CHAPTER SIXTEEN

——— 1 ———

*May God have mercy.*

I returned to Wellington on Monday morning. All the way back on the plane I kept thinking over what Auntie Pat had told me about Uncle Sam, Cliff and Grandfather Arapeta. In particular, I couldn't get Grandfather's words, 'May God have mercy', out of my mind. I had heard or read them before — but where? Then I remembered. They were the last words in Uncle Sam's diary, but they weren't in Uncle Sam's handwriting. Had Grandfather written them? If so, why? As a last-minute act of regret, perhaps? Of penance after Sam had died? I pictured grandfather going through Sam's belongings after he'd had news about the accident. Coming across the diary. Taking up the pen, his hand quivering with emotion, and writing in it.

I tried to fit the memory of my grandfather around such an act of contrition.

'Go and kiss your Grandad,' Dad would say whenever we visited him, Nana Florence and Auntie Pat. At that time, Dad had shifted Mum, Amiria and me from the old homestead, and we lived about ten kilometres away — at the present location of Mahana Wines. Auntie Pat had elected to stay behind to look after Grandad and Nana.

Grandad was a dark man with wrinkles which looked as if they had been sliced into him with a knife. His best years were behind him. He'd transformed the farmland into vineyard country and passed the running of it over to Dad. He was bedridden from a stroke, and half of his face

267

had collapsed. His eyes were always watery, and he had a permanent drool of saliva from the right side of his mouth. Perhaps the stroke had tamed his temper. All I know is that I associate him with Sundays — the days we visited — and that I always kissed him on his left cheek or forehead to avoid his sticky slick of drool. I think he was proud of me — and he sometimes allowed me to hold his medals and swagger stick.

Grandfather died when I was eight. I thought:

'Hurrah, I've got the day off school.'

His tangi was huge, with representation from all the tribes of Maoridom. His erstwhile opponent, General Collinson, now retired, turned up with Army officials from Wellington. I heard grand speeches extolling his virtues and recalling his great army career. His mates from the Maori Battalion did a haka — a raging, eyeball-rattling, vein-popping expression of their grief. While the men were shouting their anger, the women set up an intense wailing, the likes of which I have never heard since. Throughout the haka, Nana Florence and Auntie Pat sat by the side of Grandad's coffin, stroking his hair and face.

Surely somebody who people revered like that could redeem himself by being sorry for what he'd done to his son. Surely —

––––––– 2 –––––––

Roimata was waiting for me at Wellington airport.

'Have you got a passport?' she asked. 'Is it valid? Our trip to Canada's only a week away and I want to make sure you're on the plane with me!'

We went immediately to the office of Toi Maori where we were scheduled for a strategic planning session with her trustees. Our nickname for them was the Maori Jedi and we called the chairman Obi Wan Kanobi. His name was really Piripi Jones, a farmer from Eketahuna, and his gentle manner belied his history as a Maori activist from way back.

'Okay, people,' he said. 'Let's hear how our submission has fared. Roimata, do you want to kick off?'

Roimata preened and purred.

'I'll ask my colleague Michael, whom I asked to write my report, to brief you.'

I smiled at the lovely Roimata with my teeth.

'As you know,' I began, 'our submission proposed that Maori art was

268

too important to be funded via the Arts Council and that we should receive our allocation direct from government. Despite good support from the Minister of Maori Affairs, the Arts Council have managed to persuade the Prime Minister our proposal is dangerous. We have a fight on our hands.'

'A fight?' Obi Wan Kanobi asked.

'They're spouting the usual arguments. They say their own funding framework accommodates Pakeha and Maori, so why should there be a separate funding structure —'

'The issue is that Pakeha still get all the funding and we get the crumbs,' Roimata added.

'They say that if Maori move outside the framework, it is tantamount to separate development —'

'The usual apartheid argument,' Roimata said.

She could never resist tacking on comments just to show she was boss.

'And they've asked how can you split arts funding along racial grounds when some of our Maori artists are ballet dancers, opera singers or actors?'

'Worst of all,' Roimata added, the fire of battle gleaming in her eyes, 'is that the Council have marshalled some of their friendly Maoris to speak against us. That funding should be on the basis of quality, not race. Sure, a Maori artist can succeed within the Pakeha model, but as long as he paints, sings or performs like the Pakeha.'

Roimata was steaming, and the Jedi Knights knew it. They took on board our briefing, humming their words, and debated the issue between them. Obi Wan Kanobi turned to me:

'What's your recommendation, Michael?'

I decided to give it to him straight from the hip.

'It's time for us to walk the talk. Why should the Arts Council be the only ones to talk to the Prime Minister? They're probably hoping to stall us and expecting that we'll write a response. No, we must get into direct action. If we don't, we won't secure separate funding in this year's Budget.'

'And you, Roimata?' Obi Wan Kanobi asked. 'Is it your recommendation that we go directly to the Prime Minister?'

Roimata was looking at me with stars in her eyes.

'Yes,' she nodded. 'Michael has taken the words right out of my mouth.'

Obi Wan Kanobi leaned back in his chair. He never minced his words either.

'When do you two get back from Canada? Make an appointment with the Prime Minister. Let's try to cut through all the bullshit.'

The Maori Jedi nodded in agreement.

'Those people in Canada had better watch out,' Piripi added, eyes twinkling. 'Aren't you both going over there to speak about the same issues as are happening here? They better start running for shelter. You two are dynamite!'

———— 3 ————

It wasn't until mid-afternoon that I was able to address the business of finding Cliff Harper. To be truthful, I had needed the time to think about it. There was a certain amount of sentimentality driving the idea, but there was more. Auntie Pat herself had referred to the need to 'put something right'. My reasons, I suspected, were more complicated. So long denied knowledge about Uncle Sam, I wanted to do something for him almost as a way of recognising myself.

By four o'clock, the rational part of me had begun to set up counter-arguments to proceeding. Cliff Harper would be in his mid-fifties by now. He might not even be alive. He might not welcome a call from somebody he didn't know about something that had happened thirty years ago.

There was also the matter of whether I could trust Uncle Sam's diary and my interpretation of what had been written in it. Could I even trust Auntie Pat's version of events? Uncle Sam may have been in love with a man called Cliff Harper, but had Cliff Harper been in love with him? Did he even exist! Perhaps Uncle Sam had made him up. What if Cliff Harper couldn't remember Sam after all these years?

I guess that last question was the one I really feared. But I had to chance it. I had to believe in Uncle Sam's diary. I wanted to believe in it. I saw Sam and Cliff Harper in Madame Godzilla's, Sam impishly moving his fingers and Harper spraying beer from his mouth in astonishment:

*You can read me?*

*Didn't you know? Sign language, like basketball, is a Maori tradition.*

Then Sam turned to *me* and winked.

*That's right, isn't it, Michael?*

I closed my eyes, and felt ashamed of myself. I knew I had to do this for Uncle Sam. If I didn't do anything, his story would indeed end on a road thirty years ago. Who knows? Perhaps there was also a part of Cliff Harper that was still waiting at the airport for a man who would never arrive —

I chastised myself, 'Michael, get over yourself.' Counted to three. Picked up the telephone and dialled directory service:

'Could you give me the telephone number of the American Embassy?'

A few seconds later the Embassy's answering service clicked on. The usual instructions: If you want to speak to the Ambassador's secretary, press 1, if you want the Political Division press 2, if your query is about entry into the United States press 3, if you want to speak to someone in the US Information Agency press 4, if you want to speak to the operator (i.e. a real live person) please hold.

I decided to wait for the real live person.

'Good morning,' the operator's voice said. 'How may we help you?'

'I would like to speak with someone who can tell me how I go about locating an American citizen who was a helicopter pilot during the Vietnam War.'

My mouth and throat had gone dry.

'Let me see,' the operator said. 'Let me put you through to Mr Harding, the counsellor in our Defence office, and do have a nice day.'

A few blips, whirs and bleeps later, Mr Harding was on the line. He was pleasant and helpful.

'Now your best bet would be to get as much information as you can and then get in touch with the American Vietnam Veterans Association in Washington. I guess you'll be wanting the fax, phone number and address, huh?'

'Thanks. Yes.'

'All rightee. Here we go.'

Half an hour later, I was talking to Frank De Castro in the Vietnam Veterans' office in Washington.

'Uh,' Mr De Castro asked, 'can you give me any further information? Company number? Battalion? Head of Command?'

I ruffled through Uncle Sam's papers.

'That's all I have,' I said. 'I don't even know if Cliff Harper's still alive.'

'Well,' Mr De Castro paused. 'You say this Cliff Harper came from the

Chicago area? Tell you what, ring the Chicago Vets office direct. I'll get back to you possibly tomorrow with the number. Thank you for calling.'

I put the telephone down. I felt elated. I had put things in motion. Wheels were starting to turn. Something unfinished from thirty years ago was moving towards possible closure. I saw Cliff Harper's face — and something about his looks struck flint. For a moment I couldn't place my finger on what it was. I remembered Auntie Pat's reference to her favourite scene in *Till the End of Time*. The movie was set just after the Second World War, and was about a young discharged American GI returning to his home town. It was just the sort of movie that Auntie Pat's sentimental heart responded to:

'Here he comes! Here he comes!'

A bus and a young man getting off.

'That's him —'

The same crooked grin. The same matinee idol look of disarming carelessness.

When Cliff Harper arrived on the bus in Gisborne to see Uncle Sam he was wearing his American Airforce uniform.

'Looking for me?' he asked.

He must have looked to Auntie Pat just like Guy Madison.

———— 4 ————

By the time I reached home it was after six. The night was dark and drenched with impending rain. I had an hour to change before my date with Carlos. First we'd go to Jordan's for a drink, then I had booked us a table at a new restaurant at the top of Cuba Street and then —

I put the key into the door. Flushed with expectation of what the night might bring, I ran up the stairs two at a time. I reached the landing — and that's when I realised that things were missing from the flat.

A painting which used to hang on the wall of the stairwell. A piece of pottery Jason and I had purchased at an art gallery.

My mood changed. I began to shiver. I walked into the kitchen and opened the cupboards. One of the dinner sets was gone. In the bedroom closet, bedding, linen and towels had disappeared — small items but, oh, the big gaps they left behind. All gone. All the signs were there of the physical removal of everything that was Jason's or associated with him.

He had done this while I was in Gisborne — Graham had probably come with him. While I was out. They'd come in like thieves — and I felt violated. Not even the courtesy of a note to say they'd been.

I sat down on the bed, trying to take it all in. The telephone rang and, for a moment, I hoped it was Carlos cancelling out.

'Hello,' I said.

'Is that you, Michael?'

It was George.

'I had a call from Patty earlier,' he said. 'Is it true? Are you really going to try to find Woody Woodpecker?'

'Yes, it's true.' I wished George would go away.

'Good,' he said. 'Anne-Marie will be pleased.'

I was puzzled. Who was Anne-Marie?

'She was the girl involved in that car accident when Sam got killed. Did you know he was driving my car? Well, during the police investigation after the accident, that's when I met Anne-Marie. I still see her now and then, when she comes over the hill from Upper Hutt to visit her daughter in Porirua. She's never forgotten that night — or Sam. She still feels guilty about what happened.'

'Why guilty?' I asked.

The telephone went silent, and I thought we'd been disconnected. Then — was that George sobbing?

'God dammit,' he growled as he blew his nose. 'We've all felt guilty about Sam. All of us, for our own reasons. Patty, for what she did. Anne-Marie, for the accident. Me, for —'

I felt as if something was squeezing my heart. 'For what, George?'

His voice burst like a grenade over the phone.

'We were supposed to take utu,' he said. 'We were supposed to avenge Turei's death. But we didn't. Neither Sam nor I made another kill when we were in Vietnam. That's why the owl tracked us down when we returned to New Zealand. Why didn't it take me, Michael? Why did it have to take Sam? I'm a cursed man, Michael. Everybody around me dies —'

I put the telephone down. Went to have a shower. My mind was in a whirl. There was so much to deal with. All the puzzles in Sam's life were getting bigger. And in my own life, just trying to work out what was happening around me was taking all my strength. I huddled under the water for what seemed like hours. I didn't want to think about anything. I wanted the world to go away for a while and leave me alone. By the time I got out of the shower it was almost seven — and the doorbell was ringing. I grabbed the bathrobe and ran downstairs.

'You're on time,' I said, as I opened the door.

But it wasn't Carlos. Instead, Jason was standing in the rain.

'Jason, this is the wrong time,' I said. 'If you stay, I'll say or do something I'll regret.'

'This won't take long,' he said. His face was as grim as mine must have been. 'I've been around to collect the rest of my things —'

'So I've noticed. It really hacks me off that you did this without letting me know.'

Jason flared. 'I told you that you would have to pay,' he said. 'And this is just the beginning, Michael. I'm taking you to court —'

I leaned against the door jamb. I gave an incredulous laugh.

'What for!'

'I'm legally entitled to half of everything that I put into our relationship. Half of everything in the flat, not just my own stuff. Half of everything we had in our joint bank account.'

I stood staring at him. Rain squalls were sweeping across Wellington like spiders' threads. Was this the way all relationships ended? With this extracting of every pound of flesh? I made a gesture of helplessness.

'All you needed to do was to ask,' I answered. 'You can have everything if you want —'

'I want my day in court,' Jason answered. 'And I'm going to have it.'

I felt myself losing my cool. I flipped.

'Give me your set of keys, Jason. Give them to me now. If you want to come back for anything else, you can arrange an appointment.'

At that moment Carlos arrived, the headlights of his car sweeping over us. As soon as he stepped out of the car and walked across to me, Jason put it together.

'You arsehole,' he said. 'You couldn't even wait a week, could you?'

Jason threw the keys at me. They clanged against the door and fell to the ground. Carlos gave him a quizzical look as he shoved past. He bent down and picked up the keys.

'Are these yours?' Carlos asked. He was good-humoured, relaxed.

'Yes,' I answered. 'Thanks.'

'Do you always answer the door half undressed?'

I was trying to put myself back together again. I didn't know what to say. Carlos gave me a hint.

'I think,' he said, 'that this is the moment when you're supposed to ask me if I want to come in and look at your CD collection.'

'And what do you say?'

I was warming to his being there. Carefree. Not asking any questions. Uncomplicated.

'I say I'd love to.'

'And then what do I say?' I asked.

To Hell with everything. It was time for me to live the moment.

'You show me into the house and along the corridor to where the bedroom is —'

'No, that's where the kitchen is,' I said. 'I make you a cup of coffee and we talk and —'

'So the bedroom's upstairs?'

'Yes.'

Carlos was leaning in to me, staring me down with his sexy eyes. God, he was so pretty, like a mustang, nostrils flaring, impudently posing against the darkness.

'Let's skip the coffee,' he said. 'Let's fast forward to the part where we go up the stairs.'

Carlos had his hands under the bathrobe and around my waist. I gasped at their coldness as he slid them between my thighs.

'Is that the remote?' he asked.

He pressed it. Looked at the stairs.

'Stairs are *good.*'

Around two in the morning, I nuzzled at Carlos's armpits. He had such silky hair there and, when it was wet, it curled into tight, dark fronds like a fern. With a murmur he moved away and I was able to get out of the tangle we were in and go to the kitchen for a glass of water. On the way I saw the light winking on the telephone, and picked up the message.

'Hello?'

An unfamiliar voice. A woman's — quavery, old.

'Is this the residence of Michael Mahana? My name is Anne-Marie

Davidson. I understand from George that you are the nephew of Sam Mahana —'

Of course, the woman involved in Uncle Sam's car accident.

'Would you be so kind as to come to see me when it is convenient for you? George tells me you may be seeing Sam's friend when you go to Canada. I have something which belongs to him. Thank you.'


Later that morning, when I awoke, Carlos was gone. A note was taped to the bedroom door:

'Congratulations! You threw three sixes in a row, keep your hotel on Mayfair and pick up a Chance card. The card reads: You still owe me a meal. I could eat a horse, so I'm coming by your office at midday and you can take me to lunch. Carlos.'

I smiled at the message. Remembered the earlier call from Anne-Marie Davidson and telephoned her back.

'Hello, Mrs Davidson? I'm Michael Mahana. Yes, this afternoon would be convenient. Three o'clock? Yes, I have a car —'

———— 5 ————

I had the morning to myself at Toi Maori. Roimata was out of the office giving a lecture entitled 'Maori Sovereignty in the Arts' at Victoria University. Not that I minded. Things were coming at me so fast that I didn't know whether to keep standing or duck.

For instance, no sooner had I sat down than Auntie Pat telephoned.

'Have you found Cliff Harper yet?' she asked.

'Auntie, it takes you thirty years to tell me and then you expect me to find Cliff Harper in a couple of days? Give me a break.'

Next on the line was a surprise caller — Margo, Jason's therapist — and she was rocking.

'Do you realise what you've done?' she asked. 'By moving so quickly to a new boyfriend —' she could hardly keep the sarcasm out of her voice '— you've destroyed all Jason's confidence in himself.'

'Margo, I haven't a clue what you're talking about.'

'You've put him back ten years —'

I decided to short-circuit her.

'Look, Margo, what have you done to Jason?'

'I'm sorry, Michael. You know I can't discuss my client with you. I gave Jason permission to explore who he is and who he wants to be. You've taken that permission away from him and we're back at the beginning again. Just when Jason thought he was winning —'

'Oh, so that's it,' I interrupted. 'Well, Margo, I've had enough of your mumbo jumbo. You go ahead and help Jason take control of his life. Obviously, you've helped him to the point where he's been able to give me the flick. Well, whether you like it or not, and whether Jason likes it or not, we had a great relationship. It was based on love, not on dependency. As for me, I'm nobody's punching bag. I've got my own life to get on with.'

I put the phone down. I thought about my forthcoming visit to Mrs Anne-Marie Davidson. What would she tell me to add to Uncle Sam's story? And when would I hear from Frank De Castro in the Vietnam Veterans Office, Washington?

At 11.30, the call from Washington arrived.

'Okay,' Mr De Castro began. 'Here's the number for our office in Chicago. Good luck. I hope you find who you're looking for.'

I dialled, and Mrs Ada Sylvester answered my call.

'Gosh, honey,' Mrs Sylvester said, 'you're not leaving us much time, are you! When did you say you're leaving Noo Zealan'? In five days? We better get a move on, right? Lemme see, I'll run a check on our database.'

'Thank you, Mrs Sylvester. I hope this isn't too much trouble.'

'Call me Ada, and no, it'll only be trouble if I can't find Mr Harper on our master list.'

Ada was cracking gum, sending small explosions down the line, and giving me a running commentary on everything she was doing:

'I'm going into our database now. I'm entering Mr Harper's name. Do you spell that H-A-R-P-E-R?' Gum crack, double crack, click of teeth, crack. 'O-kay, so I am now into the haitches — and how is the weather down there in Noo Zealan'? I hear it's mighty pretty.'

'You should come down and see us sometime,' I answered. 'It's summer right now and the weather is really warm.'

'Honey —' crack, crack, click clickety click — 'you give me the money and I'll give you the time. So here we are, Harper, Harper, Harper B, Harper C. We're freezing over here so you better bring yourself a nice warm coat. God Almighty, these old computers are mighty slow today, Harper D —'

I could feel the tension rising. I imagined Ada in front of a screen, scrolling down a list of names. Every man on her list had gone to Vietnam. They all had stories to tell.

'Damn, gone past him,' Ada said. 'So here I go, I'm pressing the Page Down button to get me back to the Cs. Got it! Here we go. Harper Carlos, Harper Cecil, Harper Charles. Sorry it's taking so long, honey, I'm scrolling as fast as I can. Hey, did you ever know that song, "Harper Valley PTA?" Bobbie Gentry, she was one of the greats. You like country & western music, honey? O-kay, we're coming in for a landing now. Harper Christian, Harper Clarence, Harper Conal, Hatfield, Havers, Hawley, Hay —'

I felt disappointment well inside me.

'Let me just check again now,' Ada said. 'Nope, honey.'

Her voice was kind and sympathetic.

'He could have moved. Thirty years is a long time in the life of a Vet. Are you sure he's still alive?'

'No, I'm not sure.'

Pause, click click, crack.

'Listen, honey, you leave this little mystery with me. I'll try to get some information on Mr Harper. I was always a sucker for a man with an accent like yours. I'll get in touch with Mr Harper's Command. Send out an All-Points Alert. If he's alive, if he's in this country, we'll locate him. Call me next week, okay? And do have a nice day.'

————— 6 —————

I leaned on my elbows. So where to now, Michael? I would just have to wait — and hope. When I looked up, I saw that Roimata had returned from giving her lecture. Carlos had also arrived, talking on his cellphone. He saw me, grinned, waved and made signs that he would only be a couple of minutes.

Roimata watched Carlos, arms folded. She knew we had got it on, and she was furious.

'How could you! I had plans for you, and now you've ruined them! Here I was, thinking that Jason splitting from you would give you the

278

chance to decolonise yourself, regain your sovereignty as a Maori gay man, and what do I find? You've gone and colonised yourself again.'

Sometimes it was very difficult to know just where Roimata was coming from — as if she had dropped the first three pages of a speech and gone straight to page four.

'Roimata,' I sighed, 'what are you talking about?'

'All your White lovers!' she said. 'And now look at this one, this Carlos. Straight off the White gay assembly line and out of a White gay boy magazine. Can't you see what's happening? Yet again you've gone for an assemblage of body parts, pumped-up pecs and penis. Sure, I can see why that boy would lift your skirt. Well, he may have a six-pack and he certainly does pack a lot of lunch — but when are you going to go for mana Maori!'

Roimata always had a loud voice. It carried out to where Carlos, who had finished his phone call, was sitting. He stood up, came to the door and waited for her to finish her rant. He was very pleasant about it all.

'I thought you liked me,' Carlos pouted. 'And, actually, you'll be pleased to know that I do have Maori blood.'

Roimata had the grace to appear flustered. As for me, did Carlos really think I believed him? Green eyes, blond chin stubble, white skin from the tip of his shaven head to his toes. Ha.

'So how much Maori blood have you got?' I asked sceptically.

'My grandmother was Parehuia Te Ariki. My tribe is Kai Tahu and I come from Otakou.'

That really had me floored. I stared at Roimata and saw her mouth was hanging wide open. Then she put up her left hand, Carlos put up his, and they did a high five.

'Put it there, brother!' Roimata laughed and turned to me. 'Hey, Michael,' she said, 'I like this boy.'

But she wagged a finger at Carlos in warning.

'If you know what's best for you, don't come between me and —' She pointed at me. 'Him. And don't forget I'm from Porourangi and you Kai Tahu are descended from Porourangi's younger brother, Tahu Potiki, so I'm from the senior line! Apart from which I saw Michael first and I've known him longer than you have.'

I thought that Roimata was referring to our close friendship. Carlos

279

knew better. He looked at Roimata closely and nodded in tacit understanding.

'Done,' he said.

Later, at lunch, I quizzed Carlos more about his ancestry.

'I thought you already knew,' he said. 'I work for the Maori Fisheries Commission. They employ me to go up and down the country checking on fisheries quotas. That's why I'm on the phone all the time. When I'm not doing that I like to go out dancing or, even better, spearfishing.'

'Well, there's lots I don't know about you, obviously,' I answered.

Like how hungry he was. He was wolfing down his food.

'Yeah, well, I know a lot about you,' Carlos said. 'I've had my eye on you for some time. But you were always with somebody else.'

Uh oh. 'So this is not just about sex, is it,' I asked. 'Listen, I don't want any complications. Right now I've had all I want of —'

Carlos put down his knife and fork and smiled very dangerously.

'I want you to put your hands on the table, lay them flat and keep them where I can see them. Do it now.'

He sounded like the bad guy in a Jean-Claude Van Damme movie so I did as I was told. Under the table I felt his fingers undoing my zip. I began to protest, and moved my hands to stop him.

'Oh, no you don't,' Carlos said. 'Keep them on the table.'

His fingers dipped, opened and *pulled*. My groan must have been heard by everyone in the restaurant. Satisfied, Carlos went back to eating.

'Now what were we talking about?' he asked. 'Was it about your needing me to come to see you tonight?'

He chopped a very large piece of steak and lobbed it into his mouth. Chewed. Swallowed in a single gulp. Looked at me with those big innocent eyes of his.

My answer was a strangulated squeak.

'Okay.'

Back at Roimata's office, I looked at my watch: 2.30. Time for me to go out to meet Anne-Marie Davidson. I gave Roimata a kiss on the cheek. She held my face a fraction and smiled.

'I like your Carlos,' she said. 'So will Tane Mahuta. Did I tell you he's back in town tomorrow? Are you free for lunch?'

The Noble Savage. Yes, it would be great to see him.

'Sure,' I answered.

Then I was out of there, into the carpark and driving away from the city — and it was so good to see the sea, the highway curving around Kaiwharawhara, and the Hutt Valley opening up ahead. For a while I raced the suburban train. Two small children were crowded at a carriage window, waving at me. They made me remember my sister Amiria and me, and how we had been on those days before —

The train disappeared into a tunnel.

When I had a mother and father —

Then, there the train was again, away in the distance. Two small arms waving.

A mother and a father . . .

Sometimes it happens like this. These glimpses of the past. Before you know it, you're stopping the car and weeping because, no matter how strong you are, separation really hurts. It sucks.

––––––– 7 –––––––

Three o'clock. Right on time.

Mrs Davidson was widowed and living in a two-bedroomed unit, one of six in a tidy row in a quiet Upper Hutt suburb. She was a keen gardener by the look of her roses. They were beautiful, rich red and carefully staked.

Ah well, here goes.

I rang the bell. Heard it go ding dong. A young woman, around my age, answered the door.

'Yes?' she asked.

A voice called from behind her.

'That'll be Mr Mahana, love. Do show him in.'

The young woman asked me to come in. The doorway opened onto a large open-plan sitting room with a breakfast bar. Mrs Davidson had her back to me. She was preparing a tea tray for my visit. She picked it up, turned with a smile on her face and began to introduce me to the young woman at the door.

'Thank you for coming, Mr Mahana. This is my daughter Fran. She just popped over to see me and —'

Mrs Davidson froze. She looked at me and:

'Oh, my.'

She gave a helpless cry. The tea tray fell to the floor. She swayed, and her daughter reached her just in time to catch her.

'Fran, love, I have to sit down.'

Fran took her to an armchair. As she settled her mother, plumping up the cushions to make her comfortable, she glared at me.

'I don't know who you are, or what this is about, but I want you to leave immediately.'

'No, love,' Mrs Davidson intervened. 'It's been so long. And this boy here, he looks just like Sam did. Sam was his uncle, love. He died in my arms. He was looking up at me, and I was holding him and then —'

She had been Anne-Marie Du Fresne in those days. She was twenty-five and worked as a nurse in Tauranga during the week, but she liked getting back to Auckland for the weekends. Tauranga was such a bore, with nothing to do on Fridays and Saturdays, and the boys weren't much cop either. She had bought a small car, an Austin Mini, which could get her up and over the Bombay Hills onto the Auckland motorway in a few hours.

'That Friday I was supposed to be on the afternoon shift but I swapped places with Joanne, one of the other nurses, and did the morning shift instead. This was because Barbara, a good friend of mine up in Auckland, had arranged a blind date for me to go to a ball in Auckland. The way she described him, he sounded like he was tall, dumb and single, which was how I liked my men in those days. I didn't want to settle down. I'd already been married once, and once was enough, thank you very much.

'What with one thing and another, I didn't get off my shift until two in the afternoon. I'd brought my ball gown with me and got changed, intending to drive straight to the cabaret in Auckland. Joanne did my hair for me, piling it all on top like Audrey Hepburn's in *My Fair Lady*. Well, it might have looked good on Audrey Hepburn but I must say I didn't think it did much for me! Joanne used a whole can of hairspray to keep it up there, and didn't we have a laugh when we realised that my car was so small that the hair couldn't fit! By the time we re-styled it, it was about 3.30 and I was running very late. So I zipped up my long dress, a sexy white thing down to the ankles, and said to Joanne, "I've got to go! Prince Charming's waiting!" I grabbed my high heels and ran barefoot through the hospital. Some of the male patients gave me a right royal send-off, the cheeky blighters —'

'Hey, Cinderella, take me to the ball!'

'Sorry, boys!' Anne-Marie laughed. 'I've already got my date for the night and he's on two legs, unlike all you lot.'

'It's not his legs you should worry about. It's what he's carrying between them you'll have to watch out for —'

'Especially in the waltz —'

'And watch out if he wants to dip in the foxtrot!'

Anne-Marie laughed again. In her white sequined dress she knew she looked gorgeous. She struck a pose at the front doors, blowing kisses to all and sundry.

'Jealousy will get you nowhere,' she said.

Then she was out into the cold night, looking for her keys in her bag, unlocking the door of the Mini and stepping in. A flick of the switch and she was off, careering out of the hospital car park.

On the main road she became aware of the darkness. She looked north and saw that grey clouds were broiling overhead. A few minutes later rain started to hit the windscreen. She put on the wipers and, a few seconds later, the headlights.

'I was making good time,' Mrs Davidson said, 'and had adjusted my driving to the road and the weather conditions. The traffic was pretty busy. That highway between Tauranga and Auckland has always been heavy with traffic. People heading up to Auckland for the weekend. Big trucks wanting to get back to their yards before they closed. Some fools trying to pass on bends or taking risks when there's oncoming traffic. I had one impatient driver tailgating me for quite a while and, when he passed, he pressed his horn almost as if to say I shouldn't be on the road with my little Mini. So I gave him the fingers. Anyway, the heater was working, the windscreen wipers were doing their job and I was feeling pretty good, and quite excited about a date with somebody I'd never met.

'Let me think, it must have been about quarter to five when I saw the crossroads where the Tauranga highway joins the main highway from Hamilton to Auckland. I was checking my lipstick in the rear-view mirror and humming to myself. I was going around a bend when I had the

283

puncture. I heard a bang and, next minute, the car was sliding all over the road. I managed to get it under control and pulled over to the side. At the time I didn't realise how dangerous my position was. On a bend. The rain and darkness. I kept waiting for somebody to slow down and help me. No such luck. There were certainly no gentlemen on the road that night! All those cars kept on streaming past, swerving to get around me, horns blaring. Mind you, who could blame them? The rain was really atrocious. So I thought to myself, "Oh, well, there's nothing for it, Anne-Marie, except to get out of the car and change the bloody tyre yourself." In one second I was drenched. My dress was soaked. My hairstyle flopped across my forehead like wet candyfloss. My shoes were ruined. But I got the spare tyre out, and the jack, and was just about to get to work when, among the stream of cars going past, one stopped. It's rear backing lights came on. It backed up fast. A young man jumped out. He was Maori. It was your Uncle Sam.'

'What the hell —'

Sam swore as he saw the car in front of him brake, swerve and narrowly avoid a small car that had broken down on the side of the highway. He braked too, swung hard on the steering wheel and, in the headlights, caught a glimpse of a woman in a white-sequined ballgown. She was struggling with a spare tyre. Her dress sparkled in the light and then was gone like small glowing stars falling to earth. For a split second he almost kept driving. He thought of Cliff, waiting at the airport, but then braked, reversed and switched off the ignition. He glanced quickly at his watch. He could spare five minutes. He got out of the car and ran through the rain.

'I could never resist a woman in a white dress.'

'Thank God,' Anne-Marie said. 'I was thinking that nobody would stop.'

'You look like a drowned cat,' Sam said. 'Why don't you go and sit in my car out of the rain. I'll have this done in a jiffy.'

'I think I'm past caring. I'll get the torch out of the glove box. You might need some light.'

'The sooner we get you off this bend the better,' Sam nodded.

With that, he was cranking the car up, slipping the jack underneath and unscrewing the wheel nuts. Anne-Marie came back and shone the light on the hub of the tyre. She saw Sam's face, the rain falling into it, as if he was transparent. He had a strong profile and lovely dark eyes.

'How come you're dressed like that?' Sam asked.

'I'm supposed to be going to a ball tonight,' Anne-Marie answered. 'I doubt my partner would want me to accompany him now. I mean, look at me.'

'You look gorgeous,' Sam said. 'If your boyfriend doesn't like you wet, ditch him and find somebody else. So what's your name?'

With a yank, Sam pulled the punctured tyre off the hub.

'Anne-Marie.'

'Pleased to meet you, Anne-Marie.'

Sam positioned the wheel. Reached for the screws and began to tighten them on.

'And you?' Anne-Marie asked.

'I'm Sam Mahana. I'm on my way to the international air terminal to meet up with my mate. I've got plenty of time.'

At that moment, another car stopped and backed. An elderly man stepped out with an umbrella and hazard light, and ran to join Sam and Anne-Marie.

'Goodness me,' he said. 'Are you just about done? I'd better go up the road a bit and try to get the traffic to slow down until you've finished.'

'But it was too late,' Mrs Davidson said. 'From out of the rain came one of those big long trucks with trailers. It was festooned with lights. I saw the old man almost disappear into them, almost as if the truck had eaten him up. Luckily he was able to leap to one side out of its way. I can still remember how the lights from the truck blazed on Sam. He was kneeling. He had the wheel brace in his hands. He was screwing one of the screws on the tyre. Then everything seemed to happen in slow motion. Sam cried out my name, "Anne-Marie." All of a sudden he was reaching for me. Picking me up. He threw me across the bonnet of the car and out of danger. I can remember, as I tumbled in the air, thinking how strong he was. I heard the screech of brakes. The klaxon of the truck blaring like an air-raid siren. I had a brief glimpse of Sam in its headlights. He was beating at something in the air. Then the truck slammed into my car, and Sam disappeared.

'I must have hit the ground at that point. When I stood up all I could

285

see was this mangled mess on the highway. The truck had stopped. Everywhere, traffic was stopping. I ran back. I couldn't see Sam at first and I thought, "Thank God, he's been thrown clear." Then I heard a groan and I saw him. The car was on top of him. I've seen accident victims before. I knew there was no way in which he was going to live —'

'God have mercy.'

Sam saw the headlights of the truck bearing down on him, and he remembered the owl on the night he and Cliff had driven from the wedding. The owl had cried out a name — Sam hadn't been too sure whose. Now he knew it had been his. He was glad that it wasn't Cliff's.

The truck hit him. It came out of the dark, blazing like a Christmas tree. The impact was loud, fast, blinding.

For a moment Sam thought, 'Why, that doesn't hurt at all.'

A second later his body was in agony as the truck shunted Anne-Marie's car over his chest. He tried to scream out with pain but found that he couldn't. He felt something squeezing at his heart and knew it was Death. He turned his head a little and saw Anne-Marie's shoes. She was crying out his name.

'Sam? Oh, God, Sam.'

He heard other footsteps. The elderly man. The truck driver slamming the door of his truck as he got out. All the sounds were magnified. He could hear them clear as crystal. He groaned.

'Oh, my God,' he heard Anne-Marie cry. 'He's under the car.'

Then she was there. Reaching for him. Sliding under, her face so close to his that he could have kissed her. Lifting his head onto her white dress. As she did so, something rattled inside his chest as if he was broken. He screamed when he heard it, the blood flying like spray and splattering Anne-Marie's dress.

'No —'

Anne-Marie tried to motion to him that it was nothing to worry about. Her eyes were streaming with tears.

'You shouldn't be the one who's crying,' Sam said. 'After all, I'm the one who's stuck under your car. Unless — you want to change places? And you mustn't cry. I hate it when a pretty girl cries.'

He tried to reach up and wipe Anne-Marie's tears away but ended up in another paroxysm of spouting blood.

'Oh, God!' he screamed. 'It hurts. It *hurts*.'

The elderly man whispered to Anne-Marie:

'The truck driver has just radioed for help.'

Sam shook his head.

'That's not going to do any good,' he said. 'I've served in Vietnam and I know when a man's bought it. And I've bought it.'

Then death really squeezed Sam's heart. In panic, he turned to Anne-Marie.

'There's a man you must find. He's waiting at the airport. I was supposed to meet him there. His name is Cliff —'

Sam's voice was getting weaker. The name sounded like Chris.

'Please find him. Give him this.'

He pressed a greenstone pendant into Anne-Marie's palm.

'I'm not leaving you,' Anne-Marie cried. 'You can't die. I won't let you.'

The rain was falling. Everywhere, people were moving, shadows in the light.

*Cliff, where are you? You said you never left anybody behind. Come and get me, Cliff, come and get me.*

The rain, only the rain. And strangers, only strangers. And a strange woman in a white dress. Why was she crying?

In his mind Sam could hear himself saying the words:

'You must find Cliff for me. Find him for me. Please. Tell him that —'

But Sam knew his voice wasn't working and the woman couldn't hear him. Desperately, he began to move his fingers in sign.

*You must find Cliff. Tell him, tell him that I was coming and that I loved him, oh how I —*

Then there was nothing. Only darkness and rain.

———— 8 ————

I was sitting in Mrs Davidson's small unit in Upper Hutt. Fran excused herself to make us a cup of tea.

'Sam died in my arms,' Mrs Davidson said. 'Neither of my two husbands died in my arms. That's why I remember him. He was so beautiful when he died. The police came. The ambulance came. The police needed a statement. After it was over, they wanted me to go to hospital for observation. I convinced them I was all right. I asked the elderly man to help me. I said to him, "Could you please drive me to the international terminal?" He was such a lovely man. He waited for me as I wandered around the building. God, I must have looked a sight in that ball gown, covered in blood. I kept on calling "Chris! Chris!" The airport security people came up to me. They couldn't have a mad, demented-looking woman walking around and scaring everybody. Not until later, when I met George, did I know his name was Cliff. When you do find Cliff, please tell him how sorry I am. I feel so responsible for Sam's death. If he hadn't stopped to help me —'

An hour later, Mrs Davidson saw me to her door.

'Could you do something for me?' she asked. 'Could you telephone me when you get back from America and Canada?'

'Yes,' I promised.

I started to walk away — then I remembered something. I turned to Mrs Davidson.

'You said you had something that belongs to Cliff Harper.'

'Oh, yes. I'll go and get it.'

She was away only a minute. But my heart was beating loud enough to split the world open with sadness. When she returned and I saw what she was carrying, I couldn't help it. I burst into tears. And Mrs Davidson began to cry too.

'The thing is,' she wept, 'I tried to return this to your grandfather, but he said that it had been defiled and he didn't want it back. I didn't know what to do with it. I asked George, but he didn't want anything to do with it either. When Sam was dying he wanted me to take it to Cliff Harper at the airport. But —'

In Anne-Marie's hand a box with its lid off.

'Anyway, here it is.'

Nestling in the box, a greenstone pendant. Cliff had thrown it to Sam on the night he had left the farm. It had twisted and tumbled, catching fire and turning into a flaming bird.

*Bring it back to me, Sam. You son of a bitch, you bring it back to me.*

And I was sobbing while Mrs Davidson held me, sobbing for something that should have happened but didn't.

*You hear me, Sam? Bring it back.*

Tunui a te Ika.

CHAPTER SEVENTEEN

———— 1 ————

Midnight. Carlos' flat.

I slipped out of bed and left Carlos to his dreams. I couldn't believe how uncomplicated he was. I'd taken him to a restaurant where he'd ploughed through the menu with gusto, eating everything in sight.

'I go to the gym every day,' he explained. 'That's how I keep my weight down — and that's where I first saw you. I can't believe that you don't remember me!'

'I wish I could say I did —'

'Couldn't you lie?' he pouted. 'But I hadn't shaved my head then.'

He downed his food with a good bottle of red, and then looked at his watch:

'I've got a meeting in the morning, so I have to get up early. We'll have to give the dance clubs a miss. Even though you don't deserve it, having such a bad memory and all — your place or mine?'

'Let's go to yours,' I answered.

I'd expected to see the usual bachelor shambles: unwashed plates in the kitchen, the bed still unmade, clothes lying all over the place. Instead, the apartment was austere, minimalist. Polished wooden floorboards. Bare walls with a scattering of paintings. Some interesting books on philosophy and religion. The bed was a platform on the floor. All the windows were wide open. I'd looked at Carlos, intrigued. He showed me a small room where there was a shrine.

'I'm a Buddhist,' he said.

I laughed, incredulous. 'A Maori who's a Buddhist?'

*Temple not far from here. Go before rain comes.*

'It happens.' Carlos shrugged. 'Trouble is, there are still many things of the flesh I still crave. Like food and —'

He took me in his arms and began to undress me. Once all his appetites had been appeased, he slid easily into sleep.

I slipped through the moonlight. I was still perplexed as to why Carlos hadn't asked me about Jason.

'You have a past,' he'd said, 'and so do I, but we live in the present. If you're asking if I'm jealous of anybody in your life, no, I'm not.' Then he said something that intrigued me. 'I can share you, Michael, if I have to. Roimata and I have already talked about that. We'll work something out —'

Tunui a te Ika was in my jacket. I fumbled in the pocket for it. My fingers touched the greenstone — so cold, so cold. But, before I knew it, it began to get warm and slid itself into my palm.

I took the greenstone out and held it by the cord to the moonlight. A small breeze from the window made the greenstone start to twirl. Slowly, at first. But soon it was spinning, scattering the light, and I imagined it chuckling like a child for joy.

'Ae.' I nodded. 'Do you recognise me? Do you see Uncle Sam in me? You are of my people! For thirty years you've been waiting, haven't you! I'm sorry it's taken so long. Forgive me —'

I traced the whorls of Tunui a te Ika. The face, the body, the penis with its white marks like a comet's tail. The greenstone seemed to come alive at my touch, glowing with contentment. I felt it trying to leap from my hands and take its place close to my heart — but I thought of Cliff Harper.

'No,' I said. 'You've been promised to somebody else. I'll take you to him soon.'

———— 2 ————

The next morning, Carlos woke me up with a cup of tea.

'I've gotta go. I'll catch up with you later. I heard you get up in the middle of the night. I thought you were leaving. I'm glad you stayed.'

'Maybe you're getting to me.'

'Good!' he beamed. 'I've been trying hard enough! I heard you talking to somebody —'

I told him about Uncle Sam, Cliff Harper and Tunui a te Ika.

'I'm leaving for Canada and America in a few days.'

'As long as you come back,' he answered.


Full of hope, I arrived at Toi Maori and awaited the telephone call from Ada Sylvester in Chicago. Her news came as a terrible blow. Having heard from Anne-Marie Davidson about how Sam died, I wanted to hear Ada tell me she'd found Cliff Harper. I wanted to be able to tell Tunui a te Ika, 'We've found him.'

'Sorry, honey, we've located seven Cliff Harpers in our all-points request, but none of them is the one you want. You sure you've got the right name?'

'Yes.' My brain was racing as I tried to remember any other relevant details that might give Ada a better lead. 'He mentioned a place called Back of the Moon —'

'Anything else?' Ada asked. 'Anything more substantial? His call-up papers? Name of the helicopter squadron? If you have any further information that might help me out, let me know and I'll try again. Meantime, it's a dead end, honey.'

'Thanks, Ada, I really appreciate your help.'

'We mean to be of service and do —'

'Yes, Ada, I will have a nice day.'

It was so unfair. So unfair. When Auntie Pat called, I didn't have the heart to give her Ada's news.

'Have you been able to find Cliff? Is he still alive?'

'Not yet,' I answered. 'Can you think of any other details about him? Anything?'

Auntie Pat's voice became edged with hysteria.

'You've got everything I had of Sam's, the diary, everything. You're leaving in three days! Do something —'


Around mid-morning I was still depressed about Ada's telephone call.

'I'm going back to the flat,' I told Roimata. 'I want to look at Uncle

Sam's diary. Perhaps there's something in it that I've missed. Some clue about Cliff Harper.'

'Okay,' Roimata answered. 'But don't forget to be back for lunch with Tane Mahuta.'

I walked out of the office. Just as I got to the door, Jason came in. I took one look at him and realised that Margo had been right. He was in a bad state, back at the beginning again.

'Aren't you expecting me?' he asked. 'I left a message at the flat that I'd come around.'

His voice was ratcheted up a few notches. He was like a cat on a hot tin roof.

'I wasn't home,' I answered.

'Oh, I see. So how's your new toyboy?'

I should have been kind and conciliatory, I know, but I'd had just about enough of everything. And I'd had enough of Jason, the things he said, the things he didn't say, the things he meant, the things he really meant.

'So it's all right for you to have a new lover, Jason, but it's not all right for me?'

Jason was so angry.

'Why couldn't you have waited?' he asked. 'Until I was through all this? Graham doesn't mean anything to me. How do you think I feel about myself knowing no sooner am I out of the house than you've found someone to replace me? It just proves, doesn't it, that you never loved me, ever. Well, there goes your last chance of ever having me back again.'

God, that really hurt. Jason still had the power to put his knife in the wound and twist it. Why didn't our relationship end while it was still at its height? When we both felt that there were only the two of us in the world and we were all that mattered? Much better to have ended things at its height than have this long descent out of passion and love, feeding on its own flame and burning out in this tortuous consuming of each other. Better that than the onset of recriminations, accusations or terminal boredom — the lies, the simulation of love, the dissembling. The equivocation.

'What do you want, Jason?' I sighed. 'All your signals are mixed up.'

He wasn't listening. 'I won't let you off so easily,' he said. 'You think you can do whatever you want with impunity. Well, life isn't like that. I want you to share my pain. Only then will you be able to face up to what you've done to me. You've ruined my life, don't you know that? I hope you treat your latest trick with more respect than you did me.'

That was *it*.

'You keep saying I ruined your life, Jason, but I won't take the blame. *You* ruined it yourself. You left me, you made your decisions and now *you* live with the consequences. Look, I really do care for you. I don't know what you're searching for. I don't know what you want. I suspect that when you find it you'll be so fried in your brain with all your therapy you won't even recognise it. I won't be the villain in your psychodrama.'

I cupped Jason's chin in my hands. Jason struggled against me but I stopped him and looked deep into his eyes.

'Where are you, Jason? Somebody has stolen you away and put another person in your place. The man I'm looking at looks like you, talks like you, walks like you. But he isn't you.'

Jason pulled away. 'You think you're clever, don't you. Well I've given you your last chance and you haven't taken it. I'll see you in court.'

He walked in one direction. I walked in the other.

Back at the flat I went through Uncle Sam's diary again. I looked at Cliff Harper's photo:

'Tell me,' I yelled. 'Tell me how to find you —'

---

3

---

I was running late by the time I returned to Toi Maori. Tane Mahuta was sitting on my desk. Bronzed skin, eyes as bright as the sun. In his ear, a shark's tooth pendant. The Noble Savage.

'Kia ora, Michael. You look as if you need a beer. Let's go over to the bar.'

'Great.'

I looked around for Roimata but she had disappeared.

'It's just us.' Tane smiled. 'It's man-to-man talk and, this time, I have been properly briefed.'

The bar was crowded and Tane was so well known that people stopped at our table to say hello and to wish him well.

'This is what happens when you go public,' he said. 'It takes some getting used to but it comes with the territory. You can't get any more public than doing Aids work.'

He looked at me quizzically and I had the feeling he was dropping a hint of some kind. To change the subject I told Tane about Uncle Sam. The story intrigued and excited him.

'You say your uncle was both gay and a soldier? You know, if his story was known, he could become a pretty potent symbol. He would prove that you can be gay — and a warrior. If we could take that message to every marae in the country it would be a breakthrough, because if there's anything our people understand it's the warrior spirit. They may not like what gay Maori men are, but they've always admired bravery and strength. In the past nobody has been able to make a bridgehead because we've always acted on our own and without a precedent. But —'

Uh oh, I thought. Here it comes.

'I'd better get down to business,' Tane said. 'As you know, Maori have always had this tradition of arranged marriages, taumau unions. In the old days they were used for political reasons — to begin or maintain tribal alliances. In my case, I was the only son, and my mother didn't want the line to die with me. Our whakapapa is a distinguished one, and she refused to think of it coming to an end. Six years ago, when I was with Mum at the funeral of a distant uncle, Mum noticed Leah, who had nursed the old man in his last years. She made some judicious inquiries, spoke to Leah's family, and the marriage was agreed.'

I nodded, smiling at Tane's story. I knew it well.

'I didn't know anything about this,' Tane chuckled, 'until the following New Year. I was at home with Mum, fixing the tractor, and she said to me, "We have to go down to the marae." She didn't even tell me what it was all about! I was still in my hobnail boots and black singlet when, all of a sudden, I heard Mum karanga to these people. I looked at the gateway and there was Leah and her tribe. They had brought her to me! Well, I was angry at first. I could hardly speak to Mum. She had jacked the whole thing up with the tribe, and the next thing I knew was that we were all in the meeting house discussing the marriage! I told them it was impossible. But you know what our people are like. It goes in one ear and out the other. One of my uncles asked me, "Do you have a person in your life at present?" I said, "No." And he said, "So what's the problem?" Our people think being gay is just a momentary aberration. Something you get over when you come to your senses. Anyway, we were getting nowhere until Leah stood up. She said, "I would like to speak to Tane."

294

She laid it all out to me. To my surprise she wasn't a doormat. She was strong, articulate and passionate —'

'She sounds like Roimata,' I said.

'I see you're getting the picture,' Tane answered, his eyes twinkling. 'Anyway, right there in the meeting house, Leah said to me, "I haven't come here, Tane, against my will. I have come of my own accord. I would have come to see you by myself, except that my relatives wanted to turn it into a circus as usual. I know you are a homosexual —'

'At the word, everybody in the meeting house coughed and pretended not to hear. "So I do not come to this blind to your physical desires. But my womb is crying for children, as greatly as your mother weeps for grandchildren. And I want to ask you a question, Tane. Just because you're gay, does than mean you can't be a father? I think not. I hope not. You are a fine man and your sexuality has a strength of its own which you can bring to a relationship not only with me but with any children we may have. We are both too old not to accept this arrangement. I want a son. I can give you a son. I don't even know if I could love you. I admire you for what you do and the courage you have. Those are the qualities I am looking for in a husband and a father. You are my last chance. I am yours —"'

Tane shook his head with wonderment. It wasn't too difficult for me to see what Leah saw in him. His body was carved from earth and sky. Its angularity had been made for holding children. Its strength for sheltering a family.

'When Leah said it like that,' Tane continued, 'she blew my socks off. I realised she was right. I made my choice. After all, I was born a Maori and that is how my people will bury me. I owed it to them. Two kids later, I thank Leah every day for having given me my sons. They and she are more important to me than anything else in the whole world.'

Tane ordered two more beers. He downed his in two gulps as if to fortify himself.

'So here's the thing, Michael,' he said. 'I'm here as a go-between. Don't shoot me because I'm just the messenger. Just as my mother arranged my taumau with Leah, I am here to ask you to consider such an arrangement with Roimata.'

I should have been surprised, but I wasn't — and Tane moved swiftly on.

'Marriage should be an option for gay Polynesian men and women. With it we can establish a tribe — a tribe based not just on sexual identity but on family. A tribe must have children to survive. It must also have parents, grandmothers and grandfathers. Even though the children may not be gay by practice, they will be gay by genealogy through their fathers and mothers. When my own children grow up, I want them to think of themselves as belonging to a great new gay family, a wonderful new gay tribe —'

'What about other partners?' I asked. 'Gay or lesbian lovers?'

'It will be difficult,' Tane conceded. 'But we come from a tribal people and surely the tribe should be able to accommodate —'

His voice faded. He knew that what he was talking about was some ideal that might exist way in the future, if ever. He also realised he was talking too much, pushing too much. He backed off, leaving me some space to think. The seconds turned into minutes and:

'You don't need to give me an answer right now, Michael,' he said.

'It's not that,' I answered.

For some reason I thought of Carlos. He *was* getting to me.

'It's just that I don't know where my life is going right now. There's so much to sort out. The timing isn't right —'

'Michael,' Tane said gently, 'it never is.'

I returned to the office. Roimata's eyes were red, as if she had been crying. When I took her in my arms she clung to me as if her life depended on it.

'I'm so embarrassed,' she said.

'You embarrassed?' I asked. 'That's a new one. Really, I'm honoured. Who knows? This might just be the way to win back the family.'

'Yours and mine,' Roimata said. 'So you'll think about it?'

'May as well.' I shrugged. 'My life is already ratshit. One extra thing on top of it won't make it any worse.'

Roimata knew I was joking. She dabbed at her eyes with a handkerchief.

At that moment, the telephone rang. It was Auntie Pat.

'There may be more information about Cliff up at the old farmhouse,' she said. 'But I'm not going up there by myself. So I've booked you to come back up to Gisborne. I've already paid for your ticket. Pick it up at the airport. You're on the last plane out of Wellington tonight and the mid-morning plane back.'

'Great,' I answered.

But Auntie Pat hadn't finished with me:

'Michael,' she said, 'I'm so afraid. I haven't told you everything.'

—————— 4 ——————

It was pitch black when I arrived in Gisborne. I was one of only a handful of passengers on the plane and we dispersed quickly into the night.

'This is getting to be a habit,' I joked when I saw Auntie Pat waiting by the car.

She offered her cheek for a kiss. This time she was in the driver's seat. When we reached Gladstone Road she turned left on the highway out of town.

'We haven't got much time,' she said, 'so I thought we'd go straight out to the old farm and stay there overnight. I've cleared it with your father, though I didn't tell him you'd be with me. He was curious why I would want to go out there. Neither of us has been there for years. I told him I was going up with Kara — you know, Bully's widow — to collect some of their stuff.'

When Grandfather Arapeta had died in 1983 he left the farm to Auntie Pat and my father. But Dad didn't want to move back there and Auntie Pat had taken Nana Florence to live in Gisborne. Bully became the manager of the farm and, as the years went by, his role dwindled to caretaker. Six months ago he had passed away.

We arrived at the farm. PRIVATE PROPERTY and DO NOT ENTER signs had been wired to the gates. Auntie Pat gave me the keys to unlock them, and she drove through, towards the old homestead. The moon had come up above it, glinting on the windows and transforming the verandah posts into white teeth. I'd forgotten how big and imposing it was. In its day it had been one of the largest homesteads in the valley.

By the time I caught up with her, Auntie Pat was out of her car with the torch, and going up the front steps to the door.

'Can you bring the stuff in the boot?'

I nodded and lifted the box with its overnight supplies: sheets, bedding, milk, food, soap and other toiletries. Auntie Pat unlocked the door and went into the pantry. There, she found some candles and a box of matches.

'I hope you don't mind, Michael, but I didn't get the chance to have the electricity switched back on. We'll be using candles tonight.'

Auntie Pat scraped a match. It flared as she applied it to a candle. I thought that her fixed stare as she lit one candle after another, and ordered me to take them into all the rooms, was simply a matter of concentration. Later, I realised that Auntie Pat wanted to make sure there was not a dark corner anywhere. Only when the house blazed with light did she step from the pantry. Even then, I could see the terror in her eyes as her childhood came rushing back to confront her. For me, it was different. The homestead was just an old house, derelict, standing in the middle of dark bush. But for Auntie Pat it was filled with ghosts. Perhaps ghosts she thought she had exorcised years ago.

'All right,' Auntie Pat said. 'Let's see if we can find anything. When Mum, Monty and I left here, Bully was told there were two rooms that were always to remain shut. One of them was Sam's bedroom. The other was the room that Dad used as his office and where he kept his accounts, whakapapa books and all his military records. You look in Sam's room, Nephew. I'll do Dad's office.'

She gave me the key to Sam's room.

'I wish we'd brought a radio,' she shivered. 'If we had, I would have put it on the loudest rock 'n' roll radio station I could find.'

I walked along the corridor to Uncle Sam's bedroom and unlocked the door. The room was absolutely bare. No bed, no bedside furniture. Just four walls, a curtained window and a linoleum floor. Any suggestion that anybody had ever slept in here had been stripped away. Except, that is, for the wardrobe, which had been built in and could not be dismantled.

I went to the sitting room, got a chair, and took it back to Uncle Sam's room. Perhaps I might find something on the top of the wardrobe — some letter, something that might have been overlooked in the clean sweep of the room. No luck. I opened the wardrobe and tested the flooring, knocking at it with my knuckles. Hello, hello, two of the boards were loose and the reverberations from my knuckles indicated an empty space beneath them. Just the kind of space where a young boy would put special things — a pocketknife, a treasured Western comic, a blue bird's egg. Or, as a teenager, his stash of X-rated magazines. Or, as a young man, his birth certificate, Army discharge documents, letters from a lover, photographs —

Nothing.

I heard weeping. At first I thought it was the wind. My blood ran cold as I wondered whether I had disturbed Uncle Sam's spirit. But the weeping wasn't coming from his room. I followed the sound down the corridor to Grandfather Arapeta's study.

Auntie Pat was slumped in an old chair. She looked like a golden moth trapped within the aureole of candlelight.

'This was a bad idea,' she said.

In her hands was the old family Bible where family births and deaths were registered. The page where Uncle Sam's name should have appeared was ripped out. On a fresh page, Auntie Pat's name and Dad's had been re-inscribed. Immediately following were mine and my sister's.

I took the Bible from Auntie Pat's hands.

'Why don't you go and make us a cup of tea?' I asked. 'I'll finish this.'

When she had gone I looked everywhere — for a letter Sam may have written from Vietnam. Newspaper clippings. Photos. Anything.

I found nothing.

I went to join Auntie Pat.

'It was worth the try,' she said.

I thought of the barn. I went along the road. The stables were deserted. The door to the barn was swinging in the wind. I went in. Saw the ladder to the loft. Thought of Uncle Sam and Cliff together, and Cliff laughing:

*Well, what do you expect? I'm, a healthy mid-Western boy —*

'I can't find him, Uncle Sam. I'm so sorry —'

———— 5 ————

The next morning, the alarm went at dawn. Auntie Pat, reverting to childhood, had bunked down in the bedroom she had slept in as a child. When I went to find her, there was only a note pinned to her door:

GOOD MORNING, SLEEPYHEAD. BREAKFAST IS ON THE TABLE. AFTER YOU'VE EATEN, SADDLE UP ONE OF THE HORSES AND COME TO THE EAST PADDOCK.

I grabbed some toast and coffee, changed quickly and went down to the stable. I saddled a grey and, a few minutes later, hit the track which took me diagonally across the flatland and into the valley leading to the river. This was where Uncle Sam loved to hold a boulder and jump in. I could almost imagine him sitting there, looking up at me as I passed, smiling to himself that I didn't know he was there.

I crossed the river, remembering the wild mustangs that Cliff had headed off, and took the trail up the ravine and into the hills that formed the rugged eastern boundary of the farm. The ride took just on half an hour and, by the time I had crested the hills, the grey was panting with the exertion. The land was mainly covered with pines and scrub. It was the worst land on the farm.

I looked up to the skyline. Auntie Pat was silhouetted against the sky, waving to me. When I reached her I saw she had a chainsaw tied to her horse.

'See that pine tree, Michael? Saw it down, please.'

I did so, and the tree toppled. The space opened the bottom of the slope to the light.

'See that patch down there?'

Tears were running down Auntie Pat's face. She pointed to a spot which must once have been shadowed by the fallen tree. It was marked by a small cairn that had been piled by hand.

'That's your Uncle Sam.'

She resumed her story.


'After Sam was killed,' Auntie Pat began, 'and the coroner had finished his investigation, Sam's body was brought back to us. You'd think Dad would have relented of his anger, but he was such an unforgiving man. The local people wanted Sam to rest on the marae but Dad said "No". The local people assumed that Dad would bury Sam in our family graveyard. Again, Dad said "No". He and Mum argued. She had tried to stand up for Sam in life. She tried again in death. She said to Dad, "All right then, I will take Sam back to my own people and he can rest in our graveyard." Before she could do it, Dad lashed Sam's coffin to the sledge and brought him here. He told all of us to stay behind, and the last we saw of our brother was Dad taking him off across the farm. But Mum said to me, "Patty, darling, you go and follow your father and see where he buries my son. Don't let him see you though."'

It was as if Auntie Pat had forgotten I was there — it was Sam she talked to now.

'Fancy our own father, Sam, doing this to you. Bringing you here as if you were a murderer. Putting you in this unconsecrated ground, in this dark place, and leaving you here. But he didn't know I had followed him, did he? He didn't know that I watched from up there, among the trees, as he dug this grave for you.'

Auntie Pat grabbed my shoulders, and her fingers were like claws digging into me. She was trembling all over and her eyes were wide and staring.

I tried to calm her down.

'Auntie Pat —'

She looked at me, puzzled, and I knew that she had gone, gone, gone into her memories. Then she gasped and hugged me.

I knew that *I* had become Sam.

'Dad never even saw me,' she said in a girlish voice. 'Wasn't I clever? I followed the sledge on foot all the way! I kept parallel with Dad, hiding in the bushes. Maybe he suspected I was there. Sometimes he stopped and looked in my direction. "Patty, I can see yoouuuuuu —"'

Auntie Pat giggled conspiratorially.

'You would have been proud of me, Sam. I made myself small. I blended into the landscape the way you wrote you used to when you were on patrol. Dad crossed the river, and I slipped in, swimming underwater after him. Did you know I even swam under the sledge, and he didn't know I was there? I re-surfaced over by some rocks and, when Dad went up the ravine, I followed. My dress was cold and clammy from the water . . . my hair was wet . . . I was so tired by the time Dad reached this place . . . yes, just as the sun was going down . . . and he took out his spade . . . and began digging . . . and . . .'

'Auntie Pat . . . Auntie *Pat.*'

Auntie Pat began to scream and scream. She stood up and looked down at the cairn. 'Why did you do it, Daddy? Why did you have to bring Sam here? I saw what you did . . . the way you buried Sam . . . the way you placed him on the side of the hole . . . and then . . . you pushed him in with your foot . . . and he went tumbling in . .'

*Please, not eternal darkness.*

'Why, Daddy, why . .'

I don't know how long Auntie Pat and I stayed up there, on the side of the hill, looking at Uncle Sam's grave. It took me a long time to quieten her down. Then, without a word, she stood up and went to a saddlebag and took out some flowers she'd brought with her. She went down to the cairn and started to place them on the grave. I joined her.

'I saw it all, Michael,' she said. 'I watched Dad shovel dirt over Sam. Once it was over, I ran like the wind to get back to the homestead before Dad. When I arrived, Mum was waiting for me. She was out of her mind with grief. "Did you see where he buried Sam? Did you?" she asked. I told her, "Yes, Mum." She asked me, "Will you be able to find the place again?" I said, "Yes, I'll be able to find it." Half an hour later, Dad arrived. When he had washed up he said, "Florence bring the family Bible to me." He tore out the page which had Sam's birth details on it, and he said, "Nobody is to mention Sam's name in this house again." Then he told us we had to burn all Sam's things.'

Auntie Pat paused for a moment. I thought she might start weeping again but —

'No, I'm all right, Michael.'

Her memory went back to that night again.

'Mum tried to stop Dad. She followed him into Sam's room, and when he started to throw everything out of the window — the bedding, Sam's clothes, Sam's records and Sam's books — she ran at him and started to hit him with her fists. "You bastard," she yelled, over and over. Then Dad found Sam's secret place under the floorboards where he'd kept his diary, photos and letters, Mum launched herself at him and started to scratch his face. While they fought, I saw Sam's diary fall from Dad's arms. I picked it up quickly, and hid it. Monty saw what I did. "Sshh, don't tell Daddy." A few letters fell also, and the photograph. Next minute, Dad threw Mum off him and walked out the door. He went to the car, opened the boot and took out the can of spare petrol. He splashed the petrol over Sam's things and set a match to them. There was a whoosh and, next minute, the sky was alight — and the updraught was carrying burning ash into the air like they were birds on fire. I heard Mum say to Dad, "You've told us we are never to speak Sam's name again. Let me tell you what I have decided. You will never hear me speak your name again, ever." Dad just looked at her. "Do what you like," he said. He'd long passed caring about her. After a while, he stopped caring about me too. All he really cared about was Monty.'

Auntie Pat wiped her brow.

'My father broke Mum's heart,' she said as she stood up. 'But he never broke her spirit. Every year while Dad was alive we always brought flowers to Sam's grave. Dad must have wondered how we knew where Sam was buried, but he said nothing. When he died, Mum was no longer tied to the farm — or to him. People think I was the one who decided to shift to Gisborne, but it was Mum's idea. We still kept bringing flowers to Sam. Every anniversary of his death. Mum would say to me, "Patty? Patty! Hurry up and bring the car around to the front! It's time to see Sam —"'

Auntie Pat looked up at the sky.

'You never stopped loving him, did you, Mum. Neither did I, and don't you worry — I'll still come back out here every year.'

Then Auntie Pat put her fingers to her lips and placed a kiss on Sam's grave.

'I'm sorry, brother. It was all my fault. Everything that happened was all my fault.'

I held Auntie Pat close to me.

'You mustn't blame yourself,' I said. 'You loved your brother. If you'd been able to, I know you would have tried to save him.'

Auntie Pat sighed, took my hand, nodded and addressed Sam:

'Well, at least you'll have some sun this winter, brother.' She turned swiftly to me.

'When I die, you are to bring me up here and bury me next to my brother. The others can go to the family graveyard if they want to. But my brother is not to lie here alone. Do you hear me, Michael? Do you hear me?'

Auntie Pat called me Michael only when she was angry. Boy, was she getting her wild up now.

'Okay, Auntie,' I answered. 'You and Uncle Sam might be starting up a family tradition.'

Auntie Pat looked puzzled.

'Well,' I continued, 'you don't think they'll be wanting me in the graveyard, do you? I'll be better off with you two!'

Auntie Pat pulled a face.

'Listen to the boy,' she said to Sam. 'God, he has some dumb ideas.'

She looked at her watch.

'We'd better get back. You have a plane to catch.'

--------- 6 ---------

Then, with a rush, it was time to go to Canada. Half an hour before Roimata and I were due to leave the office for the airport, the telephone rang. Roimata was in her usual panic and thought I would answer it, but I was having a little panic of my own and thought she would pick it up. It was just as well I realised in time:

'Hi, Michael.'

Click click, crack.

'Ada!'

'Oh, you naughty boy!' she said, crack, swallow, laugh, click. 'Why didn't you tell me that Mr Harper had one of those hyphenated names, Clifford James *Addison*-Harper! You go stand by your fax machine right now, because I'm sending down to you all the information I've got on him.'

'You mean he's alive? And you've found him?'

'Sure thing, honey!'

'Ada, I could kiss you!'

'Oh, honey, you're making me blush and that's hard for a sixty-five-year-old woman to do!'

'You're sixty-five?'

'Every bitty year.'

'I don't care. Here's the kiss!'

I blew her a kiss down the telephone. Heard her pause. Then click click clickety click, crack crack CRACK — *sigh*.

'I guess that's the closest to telephone sex I'll ever get,' Ada drawled. 'Take care, honey, and here's Mr Harper's details coming at you.'

A few seconds later the fax machine began to spit, curl and hum with Cliff Harper's telephone number and address: Back of the Moon, Muskegon Harbour, Illinois.

I rang Auntie Pat. 'We've found him, Auntie Pat.

'We've found Cliff Harper.'

# PART SIX

# Brangäne's Warning

CHAPTER EIGHTEEN

———— 1 ————

'Oh, no,' Roimata said.

Auckland International Airport on a Friday evening was absolute bedlam. Loud, noisy and full of people queueing at the check-in counters. The lines for United Economy in particular were very long, and that meant a full flight to Los Angeles. There was nothing for it but to try to be patient, shuffle forward in line and, once we'd finally made it to the desk, pass over our tickets and passports and wait for our seat assignments — right at the back next to the toilets.

'At least we'll be the last to die if the plane goes down,' I said to Roimata.

She batted her eyelids. 'And we'll be together, up close and personal.'

Even so, I was puzzled at the length of time it was taking to check us in. I often wondered exactly what counter clerks tapped into their computers. I suspected that by the time each passenger had been processed, their names went out the window and were replaced by fifty-digit bar codes. Finally the clerk stopped tapping and smiled at us encouragingly:

'Mr Mahana? Your upgrade has been confirmed. You and Miss Williams have seating in business class.'

'Upgrade? There must be some mistake.'

'No, Sir. It's been arranged by Mr Carlos Poulsen. Best wishes at your international fisheries conference, and enjoy the flight.'

Roimata's mouth dropped open. 'That boy has class,' she said as we beat a fast track through Customs and into the business lounge. There Roimata kicked off her shoes, helped herself to a drink and pretended to be a film star. I picked up the phone and dialled Wellington.

'You're full of surprises,' I said to Carlos when he answered.

'I'd much rather you were up front where you've got flight attendants to look after you than at the back with Roimata in the dark. You tell her to keep her red-painted fingernails to herself.'

I looked across at Roimata. 'Carlos sends his love.'

'I'll bet,' Roimata said. 'Do tell him, however, that his attempts at bribery last only as long as the flight. All's fair in love and war.'

'I heard that,' Carlos laughed. 'You tell Roimata her privileges have just been revoked for the trip back. And as for you Michael, have a great trip, be a star, do what you have to do but don't miss the plane back from your, er, fisheries conference, you hear?'

'Okay, you're the sheriff.'

I put down the telephone and, buoyed by my conversation with Carlos, excused myself from Roimata and went into the business room. I put my Mastercard in one of the telephones. Dialled the country code for the United States, the city code for Chicago and the number that Ada had faxed me.

There was a faint pause, a dial tone, then another. I counted each one. After the fourth I realised the call wasn't going to click over to an answerphone. I waited another six rings, and was about to put the telephone down, when:

'Hello?'

The voice was bright. Breathless. For a moment I simply held the phone, not knowing what to do. My mouth was dry.

'Is this Cliff Harper?'

'Yes. May I ask who's calling?'

My heart pounded. I couldn't go on. It seemed so ridiculously easy to be speaking with Cliff Harper after all the time it had taken trying to find him.

'My name is Michael Mahana and I'm calling from New Zealand —'

'New Zealand? Wow.'

I collected my thoughts.

308

'Mr Harper, I was given your number by your American Vietnam Veterans' Association and —'

'Oh, wait up.'

Wait up? My breath caught in my throat.

'You're wanting my Dad,' the voice said. 'Cliff senior. I'll see if he's in.'

I heard Cliff junior leave the telephone and call:

'Dad, are you downstairs? Mom, is Dad down there?'

Cliff Harper was married? Had a wife and a son — perhaps other sons and daughters?

I felt a sense of alarm, and then anger at myself. What should I have expected after thirty years? Some absurd romantic part of me had assumed that Cliff Harper was still single and had been waiting every day for this telephone call. I had never expected he would be married with a wife and children. I may have countenanced a relationship — but a male one with someone who would, surely, have looked like Uncle Sam.

Something told me to hang up. But it was too late.

'I'm sorry, Dad's just this minute left the house. Can I tell him you called? Is there a return number in New Zealand?'

My body flooded with both relief and disappointment.

'Look,' I answered. 'Could you tell Mr Harper senior that my name is Michael Mahana and I am a nephew of Sam Mahana. I'm actually on my way to Canada via the United States tonight. I'm flying United —'

'The Friendly Skies?'

'I'll be transiting Chicago on my way to Ottawa. If possible I am hoping to meet Mr Harper in Chicago. Please tell him I'll call again during my stopover in Los Angeles to see whether a meeting can be arranged.'

'I'll give Dad the message. Wow, New Zealand!'

Two hours later, I was on my way. Roimata and I settled into our plush seats with champagne and nibbles. United's signature tune, Gershwin's 'Rhapsody in Blue', was playing as the plane taxied out onto the runway. A roar, a sense of gliding and then we lifted into the air. Below us, Auckland fell away like a necklace whose clasp had broken. Still climbing steeply, we crossed the coastline, heading north-east across the dark night sea.

I have always loved long journeys. The act of leaving accustomed surroundings is a release from real time, real life. You can place that familiar life on hold, freeze it, secure in the awareness that it will be there waiting for you when you come back. The journey itself becomes an opportunity to explore parallel lives, those other optional lives which have always been there.

My trip with Roimata to Canada seemed ordinary enough. But something was closing behind me — the way I had been, the seemingly dutiful son leading a dutiful life — and a new Michael was emerging. Ahead, the main purpose of the trip was a conference in Ottawa — but there was also Cliff Harper in Illinois, a destination which was assuming as much importance as the conference. What had happened to him and Uncle Sam in the past would be put right in the present.

Somehow, I had the feeling that my trip would take me to another crossroad too. This wasn't just about Uncle Sam. It was also about me. There, in Ottawa and Illinois, Uncle Sam's story and mine would meet — and I had the suspicion that my own destiny would be forever changed by it. All the journeys I had taken through my life would find their answers in that encounter and help me to complete the decisions I was making. About Jason. About Carlos. About Roimata. About myself.

For the moment, I could relax, enjoy dinner with Roimata and toast the future with a fine glass or two of wine. Suspended between earth and sky, I could have my choice of twenty movies on my own personal console, and delay any decisions that needed to be made about Life.

Or could I? I wasn't alone on the flight. Nor was I the only one with an appointment to keep with Cliff Harper. I had Tunui a te Ika in my hand luggage, and I had a promise to keep for an uncle I had never known — a promise passed to a nurse in a bloodied ball dress on a night road to Auckland thirty years ago.

As well there was Auntie Pat, also seeking an ending, a resolution, and motivated by love for her brother.

Roimata's voice intruded on my thoughts. 'Are you okay?'

'Yes,' I answered. 'Just before we left Auckland I telephoned Cliff Harper. He's married. His son answered the phone. I didn't expect him to be married.'

'So you didn't speak to him personally.'

'No.'

Roimata took a sip of her wine. 'How old would he be now?'

'Uncle Sam was twenty-two or twenty-three when they were in Vietnam together. If Cliff Harper was the same age, he'd be in his early fifties.'

The thought caught me unawares and I laughed with surprise because, until that moment, I had never thought of Cliff Harper as being anything except the age he was in Uncle Sam's diary, in the photograph and the conversations with Auntie Pat, George and Anne-Marie Davidson. What nonsense to think that he would look the same! Had life treated him kindly? Was he still as devastatingly handsome as he had been in his youth? Did he even remember Uncle Sam? Perhaps Sam had been only one of a number of lovers. Cliff Harper may have been the great romantic love of Uncle Sam's life, but the reverse might not have been true.

'He'll have made another life,' Roimata said. 'He will have put all that stuff about him and Sam behind him. He may not want to see you.'

'I never thought of that as a possibility. I never wanted to admit it, but now I'm not so sure —'

'Speaking of which,' Roimata continued, changing the subject, 'I've a question about your Auntie Pat. She's never married, has she? Do you think Auntie Pat might be —'

'Might be? Might be what?'

'You know . . .'

I knew exactly what Roimata was implying.

'No *way*,' I answered.

The force of my insistence surprised me. Even if Auntie Pat was lesbian, I didn't want her to be. I didn't want even to consider it possible.

'Pity. She would make a great kuia for us.'

Roimata leaned over and kissed me on the cheek.

'I'd do more,' she said, 'but I'm mindful of Carlos's embargo. Goodnight, Michael. Do you realise that this is the first night we've slept together?'

Two hours later, most of the passengers were asleep but I was still awake. I was relaxed and at peace with myself. I had already watched one movie on my console and clicked over to *Laura*, a 1940s film noir classic directed by Otto Preminger, on the movie classics channel. This was just the kind of old movie Auntie Pat loved.

A woman is found murdered in Laura's apartment. Lieutenant Mark McPherson, played by Dana Andrews, interviews an intriguing set of ambivalent suspects and it is through their flashback stories that we — and McPherson — get to know Laura. She is played by Gene Tierney, one of the great beauties of Hollywood, and her scenes are filled with rich romantic music and camerawork. The visual centrepiece of the film is, in fact, a portrait of Laura in her apartment — and McPherson is constantly drawn to it.

A third of the way through the film came a scene filled with revelation. Watching it, a thunderbolt struck me, and I realised I could never escape from Uncle Sam's story — or Cliff Harper.

It is a wet night. Late evening. McPherson visits Laura's empty apartment for further clues about her murder. He looks at the portrait, and the soundtrack fills with haunting music. He takes out a cigarette and smokes it. He takes off his tie. He goes through the sitting room to an adjoining room where he switches on a desk light. He sits at the desk. He takes off his coat. He opens a drawer in the desk. He gets up and paces the room. He goes into the dead woman's bedroom.

The scene becomes charged with suspense and an underlying sense of the erotic. McPherson's visit is not all that it appears to be. In Laura's bedroom, he opens her dresser. He picks up a white handkerchief and holds it to his nose. He opens a small bottle of her perfume and inhales the smell. He opens the door to her wardrobe and looks at her dresses. The wardrobe door has a mirror on it and, when it closes, McPherson sees his reflection like a voyeur.

At that moment, Waldo Lydecker, Laura's mentor and elderly friend, enters. Cynically he asks McPherson whether he thinks he's acting very strangely, coming to Laura's apartment like a suitor with roses and a box of candy. He warns McPherson to watch it, or he'll end up in a psychiatric ward, because he's fallen in love with a woman who doesn't exist.

I turned off the console. My heart was thudding. I looked out the window, trying to escape the thought that was swirling inside my head. In a panic I lifted the shutter on the window and looked out at the night sky. Instead I saw a reflection of somebody behind me — and I knew it was Uncle Sam. He looked like he did in the photograph, smiling shyly, and he reached out and touched my shoulder:

*It's okay, Nephew,* he signed. *It was only to be expected* —

Then he was gone and it was only the moon, shining through my momentary lunacy, soothing my anxieties and calming me down.

'Yes, Uncle Sam,' I thought, 'perhaps it was inevitable that seeing Cliff Harper through your diary, Auntie Pat, George and Anne-Marie Davidson, I would become you and, just as McPherson had done with Laura, fall in love with Cliff too.'

The dark swirled past. The moon silvered the clouds.

———— 3 ————

The following morning, the flight arrived at Los Angeles. Roimata and I went through Customs. There was just enough time before our onward flight to Chicago to make my second call to Cliff Harper.

'It'll be all right,' Roimata said, and she hugged me reassuringly.

Instead of being easier the second call was harder. There was the usual dryness in my throat. The telephone kept on ringing and ringing. My palms began to sweat. Thirty years went by and still nobody was picking up the call and —

'Hello?'

This time, a woman's voice.

'Is this the home of Mr Cliff Harper?'

'Why, yes. Are you wanting my husband or Cliff junior?'

'Mr Harper senior.'

'I'll go get him for you.'

The telephone went silent. Then:

'This is Cliff Harper speaking. May I help you?'

Rich. Mellow. So this was what Cliff Harper's voice sounded like. This was the man who had existed only as a photograph, the man written about in a diary and conveyed through the memories of three people who had known him. The voice breathed life into the shell of memory, filled out the physical frame and gave it substance.

'Mr Harper? You don't know me, but I am the nephew of a New Zealander you knew during the Vietnam War. His name was Sam Mahana and I am ringing to —'

There was a sharp intake of breath.

313

'I'm sorry,' Cliff Harper said, 'you have the wrong number.'

'Is this Chicago 7685 —'

Cliff Harper interrupted again.

'I repeat, you have the wrong number. Please do not call this number again.'

The line went dead. I stood there, drained. But I couldn't let it go. I hit the redial.

'Mr Harper, I'm ringing from Los Angeles. My name is —'

'Son, I told you not to call.'

'Mr Harper, please don't hang up. All I want to do is pass you a message from my Uncle Sam.'

I could feel my voice beginning to crack apart with emotion.

'Sir, I'm travelling on United 51 and I get into Chicago this afternoon at 1450 hours. I go through Canadian Customs there before I catch my onward flight, Air Canada 762 for Ottawa. But I'll be on the ground for a few hours. I'd like to give you the message if I can. Please —'

Cliff Harper's voice interrupted me. He was gentle. Firm.

'Son, I am not the person you are looking for.'

There was a click as the call was disconnected.

I sat silent for most of the trip to Chicago, and Roimata understood. She had been right to remind me that Cliff Harper might not want to see me. It's funny though, how you keep hoping against hope. When the flight arrived at Chicago I told her to go on through Canadian Customs.

'You sure you don't want me to wait with you?' she asked.

'No,' I answered.

If disappointment lay ahead, I wanted to face it alone.

I took Tunui a te Ika in my hands and prayed:

'If you have any power, make him come so that I can put you in his hands.'

Tunui a te Ika was so hot, almost burning in my palms. It kicked and bucked, impatient to complete its journey. But the minutes kept ticking by and, after a while, it quietened. It knew. It knew Harper wasn't coming.

To have come all this way after all these years —

I couldn't wait any longer. I mourned with Tunui a te Ika and held the greenstone close to my heart.

I went through Customs and joined Roimata.

# CHAPTER NINETEEN

———— 1 ————

Darkness had fallen by the time Roimata and I arrived in Ottawa. We had come from the ends of the earth, and we were tired — by our calculations, we had been travelling for almost two days. It was therefore a relief to be met at the airport by a dapper middle-aged man holding up a card with our names misspelt. He introduced himself as Franklin Eaglen.

'Is this your first time in Canada?' he asked. 'If so, welcome, and I hope you enjoy the visit.'

There's a kind of recognition that happens when one gay man meets another. As soon as I saw Franklin I knew he was one of us. It was in the flicker of his eyes and the warmth of his voice. There was nothing sexual about it. Rather, there was a sense that we could start a friendship on a different kind of understanding.

'The car's just outside,' Franklin said as he led the way to the luggage conveyor.

I picked up my bag. Roimata left Franklin to struggle after her with her suitcase — and the hatbox which went everywhere with her. It never had a hat in it, but was one of Roimata's affectations — it was also good for taking the dirty washing back home in.

We walked out into the street, and when Roimata saw the car she screamed so loudly that Franklin almost dropped everything he was carrying.

'Oh, my God —'

Parked at the kerb was a limousine, sparkling white and as long as a city block. It was the kind of car movie stars arrive in at the Academy Awards.

'Quick,' Roimata said, 'we must get somebody to take a photograph of us with the car and the chauffeur.'

She gave a passerby her camera. She found a chauffeur's hat on the front seat and commanded a rather startled Franklin to put it on. Then she draped herself across the bonnet, blew a kiss, and the photo was taken.

By comparison, our hotel was small.

'Ah well,' Roimata said. 'It had to happen. Back to being just the executive officer of an organisation nobody ever heard of in a country at the bottom of the world.'

She showed Franklin where to put her bags in the room and offered him a tip.

'That won't be necessary, Madam,' he said, smirking happily.

'What's so funny?' I asked.

'Oh nothing,' he said.

He opened the door to my room, which was about the size of a cupboard.

'I do hope you enjoy Survival 2000. I am, and it hasn't even started!'


The next morning, the telephone woke me up. I thought it would be Roimata wanting to go across to the conference venue for the opening ceremony.

'Well?' Auntie Pat asked, 'have you spoken to Cliff Harper yet?'

'Auntie, I've only just arrived.'

I tried to stall, thinking fast about what I should tell her and what I shouldn't. But I knew in my heart the best thing to do was not to keep Auntie Pat's hopes up. I hated the idea of her assuming a meeting might take place when, so far, all the signs were that it wouldn't.

'Cliff Harper didn't show.'

'What do you mean he didn't show?'

She made it sound as if it was my fault.

'The man I spoke to when I rang up from Los Angeles to arrange the meeting in Chicago didn't show. He said he wasn't the man I was looking for. He may be the wrong Cliff Harper.'

'It's him,' Auntie Pat said. 'I know it's him.'

'No, Auntie,' I answered. 'You only want it to be him.' I took a deep breath. 'If it *is* Cliff Harper, he's married and has a son. He could have more children, for all I know. I can't go barging into somebody's life if they don't want me to. I'll ring him again and try to talk to him.'

There was silence at the other end of the telephone. For a moment I thought that Auntie Pat had hung up. Her voice came sliding down the line, striking me in the ear.

'Michael, you are not to let this go. Do you hear me, Nephew? Do you hear me?'

———— 2 ————

'Okay,' Roimata asked me cheekily when she finally met me in the foyer, 'are you ready to go?'

Roimata had decided to be totally glamorous. When she came down the stairs in her red dress and long greenstone earrings I couldn't help doing an appreciative wolf whistle.

'I'll tell Carlos you did that,' she said.

We took a taxi across the Alexandra Bridge to the Museum of Civilisation. The trees fringing the deep swirling Ottawa River were turning red and there was an invigorating bite to the wind. The museum appeared — and it was breathtaking. It seemed to have been layered into the land, long slabs of honey-coloured stone contoured to fit the slope down to the river.

There's nothing like the first day of a conference. The foyer of the museum was packed with people registering, meeting and greeting, shouting and rushing from group to group. Of course, Roimata, with her flair for the dramatic, couldn't just stand there unnoticed. As soon as she saw all those people — representatives of First Nations throughout the world — she was moved to karanga.

'Tena koutou nga iwi o te Ao, tena koutou, tena koutou, tena koutou —'

Her voice soared across the foyer, cutting through the hubbub. People turned to see where the spear of sound was coming from — and that is when we began to chant our way forward.

'Well,' I whispered to Roimata, 'that's one way to make an entrance.'

317

We may only have been two, but our people have always said that where there is one, there is a thousand, where there are two, there are two thousand. When we stand, we do not stand alone. We bring our culture with us.

From among the crowd came a familiar face. He smiled at me, and bowed to Roimata.

'I see that the Maori delegation from New Zealand has arrived,' Franklin said.

He took us in hand, introducing us to the organising committee and, in particular, its chairman.

There were very few people I've taken an instant dislike to, but Bertram Pine Hawk was one of them. He was young, handsome in an arrogant kind of way, and had that sense of well-oiled assurance that would one day make him an ideal candidate for State governor. Franklin went up in my estimation when I noticed that there was no love lost between him and Bertram either.

'Would you mind,' Franklin asked me, 'if I introduce you and Roimata to some of the other delegates? They will look after you.'

Lang, Sterling and Wandisa were all around my age. Having grown up with Western movie images of Indians as tall, muscular and looking as if they could eat six white folks a day, I was surprised to find how small they were in stature and how unassuming in appearance. Certainly, I was not prepared for the sly irony of their wit and banter.

'I'm Okanagan,' Lang said.

'And I'm Dakota,' Sterling said. 'Lang's a mountain Indian, I'm a plains Indian. Plains Indians generally stay clear of those mountain people.'

'If I was you,' Wandisa said, eyes twinkling, 'I would stay clear of them both and just stick with us Inuit.'

I couldn't help laughing. 'Sounds just like home.'

'So how come you're all friends?' Roimata asked politely.

'Us? Friends?' Wandisa answered with mock horror. 'Oh, no, we just happen to be standing together.'

At that moment a drum began to beat. A woman in ceremonial Indian dress appeared at the top of the escalator and began to call us to the First Peoples' Hall. I saw an old man look across at Lang and frown.

'That's my grandfather,' Lang said. 'He's the chief of my tribe. He

318

doesn't like me consorting with a plains Indian and an Inuit.'

'The thing is,' Sterling whispered conspiratorially, 'the three of us all met at university and Lang's grandfather thinks Wandisa and I are responsible for having made Lang, well, stray from the beaten track.'

The way Sterling said it made me wonder whether there were other meanings within his words.

'Oh, Michael, look —'

Roimata was gasping as we went down the escalator.

We seemed to descend into the past. The First Peoples' Hall opened before us, a spectacular row of totems, carvings, canoes and great houses commemorating the ancestral cultures of Canada's West Coast: the Tlingit, Nishga, Gitksan, Tsimshian, Haida, Haisla, Heiltsuk, Nuxalk, Oowekeno, Kwakwaka'wakw, Nuuchahhnulth and Coast Salish. As we descended, the totems and great houses rose above us. I was unprepared for their scale, their sheer size and psychic impact.

'We used to live in a world that must have looked like this,' Lang said, taking Roimata under his wing. 'It was inhabited by Beaver, Thunderbird, Lightning Snake and other supernatural beings, and they supplied us with all our needs. We fished the seas for whales, seals, sea lions, halibut and codfish. The spring rivers gave us shoals of oil-rich eulachon, and salmon returned to spawn in the streams where they were born. Seaweed and shellfish were gathered along the shore. We culled the tall dense forests for the massive cedar and yew to build our villages; we cultivated spruce roots for weaving, and salal, thimbleberry and huckleberry. Then Europeans arrived in the 1770s —'

I lagged behind with Sterling and Wandisa.

'The reason Lang sounds like a textbook,' Sterling said, 'is because he took his degree in Art History. He hasn't spoken like a real person since.'

We took our seats in the hall. People who had heard Roimata and I make our entrance came to shake our hands and to say hello. Over three hundred delegates were in attendance. The majority were representatives of all the Indian tribes of Turtle Island, the name they gave to North America — for them, the distinction between Alaska, Hawaii, Canada, the United States and Mexico was a colonial fiction. A few delegates, like Roimata and myself, had come from other countries: New Zealand, Australia, South Africa and Iceland.

319

The noise in the hall receded. The organising committee took the stage. Roimata was surprised that Franklin was among them.

'I'm getting a terrible feeling,' she whispered. 'Franklin was driving this huge limousine last night and —'

'Franklin?' Wandisa answered. 'He's one of the sponsors of the conference. He's a millionaire, probably the richest Indian in this room. Of course, that's because he's an Inuit.'

Roimata's jaw dropped.

'Oh, no,' she said. 'I thought he was a chauffeur. We had a photograph taken. I made him put on a cap. Oh, I could die.'

Before Roimata could do that, Bertram Pine Hawk motioned that the opening ceremony should begin. Two elderly women came out and, beating drums in a steady rhythm, offered prayers of thanksgiving and hope. They were joined by Lang's grandfather, Albert Pentecost, who had similar status as a kaumatua in Maori proceedings.

Bertram Pine Hawk approached the rostrum. As he did so, a small fact stuck in my brain. Bertram, Franklin, Lang's grandfather Mr Pentecost and the two women elders were First Nation, but they were outnumbered on the stage by European officials of the organising foundation.

'On behalf of the Canadian Council for the Promotion of First Nation Arts,' Bertram Pine Hawk began, 'I am pleased to welcome you all to Survival 2000. The Council is funded by the Canadian Government and some of the members are on stage with me today. The Council wants you to know that they totally support the objectives of this conference and have asked me to announce that a fund of $2 million is to be established to further the arts of our people.'

Bertram Pine Hawk's words were greeted with a murmur of pleasure, and he himself led the applause. He motioned to the members on the stage to receive the acclamation.

'I am the First Nation representative on the Council,' he continued, 'and I want you to know that without the Council's support this conference wouldn't be happening today. Without their funding, we wouldn't have distinguished guests from around the world to provide insight into how the indigenous arts are supported in their own countries.'

Roimata banged me with an elbow.

'Hmmn,' she said. 'I hope he doesn't think he's bought us —'

Delegates from all over the hall were leaping to their feet to acknowledge Bertram Pine Hawk and the Council. With a theatrical flourish he opened his arms:

'Let the conference begin!'

I looked at Roimata. She nodded to me and we stood to join the applauding crowd. We stood out of respect for our Indian hosts, but not for what had been said. We'd both seen this kind of thing before.

A puppet out front.

Behind, people pulling the strings.

———— 3 ————

The next morning Auntie Pat rang again. She was agitated and seemed to need reassurance.

'I'm sorry, Michael,' she said, 'for always being on your case about Cliff Harper.'

'You don't need to be sorry, Auntie, I understand.'

'I've been carrying Sam's story around with me for so long. The burden of it has been so heavy. It's been a burden I have carried with love, but I don't know how much longer I can do it. I guess we'll just have to keep on hoping, won't we? Keep on going until it is resolved. And if it isn't, well, we will have tried our best. You will try your best, won't you, Michael?'

'Yes, Auntie Pat. You know I will.'

I put the telephone down. It was too early to telephone Cliff Harper and try once more to talk to him. I resolved to do so that evening.

Depressed, I dressed for the day. I looked into the mirror, and I felt like shattering it with my fists. Who could I turn to for help? I couldn't even pray to God, because why pray to a god who denied his kingdom to gay men? His prophets had established homosexuality as a sin. They had all denied gay men and women a place in the main narrative of the world — God, his prophets and his followers.

My grandfather had been such a follower. He had tried to remove Sam physically from the family and to obliterate all traces of him. How I hated him for that. I wanted to picture him collapsing beside the broken body of his son on that day he had taken Sam out to the burial place on the

321

farm. I wanted the bastard to weep, 'Sam! Oh, my son!' — to weep so hard that after he'd used up all his tears he would begin weeping blood. I wanted to hear him wail as he pushed Sam's body into the pit he'd dug for it. Throughout all the years afterwards I wanted his eyes to rot from the constant weeping.

Most of all, I wanted to curse the God that Arapeta believed in:

*Yes, better indeed to rule in Hell than to serve in Heaven.*

I hoped that when he died Arapeta had gone to a worse place than that to which he had consigned his son. I wanted crows to come out of the sky to take their retribution, to slash and claw and rip my grandfather, to spill his entrails open in some sacrifice for his unbending righteousness. I wanted him to be denied any possibility of redemption.

Grandfather Arapeta had consigned Uncle Sam to Te Kore, The Void. He had disconnected him from the umbilical cord of whakapapa, and sent him falling head over heels like a spaceman trailing his severed lifeline through a dark and hostile universe to oblivion.

This was how it was done to all gay men and women. But if we were lucky, oh if we were lucky, someone remembered who we were. Someone stopped us from becoming invisible. Expunged from memory. Deleted from the text.

Auntie Pat had, at the last moment, caught the lifeline:

'I'm here, Sam. Hold on, brother.'

If we weren't lucky, however, we were gone.

Forever.


I met Roimata and she was fury incarnate.

'The whole conference is a jack-up,' she said. 'It's been rigged and we've been hoodwinked into coming.'

When Roimata was angry, watch out. But we had a dilemma. The paper we had come to present, 'The New Zealand Perspective: The Maori Experience', was scheduled to take place in the afternoon. Immediately after the opening ceremony Bertram Pine Hawk himself had asked us to err on the side of the positive.

'We must honour the millennial spirit,' he said. 'The theme must be on the achievements of indigenous peoples and on reconciliation. You understand, don't you?'

To be fair, there was nothing wrong about celebrating indigenous achievement — and the concert after Bertram Pine Hawk's address had been a spectacular showcase of indigenous dance, theatre, literature and music. Writers Lee Maracle, Thomson Highway, Jeannette Armstrong and Kateri Akiwenzie-Damm had shown that First Nation literature was in superb hands. The fantastic Chinook Winds dance company had brought the house down with their 'From the Mayan to the Inuit' production. But I knew when Roimata began to sing under her breath that she hadn't been fooled one bit:

'You've got to accentuate the positive, eliminate the negative —'

She looked over at Bertram Pine Hawk, who was laughing unawares.

'Well,' she said, 'I have news for you, Mister In-Between.'

'Perhaps things will be different today,' I said to Roimata, not very hopefully.

We hastened over to the museum, and mingled with the delegates in the foyer again. Such proud people — Inuit, Anishnaabe, Chippewa, Tutchone, Okanagan, Algonquin, Saulteaux, Mohawk, Inuvialuit, Cree, Ojibway, Metis, Cayuga, Teme-Augama, Seneca, Kwakiutl, Inuk, Maliseet, Dogrib, Dakota, Huron — should not be denied their sovereign right to speak out, speak against. Even if it destroyed the orchestrated harmony established by the Council.

Roimata decided we should split for the two plenary sessions on offer. On the way into her session she bumped into Lang, Sterling and Wandisa, who just happened to be standing next to each other again. They took her immediately under their wing.

I hurried to the other session but stopped when I heard a voice calling:

'Michael, can you spare a moment?'

It was Franklin, looking shy and rather diffident.

'I know this is short notice, but I wonder if I might ask you to accompany me this evening.'

'Where to?'

'The opera. A benefit. Everybody will be there and I am in the VIP party. Unfortunately, I have been let down by my partner —' Franklin's eyes flickered. 'The opera is Richard Wagner's *Tristan and Isolde*. But perhaps you've got other plans —'

Franklin sounded so sad and disconsolate that I felt I had to accept.

'I'd be delighted to come with you,' I answered.

Then it was lunchtime, and Roimata and I met in the cafeteria to exchange notes.

'Well,' she said, 'we hoped that things would get better. Not in my session. The Council is playing the conference very close to its chest. All they want is to be supported in their programmes. They're good programmes, mind you, but I will not bribed. So what happened at yours?'

'It's the same as at home,' I said. 'Everybody's playing Happy Family. Nobody wants to bite on the bullet.'

'Oh, well,' Roimata said. 'Bertram Pine Hawk and his organising committee, they are such dears, but it looks like we'll have to do our usual Maori thing.'

'And what's that?'

'I'm going back to the hotel to get dressed to kill. You and I will just have to hijack this conference and take it to the place it's supposed to go.'

'And where's that?' I asked, feeling very afraid.

'To the cliff and over.'

———— 4 ————

Two hours later, we were on.

The location was the First Peoples' Hall, and it was crowded. Roimata was looking radiant, but there was a cutting edge to her beauty. She had dressed entirely in black and had placed three white feathers in her hair. I was reminded that her mother was from Taranaki and that, by wearing the feathers, Roimata was acknowledging her ancestral links with Parihaka, the village which had been the great site of resistance during the Land Wars.

I felt a momentary lapse of confidence. In the front seats I saw Bertram Pine Hawk and some of the members of his committee. Lang's grandfather, Albert Pentecost, was with them also, dignified and compelling in his authority. Further back, I saw Lang himself, Sterling and Wandisa.

'Are you sure we're doing the right thing?' I asked Roimata.

'Probably not,' Roimata answered. 'But we're not here to be liked. We haven't come all this way to say things that people expect to hear or because we want them to love us. We have to tell it the way we see it.

The way our heart and our history wants us to say it.'

With that, and before we could be introduced, Roimata launched into a strong and passionate karanga. She took three steps forward, raised her hands, and began to call in the direction of the south. She asked the Gods of Maoridom to come to Canada and to help us deliver our korero.

'Haramai nga Atua o Aotearoa ki tenei powhiri ki a koutou —'

Caught unawares, the delegates quickly took their seats. They heard the blazing passion in Roimata's voice, the anger and the love. As for me, I had forgotten how powerful the karanga could be. With it, Maori women could say whatever they wished and go wherever they wished. The karanga was their song. It was their voice. It could soothe, it could defy, it could caress, it could kill.

'E nga taonga, tu mai, tu mai, tu mai —'

Roimata turned to the great houses in the hall and the totems that were standing so tall, holding up the sky. She made our Maori greetings to them. She prayed for their forgiveness should she and I in any way offend them. Then she turned to me and passed the kaupapa, the purpose, from her heart into mine. The ihi, the wehi, the mana rushed into me. And I began:

'Today Roimata and I are going to commit a crime. The crime is called aroha ki te iwi, love of the people. It is a crime of passion. In the past our ancestors were shot, killed, maimed, murdered and hanged for it. So were yours.

'We are doing this against the grain of the conference which has looked so positively at all that is being achieved. But we have disliked from the very beginning the implication that the Canada Confederation of the Arts has been responsible for these achievements and should be congratulated. We cannot congratulate the oppressor, no matter how benign they might appear to be. We cannot congratulate a system which calls the shots on what should be funded and how much it should get. The $2 million announced for Indian arts at the beginning of this conference is terrific but we are suspicious of it. It looks like a bribe, it smells like a bribe and if we were you, we would not trust it.'

In the front row, Bertram Pine Hawk was crimsoning with anger. On stage, Roimata was performing the pukana, her fingers quivering in the movement of attack. Elsewhere, there was absolute silence.

'In this murder, Roimata and I shall be calling in our defence on the burden of history. We wish to plead extenuating circumstances. Our kind has been hunted in Tasmania, moved onto reserve lands in Canada and the United States, assimilated in New Zealand. Although our retaliation is an indictable act, the real criminal, the one who should be in the dock is not us. It is the White man.'

There, it was out. It could not be taken back. The words took physical shape and fluttered on the wings of eagles above the crowd.

'This is the case that Roimata and I put before you. We have been dispossessed. We have been marginalised. In many places our cultures, yours and mine, have been destroyed. We occupy the borderlands of White society. We live only by the White man's leave within White structures that are White driven and White kept. Our jailers might be kindly, but they are still our jailers.'

I motioned Roimata forward. Her voice took over.

'White mainstream policies do not honour the rights of indigenous people,' she said. 'The domination of the majority over the minority must be put to an end. This is why Michael and I have committed murder today. Not only that but, from our positions in the dock, we incite you to join us in this act. How can we, as indigenous people, grow under such oppression? We must regain our right to rehabilitate, reconstruct, reaffirm and re-establish our cultures. We must disconnect from the White umbilical.'

Roimata always had a flair for the dramatic. She threw the spear of her korero back to me to carry forward.

'Our counsel has suggested that we should plead innocence,' I said. 'But we do not make such a plea. We are guilty of the crime we stand accused of. We admit our guilt also on behalf of all those who commit to indigenous causes. Although we are minority cultures in the eyes of the White world, we must all continue to dream majority dreams. We must be let through.'

I returned the korero to Roimata. She caught it and continued it in an unbroken line.

'The past is not behind us,' she said. 'It is before us, a long line of ancestors to whom we are accountable and with whom we have an implicit contract. There is no future for indigenous people unless you obtain your sovereignty. This is the lesson we have learnt in our country. Maintain your sovereign goals, do not let go of your inspiration, hold to

326

your strength. Remember your warrior spirit.'

Then for the final time she placed the korero in my hands. I looked to the south. I looked to the north. I looked to the west. I looked to the east. I looked at Albert Pentecost, hoping he would understand.

'If you must bow your heads, let it be only to the highest mountain.'

For a moment there was silence. Then a moan which I first mistook for anger. But people were standing, and the applause was like the waves of the sea. Roimata came forward and took my hand. She was exhausted. It was true, what the old people said — in giving of your own life there was a corresponding diminution of it.

'We've done our job,' she said. 'Now let's get out of here.'

Immediately we were retreating with a haka.

'Turuki turuki! Paneke paneke! Turuki turuki! Paneke paneke!

'Tenei te tangata puhuruhuru nana i tiki mai whiti te ra!

'A haupane, kaupane! Haupane, kaupane whiti te ra!'

## CHAPTER TWENTY

——— 1 ———

And after all that, Roimata and I weren't tarred, feathered and run out of town. Bertram Pine Hawk suggested a recess and his Council retired to discuss what had occurred.

Meantime, the First Peoples' Hall echoed with excitement.

'All we had to do was light the fire,' Roimata said. 'Can't you hear what everybody is talking about? They're talking sovereignty. They're talking tino rangatiratanga. Delegates have been going into the Council's meeting to insist the agenda be changed. Everything's moving so fast that you and I have been forgotten in the rush! That's how it should be. This is their kaupapa, not ours.'

Half an hour later, the Council returned to the hall. Bertram Pine Hawk stood up to speak.

'Well, ladies and gentlemen,' he began, 'you have spoken and we, your Council, have heard and heeded your words. I want to applaud you all for allowing us to respect your wishes. That is what we are here for.'

He responded to the scattered applause with a shy smile.

'So what we, your Council, want you to discuss today and tomorrow is —'

He paused, dramatically, and then pushed on, his voice ringing through the hall.

'What do you want your Council to do? What is your action plan for the new millennium? This may be your last chance to get it right. Go, people —'

This time the applause was thunderous. As Bertram Pine Hawk received it, I felt a grudging admiration for the politician, the consummate diplomat.

'Yes, Bertram Pine Hawk,' I thought, 'you will go a long way.'

He saw my look and inclined his head in acknowledgement. I may have put him in a tight spot, but he had negotiated his way out of it.

If you can't beat 'em, join 'em.

——— 2 ———

The lid came off the conference. The lid came off other things too. That afternoon, Lang, Sterling and Wandisa told Roimata and I that they were gay. They didn't exactly come right out and say it. They did it in a tangential way by taking Roimata and me to a club where a young man wearing nothing but a smile and a g-string was dancing on top of the bar. When he knelt in front of Roimata, inviting her to put some money in his pouch, she turned to me:

'You do it, Michael. He's more your kind of person than mine.'

Sterling screeched with excitement.

'I told you,' he said to Lang and Wandisa, 'that they were people of two spirits!'

Roimata gave a sweet smile.

'And you guys are more than just friends, right? Don't give me any of that stuff about how you just happen to be standing together!'

'Well,' Wandisa said, 'it is true that we went to university together, and it is true that Lang's grandfather believes me and Sterling are a bad influence on him.'

'But I'm not on with Lang,' Sterling said. 'He's a mountain Indian.'

'Nor am I on with Sterling,' Lang continued. 'He's a plains Indian.'

Roimata and I listened, bewildered. Sometimes, Indian people could be so maddening. They talked not in a straight line but always in circles.

'But we are gay,' Wandisa confirmed, 'although we prefer to use our own First Nations' definition. We call ourselves people of two spirits.'

'There are a few others at the conference,' Lang said, 'but they're not out like we are. I think they would like to be but —'

'I mean,' Sterling asked us, 'have you ever heard of a gay Indian? We're not supposed to exist!'

The three friends began to squabble.

'Excuse me, Sterling?' Lang interjected, 'Aren't you forgetting the berdache tradition?'

Roimata was in the middle of her drink. She put it down, and her eyes gleamed with interest.

'I've heard of that —'

'Among *my* people,' Lang explained, 'they were holy people. Their two-spirit identity did not bring them disapproval or denial —'

'On the contrary,' Sterling said, 'they held a respected position in tribal society. They were shamans, and they acted as intermediaries between man and the gods. Only they could go out onto the battlefield to collect the dead and carry them to the world after this one. They travelled in their dreams —'

'They existed,' Lang interrupted, 'beyond the laws for men and women. In particular, twins —'

'I'm a twin,' I said. 'I have a twin sister.'

'There are two of you?' Wandisa's eyes widened. 'Brother and sister?'

She exchanged looks with Lang and Sterling.

'Twins, if one was male and other was female, were particularly favoured by the gods. The male twin especially, if he became a berdache, was destined —'

'Destined?'

'To lead the berdache tribe,' she said.


I returned to the hotel to get ready for my date at the opera with Franklin. I thought back on Wandisa's words.

Great, so now I was going to become a gay Maori Moses.

I looked at my watch. Time, first, to make the call to Cliff Harper. Make it third time lucky. I took a deep breath and dialled Chicago.

I heard the phone ringing. Once. Twice. Thrice. Part of me wanted somebody to pick it up. The other part of me didn't. I felt the usual apprehension, the usual dread.

'Hello?'

This time, Cliff Harper himself.

330

'Mr Harper, please don't hang up —'

'It's you again. Son, I asked you not to call.'

'Mr Harper, all I want to do is give you a message but it's not one I can give over the telephone. Sir, I am coming back through Chicago International Airport in two days' time. Please, may I see you.'

'There is nothing I can help you with, I'm sorry. Now I'm really going to have to spell it out loud and clear to you for the last time. I do not want you to continue to bother me in this way.'

'All right, Mr Harper,' I answered. 'I hear what you're saying. But I must ask you one question. Sir, did you know a New Zealand soldier named Sam Mahana? I have to know, because if you didn't know my uncle I have to keep on trying to find the Cliff Harper who does. I can't give up on this, Sir, I can't. If you are that Cliff Harper and you still don't want to see me, fine. That's your call and your decision and I will respect it. Please don't consign me to eternal darkness trying to find you.'

I don't know why I said it like that — but at the other end of the telephone I heard a deep moan. It seemed to come out of Te Kore, The Void. Then somebody else was in the room with Cliff Harper, asking if he was okay, and he replied, 'I'm fine, son. I'll be down soon.' Seconds passed. It was like waiting a thousand years.

'Yes, I knew a soldier called Sam.'

My heart burst with relief. This was where Uncle Sam's story would end, but at least I had taken it as far as Cliff Harper wished it to go.

'Thank you Mr Harper,' I said.

I don't think Cliff Harper heard me. He was weeping. I hung on, hoping he might change his mind and say, 'Yes, I'll meet you at the airport,' but he didn't. I thought to myself that there was nothing worse than hearing a grown man cry. Gradually, Cliff Harper began to recover. I heard him sigh and blow his nose.

'I have to go now, son.'

There was a click as he disconnected the call.

Was that *it*? Was that the end of Uncle Sam's story? I stood there, motionless, disbelief working its way through my mind. I don't know how long I stood like that. Then I finally realised — yes, that was it. The end. We could all leave the theatre now and go home.

I took a long hot shower. Afterwards, I towelled myself down and began to change for the opera. I was standing in front of the mirror trying to put on the bowtie when there was a knock at the door. It was Roimata, and Lang was with her.

'Just in time,' I said, waving the bowtie at her.

But I couldn't keep up the pretense.

'Cliff Harper doesn't want to see me.'

Roimata tried to give me sympathy. She and Lang propped me up against the wall, and she began to knot my bowtie.

'We knew this might happen. We win some, we lose some.'

'I know,' I sighed, 'but I was so close —'

'Perhaps I better go,' Lang said.

'No,' Roimata answered.

She turned to me with a look of determination.

'Listen, Michael,' she said, 'this may not be the right time to bring this up but there's another matter we have to attend to. Our job isn't over yet.'

'What do you mean?'

I was suddenly aware that I was standing there just in white shirt, bowtie and underpants, and went to the closet to get my trousers. I saw Lang exchange a glance with Roimata.

'We who are people of two spirits,' Lang said, 'want to make a stand. We want to introduce a resolution at the final session tomorrow, calling on the conference to recognise the contribution made by gay and lesbian men and women to our cultures.'

Lang's words took my breath away.

'Michael,' Roimata continued, 'the time has come to make a stand. We've got to start fighting all the homophobia. All the prejudice. It's time we came out into the full light of day.'

'But we need a leader,' Lang said, looking at me.

'This is something that you should do,' I answered gently.

'I can't. My grandfather —'

I sat down. I tried to think it through. I finished dressing. I took my black jacket out of the wardrobe. A thought flicked through my head:

'Yes, the time had come to start fighting. For all the Sams and Cliffs of the world —'

'Oh what the hell,' I said. 'We've already lit one fire. Another won't make a difference. I've grown accustomed to playing with matches.'

Then it was time to go to *Tristan and Isolde*. Franklin was waiting downstairs.

'Thanks for helping me out,' he said.

We walked out to the limousine. In the distance I saw spotlights circling in the sky.

The street outside the theatre was crowded with operagoers. When our car came up to the red carpet, flashlights popped all around us. I could just see my photograph in tomorrow's newspaper and the caption:

'Millionaire benefactor, Mr Franklin Eaglen, arrives at the opera with an opossum from New Zealand.'

We made it upstairs to the Green Room and Franklin smiled at me, amused.

'You're doing this to the manner born,' he said. 'I appreciate it.'

I caught sight of the upwardly mobile Bertram Pine Hawk.

'Why, good evening, Franklin,' Bertram said. 'Mr Mahana, I wasn't aware you loved the opera.'

'Kiri Te Kanawa is my aunt,' I lied, 'and I go all the time.'

'We must have our little talk, Franklin,' Bertram continued. 'Once the conference is over and we're not so busy.'

He turned to me again, before gliding off.

'Meanwhile, Mr Mahana, will you let me know before we cross swords again? I managed to get out from under this time, but —'

'Thank God that's behind us,' Franklin said when Bertram had moved off.

He told me the full story. He had met Bertram five years ago, and they had lived together until six months ago, when Bertram went on to somebody older and better placed politically to provide him with more possibilities of advancement.

'This is the first time I've been out for months,' Franklin said. 'I didn't think I could bear the ridicule. But look at me now! Here I am, with the handsomest young man in the room and Bertram is seething. I've come out with a guy who's prettier than him, who's obviously got a gun in his pocket and isn't a hairdresser.'

We took our seats and the curtain went up. On stage was a ship with sails billowing, cresting the wild sea from Ireland to Cornwall. A young sailor was singing a taunting song. Enraged, Isolde appeared, hair wild and long blood-red dress flowing in the wind.

'Who dares to mock me?'

She called for her maid, Brangäne.

It happened just like that, almost as if Fate had snapped her fingers. Brangäne looked just like Auntie Pat, and I could not help but think again of the story of Uncle Sam and Cliff Harper. It was not just the plot that triggered the memory — the fatal love between Isolde, an Irish princess betrothed to King Marke, and Tristan, a knight in service to him. It was also the volcanic and propulsive nature of the music. I had never heard an orchestra surge and glow with such sound. Nor voices that could soar above the orchestra and deliver such glorious radiance. And before I knew it —

*We haven't much time, Sam said.*

The lovers drink a love potion. Now arrived at Cornwall, they cannot stop their desire for each other.

*Don't move, Cliff hissed. Sam groaned and arched and, stretching both arms, reached for the rung above his head. The light showered around him like a waterfall.*

In the distance, you can hear the retreating sound of hunting horns as King Marke leaves the castle. Tristan and Isolde take the reckless chance to be together. Night and darkness give a private world for the lovers. In it they can sink down into the miraculous realm of passion.

*Oh, God, Sam. I thought this would never happen to me again.*

The two lovers consummate their ardour to music of great romantic power. But there are already hints in the orchestra that their love is also associated with death.

*Cliff's voice was smoky with lust, and Sam realised there could be no going back. He had to keep on going forward with Cliff and hope that there was a way of escape from whatever destiny was lying in front of him. And he was gone, gone, gone beyond the point of no return.*

While Tristan lies in Isolde's arms, Brangäne keeps the watch. Her aria, known as Brangäne's Warning, is full of beauty and yet underscored by a deep sense of tragedy:

'Alone I watch in the night

Over you who laugh in your dreams

Listen to my warning for someone comes . . .

Sleepers, wake up! Take care!

Soon the night will pass —'

But the lovers are discovered. By the end of the opera, Tristan dies and Isolde sings her great Liebestod before she also dies of love in his arms.

'Mild und leise wie er lachelt —'

The aria is like a sea, one great swelling of sound cascading after another, higher and higher to a magnificent climactic peak. In the final moments, though, the sea calms, smooths out, and Isolde's voice is a star, shining over the waves.

*I will always love you, Cliff. From the first moment I saw you I loved you. You're in my heart and nobody will be able to take you out.*

*You're there forever.*

I stayed with Franklin for the reception after the opera, but I was impatient to be away. Moments of the opera kept coming back to me: the doomed lovers, the titanic love duet, Isolde's final, incandescent aria.

In particular, I couldn't get Brangäne's Warning out of my mind.

Like Brangäne, Auntie Pat had kept watch over Sam and Cliff all these years. She had carried their story faithfully and against all odds. That it should all end like this, with a few telephone calls and Cliff Harper unwilling to let the story have its completion, was unbearable.

*May God have mercy.*

When Franklin and I finally left the reception and were driving back to the hotel, I told him about Uncle Sam and Cliff Harper.

'I don't know what to do,' I said. 'I think I need to make one more effort, one which Cliff Harper can't turn away from. But the timing's all wrong. He lives out at a place called 'Back of the Moon', maybe two hours drive from Chicago, near Muskegon Harbour on Lake Michigan. My stopover in Chicago will be too short. I can't do it. I've run out of time.'

Just before I got out of the car Franklin embraced me and then patted me reassuringly on the shoulder.

'Things have a habit of working out,' he said.

I didn't think any more about Franklin's comment until the hotel receptionist woke me next morning with a message that an urgent delivery was waiting for me. It was an envelope with my name on it. Inside was an air ticket for Muskegon Harbour and a rental car voucher. With the envelope was a letter:

Dear Michael,

You need a fairy Godmother, and I hope you don't mind if I cast myself in that role for you. My driver is waiting downstairs to take you to the airport to catch the 8.30 a.m. flight to Chicago. From there you have a short commuter flight to Muskegon County Airport. A rental car has been booked for you to pick up on arrival. I hope you can accomplish your task in time to return to Ottawa via Chicago for the final session of the conference. Please allow me to wave my wand. Your uncle's story needs a happy ending.

Kind Regards,

Franklin

There was a knock on the door.

'Franklin's just rung me,' Roimata said. 'Don't worry about me, I'll be fine. Just make sure you're back by the final session when we have to put the remit. So don't just stand there! Go, Michael, go.'

———— 4 ————

And then the plane was swooping low over dazzling lakes and forests, turning onto its glide path into Muskegon County Airport. I had just on three hours before I needed to catch my flight back to Ottawa. Would I be able to accomplish my task in time?

'Welcome to Muskegon,' the bright, young receptionist at the car rental desk said. 'Would you like me to trace your route on the map?'

Five minutes later, I was on the road heading for Cliff Harper's place. The drive was incredibly beautiful, and surrounded me with the sense of history — of the times when Muskegon had been inhabited by the Ottawa and Pottawatomi tribes. First contact had come with the French during the 1600s, when trappers and hunters came to this land of tall trees and lakes. During the bustling adventurous 1800s, timber felling made Muskegon famous as the 'Lumber Queen of the World'.

I thought to myself that Uncle Sam would have loved Muskegon and its history. He would have loved it now. Muskegon had become a popular tourist destination — Native American reservations, forests, parks, wetlands and picturesque villages dotted the shoreline. The fall was coming, and the leaves drifted across the landscape, red, yellow, purple, like dreams.

Indeed, I felt as if Uncle Sam was riding with me. Or as if *I* was Uncle Sam on my way to a rendezvous that was already thirty years overdue. Every now and then I came across marinas and gaps in the trees where the sun sparkled on the lake and pleasure boats etched the water with arrow patterns.

Beside me, I had opened the box containing Tunui a te Ika. The greenstone was lustrous with an inner light, as if it was bursting with happiness.

'Almost there, little one. Almost there.'

I came to the lakeside village that the car rental receptionist had marked on the map. I stopped for more precise directions at a small shop near the jetty selling boating supplies. The proprietor was a grizzled old-timer and he pointed the way.

'Go down the highway until you reach the left fork. The Harper place is on the second bend.'

Quarter of an hour later, I saw the letterbox:
BACK OF THE MOON
C. & W. HARPER

I turned in at the driveway. The road took me through natural pastureland and down into a broad shallow basin around the shores of the lake. I could imagine two brothers playing there, one signing to the other: *I'll race you, Johnny!* There, among a scattering of trees, was the house. It was sturdy, two-storeyed, and its windows flashed in the sun. It looked as if it had been standing forever, having sprung from the ground hand-hewn and shaped by determined hands to keep generations safe through all the seasons — the kind of house that an Illinois country boy would grow up in.

I walked up the steps to the front door. The house had been recently painted. To one side was a garage and farm sheds. A ute was parked in the garage. I knocked. Knocked again. No answer. I walked around the back and rapped on the back door. A radio was playing inside. Somebody was at home.

From the lake, I heard dogs barking. I looked up, shading my eyes from the glare. Across the water and out of the sun came a man with two small dogs in a runabout. The man waved at me, and docked at the jetty. His dogs came bounding through the trees and up the slope to the house, barking. I knelt down and waited for their arrival:

'Hello, boy! Hello, dog! How are you, fellas?'

My heart was beating in anticipation. I didn't want to look up. I heard the man whistle and call his dogs off.

'Hi there,' he yelled. 'I saw your car coming along our road. Can I help you?'

The sun was dazzling. All I could see was a shape — golden hair on fire with the light. All I could hear was a voice — light, friendly, but guarded. He put out a hand. Strong, firm, lightly filmed with sweat. And all the while, the dogs were barking, jumping at us both.

'The name's Cliff Harper,' he said.

He stepped into my vision.

'But people call me by my middle name, Sam, to distinguish me from my Dad, Cliff senior.'

The son, not the father. With the look of the father, made from the same clay. But where God had breathed divinity into the father, the son was more of a mortal. The ahua, the appearance was there, but the ihi, the energy that gave the body it's own sense of self, was different. Or, perhaps, I had been living with the dream of Cliff Harper, the father, for too long. Had idealised him, made him charismatic, impossible to replicate. Yes, perhaps that was it. It was difficult not to feel disappointed.

'I was hoping to speak to Mr Harper senior,' I said.

'I'm sorry, but Dad's gone to Indiana,' Sam Harper answered. 'Both he and Mom are there to see Mom's parents. Grandpop's not too well.'

He looked at me curiously. Then his eyes narrowed, as if he was puzzling something out. He snapped his fingers.

'That's *it*,' he said.

I doubt if Sam Harper even thought about what he was doing. He opened the back door and motioned me to follow him.

'Come in,' he said. 'There's something I'd like you to see.'

The dogs tried to come inside with us but he ordered them out. He was on the run through the house and I didn't get much of a chance to see what the interior was like. A hallway. A sitting room. Up the stairs. Past a bedroom. Another bedroom. A study.

'This is where Dad does his paper work,' Sam Harper said. 'You know, all the bills, correspondence, his Vietnam Veterans' stuff —'

Books. Deer horns mounted above the doorway. A huge trout and, underneath, a photograph of a father and son proudly holding the fish after they'd caught it. Other photographs in silver frames — a family portrait, a beautiful young woman, a photo of Cliff Harper himself.

Sam Harper was reaching for an album from his father's book shelf. I couldn't take my eyes off the photograph of Cliff Harper. He had grown older, but his looks were intact. Blond, clean cut, still devastatingly handsome. Although his unswerving gaze had lost its innocence, he still possessed his boyish grin and mysterious half smile.

Sam Harper clambered down and stood beside me. He flicked through the pages, then stopped. He looked at me and pointed to a photograph.

'Do you know who this is?' he asked.

The photograph was dated Vietnam, 1969. I knew it well. Uncle Sam and Cliff Harper look as if they've just come up from the beach after taking a swim. The photograph must have been taken when they were on leave at Vung Tau. Someone, I don't know who —George maybe — had taken it. Cliff Harper is sitting on the sand. Uncle Sam is resting in the harbour of his arms. His upper body is strongly developed. Around his neck is a greenstone hei tiki. Tunui a te Ika.

'Yes,' I nodded. 'That's my uncle.'

I was trying to keep my emotions under control but it was so hard.

Once I had thought that the one who really drew your attention in the photograph was Cliff Harper. It was he who looked directly at the camera. Now, seeing the photograph again, I realised that while Cliff Harper was the looker, Uncle Sam was the one who eventually held your fascination. His eyes were looking somewhere else, at some point beyond the camera. His beauty was more subtle. It had less to do with the externals of high cheekbones and chiselled planes and more to do with a deep inner sadness. Uncle Sam was like the moon, veiled and evanescent.

'I'm named after him, aren't I?' Sam Harper said.

His voice sounded breathless with wonder. For a moment I thought everything was going to be all right. Then:

'You're the guy who phoned Dad from New Zealand.'

'Yes. You're named after my Uncle Sam. And, yes, I phoned your father from New Zealand.'

'And again from Ottawa? It was you, wasn't it. You.'

Sam Harper's voice had taken on an angry tone. When I looked at him I could see he had become afraid. He put the album back in its place and, arms folded, sat on his father's desk.

'What's this all about? Why has Dad been acting the way he has?'

What could I tell him? That his father and my uncle had been lovers? No.

'I shouldn't have invited you in,' Sam Harper said. 'I want you to leave. Now.'

I saw him looking at a rifle leaning against Cliff Harper's desk.

'That won't be necessary,' I said. 'My business was with your father. If he isn't here, of course I will go.'


It all happened so quickly. Even now I'm not too sure if I handled it right. Perhaps there was no way of handling it so that Sam Harper would feel comfortable. Even when we were outside and I was walking to the car I saw that he was still afraid. I smiled at him, trying to soothe his fears.

I reached through the window and picked up Tunui a te Ika.

'I'd like to leave your father a gift. Would you give it to him when he returns?'

Tunui a te Ika bucked and twisted in my hands.

*Bring it back to me, Sam. Bring it back.*

I handed the greenstone to Sam Harper.

'It's beautiful. What is it?'

'It's something that Uncle Sam gave your father in Vietnam. It's a long story. Your father returned it to Sam —'

'He's dead then? The man I'm named after?'

'Yes. That's why I came to see Mister Harper senior. To tell him and give him the greenstone.'

Sam Harper began to relax. He smiled cautiously.

'Look, I'm sorry. If that's all this is about I've reacted pretty badly, right? You feel like a coffee?'

I was feeling embarrassed now. 'I've already presumed too long on your hospitality,' I said, 'but would you mind if I left a letter with the gift? It won't take me long to write —'

'Sure. Do you have pen and paper?'

'Yes. It won't take a moment.'

It had been foolish of me to come. What had I expected? Why hadn't I understood why Cliff Harper had been so evasive and angry? He had built another life. He did not want to revisit the past. I hoped the letter would explain why I had come, even when he had not wanted me to:

Dear Mr Harper,

I am sorry if I have invaded your privacy and, as soon as I've written this letter I'll be on my way and you will not hear from me again. I have not wanted to cause you stress by pursuing this matter but I am not only acting on my own behalf. I am also under instructions from my aunt, whom you knew as Patty, who wanted me to advise you that Sam was on his way to meet you at Auckland Airport on the evening you left New Zealand in 1971. He was killed in a car accident.

I realise it was a mistake to come here uninvited, but I had an obligation to fulfil. I am leaving with this letter the greenstone pendant, Tunui a te Ika. Uncle Sam wanted you to have it. Had he been able to, he would have brought it to you himself in Auckland.

I leave you and your family my best wishes,
Michael Mahana.

I gave the letter to Sam Harper. Tried to smile. Shook his hand.

'Should you or any of your family ever come to New Zealand, please let us know. My aunt and I would be happy to extend to you all the hospitality we can.'

'Listen,' Sam Harper said. 'Are you sure you don't want that coffee? How about lunch?'

'Thank you, but no. I've already stayed too long. I have to get back to Ottawa.'

'You came from Ottawa for just a few hours?'

'It was all the time I had available. Please tell Mr Harper senior I'm sorry I did not meet him personally. Goodbye.'

I stepped into the car. I saw Tunui a te Ika trying to leap the distance back into my hands, and I felt the onset of tears.

'No, little one. Stay.'

I had to get away. I backed out of the drive and drove as fast as I could from the house. At the top of the rise I stopped and looked back.

Had Uncle Sam met up with Cliff Harper, perhaps this was where they would have ended. Together, in Muskegon County, on a small Illinois farm. A valley with a river running through it, or a place overlooking a lake, where they could last out all their days. A time when they could celebrate, every evening, the secret embrace that comes at the end of the day. But they had never found that safe place that is the right of every human being.

All of a sudden the wind came out of nowhere. The dust swirled high. The trees began to sigh and whisper, showering petals. At first they were like tears, but as they continued, I knew they were like a benediction.

*No, Michael. Don't grieve, Nephew. You've done your job. Thank you.*

There was a flare of light and the sky became transformed into a sea of opalescent waves, tinged with red, stretching to the end of forever.

The mackerel sky —

From east to west stretched a broad band of cloud broken into long, thin, parallel masses, as if shoals of fish were teeming just below its surface. Everywhere silvered mackerel were leaping. They had been disturbed by a young boy on a wild palomino, urging his horse to the place where the hills cut sharply into the blue.

My eyes blurred with tears.

'Yes, Uncle Sam, *go*. Go, dammit, go. Don't look back, you're free now —'

With a hoarse cry the boy kicked the stallion to jump into the sky. The mackerel shoal opened up and scattered, flash, flash, flash around him. The sky filled with a sparkling radiance like silver rain.

'It's done, Auntie Pat. It's done.'

'You're back just in time,' Roimata said.

The First Peoples' Hall was crowded for the final session. It was time to light the second match.

'I understand that we have a late remit,' Bertram Pine Hawk said. 'Mr Mahana, I see it's you again.'

The conference murmured with laughter, but I was in no laughing mood. Even Roimata was anxious as I hugged her and made my way to the podium. All I could think of was Uncle Sam. I had reached the point of emotional exhaustion. When I put the motion which Lang, Sterling and Wandisa had prepared, I did it with too much anger.

'In the beginning, our Maori legends tell us, Earth and Sky were lovers who embraced each other so tightly that there was no space between them. When they had children, who were gods, those children were squeezed within whatever cracks they could find. It was one of those gods, Tane, who conspired with some of his brother gods to separate Earth and Sky. When the Great Separation was achieved, that was the beginning of our legacy. The light came flooding in. We, the children, were able to walk upright upon the bright strand between.

'Many people have seen, in this myth, a metaphor applicable to all kinds of situations. That independence does not come without sacrifice. That fighting for space and for light, the universal image for knowledge or enlightenment or freedom, is the continual challenge for all peoples who cannot see the sky. I would like to deploy this myth in another manner.

'I am a gay man. Of all the children of the gods, my kind — gay, lesbian, transvestite and transsexual — inhabited the lowest and darkest cracks between the Primal Parents. We, now, also wish to walk upright upon this bright strand.

'To do this, we must make a stand. For those of us who are First Peoples, this is not something to be done lightly nor without knowledge of risk. In my own country, my own Maori people are among the most homophobic in the world. They are a strong, wonderful people but their codes are so patriarchal as to disallow any inclusion of gay Maori men and women within the tribe. As long as we do not speak of our sin openly, we are accepted. But if we speak of it, if we stand up for it, we are cast out. My own uncle was cast out. I have been cast out. Many of us, in all our cultures, have been cast out. There is nowhere else for us to go except into the borderlands and there create our own tribe. But there is another way. Only you, however, can sanction it. This is why I am standing today.

'The issue here is that for too long all of you who come from traditional cultures have profited by the efforts of those gay men and women who, for love of their nations, developed the songs, the poems, the dances, the arts of all of us. You need only to look in your hearts to know that what I say is true. You need only to look into each other's eyes to know that all our genealogies are intertwined with people of two spirits. But they are people who, to do their work, had to pretend they did not exist. They had to deny themselves the right to walk proud among us. You *knew* they were two spirited. You knew that they were giving you gifts of their talents. You knew —'

I couldn't carry on. I thought of Uncle Sam, and I wanted to tell him that what I was doing was for him as much as for anybody else.

It's still a war zone, Uncle Sam.

I closed my eyes and began to weep. I didn't give a damn that I was making a fool of myself. I was aware that Roimata had come to join me at the podium. Then Lang joined her with Sterling and Wandisa.

Oh, such a small tribe in that hall so filled with history.

Lang claimed the microphone.

'Michael has been brave to bring this matter before us,' he said. 'But in this country it is our fight, not his. I ask this conference, in the name of all two-spirited people, to recognise the achievements of our two-spirit ancestors to all our traditions.'

There was a silence. Bertram Pine Hawk, without looking at us, got up and said:

'A motion has been put to this plenary. I need two delegates to second the motion before I can put it to the vote. I ask for the first —'

There was a murmur and then a receding of noise into silence. I felt ashamed that I had pushed too strongly. Had I been more accommodating, I would not have alienated the audience from the remit.

'You've all known I was a gay man,' Franklin said. 'I may as well come out now. I will support the motion.'

He was trembling, but then he lifted his head and seemed to grow in stature. Growing, growing like a tall tree of the forest.

'I need a second person to support the remit,' Bertram Pine Hawk persisted. 'May I ask for a second?'

This time the silence was so deafening that I knew we had lost. My heart went out to my small gay tribe — Wandisa, head bowed to the floor. Sterling, unable to look anyone in the eye, and staring at his feet. Roimata and I, we were leaving Canada in the morning. But they lived here. For them there was no easy escape. For the rest of their lives they would be damned for standing up this day.

From the corner of my eye I saw Albert Pentecost whisper to Bertram Pine Hawk. The old man stood up, came forward, and I heard Lang groan in despair.

'You all know me,' Albert Pentecost began. 'You all know my grandson. I apologise to you all, because it was wrong of him to stand up and to ask you to support and to vote on this thing which recognises people of two spirits. It was wrong.'

I thought the old man was disciplining us. I thought he was against us. Lang thought so too. He shaded his eyes and stepped into the arms of Sterling and Wandisa. But the old man's voice changed. It was like the wind had turned and was blowing from another direction.

'It was wrong of Lang because he was not the one who should have done this thing. It was *I* who should have done it. Me. I am his chief. It is my job to do these hard things and to make the hard decisions.'

The old man pointed at Lang.

'Look at my grandson. He is just a boy. *I* am a man. This was a man's job and a boy has done it. I am ashamed of myself but I am proud of him. He has shown more courage than many men in exposing himself in this battle. He and all who stand with him have exposed themselves to us. They have formed their war party and what are their weapons? Where are their bows and arrows? Where are their spears? Where are their other braves and warriors? They have brought only themselves to their battle. They are foolish, but I salute them for their courage. And I salute them for bringing to our attention something we have known for years.'

Albert Pentecost turned to Bertram Pine Hawk.

'I join my co-committee member, Franklin Eaglen, in seconding the motion.'

Bertram Pine Hawk would not look at me. At us. He was one of us, but he would not look at us.

'I will ask for the vote. All in favour, please raise your hands and say Aye.'

For a moment there was silence. Then from every part of the hall came scattered 'Ayes.' Surely the 'Noes' would outnumber us.

'You don't know First Nation people,' Sterling whispered.

'All those against, say No,' Bertram Pine Hawk said.

There was silence.

In the end, it was as simple as that. No thunderous acclamation. No dancing around the totem pole. Change is not always telegraphed in big ways and with grand gestures. Sometimes it comes quietly from the silent places of the heart. Even so, I couldn't believe it. I heard Bertram Pine Hawk turning to the next remit as if it was the most ordinary thing in the world to do.

'Can you confirm for me,' I asked Roimata. 'Have we won?'

Roimata's eyes were shining.

'Yes, you dumb ox, we've won.'

# Liebestod

## CHAPTER TWENTY-ONE

——— 1 ———

'Okay, babe,' I said to Roimata, 'it's time for you to get on your plane.'

The conference was over and Roimata and I were separating. She was going on to London, and I was leaving half an hour later for Houston, Texas, to spend a few days with Amiria and Tyrone.

'Are you sure you're going to be all right without me?' she asked.

'You're talking like a wife already.'

'Look,' she said, 'I've had strict instructions from Carlos. If you don't get back in one piece and on time, he's pulling my business class ticket from London to New Zealand. I'm sorry, dear, but when it comes to your welfare or my ticket, the ticket wins. Oh, you —'

Sometimes, when Roimata can't express herself verbally, she resorts to physical stuff. Usually a furious hug and a badly aimed kiss. While I was wiping her lipstick off my nose, she said her goodbyes to Lang, Sterling, Wandisa and Franklin.

Surprise, surprise, Bertram Pine Hawk joined us.

'This might be unexpected, Michael,' he said, 'but I want to thank you for all you and Roimata have done. Not only did you shake us up once, you shook us up twice! The irony is that I have benefited on both occasions. The Council is going to have to change, and it looks like I'll be up for a more important position either there or higher.'

'You?'

Bertram laughed and shook my hand.

'Goodbye, Michael. Some future time, somewhere in the world, we'll cross swords again no doubt.'

With a nod to Franklin and the others, he turned and left and — Roimata was hugging me again.

'Come on, Roimata,' I soothed. 'We'll see each other back in New Zealand.'

'Oh, I'm not emotional about that,' she answered. 'I'm so happy at what we did here in Canada! Bertram knows it, I know it, you're the only one who doesn't! And this is just the beginning, Michael. Don't you understand how much you've changed, how much you've grown? When we get back to Aotearoa, we'll have to make our stand there too.'

Then she was gone, running through Customs, a whirlwind of beauty and strength.

I turned to Franklin.

'Goodbye, Fairy Godmother,' I said.

'It's been an honour, Michael.'

I turned to Lang, Sterling and Wandisa.

'Be strong,' I said. 'You all have a long and hard road ahead of you, but together you'll get there.'

Lang laughed.

'Are you talking to us? We don't know each other. We only happen to be standing next to each other. I'm a mountain Indian.'

---

2

---

A few hours later, I exchanged the cool of Canada for the heat of Texas. The first person I saw when I got off the plane was Amiria. Who could miss her? She was as big as a house.

'I'm pregnant,' she wailed as she hugged me.

'Gee, Sis, tell me something I don't know,' I said.

'I can't even fit behind the steering wheel any longer.'

I saw Tyrone, grinning from ear to ear. I shook his hand and whispered:

'I suppose it's twins, right?'

'Even better,' he said. 'Triplets. I was wondering how I was going to keep Amiria off the freeways. Have you seen her drive? Man, she's lethal — still hasn't remembered which side of the road she should be on. Now she'll be so busy with the kids and America will be able to breathe easy.'

Tyrone and Amiria's uptown apartment was lavishly decorated and had a balcony view of the city to die for. In the early evening Tyrone excused himself, and left for work at the casino.

'Anyhow,' he said, 'I'd only be in the way. You two have a lot to talk about.'

Amiria and I sat on the balcony and watched the sun go down. Amiria told me about her life in Texas and how everybody was overjoyed about the triplets, especially Tyrone's ex-girlfriend.

'She thinks this is her chance to get Tyrone back. No way! All he wants to do at nights is to come home, put his head against my tummy and listen to the three little buggers fighting in there. He goes all cross-eyed and goofy-looking, and he's full of plans for them. I can't stand it!'

Amiria made dinner and we sat in the candlelight munching on the diet to which the obstetrician had confined her: lettuce, carrots, fish, no dairy products or fatty foods whatsoever. I told her about my split with Jason, meeting Carlos, and Roimata's proposal that we should think of getting married.

'Give me that girl's telephone number,' Amiria said as the triplets kicked inside her. 'There's something somebody better warn her about *fast.*'

She gave me a quizzical look.

'You're moving, aren't you Michael. I can see it in the way you are, the way you look, the way you act. It's like you were in soft focus before you came out. Now you're more defined, more clear, more purposeful. I can see you now.'

Amiria, my twin, had always been able to go straight to the heart of things.

'Yes,' I nodded. 'I think you're right. It's taken me some time, but right now, I have embraced being gay. I'm no longer scared of it or ashamed of it. I'm glad of it and proud of it. And —'

'And?'

I stood up. I looked at the darkening city.

'Amiria, it has to stop. All this hatred of gay men and women. All the pain that it causes. I can help make the difference. I have to get out there in the front line.'

'Mum and Dad won't like that. I was talking to Mum on the telephone

351

last week. I told her you were coming to see me. She and Dad are hoping for a reconciliation.'

'That's what they say, but that's not what they want. What they want is for me to go home and tell them I'm sorry, I'll be a good boy and that I won't do it again. But that's not the way it's going to be, Sis. They're going to have to accept me as I am. On my own terms.'

By late evening Amiria and I were like old lovers. There was only one last thing to tell her. I breathed in deep, saw the stars spinning in the night sky and began.

'Amiria, I need to tell you about someone you don't know. He was our uncle. His name was Sam —'

That night, speaking Uncle Sam's story to Amiria, singing and crying his story into the dawn, was the First Telling.

———— 3 ————

I had a wonderful few days with Amiria. She and Tyrone had an invitation to go to the opening of the Dan Flavin art installation down at Marfa, and they insisted I go with them. We booked into the El Paisano Hotel, where the cast of *Giant* had stayed while making the film. Amiria and Tyrone had Elizabeth Taylor's room, I had James Dean's, and I imagined Auntie Pat's face when I told her. The Flavin installation was stunning — awe-inspiring fluorescent gateways illuminating tunnels of darkness. All too soon, however, it was time to go home.

'Will you come back?' Amiria asked.

'I'll come when the triplets are born.'

We hugged and kissed. Amiria didn't want to let me go.

'Tell Roimata not to bother to have a kid of her own,' she yelled, as I ran to catch my flight. 'She can take one of mine!'

It's strange how these things happen. On the flight to Los Angeles the plane ran into a lightning storm. The lightning flashed and zinged and crackled across the sky in a display of awesome power. I kept thinking of fluorescent gateways, opening and opening, one after the other, a limitless set of doors leading to some great mystery.

Was the lightning display just to be admired for itself, or was it a portent of some kind? Was there something in what Sterling had told me about people of two spirits and the berdache culture:

'People of two spirits were shamans. The berdache were the ones to go out onto the battlefields to collect the dead. They could communicate with the gods. They were dream travellers —'

Somewhere between Houston and Los Angeles I tapped into my second spirit. I saw myself holding Uncle Sam's body in my arms and carrying it through a pyrotechnic storm of lightning strikes and fluorescent gateways. Ahead, in that fearful universe, I saw an altar. I placed Uncle Sam's body on it and uttered a prayer to any gods who were listening:

'Have mercy. Have pity. Please, not eternal darkness —'

Was that it? Was that what happened?

All I know is that it was stifling and hot in Los Angeles. My throat was dry. There was a water fountain near the airline's lounge, but I wasn't quite sure how to operate it. There was no hand button or foot pedal to activate the flow. A teenage girl, watching, put me out of my misery.

'It works automatically,' she said. 'You lower your face to the fountain and —'

Yeah, the water comes out and spits you in the eye.

I heard a ripple of amusement as I drank. The water was cool. I scooped some in my left hand and rubbed it on my neck. I began to stand.

That's when I felt the presence of the past.

Perhaps the music being piped through the terminal had something to do with it: 'Rhapsody In Blue', redolent of the Big Band era, American nostalgia, Fourth of July. The 'Rhapsody' reached that point where the big melody comes in. It soared above me and I followed its path —

And a flight of helicopters came out of the music, circling down through the blue sky over Vietnam, to land at the far end of the concourse. The lead chopper was already on the ground. The rotors slowed to a halt. A pilot stepped out. He saw me, waved, smiled, took off his sunglasses. His eyes, so green. His teeth, so white and even. His boyish grin. He looked so handsome in his flyer's kit.

'Hey! Sam —'

Cliff Harper.


'This can't be happening.'

The water from the fountain was still fresh on my hands. I swayed, closed my eyes and spread the water with my fingers across my lips.

*Ah, rainwater, it is always so cool.*

When I recovered, I looked back down the concourse. My heart was pounding — had it just been my imagination? People were rushing backwards and forwards, obscuring my vision. Then I saw him again, the handsome, smiling pilot walking towards me. It *was* happening. But something was wrong. At every step, at every move as he tried to get through the press of people, he became older. His youthful stride began to falter — and I began to feel an extraordinary sense of aroha for him.

Time had indeed been kind to Cliff Harper. The devastatingly handsome pilot whom Uncle Sam had known had become a middle-aged man who still had an immense physical charm. It was not just a matter of matinee-idol looks. It was also a matter of charisma.

Cliff Harper stopped some ten metres away. He still carried himself with grace and strength. I realised he hadn't seen me. He had taken off his glasses and was wiping them with a handkerchief.

I stepped into his line of vision. For some reason I became so angry:

'Why now, Mr Harper? Why come now?'

Cliff Harper gave a gasp.

'Oh, God,' he said. 'My son told me you looked like the photograph, but —'

'Why didn't you stay in the past where you belong?'

Cliff Harper didn't hear me. He took a step forward, his walking stick slipped on the tiled floor and he fell into my arms:

'I never expected you to look so like Sam —'

I helped him to a nearby seat. Some passersby stopped and asked if I needed any assistance.

'No,' I said. 'But perhaps a glass of water?'

I turned to Cliff Harper. I was still angry.

'How did you find me?'

'I have friends in the airlines. When I came back from Vietnam I became a commercial pilot. My friends were able to check on the incoming flight details you gave me on the telephone and tell me when you were flying out.'

He was still looking at me as if he couldn't believe — or was afraid to believe — who I was.

'So why now? Why?'

354

'Young Cliff gave me Tunui a te Ika and your letter. I knew then that I couldn't keep on closing Sam out of my memory.'

He began to talk fast, almost as if he was pleading for me to understand.

'This might be hard for you to understand, but whenever memories of those war years threaten to come into my mind, I close them off. It's the same with Sam. I dare not think about him. If I do —'

He was expecting me to reply, but I remained tight-lipped, refusing to give him any quarter. He tried again.

'You live your life, son, that's all I can say. When I left Sam, and your country, I closed the door. I thought, 'Sam's made his decision to stay with his family.' I was stubborn. I was too proud. I kept going forward. Day by day. Month by month. Year by year. And, you know, all of a sudden I'd made it to the other side. I met Wendy. A really good woman. We got ourselves three kids. All boys. Eldest is twenty-five now, Cliff junior, whom you've already met.'

'You still haven't told me why you decided to come to see me now.'

Cliff Harper looked up. His eyes were brimming with tears.

'Do you know anything at all about love, son? Do you know what it is like to close it away, lock yourself up so damned tight and throw away the key? Sam and I, we were going to be back to back together against the rest of the world. I believed it would happen. He believed it would happen. When it didn't, I didn't blame him. I blamed myself. I've been blaming myself these past thirty years. And I know this sounds crazy, but I got to thinking that Sam, he blamed me too. When you began to telephone me, I just didn't want to know. I didn't want to know anything. Don't you understand? I should never have left Sam behind.'

Then he became angry. He pulled Tunui a te Ika out of his pocket.

'No, you wouldn't know anything about love, you son of a bitch. And you had to bring me the goddam key, didn't you —'

His face grew grim.

'You had to disobey me and you've left me with a lot of explaining to do to my family. That's in the future, but right now I want to know about the past. So you start talking, son, and start talking fast. I want to know the details of what happened to Sam. You said in your letter there had been a car accident —'

'He was coming to meet you at the airport. There was a woman

355

changing her tyre on the side of the road. Uncle Sam stopped to help her. It was raining. The traffic was heavy. While Uncle Sam was changing the tyre, a truck smashed into the car. It fell on him. He died instantly.'

Cliff Harper gave a sharp cry. He groaned and hunched forward.

'Dear God —'

———— 4 ————

Five minutes later, I was sitting with Cliff Harper in the business class lounge. We had managed to make a kind of peace with each other, and Cliff Harper was making peace with his past. It was strange how it happened. The story of Sam's death may have been a tragedy, but in some wonderful way it was also an affirmation that Cliff Harper had been waiting for all these years.

'So he *was* coming,' he whispered to himself. 'And he stopped to help somebody who'd broken down on the road? That was just like Sam. I wouldn't have expected him to do anything else.'

Cliff Harper turned to me and sighed.

'You'll never know the hell I went through when I left your grandfather's farm. When I arrived in Auckland I tried telephoning Sam, but Arapeta always answered. He would never let me speak to Sam. I tried to get through to George to see if *he* would get a message through to Sam. But that never worked either. By the time Friday night arrived I was going crazy with anxiety. I checked in early and I waited and waited. I died a thousand times thinking "There he is!" when it was somebody else. That night, waiting there for Sam while everybody around me had someone they were saying goodbye to or travelling with, was the loneliest night of my life. I heard the first boarding call. The second. The third. Then —'

The loudspeaker crackled.

'Would Mr Harper please go through Customs and board his flight immediately at Gate One.'

Cliff was going out of his mind. He couldn't wait any longer. In desperation, he turned to the Customs officer at the gate.

'Sir, I need to leave a message. There's a friend of mine, his name's Sam, he's supposed to be here. If he arrives, please give him this note.'

Cliff scribbled his Illinois address and phone number: Back of the Moon, Muskegon County, Illinois. He folded the note and put Sam's name on the front.

'Please tell him to call me as soon as he can,' Cliff said.

The loudspeaker crackled again:

'Mr Harper, Mr Cliff Harper, your plane is waiting for immediate departure.'

Across the departure hall, Cliff Harper saw something strange, almost surreal. A young woman was stumbling through the crowd in a dazed manner. She looked like a madwoman. Her evening dress was spattered with the brown rust colour that Cliff knew was dried blood. She was calling for somebody:

'Chris? Chris —'

An airport security officer went over to her, and tried to get her to leave. She kept resisting, saying:

'No, I must find him.'

An old man approached the girl. He cradled her and she collapsed into his arms.

Once more the loudspeaker:

'Mr Harper? Mr Cliff Harper —'

Cliff's heart was beating with pain. He thought of the time when Sam had come along on the rescue mission to bring out a downed F-4 fighter pilot. Sam was on the ground with the pilot. The enemy were closing in. Suddenly there was a whump and the chopper juddered in the air:

'They've got a rocket launcher!' Seymour yelled. 'We're hit! We're hit!'

Cliff's body flooded with adrenalin: 'God, don't let me go down like Fox.' He was checking his gauges, his training automatically initiating the procedures to ensure damage control. To his right he heard the Skyraiders begin high-speed strafing of the area from which the rocket had been launched, walking their incendiary shells down the slope. The forest flamed and smoked.

Sam was still on the ground with the wounded pilot. Only, it wasn't a pilot any more but a girl in an evening dress. And MacDuff was radioing:

'Your call, Woody Woodpecker.'

Bullets were whanging around the chopper. Seymour was yelling that they had to exit the area. But Cliff couldn't leave Sam. Not like this. He looked down to the ground. Saw Sam moving his fingers in sign.

357

*Hey, Harper! Do you know what haere ra means?*

Cliff cried out,

'Sam, *no* — '

He worked the controls, seesawing the chopper back and forth across the tops of the trees, mowing through the upper density.

Suddenly there was a sunlit space. Sam's eyes were glowing with love.

*I will always love you, Illinois country boy. You're in my heart.*

And he was gone.


Thirty years later, and I was sitting in an airport lounge with Cliff Harper. Our conversation had circled and spun between past and present. Somehow we managed to stitch together what he knew of Sam and what I knew of what had happened to him. Somewhere in all that circling we found a kind of friendship, a kind of reconciliation with one another.

From talking about Uncle Sam it only seemed natural to talk about Auntie Pat.

'How is she?' Cliff Harper asked.

He had a strange look in his eyes, almost as if he didn't want to know, but he relaxed as I told him she was well.

'Is she still unmarried?' he asked.

To my surprise, Cliff Harper then turned the attention to my life.

'Tell me about yourself,' he asked.

I told him I was gay. 'Once,' I said, 'I was ashamed of it. I'm not any longer.' I told him about my break-up with Jason, my meeting Carlos, and the interesting shapes that were emerging out of the dynamic of Roimata, Carlos and myself.

'Most of all,' I said, 'I've made a political commitment to change my world. To change the Maori world. I owe it to myself. I owe it to Uncle Sam — and to you —'

Cliff Harper nodded.

'You know,' he said, 'when you talk like that, you take up a particular posture, a way of standing that reminds me of Sam. Leaning slightly forward. Ready to take on all comers.'

The business class supervisor tapped me on the shoulder.

'Mr Mahana, your plane is boarding now.'

I stood up. Shook Cliff Harper's hand.

'I'm glad you came to Los Angeles.'

'So am I, son,' he answered. 'So am I.'

'Would you do me a favour? Some day, would you tell your son, Cliff Junior, about you and Uncle Sam? It might be a hard ask right now, but you were the one he loved, the one he wanted to be with. I don't think I'd be able to take it if I knew that of all the people in the world, you denied him, Mr Harper. It doesn't have to be tomorrow or next week or next month. But tell your son sometime?'

'Yes, I will,' he promised

I turned to walk away. I don't know why, but something made me turn back. Something to do with gladness, with joy, with grief. I grasped Cliff Harper fiercely and pulled his forehead against mine, his nose against mine in the hongi. Mourned and keened over all that could have been between him and Sam.

'Goodbye, Mr Harper.'

'Wait,' he said.

His face was blanched with grief, as if he didn't want to let me go. As if he should do something to keep Uncle Sam alive between us. Then he found the way.

He took Tunui a te Ika out of his pocket, lifted it up. The light glowed through it, showing its upright penis, its mana, its strength. The greenstone twisted and flashed in his fingers.

'I know you brought this all the way to give to me. But I need to return it to you. Your uncle would have wanted you to have it. You will need it more than I do if you are to achieve all the things that lie ahead of you.'

He placed Tunui a te Ika around my neck. At first the greenstone was cold, as if only just awakening. Then it began to take warmth from my skin, and I felt it searching for a place to settle. A place from which to begin battle.

'Tell Patty,' Cliff Harper said, 'I forgive her.'

---

5

---

The flight soared across a midnight sea. The sky was still sunless as we made our descent to New Zealand. Mist was streaming across the land, spilling over the cliffs at the end of the world. Mist, sea, land, all spilling over into oblivion.

Carlos met me at the airport. 'Welcome home,' he said.

We drove to the apartment. Made love. Talked about what had happened in Canada. Talked about his skindiving while I'd been away. I told him about Cliff Harper. He asked about Roimata. We made love again.

That night I tossed and turned in the tightening noose of jet lag. My dreams were fractured, cut glass tearing at the dreams and letting the nightmares in. Once more, I felt that tremendous dread as, all of a sudden, a thousand shards fell about me and I saw that black highway at midnight. I fell to the tarseal and listened to the ground throbbing with hoofbeats. The thrum thrum thrum of the black stallion. It had pursued me all my life, through countless years, countless beds and countless dreams.

You know what it's like in nightmares. It's dark and you're always alone. It's like those horror movies where the actor is in a perilous position and there's never anybody around.

And so, once again, I began to run. I could only move in slow motion. I could hear myself grinding my teeth. I heard myself moaning, willing myself to run faster, get out of there, escape from the blackness. I felt my pores pop with explosions of fear, and I was drenched with sweat.

I looked back again. I could see the stallion. Its eyes were on fire. Its hooves struck sparks like flints, taunted me, circling me in the blackness, choosing its moment. The thrum, thrum thrum was all around me and then —

There it was. Coming towards me. There was nothing I could do.

I cried out to myself, Wake up, wake *up*.

But the stallion was rearing up on its hind legs. It was screaming its rage and slashing out its hooves like steel blades. It shredded the blackness with arcs of fire. Its eyes were bulging. The veins on its neck were like ropes.

The hooves descending. Slashing.

Then I heard myself saying in my dream, '*No*.'

The stallion was standing on its hind legs. For a moment it was motionless, looking down at me. Its eyes were wild, unwavering. It whinnied again, surrounding me with its rage and fetid breath.

'No,' I said again.

All of a sudden, I saw that there was a bullwhip in my hands. The whip was covered in blood. And all the fury, sadness and anger of the

360

world rushed into the whip as I raised it and began to crack it at the stallion.

'Get back. Get back.'

The whip arced through the air. At each snap it showered sparks through the dream. The sparks fell upon the stallion, making it cry with pain. Then the whip began to sing. Its song was one of strength and power. It said, 'I will take this no longer, I will no longer let you have power over me. From this day I will fight back and I will win.'

I brought all my rage to the bullwhip.

'Oh, you bastard world!' I called.

My eyes were on fire. My feet struck sparks like flints. At each crack of the lash the stallion began to diminish, to squeal with confusion and pain. It began to retreat. Slowly. Giving ground.

In the dream I heard the whip singing. I saw the stallion retreating. The arc of the whip shredded that dream until it no longer existed. Then I woke up. How Carlos had slept through my tossing and turning was beyond me.

I got out of bed, went to the bathroom and had a long hot shower. After a while an extraordinary sense of release and calm came over me. I went out into the kitchen, made myself a cup of coffee and took it out onto the balcony.

'What's up?' Carlos asked, yawning and scratching his armpits.

'I couldn't sleep.'

He put his arms around me. 'Well, seeing that we're both wide awake —'

We had a race back to bed. He won.

## CHAPTER TWENTY TWO

—— 1 ——

There was still one thing left to do to complete my uncle's story.

But first there were more immediate matters to take care of. One of them was to formally end my relationship with Jason.

'I'll see you in court,' he had said. He wanted his day there — but I instructed my lawyer to give him the property or money he wanted. Half of everything, all of everything, it didn't matter any longer. His lawyer persuaded Jason to settle out of court, and we met for the last time in his lawyer's office.

'Do you want me to come with you?' Carlos asked.

'No,' I answered.

It was better for me to face Jason alone. But I hadn't expected him to bring along his cheerleaders, Graham and Margo.

I can't begin to tell you how difficult the meeting was. On my part, I was sad that our goodbyes had to take place within a legal framework. Jason was ballistic, out of control, wanting his pound of flesh.

'You owe me more than half of everything we had together,' he said. 'You owe me my life back. All those wasted years with you —'

He was still spiralling, on a descent to confront whatever demons Margo had found lurking in the shadows of his life. Angry, I turned to her and Graham.

'You are responsible for Jason now. And you both better look after him.'

I had brought roses to give Jason. He laughed with incredulity and threw them at me.

'Keep your roses.'

The petals scattered in the air like blood.


Another matter involved Carlos. Whatever was going to happen to Roimata and me, marriage, children, would be in the future. And it would have to take into consideration the fact that I had decided to let Carlos into my life.

'How about going to the next level?' he asked.

I think he was surprised at my answer.

'You give me Mayfair, Piccadilly, $5000 cash, a Chance card and a card to get me out of jail — and I'll think about it.'

His eyes brightened.

'Can we be a bit more specific? Is that a yes?'

'Well, okay,' I said, 'but I'll have a crayfish with that.'


———— 2 ————


Then Tane Mahuta rang me and gave me the opportunity to go to Gisborne and to settle the matter.

'A young gay boy has died of Aids,' Tane said. 'His name was Waka. He comes from the Gisborne area and somebody needs to lead an ope to take his body back to his marae. Will you and Roimata do it?'

'Yes,' I said. 'It's time, and I will be proud to lead the group.'

Tane conveniently forgot to tell me that Waka had been a rent boy on Vivian Street and that the ope, in consequence, wasn't going to be conventional. Quite the opposite — and when I called all his friends together to discuss the travel arrangements, I gulped at the enormity of the task. Talk about a dog's breakfast. There were about thirty who wanted to accompany Waka's body to his marae — an assortment of other boys who were on the game, two trannies, some street kids and other teenagers with green hair, pierced noses and chains hanging from their belts.

I called Auntie Pat.

'I need your help, Auntie Pat! Can I count on you to be at Poho o Rawiri to do the karanga when we go on?'

As for Roimata, she tried to back out. 'Oh, no you don't,' I said.

Carlos promised to join us in Gisborne after attending a fisheries hui in Christchurch.

The ope started out from Wellington during the weekend. Waka was accompanied in the hearse by his boyfriend, Jewel, and a cousin, Tim. The rest of us were in cars of all descriptions, and one of them, a flash Jaguar, had been stolen — though I didn't know it at the time. When we arrived in Gisborne, Auntie Pat said it looked like a circus had come to town. She was waiting for us at the gate to Poho o Rawiri.

'Boy, oh boy,' she warned. 'There's a big row taking place in there and you started it. Some of the dead boy's family don't want him back here. They may not welcome you onto the marae.'

'We'll wait all day and all night if we have to,' I said. 'It is Waka's right to be buried in the place where he was born. He is Maori as well as gay. We're here to make sure his right is honoured.'

Oh, I felt so proud of our ope. I didn't care that we looked a rather odd tribe. It took courage to front up to a culture as forbidding as ours. The meeting house with its warrior carvings. The welcome ceremonies with all their strict protocol. In the old days, one false move and you could die. And the local people didn't even want us there.

Roimata took charge of the young girls, explaining the rituals of the tangihanga and what was required of them. When Carlos arrived he gave the boys, including Jewel, a five-minute lesson on haka. None of them had been on a marae before. The bravado in Wellington had evaporated into absolute terror.

We waited and waited. One hour later, the arguing was still going on in the meeting house.

'Well, we've been here two hours,' Roimata said. 'If the local people don't come to a decision, you'll have to force the issue.'

That's what I like about Roimata. She is such a dear, always implying that I have to make the decisions.

'We'll give them five minutes more,' I said. 'If we aren't called on, we're going on, and to hell with them. Tama tu tama ora, tama noho tama mate. If we stand, we live. If we lie down, we die.'

At that, some of the ope wanted to bolt. Not that they would have got far. I had told them to wear black, but I had forgotten to tell Jewel and Tim to leave their high heels at home.

'Okay,' I said to Roimata. 'You and Auntie Pat begin the karanga. We're going *in*.'

And after suggesting it herself, you know what Roimata asked?

364

'Are you sure?'

'Yes,' I answered. 'We are a people. We are a tribe. We bring our dead. If tradition has to be broken, then I will break it. Nobody will stop us from burying our own among the people where they belong. The time for hiding ourselves and our dead is past. The time for burying them in some anonymous cemetery is over. '

Roimata went to the gateway to begin the call announcing that we were coming in no matter what.

Just then, an old woman, walking stick in her left hand, came out of the doorway of the meeting house and approached us.

'I didn't know Lilly was the grandmother,' Auntie Pat said.

'Lilly? Turei's mother?'

Immediately, three men came running out after Lilly — and, oh no, now they were having a row with her in broad daylight. In a temper, Lilly raised her walking stick and began to hit them.

'Get away you mongrels —'

The men backed away. One of them swore loudly at her and gave us the fingers. Lilly didn't care and neither did we. We'd had worse.

Lilly straightened up. She looked at us. I think we probably gave her a bit of a shock. She knew we had brought Waka's body back, but she was trying to figure out some tribal reference point. E hika, we were like no tribe she had ever seen. Ah well —

Lilly raised her right arm.

'Haramai ki te ope tane me wahine takatapui —'

Listening to her, I thought: 'Yes, this is only to be expected from a woman who once took an axe to her son's coffin so she could see his face.'

'Welcome to this marae,' Lilly called. 'Welcome you strange tribe I see before me! Come forward, you tribe of men who love men and women who love women! Welcome, you brave gay tribe, whom none have seen before! Come! Bring your dead who is also our dead —'

Our tribe was born that day. It was born out of a grandmother's compulsion to take her grandchild back to her bosom. Out of a need to accept that a new tribe was coming. That day we signalled, 'Make way, we are coming through.'

We would not be stopped.

Yes, there was still one last thing to be done, but I didn't get a chance to do it until late that evening. By that time we had been formally welcomed, even if reluctantly, and all the speeches were over. Waka was now lying in state in the meeting house, and the anger against us had begun to dissipate as locals mixed with our new gay tribe and we got to know each other. Bedrolls were being spread in the meeting house. Dinner was over in the wharekai. If it wasn't for the green hair, garish clothes and pierced noses and eyebrows, you wouldn't have known that this wasn't your usual crowd at a tangi. Or that something extraordinary had happened.

Auntie Pat had gone home early. There had been a moment, just after the welcoming ceremony, when she knew I was on to her. I had been following her, waiting for the moment to confront her. When it came, she had been talking to Lilly. I tapped her on the shoulder and she turned and beamed a smile:

'Yes, Michael?'

For a moment I couldn't speak. Then:

'Cliff Harper asked me to give you a message —'

*Tell Patty I forgive her.*

As soon as I said the words, Auntie Pat knew she had been found out. Her eyes gleamed with sorrow.

'Do we have to talk about this now, while I am defenceless, Michael?' she asked. 'Come and see me at home —'

I went to check that things were okay with Roimata. She was sitting with Waka's family, beginning the vigil over his body that would continue until he was buried. Then I sought out Carlos, who had gone to check the toilets to make sure the kids weren't snorting coke or doing anything else illegal in there.

'Can you look after everybody?' I asked. 'There's something I have to talk about with Auntie Pat.'

'Sure,' he said. 'But get back soon. When I asked you if we could go to another level, this wasn't exactly what I had in mind —'

I hopped into the car and drove away from the marae towards Auntie Pat's place. Gisborne was bright with streetlights and, as I drove along the main road, I remembered Auntie Pat's description of the first time she had met Cliff Harper. Was that when it had begun for her?

*I loved my brother. People used to take us for girlfriend and boyfriend. Then Cliff Harper came. I had my face pressed tight against Sam's chest and I felt and heard his heart beating. It was going* der *der* der *der* der *der. But when he saw Cliff it changed to* der *der* der *der* der *der —*

My mind was whirling. No, perhaps it had all begun down at the waterhole. Sam was singing the Woody Woodpecker song, and Cliff was making mock poses, green eyes like the river, hair set on fire by the sun. Auntie Pat was with Anita and Kara, and they had wanted to take revenge on the men for stealing their clothes.

When *had* it begun?

I arrived at Auntie Pat's place. All the lights were off except for the blue illumination of the television screen in the living room. She was still up, watching one of her old movies.

I walked to the open front door. I went past the poster of *Till the End of Time*. Auntie Pat was sitting in her favorite armchair, and her face was aglow with excitement.

'Hello, Nephew,' she said. 'You've come just in time! There he is! There he is —'

On the screen, a young man in American uniform was getting off a bus. A young man who could have been Guy Madison or Cliff Harper. Guy Madison playing Cliff Harper. Or Cliff Harper playing Guy Madison.

I walked over to the television set and switched it off.

'No,' Auntie Pat pleaded.

I whirled on her and she shrank back, huddling into the armchair to get away from me. I looked at her — and at the house to which she had escaped for thirty years.

It was time to bring her out.

'Why did you do it, Auntie? *Why?*'

'I don't know what you're talking about.'

I grabbed her by the wrists and she fought me, striking out at me.

'You know nothing, Michael,' she yelled. 'You know nothing.'

Auntie Pat has always disliked physical contact. I used to joke that maybe it all had to do with those slobbery kisses you get when you're on the marae. But despite her screaming and raging against me, I held her tight.

'Let me go, Michael, let me *go* —'

She was kicking, scratching and biting. All of a sudden she began to scream and scream. Before I knew it, the dam inside Auntie Pat burst apart.

'They should have told me, Michael. They should have told me the truth. I thought that Sam and Cliff were just friends. That's what Sam told me. But it wasn't the truth. If I'd known about them I wouldn't have —'

'What, Auntie, what —'

*George's wedding. The dancehall, 1971. Patty was drunk and giggling because she had played a trick on Cliff and run to the bandleader and told him, 'Get Cliff up to do a song for us.' And Cliff had been positively fabulous, singing 'Heartbreak Hotel' just like Elvis. And Patty knew that she loved him, had loved him ever since he had stepped down from the bus, ever since she had seen him at the river, ever since the beginning of Time. And she screamed herself hoarse as Cliff scorched the hall with his number.*

Auntie Pat's eyes were wide and staring. 'Then the song was over, and I saw Cliff running out the door with Sam, and I remembered that they were going home that night, back to the farm. I yelled above the crowd, 'Cliff, don't go!' I wanted to tell him to stay. I wanted to tell him I loved him.'

*And Patty couldn't let Cliff leave just like that. She pushed through the crowd to the doorway. Where had Cliff and Sam gone? She saw them stumbling down to the rental car and, next moment, they had fallen. 'Cliff! Cliff! Don't go, Cliff!' She ran after them and heard them laughing. And she too was laughing with happiness that she had caught up with Cliff, and then —*

Auntie Pat turned to me. She touched her lips.

'And then I saw you kiss him, Sam.'

Her voice was hushed, almost with awe.

'I saw you kiss each other and I didn't know what to think . . . I didn't know that men would do that, kiss like that . . . and Cliff saw me and

368

later, he must have realised I was the one who . . .'

'Who did what, Auntie?'

*And all of a sudden, Patty was vomiting. She ran back to the dining hall. Daddy was there. He asked her, 'What's wrong with you, Patty? What's wrong?'*

'I told Daddy, Sam,' Auntie Pat's voice was small, plaintive. 'I told him I saw you kissing Cliff. You should have told me the truth, Sam. If you had told me the truth about you and Cliff I would never have fallen in love with him. Or become so angry as to tell Daddy.'

I remembered the last words in Uncle Sam's diary.

*May God have mercy.*

'So who was it who wrote those words, Auntie? Was it Uncle Sam?'

'Of course it wasn't.'

'You did, didn't you?'

'Yes.'

———— 4 ————

It took me until five in the morning to calm Auntie Pat down and to help her find her way back to the present. When she did, it was like watching somebody newly arisen from a morning sea.

'Yes, Auntie Pat,' I said, 'it's done. It's over.'

'I've been carrying the guilt all my life,' she answered. 'I'm glad you know everything.'

'You have to forgive yourself. You weren't to blame. You can put the past behind you now and get on with life. And I need you.'

'Need me?'

'This is just the beginning, Auntie. There are other Sams to fight for. I'll need your feistiness, your fighting sprit.'

I watched as Auntie Pat's back stiffened and her head went up to look at the far horizon.

'Okay, Nephew,' she said, spitting on her hands. 'Just put me in the front row. You'll hear all about it if you don't put me in the front —'

Roimata was right. Auntie Pat was going to make a good kuia for our new gay tribe.

When I returned to the marae, the Southern Cross was turning just above the meeting house like a pinwheel. The meeting house had become its axis, determining the revolving of the world and stars. Roimata was sleeping next to Waka's casket. Some of the kids from Wellington had crawled into her arms.

'Yes, Roimata, you will make a fine mother for this great new tribe of ours. Your children will be as numerous — twins, triplets, whatever. Pity you couldn't have chosen a better father.'

I went to find Carlos in the meeting house. He was by himself, watching the stars spilling over the brim of the night.

'Keep your hands to your sides and don't move,' I said.

I stood behind him and slipped my arms under his shirt and around his chest. He shivered at their coldness.

The sky started to streak with the dawn.

'Hey,' Carlos said, 'It's going to be a great day —'

I felt Tunui a te Ika leap with expectancy against my heart. A good place from which to do battle.

A good day to begin battle from.


My mind went back to Cliff Harper when we were saying goodbye to each other at Los Angeles Airport. I was at the jetway, boarding my flight. He was at the other end of the terminal, walking away. He looked so lonely.

In despair, I called down the concourse. 'Mr Harper!'

He turned to look at me. I didn't know what to do next. Then I heard music surging like the sea, music filled with timelessness. The retreating sound of hunting horns. Two lovers taking the reckless chance to be together. Clattering down through the music, a huge chopper came through the roof. The helicopter hovered, its rotors slicing the sun.

'This is from Sam!' I called.

My voice echoed and echoed along the concourse. It seemed to open gateways in Time. People stopped, looked at me, curious.

I pointed at Harper. *You.*

I pointed at my heart. *Me.*

I made the thumbs up sign. *Love you.*

I stood tall. Saluted to him.

Cliff Harper seemed to crumple. Then he straightened. His hand snapped up as he returned my salute.

He turned and walked away.

In the roar of aircraft taking off and landing, in the sound of a helicopter suddenly jumping into the sky, I watched Cliff Harper until he was gone.

And the sun was there, bursting across the horizon.

I thought of Uncle Sam and his great love story. I made him a promise.

Uncle Sam, it is time to construct the world again, but a brave new world. Your story will become part of it and I will tell it until the whole world knows it.

I make my promise, Uncle Sam, to bind the new world's top and bottom with light. I will tell your story to everyone I meet, whether they want to hear it or not. I will tell them how you loved a man and how wonderful that love was. With that love I will bind the outer framework of the world with the inner framework.

I have realised, Uncle Sam, that the telling of our stories will bring a location and a history to the world that we build. We who are gay and lesbian must fix the stories with firmness and solder their knots with purpose so that they become part of the narratives — the foundations, walls and roof — all peoples tell about each other. We must speak our stories, we must enact them, we must sing our songs throughout this hostile universe. We must bring a new promise to life and a new music to the impulse of history.

Tuia i runga, tuia i raro.
Tuia i roto, tuia i waho.
Tuia i te here tangata ka rongo te Ao
Ka rongo te Po.
Tuia. Tuia
*Tuia.*

No, Uncle Sam, not eternal darkness.

# ACKNOWLEDGEMENTS

This book has been in my mind since 1986. However, it wasn't until 1 October 1999 that it began life as *Brangäne's Warning*. It was completed as *The Uncle's Story* on 3 July 2000. Just prior to beginning the novel the New Zealand Air Force and New Zealand Army must have been on joint manoeuvres at the military airbase at Hobsonville. All I know is that in September I kept hearing thunder in the sky: the sounds of military helicopters morning and evening coming down Auckland Harbour and over the house I live in on the harbour. The sound was a powerful stimulus to my imagination. In particular, it brought back memories of Maori relatives and friends who had died in the Vietnam conflict and, also, of two events in Washington DC, where I lived in 1987–1990, stationed at the New Zealand Embassy: witnessing the moments of grief at the unveiling of the Aids Quilt, 1997, and at the Vietnam Veterans' Memorial on Memorial Day, 1997.

In terms of research, I wish to particularly acknowledge the following texts:

*Brief History of the New Zealand Army in South Vietnam, 1964–1972*, Army Public Relations, NZ Ministry of Defence, Wellington, 1973; *Choppers: Thunder in the Sky*, Robert Genat, Metro Books, New York, 1998; *Grey Ghosts: New Zealand Vietnam Vets Talk About Their War*, Deborah Challinor, Hodder Moa Beckett, Auckland, 1998; *Reluctant Warrior: A Marine's True Story of Duty and Heroism in Vietnam*, Michael C. Hodgins, Ivy Books, New York, 1996; *Six Silent Men: 101st LRP/ Rangers: Book One*, Raynel Martinez, Ivy Books, New York, 1997; *Splash One: Air Victory Over Hanoi*, Walt Kross, Brassey's (US) Inc., McLean, 1991; *The*

*Killing Zone: New Zealand Infantry in Vietnam, 1967 to 1971*, Colin Smith 1987; *The New Zealand Army: A History from the 1840s to the 1980s*, Major M. R. Wicksteed, RNZA, Wellington, 1982; *Te Mura O Te Ahi: The Story of the Maori Battalion*, Wira Gardiner, Reed, 1992; and *Wounded Warriors, The true story of a soldier in the Vietnam wars and the emotional wounds inflicted*, Colin P. Sisson, Total Press Ltd, Auckland, 1993.

Documents about the 28th NZ (Maori) Batallion by Bruce Poananga and George Rogers were also consulted.

The First Peoples' Conference described in Part 6 of the novel is based on the 'Beyond Survival' conference, Ottawa, Canada, 1992 and the 'To See Proudly: Advancing Indigenous Arts Beyond the New Millennium' conference, Ottawa, Canada, 24–27 September 1998. The political debates that occur in the novel are extrapolated from some of the issues that arose at both conferences.

The 'Heartbreak Hotel' (Axton/Durden/Presley) © lyrics on p. 240–243 are reproduced with kind permission by J Albert & Son Pty Ltd.

The lines on p. 120 were written by Nguyen Du, an 18th century Vietnamese poet and philosopher.

As always, my thanks to Jessica Kiri and Olivia Ata, my constant inspiration. Thanks also to Jenny Te Paa, who will recognise herself, to Darling Thing, to Little Bear, who came into my life just when I needed him, to Jenny, Jaimie and Gretchen, my madcap companions on the trip through Texas, and to the boys in Hawaii.

Finally my thanks and tribute to my publisher, Geoff Walker, Jane Parkin, my editor, and Louise, Mary and Marilyn who helped me through the jungles of Vietnam.

# Sky Dancer

## Witi Ihimaera

Feisty young Skylark O'Shea is on holiday with her mother at a town on the coast. Soon it becomes clear that in Tuapa all is not as it seems. Strange things begin to happen.

What is the threat facing the town and the birds of the forest? Where do the charismatic old Maori women Hoki and Bella fit in?

Skylark becomes embroiled in an extraordinary journey. Soon she is testing her wits, her life and the fate of all she loves in a race of breathtaking dimension . . .

Witi Ihimaera's *Sky Dancer* cleverly combines a rollercoaster adventure ride with new ways of exploring Maori myth. This result is a storytelling triumph.

# The Dream Swimmer

## Witi Ihimaera

*'Eleven years have passed since I put down my pen on the story of the woman who wore pearls in her hair, my grandmother the matriarch, Riripeti Mahana whom some called Artemis . . .'*

So begins *The Dream Swimmer*, Witi Ihimaera's long-awaited sequel to *The Matriarch*, acclaimed winner of the Wattie Award in 1986.

*The Dream Swimmer* continues the odyssey of Tama Mahana, grandson and heir to the matriarch, as he takes up the mantle of leadership, along with his grandmother's battles with the Pakeha. But at every step Tama is thwarted, by deceit, deception and intrigue, and by the woman whose destiny has intersected Riripeti's and his. She is the enigmatic Tiana, his mother, the woman of no account.

Mana, power and boldness remain the hallmarks of Ihimaera's style as he negotiates a story of breadth and breathtaking climaxes, combining the passion of *The Matriarch* with the sheer storytelling ability of *Bulibasha, King of the Gypsies*.

'Witi Ihimaera's long-awaited sequel to *The Matriarch* is another blockbuster.'

Molly Anderson, *Otago Daily Times*

# BULIBASHA
## KING OF THE GYPSIES

## Witi Ihimaera

*'We crown him King of the Gypsies. Bulibasha.'*
*He took Grandfather's hand and kissed it. Then he was gone.*
*Soon after he left my conflict with Grandfather began.*

Caught in the middle of the struggle between two great Maori clans the teenager Simeon, grandson of Bulibasha and Ramona, struggles with his own feelings and loyalties as the battles rage – on many levels. . .

*Winner of the Montana Book Award*

'A marvellous story, engaging from beginning to end.'
Margaret Scott, *Dominion*

'Unexpectedly riotous, cunningly crafted.'
Dennis McEldowney, *Landfall*

'A comedy of family dislocation and cultural adaptation. . . . Ihimaera's style is so fluid and apparently simple that his jokes take you by surprise and make you laugh out loud.'

James McLean, *Evening Post*

# DOGSIDE STORY

## Patricia Grace

There is conflict in the whanau. The young man, Te Rua, holds a 'secret for life, the one to die with'. But he realises that if he is to acknowledge and claim his daughter, the secret will have to be told.

'The Sisters' are threatening to drag the whanau through the courts. But why? What is really going on?

Like Patricia Grace's award-winning novel *Potiki* before it, *Dogside Story* is set in a rural Maori coastal community. The power of the land and the strength of whanau are life-preserving forces. This rich and dramatic novel by one of our finest writers presents a powerful picture of Maori in modern times.

*Winner Kiriyama Pacific Rim Book Prize*

*Longlisted for the Booker Prize*

'In her new novel, Patricia Grace displays the kind of mastery that comes only from years of writing experience. . . . Here she's writing at the peak of her form.'

Iain Sharp, *Sunday Star Times*

'This is a writer at the pinnacle of her art. *Dogside Story* is her best novel yet.'

Beryl Fletcher, *Waikato Times*

# COUSINS

### Patricia Grace

*Makareta is the chosen one — carrying her family's hopes.*
*Missy is the observer — the one who accepts but has her dreams.*
*Mata is always waiting — for life to happen as it stealthily*
*passes by.*

These three women are the cousins of one of Patricia Grace's most popular novels. Moving from the forties to the present, from the country to the protests of the cities, *Cousins* is the story of three girls once thrown together and as women grown apart.

This is a stunning novel of tradition and change, of whanau and its struggle to survive, of the place of women in a changing world.

'. . . it is robust and powerful. I simply could not put it down. Lyrical and vibrant, smoothly paced and quietly rhythmic, Grace's language moves easily from one person to the next, as the stories unfold.'

Ngahuia Te Awekotuku, *NZ Listener*

'Patricia Grace writes with an enviable clarity and power.'

Margaret Mahy, *Evening Post*